PRELUDE TO HEMLOCK

by the same author

A Self Made Monster
Flunky

PRELUDE TO HEMLOCK

Steven D. Vivian

Published by **Boson Books**

An imprint of **C&M Online Media Inc.**

ISBN 1-932482-36-9 (paperback
IBSN 1-932482-38-5 (e-book)

Cover Design by Once Removed
Cover Image: *The Kiss* by Francesco Hayez

C&M Online Media Inc.
Tel: (919) 233-8164
Fax: (919) 233-8578

www.bosonbooks.com

For Theresa
Without Whom
Not

One: The Nothing

All I did was that crummy little stuff like support you and give you talent and hope! But I was right always right after all, always right. You are perverted skanky money grubers, even Robbie knows that and he's a MORRON and IDIOT and that makes me a morron? No a sucker!! And to think that I gave you every idea you've had, both of you!

Ive had it and that means you've had it and theres no more band because theres no more brains, I am the brains and you stole ideas and ten thousand dollars and I cannot live anymore. the slime and stink of you two. Patty's right, you are filth you are filth.

Eyes half-closed, Dr. Rebecca listened with professional concentration. She was small in the over-stuffed black chair, and her floor lamp threw a warm oval of light upon her charmingly unkempt auburn hair. She'd wanted to untie my tortuous familial knots, and I agreed. But first, I recited what I'd brought with me.

After several paragraphs, I paused for a cigarette. Hearing the flinty scratching of my plastic lighter's tiny wheel, Dr. Rebecca pointed at the "Please No Smoking" placard upon her bow-legged oak desk.

"Join me?"

"I'd love to," she said wistfully. "But it's really bad for you."

"You doctors, you're so cowed by good health."

With a halting hand, she accepted my offer. We smoked in silence, exchanging polite nods when our eyes met, and we used my empty cola can as an ashtray. Finally, cigarettes consumed, I turned again to the yellow legal pad upon my lap.

Take whats left of the money I hope it's gone in fact I know it is you bloodsucking shits, I spent the last of it on beer and chocolates and Dairy Freeze!! I would now like to publicley announce that I alone am RESPONSABLE for anything GOOD in both of you!! But now you curs your out luck because I'm giving you what's left. Nothing.
Sniff it and lick it:
Nothing.
Nothing
The Nothing

"Jeffrey...why do you enjoy reading that?"

"I like to picture the author, reciting it in her grand manner. Wish I could've read it to her just as...Well. Anyway. It's the best kind of suicide note. It's got vanity and despair and split infinitives."

"Did you dissociate that night?"

"You've got it backward, doc."

"How?"

"What you call dissociation is really making the moment last, seeing it from more than one perspective. To, you know, see and experience it more fully. Not push it away."

Doubts darkened her face. Presently, she tried to sit straight in her chair and, sinking comically into the long-collapsed seat cushion, redoubled her efforts. "You should take a few days off from the hospital visits. They've become obsessive."

My smile compelled her to abandon that particular tack. "Then at the very least, Jeffrey, I must really insist that you stop reading those notes. It's true that, uh, ritual is an important part of grieving, but ritual can take on a life of its own."

"I'm grieving," I snorted, "but not for *her*."

"It's just that, you know, there's a lot of hatred there." Chair finally conquered, she continued. "But anyway. Do you still get tired a lot?"

"...I'm about to turn the corner."

Her gaze loitered upon my eyes' dark circles. "I think so too." She smiled with professional optimism. "Your therapy, it'll go well because you're smart."

"Smart enough to stay out of jail."

"And smart enough to write lyrics for an acclaimed rock band. Not bad."

"And dumb enough to be friendless and broke and on parole."

Undeterred, Dr. Rebecca opened her purse and, after a moment's fishing, retrieved a copy of *Femme en Blanc.* "See?

"Thank you."

"I listened to it on my way into work today. Your sister's singing, it's really wonderful."

"*Was* really wonderful."

Dr. Rebecca announced that our time was nearly up. Next time, she noted, we might discuss the Westermarck theory. "And Jeffrey, consider moving out of that house. It's just not healthy to be there by yourself right now."

I waved away her concerns.

"Or consider a roommate."

"Lots of possibilities there." I pretended to hold a newspaper before me. "Wanted: One roommate for court-ordered recipient of psychiatric counseling. Must deeply love classical music (especially Rachmaninoff), must hate most rock music, and must enjoy rumors of devil worship and debauchery." I tossed aside the imaginary ad. "Females strongly preferred."

"Remember to keep up with your journal!" she cheerfully reminded as I silently shut her office door. "Write in it every day!"

Blitzing my discount cigarettes, I weaved south through the traffic jam then past the newest outcropping of strip malls, car dealerships, fast food emporiums. Bustle yielded to bucolic. I turned down the sloping county highway, and at that moment Kim's voice jumped from the radio. "Pay for my Hell" was ubiquitous, even on corporate rock radio, the aesthetic of which Kim loathed and the money of which I envied.

Finally, money for sister Kim: money she'd never enjoy.

The familiar drive soothed me...one landmark was a distant hillside upon which Holsteins grazed. Another was a failed roadside diner, its lonely parking lot now rubble beneath tall yellowing grasses. After the final hundred yards down the gravel road, I saw our rental: a Cape Cod, incongruous among the cornfields.

Stepping onto the creaking porch, I heard the music: or rather, I felt the walloping drums of Pad...and as I stepped inside, Kim's guitar greeted me: the chords fleet and sharp, the lead lines trebly and bright. Her sound was a crashing wave on a white beach, with sparkling foam and blinding sun. Then came her voice: a nearly peerless instrument, its precision heated with sass and verve.

I played her music all the time, even when I was out: it made the house more than a dank reliquary. I recalled Kim sitting upon a squeaking kitchen chair, electric guitar cradled on her lap, bottle of warm soda upon the kitchen table. She'd gesture that I join her and, grocery sacks or clothes basket in my arms, I'd step over the CD's, guitar picks, and sheet music scattered across the scuffed wood floor.

"Do you happen to have any—"

I'd toss her a nearly empty pack.

Then, cigarette in hand, she'd rise from her chair and pace in excited ellipses around the cramped kitchen. Pinkish crenulations, imprints from the chair, crisscrossed the back of her pale legs.

"See I've got this diminished minor seventh thing," she'd chatter, cigarette smoke trailing her, "this bed of chords with a kind of, uh, a spike of majors right at the end, right to punch it up."

Upon a neurologist's screen, Kim's brainwaves would appear as musical notes. She was the miraculous product—or "spawn", as our mother often shrieked—of our parents' musical genes. From our father she inherited inspired melodicism and imposing technical chops; from our mother she inherited, and greatly improved upon, an alto with power in endless reserve.

Me? From our father I inherited only apathy toward normative behavior, though—as you will see, even grudgingly—I'm capable of compassionate love, a virtue neither parent could grasp. From our mother I inherited the capacity to return to her the revulsion she felt for me. And: the gift of finding bliss in an enemy's ruin.

I picked up my mother's yellow legal pad. I imagined her, now a sepulchral heap, and recited the palsied script:

All I did was that little crummy stuff...

Two: "Your daughter's a loser."

As a world-weary sixth-grader, I'd already seen through the charade of public education and fulfilled my academic instincts by reading and re-reading comic books. Through my bedroom's wall burst Kim's vocals: she'd hit fifth grade and was already a fully committed singer. Her sheer volume, beyond most adults', often irritated me. I'd toss the comic book aside, grab one of my otherwise untouched school books as the prop of an aggrieved scholar, and storm from my room.

"C'mon Kim knock it off!"

More singing.

"C'mon knock it off I'm trying to study turn down that music Kim I mean it!"

A giggle, a pause, a new song: an hour became three.

Dad was a professional musician—low brass his expertise—and he enjoyed tenure at the university in the next town. My earliest recollections of him are composed in bright primary colors: he was cheerful, outgoing, talented, and jovially indifferent to family obligations.

I recall him playing his euphonium. He'd sit in the living room upon the scarred piano bench and practice. His musicianship was beyond dispute: I admired the thrilling notes as his fingers danced upon the silver valves with breezy precision. Then he'd pause, grin at me, and wink...the notes leapt from that Wilson's bell and danced over our heads. A few yards away, Kim lazed upon the gray carpet, humming along as the music—Sparke's shattering "Fantasy" being my favorite—buoyed our spirits. Dad sometimes indulged us with requests for another composition or just a short tune, such as "Peace, Please." And he'd rise from his chair, oblige with a comic bow, and show off with flute-like highs and stout, bassy lows. But on balance, Dad was devoted not to familial relations but to giddy feasting upon his university's co-ed population. One co-ed's father objected to

Professor Edwards's affair with his daughter. The ensuing academic soap opera left Dad with a lousy teaching schedule and a growing contempt for Mom. Increasingly, he saw Mom—dare I say "correctly"? I shall: *correctly*—as a woman of diluted affections and concentrated hatreds.

So Dad had still another motive to enjoy much younger female company...a complementary motive being that the younger female company was just that: younger, and animated by all of youth's charms, its cheerful ignorance and loud enthusiasms.

See? My home movies are lively and alarming. Let's press the fast forward button. Popcorn? (Kim powdered her popcorn with salt and grated parmesan and, after laying siege to the bowl, threatened to wipe across my face the salt and cheese that stuck to her fingertips).

The images roll by.

Christmas Eve: Kim and I fidget before the sparsely tinseled artificial tree. We're smiling as best we can as Mom struggles to compose a simple snapshot...Dad's left her again. She yells at us every half hour then demands we recite five Our Fathers. Kim tensely complies as I slyly revise: "Our Father who farts in Heaven..." Mom musters some impressive method-acting indignation, loudly hoping that I'll burn in Hell for profaning God on his Son's birthday, so I tell her to not wreck Christmas by talking about Christ. I spent that Christmas condemned to my room, with Kim on occasion sitting outside my door to complain that she was stuck alone with Mom.

More highlights: a vacation at a shabby imitation Disneyworld. Oh, and there we are trudging with a neighborhood boy between rows of apple trees at an orchard. The boy was embarrassed on the ride back home when Mom erupted at Dad about making her pick all the apples while, at a shady picnic table, he swigged beer. We never saw the boy again. And here's a vital vignette: Kim and I are late for school (again, yet again), but we won't walk downstairs and out the door because the parents are fighting (again, yet again). Kim sits on the edge of her bed, waiting for a truce. Then, spirits flagging, she tears a red ribbon from her suddenly disheveled hair, flings it across the room, and cries.

If Mom heard Kim, she'd sprint up the steps, drunk on rum and rage, meaty palm raised. Alarmed, I retrieve the ribbon, place it on the bed, and clumsily brush her hair back into place. Though merely eleven, I know that this halting gesture gives Kim hope that tomorrow will be better, that tomorrow we'd make it out the front door without tip-toeing past warring parents.

Kim calmed herself and, to obscure the bellows below, she quietly sang a currently popular tune.

"That's pretty good." For the first time, I'd noticed that she really could sing: the pitch never wavered, her tone was full and, despite her freakish pipes, she already avoided the cardinal sin of diva-style, over-the-top shrieking that should be restricted to cruise ships.

She searched my face for sarcasm and, finding none, said, "Usually you tell me to shut up."

A bright glittering crash: Mom heaving a carafe through a kitchen window.

Emboldened by my praise—after all, I really *did* usually tell her to shut up—Kim later that week gathered her nerve to sing for others: Dad & Mom, of course, and then yawning Aunt Jo and Uncle Art...even cretin cousin Robbie. And even the elderly couple next door, whom Kim once astonished with a patriotic tune as they sat on their front stoop, waiting for Independence Day fireworks.

Eventually, Kim sang in local and regional competitions, usually winning big with an alto rich and knowing far beyond her years. Irate parents at one competition demanded that Kim be barred, as her vast superiority "sent the wrong message".

"My daughter's a winner too!" a distraught mother yelled into my mother's face.

Eyebrow coldly arched, Mom corrected: "Your daughter's a loser."

Those competitions held together our family a little longer: Kim's rehearsing in the living room, our long rides to the competitions at various high school auditoriums and fraternal organizations, our post-competition fast-food dinners...these trifles postponed my family's final fracture. Now allow me to press the fast-forward button until we reach the final episodes of *The Edwards Family*.

One late Friday afternoon, a few weeks after my twelfth birthday, another of Dad's giggling galpal disciples called for

"Professor Dave." Mom dropped the handset, letting it spin wildly at the end its uncoiling cord. Then, the next morning, Mom tossed Dad's tuba and euphonium onto the front yard. His sheet music, shredded with a straight razor, followed the brass. When I looked out the window that bright Saturday, I fleetingly thought that a parade had crossed our yard: the low brass gleamed gold and silver upon the grass, and confetti was strewn about.

Roars from the kitchen snapped me from my reverie. By the time I tip-toed downstairs, Dad was gone: I caught only a glimpse of his shoulder as the heavy oak door crashed shut.

"What's, where's—" I stammered.

Mom's face contorted in crude pantomime and I thought she was trying to make me laugh.

But making people laugh just wasn't *her*: she was mocking my shocked expression. That afternoon, she celebrated Dad's departure with a pitcher of martinis, a bag of string cheese, and a half carton of cigarettes.

"This time," she croaked, "he's really gone. Forever."

So our family shrunk from quartet to trio. Kim responded by studying music even more seriously. She seemed determined to fill the musical void created by Professor Dave's absence, even doubling the length of her weekend low brass lessons. Soon she was blistering every chromatic scale exercise that Dad photocopied. And she'd learned to hold back on a tune's head, raising tension between lead line and rhythm...then she'd snap the line like a sling shot.

Eventually, her weekend visits with Dad became week-long visits, and then she was rarely with Mom and me. When Kim was home, she practiced her new love: the electric guitar. With monkish devotion, she labored over a single song for three to four hours, sitting cross-legged upon the floor, perfecting the guitar lines, then the bass lines, then the vocal lines. Finally rising, she walked comically bow-legged until regaining her sea legs.

Over time, she took to standing as she played, her bony hip pushing out the guitar's body. She ransacked decades of rock music, seizing upon its melody and texture and passion. The bands? Too many to recount, though I do recall her worship of the Pixies, with their loopy shrieking atop hooky tunes...she loved the L.A. punk band X as well, studying the guitarist's rambunctious, virtuosic riffing.

"Isn't that just *fantastic* guitar?" she demanded after making me sit through several X tunes.

I nodded.

"Just imagine if they could sing." And so for two hours she sang over the CD, pausing only to soothe her throat with strawberry yogurt. "If only X'd had the marketing machine of—" She wiped a trace of yogurt from her mouth. "—of those frauds The Strokes or, oh I don't know, any of those 90's faggot boy bands or all that *pathetic* rap and hip-hop shit." And then she was off, belittling hip hop as "made by morons who couldn't figure out Barney the Purple dinosaur music."

By the time Kim hit fifteen, her offhand *esprit* demanded one's attention: she'd stand in the middle of her CD-littered bedroom, white tee shirt loosely tucked into her jeans, black hair obscuring her face, fingers searing the fret board.

As for *The Edwards Family*'s replacement, *Mama Righteous*:

"Make me a fresh drink," she'd sneer, rising from the kitchen table to make the drink herself. Having to make her own drinks offended her, and life without offense bored her. Like an Old West gunfighter, she wielded a bottle in each hand and never missed her mark: a nearly invisible flick of the left wrist produced six splashes of vermouth in the water-marked glass, and a prolonged tremor of the right wrist topped off the concoction with soda water.

One typical Sunday night, I'd made dinner yet again, as Mom hadn't mastered kitchen arts beyond micro-waved popcorn and burnt burritos. Dad had, in fact, been the family cook by default, and in his absence, I inherited the manly duty of cooking. The night's dinner was chicken parmesan, spiced with oregano and basil. Mom agreed—barely—that the dish was pretty good.

"*Pretty* good?"

"Don't look at me that way." Her vermouth and soda slopped about and spotted her shirt sleeve. "Reminds me of someone."

"I remind you of him. So you hate me."

"I wasn't going to say that..." She glanced downward at her drink, needlessly stirring it with her lacquered little finger.

"Not yet. After another drink, maybe."

"Okay, so I *was* going to say that."

"Then I stand uncorrected." I turned to my comic book, flattened before me on the kitchen table.

"Aren't you clever." She sauntered to the living room to smoke and channel surf. "But not clever enough for your father." Mom loved making the point that she, not professor Dave, was raising me.

Later that evening, she'd sobered up enough to sample red wine. Which was fine, as red wine pushed her across the continuum of moods. The continuum ranged from choleric to maudlin to something approaching kindness.

"Finish your homework Jeffrey?"

"Yup."

She stretched upon the couch; her skinny frame barely compressed the old cushions. "I never did my homework until the last minute, and your father always teased me about that. He always got A's, even when he played all the time in the jazz band."

And so our Sundays ghost-walked into the workweek, where like so many families—rushed and splintered—we faced the mornings still fatigued by the evenings. Mom chain-smoked between micro-waved instant coffees; I subsisted on apples and chocolate bars. When Kim happened to be home, she sat before the TV with milk-logged cereal. And then with cursory wishes for a good day, we went our own ways...Kim and I to school, Mom to whatever job she held at the moment: private voice tutor or temp word processor or substitute teacher. I recall her harried preparations to sub for the diabetic French teacher...standing behind her and looking over her shoulder, I murmured the phrases, mocking her efforts to memorize the day's *mots justes*.

Each morning, it hung in the air...the heavy knowledge that *The Edwards Family* was long over. Just as well, I figured. It wasn't very good anyway: loud and lurching, just a failed vaudeville revue fueled by booze and doom.

Three: Choking Her

July's heat was merciless. Even we kids were worn down, while the adults looked pan-fried. Kim was staying for the week, as Dad was out of state on a five-day gig with his loosely confederated jazz ensemble. As I walked lazily down the sidewalk, I saw a car stop before our house. Kim got out of the passenger side and waved me over, remarking she'd been burning CD's with some friends. We glanced at the house, wondering just how low the mood would be inside. Mom was between jobs. As flat-broke drunks tend to do, she cheered herself by spending freely on booze and cigarettes.

"She's loaded already," I predicted.

"Maybe she drowned in the tub."

In the years since Dad's departure, we'd learned that both cynicism and hope spring eternal.

I pulled a meaty spliff from my shirt pocket.

"Where'd you—?"

"C'mon," I nagged. "Let's smoke it behind the shed."

"Remember how Dad used to smoke back there?"

"Weed?"

"Maybe. He smokes it now."

"With you?"

"Are you kidding? He's like Mr. TV Dad with me."

By the time we finished the joint, Kim was singing throatily, and I marveled that she could be so relaxed as we entered the house. Of course, she could get away with more: I was stuck here.

"Mom'll know you're stoned."

"Fuck her."

I went into the kitchen to scavenge for cola and chips.

A ragged piece of paper, folded into quarters, was on the kitchen counter: *Went over to David's for dinner...be back by seven or eight. There's food in the refrigerator.*

David...a balding jerk Mom met at a Parents Without Partners Friday Night Perch Dinner and Dance. He'd visited a few times, and always his visits were brief, with a tense impatience. He'd accept a drink, but his intake was limited to one while Mom's was limited to a dozen. David usually departed with vague claims of unfinished chores. She'd keep drinking of course, slinging sharp shiny glares at me, as if I'd driven David away.

Now Kim breezed into the kitchen, hungry from the joint. She snickered at the note. "Mom, she's really sleeping her way to the bottom." She was supremely stoned: heavy lids drooping over red eyes and a grin that refused to heel. She surprised me by lighting up the joint's remains right there in the living room.

"Better hope that note is wrong," I said, "about her being back by seven or eight"

She sneered, dismissing such a possibility.

And she was right: despite her note's promise, Mom didn't return at seven or eight. Kim departed when a car, headlights harshly lighting up the living room, pulled into the driveway. After a leisurely two bowls of popcorn and three bottles of soda, I fell asleep on the couch with the TV on.

Racket awoke me: I sat up and squinted in the pallid light. Before me stood Mom, bottle in hand and chip on shoulder.

"I'm still young enough to be stood up. And too young to have, to still have kids."

I offered a brief smile.

"But upon Jesus' bosom I still love my kids." She stumbled eastward, and her declaration overshot me to bounce off the ceiling. "He doesn't, but I do."

"Uh huh." Mom's righteousness was rising, a symptom of her attending Mass last month. She bent over and shouted into my face. "I do! And I can't, I mean he can't forget that!" She now listed westward and stopped a fall by placing her hand on my knee. Thusly braced, she kicked off one shoe, then another. "Where is she?"

"She went out."

"Catting around!"

Mumbling, she went to bed. I lay there a long time, listening for tell-tale din: the drunken oath or oafish tumble as big toe struck bigger dresser. Nothing. Must've been awfully tired as well as awfully drunk. Otherwise, she'd have lurched back to the couch to continue her discourse on Her Heroism in the Face of Life's Trials.

Kim arrived home smelling of menthol cigarettes and wintergreen gum. As she walked past me, she dropped upon my lap two slices of foil-wrapped pepperoni pizza.

"So how was Mom's date?" She leaned into the refrigerator, searching for a beverage.

"Not sure."

"How's the pizza?"

"Good. What'd you do tonight?"

"Jammed."

"Who with?"

"Richard."

Richard Ray: his parents were divorced—bitterly so—and they battled for Richard's favor in a spiraling game of one-upmanship: ten new DVD's from his mother, a new guitar from his father, a new amp with digital effects from mother.

"After he flunks out of 11th grade again, he'll be a Wal-Mart lifer."

"You're awful," Kim accused, tone a tad defensive. Richard Ray and Kim, I speculated, were more than a strictly musical duo. Last week, they'd headed out, two other friends in tow, across the state line into Chicago to "bear fucking righteous witness," as Kim rhapsodized, at a Pixies reunion show that had sold out, spectacularly, in five minutes.

She trundled by, cola in one hand and pizza in the other. "See ya."

She'd just closed her door a tad too loud and for a moment I thought *Goddamit Kim that's gonna wake up Mom*—then Kim appeared before me, oval-faced, as if viewed through a fish-eye lens. She grabbed my forearm but I was already on my feet and sprinting up the steps to Mom's room.

The dresser was upended, its drawers yanked out. Mom held a drawer over her head, Neanderthal-style, and heaved it through the window. Glass hung in the frame like glittering stalactites.

"Mom don't!" Kim pleaded.

A breeze rippled Mom's hair, and she transmuted from Neanderthal to gorgon, blonde-streaked locks zigging then zagging. She jumped past me and grabbed Kim's hair. Kim tried to twist free, and Mom backhanded Kim's mouth.

"Mom let go!"

Mom backhanded her again, and blood trickled from nose to mouth to chin. The blood excited Mom: with a jailer's gusto, she bounced Kim off the wall.

"Don't like my rules?" Mom roared. "Then stay with your fucking father!"

Kim choked back tears and bloody snot.

"Whore!"

Shaking away my shock, I pulled Mom off. "Goddammit, shut up!"

"And you shut *your* fucking mouth Jeffrey or—" Her eyes widened as my fist struck her mouth. Arms flailing, she somersaulted down the steps with amusing speed and came to a groaning stop upon the landing.

And I was right there with her: choking her. Her bloodshot brown eyes cart-wheeled, but I kept squeezing.

"Stop it stop it stop it!" Kim's voice was reedy and distant, as if piped through a string tied to a tin can. I jerked around to tell her to shut up and, winding up with a broad arc, she whipped an empty soda bottle across my nose. Blood sprayed brightly across the powder blue wall.

Suddenly, the hallway was bright, blindingly so...and it was silent, deafeningly so.

Four: "Hi Jeffrey and hey yourself."

During my first week in Aunt Jo's home, I'd kept to myself, appearing only at the dinner table. I was stiff and obedient. But now, on a humid Sunday morning, she and I chatted.

"This'll work out if we all do our part," she predicted. "Especially if you do yours."

We sat in the living room, me upon her sofa (gold, wrapped in plastic), her in Uncle Art's recliner (brown, draped by afghans). As Aunt Jo explained, "it had been decided that it was best" that Kim stay with Dad and I with Aunt Jo. "Of course, you living with your father just wouldn't work out, not with his new partner," she coolly noted. "It wouldn't be for the best."

I resisted the urge to rub my nose, which still occasionally throbbed from Kim's assault. Aunt Jo continued her monologue about "what's best" and "the sake of the family" and "your mother's afflictions."

Ah, mother's "afflictions": yes, her afflictions had messily climaxed on the evening Kim smashed my nose. Her boyfriend David had snickered at Mom's suggestion that he move into the Edwards home—a home that was indeed humble, I supposed, but not without its upwardly mobile pretensions. Now I knew why Mom had spent two weeks painting the kitchen and bedrooms and cleaning the windows: an outburst of domesticity foretold, or so she hoped. But on that fateful Friday at Pizza RoundUp, David jeered at the notion of his moving in, reportedly declaring that "kids drive me crazy. Not your kids specifically. Anybody's."

Mom seized upon the sweeping "Anybody's" as evidence of David's philandering. He grew indignant—especially at Mom's charge that David was interested in "that homely bitch Margaret Bronson".

David excused himself.

He didn't return.

After downing a pitcher, Mom grew philosophical. She drove to Ms. Bronson's home and—according to the police—attacked the demimondaine's SUV with a decorative rock borrowed from the garden. The SUV suffered a cracked windshield. The neighborhood dogs brayed and Mom scooted, though she helpfully dropped her billfold beside the SUV. The police came calling to the Edwards home on Saturday morning, but by then Mom had moved on to even more dramatics, such as assaulting Kim and being assaulted by me. That morning's rainy sunrise found Mom snoozing at the county hospital, where a zombie intern diagnosed her malady as depression aggravated by nonstop boozing.

"Pretty lucky that the authorities were sympathetic to both of you," Aunt Jo observed. "Your mother needs therapy, you know. It hasn't been easy for her."

"That's true."

"I mean, you could've killed her." She leaned back as if to regard me anew. "You're kind of big for your age and…" Anxiety clouded her face. "Don't you ever bully Robbie, not ever. Understand?"

I nodded.

She regarded me coldly: her tongue ran across her teeth as if honing a barb, but she abruptly shrugged and lighted a cigarette. I helped myself to one, and she did a double-take. "When did you start smoking?"

"About a year ago."

"It's a lousy habit, God knows. I've tried stopping cold turkey, but it doesn't work."

"Not really. I started cold turkey, and I've never fallen off the wagon."

"You've got a lot in common with your father. Like a smart mouth." She stalked off to the kitchen.

As Aunt Jo hunched over the scarred oak chopping block, she looked little like my mother: Aunt Jo's thick ankles and broad shoulders contrasted sharply with Mom's skinny limbs, and more strikingly, Aunt Jo didn't suffer Mom's class anxieties, such as subscriptions to wine magazines and a merry-go-round of ever pricier lawn chemical companies. Sweaty can of Budweiser in hand, Uncle Art entered the living room and flopped into the chair. "The Bears and Colts are playing this afternoon. Wanna watch?"

"Sure," I lied.

"We'll miss Mass again," Aunt Jo called, her voice more hopeful than disappointed.

"With two games on, you bet we will." In withering detail, he analyzed his enormous lead in the workplace betting pool. "None of those dumbasses, *none* of them, can even get break even on the over and under!" he enthused. "'Specially Rick. He's a gambling addict but I don't feel sorry for him."

Aunt Jo leaned in the archway that divided living room and kitchen and asked who was playing.

"Indy and Chicago."

"I'll call Robbie, he'll want to watch."

Robbie, my "cousin" of nearly identical age, soon appeared. He resembled a 17th century court jester who, after incantations and magic mushrooms, had free-fallen through a worm hole into the brave new century. He wore an incandescent red silk shirt and baggy green denim jeans. And just as he had when he was five, Robbie spoke in outbursts while pawing at his face and lap.

"Hey Robbie," I nodded.

"Hi Jeffrey and hey yourself. You've been smoking."

Aunt Jo appeared instantly. "No he hasn't Robbie, that's ridiculous. He's your age and he can't smoke. And neither can you."

"He smells like it."

I shrunk in everyone's converging stares. "That's right, Robbie," I blundered. "I don't smoke."

Skeptical, Robbie sank back in the couch and fiddled with his shirt cuffs as the football game dragged onward into the afternoon. I'd long ago concluded that Robbie was mildly retarded, though official family doctrine forbade even the possibility. Equally taboo were Robbie's origins: he was allegedly the son of Uncle Art's brother, though Kim dismissed this notion, claiming she'd overheard whispers between Mom and Aunt Jo that Robbie was a state ward taken in for an undisclosed fee.

Now, as Robbie burped loudly and moistly, I felt a pang. He'd come a long way, our Robbie: he'd stopped urinating, for instance, on the white birch in the front yard. And he'd suppressed the urge to show neighborhood girls his rococo charcoal sketches of Amazonian female wrestlers.

"Stop staring at me," Robbie complained.

I looked away.

"You stink like cigarettes."

At halftime, Robbie turned to me—his mouth packed with chocolate cake—and blurted: "Haze when's Kim groin visor?"

"Robbie don't talk with your mouth full!" Aunt Jo called from the kitchen.

"When's Kim going to visit?" he repeated.

"I don't know." I pawed my nose.

"Why'd she hit your face?"

"I don't know."

Lying in my makeshift bed that night—three old mattresses piled atop one another as if to form a sandwich—I too wondered when Kim would visit. She lived about an hour away, but miles and minutes are not the only measures of distance: resentment and envy are measures too, and I had an abundance of both. No, not because Kim broke my nose: understandably, she panicked as I choked Mom…

No, I resented the simple fact that she was the Anointed One Who Would Live With Dad. And why? I wasn't certain, but guessed that Kim's musical abilities roused Dad's interest. Years of lessons on low brass and guitar had brightly blossomed. Additionally, Kim had joined a couple garage bands: always the only girl and always by far the best musician. One of the bands had some pluck and earned several gigs: at a fair, at a car wash, at a laundry, at several dances in various counties. Kim honed an aggressive guitar style, with a ringing, neo-rockabilly verve that set hips swinging.

But my own musical abilities remained just that: nascent. I'd evaded lessons until Dad just gave up to concentrate upon Kim. And I, who could play "Chopsticks" only with a fellow hunt-and-peck pianist at my side, was apparently a bore.

Five: Lyrics

Looking back at them, my years as Jeff the Lodger were not without their pleasures. As high school gave way to college, I enjoyed enormous independence: nobody raised an eyebrow when I came in at three in the morning, stinking of beer and bong water—or when I returned on Sunday afternoon, having spent the weekend in a basement with a fuck buddy of the moment. Still, daily life was tedious: Aunt Jo enforced my domestic duties, such as washing her drab dinner dishes and mowing her weedy yard and pushing her snarling electric sweeper; I was the only candidate, apparently, as Uncle Art flatly refused and Cousin Robbie...well, he couldn't be trusted with power tools. On occasion, she even pressed me into duty as cook, and I learned— after several kitchen calamities—to create a marvelous pizza.

Even better were my hamburgers, which were out-and-out ambrosial, seasoned with a half-thimble of thyme, a rumor of garlic, and two sunny slices of Swiss. Aunt Jo's cramped kitchen, with its Clinton era white 'fridge and Bush I era black stove, grew expansive and bright in the nurturing scents of my dinners. At one point, Aunt Jo was inspired enough to replace the kitchen window's curtains, switching from morose maroon to gleeful goldenrod.

"Oh boy," Uncle Art declared when he saw me in the kitchen. "I was hoping it'd be burgers tonight." Hands humbly clasped, Aunt Jo sometimes asked for culinary guidance. I feigned mild contempt, if only to disguise my grudging pleasure in our kitchen shop talk.

Still, Aunt Jo did make good on her threats to drag me to St. Mike's for Mass, especially when I couldn't mask my irritation at Robbie. "C'mon Aunt Jo," I'd complain. "I don't need Father Homo telling me that people are sinners."

"Jeff!"

"I *know* people suck."

To rub it in, Aunt Jo let Robbie and Uncle Art stay home to watch wrestling. On one Sunday, my mood was especially sour, as Aunt Jo remarked that Mom would join us. Walking across the drab parking lot, the church looked more galling than usual and, just on the steps leading to the entrance, I refused to go in.

"C'mon," Aunt Jo insisted, smile brittle as the flock trudged past. "Do it for me. For yourself. You're a young man now, nearly an *adult*, really, and it's important that you—"

"This is, it's just *nuts*."

"What is?"

"This!" I jabbed a finger at the church and nearly poked a passing elderly man in his watery eye.

"Stop this now!" Her fingers sunk claw-like into my forearm.

"God lets a mob drive spikes through his son's hands and feet? Out of *love*?"

A half dozen worshippers paused at a discrete distance to overhear the disputation.

"Have some respect," a red-faced fatso demanded. His timorous wife lurked behind him and clutched a little boy's hand.

"Fuck off."

The crowd gasped...and it *was* a crowd now, the spectators numbering a dozen.

"Stop humiliating us," Aunt Jo pleaded, glancing about.

"Don't tell me to fuck off!"

"Jesus in a saltine? That's not *nuts*?"

The Padre, alerted to the scene upon his sanctuary's steps, pushed forward. "Jeffrey, let's talk this afternoon."

"He told me to fuck off, Father." The fatso's wife and child were in tears.

Father Donleavy placed a soothing hand upon my shoulder.

I shrugged his hand off my shoulder.

"He died for you," Father Donleavy half-whispered. His hound dog eyes were even sadder than usual.

"I didn't ask him to die for me, so don't lay that guilt on me."

"He told my Daddy to fuck off!"

Daddy shoved me.

"Punch him, Daddy!"

The fatso tried to shove me again.

I grabbed a hank of his hair and yanked him off his feet. He bounced twice upon his ample ass. Father Donleavy opened his mouth to speak, then helped Fatso to his big feet. The flock, herd animals to the end, meekly followed Padre and Fatso inside. I spun about and started walking home. Rounding a corner, I thought I saw Mom speed by in her rapidly rusting car, so I trotted to hide behind a stately oak.

Aunt Jo got home a couple hours later, not so much angry as exhausted. She began to relate her humiliation to Uncle Art, but he was absorbed by a football game. Desperate for an audience, she even turned to Robbie, but he only complained that she stunk of cigarettes.

A minor miracle ensued during my freshman college year when Kim accepted a dinner invitation from Robbie, who spontaneously phoned and badgered her into stopping by for "some really kickass pizza." I'd not seen her for seven weeks, nor Dad for three months, and I bristled with resentment. Therefore, Kim's indiscriminate friendliness maddened me all the more: yeah, she was friendly toward me, though just as friendly towards Robbie and the rest. No, Mom's therapy wasn't over, she mentioned. Her shrink had taken a job in Canada and Mom was at loose ends, therapy wise. Despite my prodding, no further details were forthcoming, and Kim smoothly shifted to another matter.

"I brought you guys something," she sing-songed. "It's in the doorway."

Robbie leapt to his feet. I tried to exploit his brief absence by asking Kim what in the goddamned hell she thought she was doing, treating me like just another relation. Her eyes narrowed to hot slits and her mouth opened—then she was all casual good cheer as Robbie returned to the living room. He carried a black guitar case.

"Is it really a guitar in here?" He sat down with the case across his lap and shook the case like an eager three year old on Christmas Eve.

"Careful, you'll wreck it," I ordered.

"Will not."

"C'mon Robbie," Kim encouraged. "Open it up."

And so he did. Inside was a shiny black electric guitar. Robbie oohhed and aahhed and Aunt Jo did her best to smile, though she already, I could tell, dreaded the inevitable racket.

"It's a guitar," Uncle Art observed unnecessarily. "That's really something."

"Are you still playing?" Robbie urgently asked Kim.

"Sure."

"Can you do it? Play it?"

Kim's hands fluttered a bit. "Not right now, not when—"

"Aw!"

"—when dinner's almost ready. Speaking of which. When do we eat?"

I stalked off to the kitchen, where my dinner—four pizzas with all the toppings—was nearly done.

Just as I leaned toward the oven, I heard an ominous crash. Aunt Jo's voice rose like a siren as she ordered Robbie to stop just standing there and help clean up. I took a few steps to investigate, but Uncle Art ambled toward me, obscuring my view.

"What happened?" I half-whispered.

"He dropped the guitar on the coffee table."

"What a moron."

Uncle Art rested a heavy hand upon my shoulder, and his easy smile was at odds with his hard eyes. "He's just an ordinary boy. Nothing more, nothing less."

"I'd say he's nothing more and something less."

Kim ate three slices of pizza. Then she was out the door, calling goodbye even as the screen door banged shut behind her.

"That was sure nice of her to stop by and see us." Uncle Art yawned from his easy chair. "And to bring you boys a guitar."

"She's looking so nice and grown up," Aunt Jo remarked, gazing absently out the living room window. She nodded slightly at Kim's parting honk of the car horn. "I hope she's getting along okay," she murmured, lighting a cigarette. "I guess she doesn't have any friends, really, and you know how hard—"

"No friends?" I interrupted.

"That's what your mother tells me anyway. Your father, he keeps her so busy with music lessons and she just stays in her room otherwise."

"But she's in a couple bands," I noted.

"I'm just telling you what your mother said," Aunt Jo nearly shouted.

"She's got *boobies*," Robbie huffed.

Aunt Jo blinked violently and turned upon her son. "Robbie!"

I was nearly out of my chair, ready slap him, but the thought of touching Robbie's sallow skin sickened me.

Indignant, he stomped upstairs. He dragged the guitar behind him, the guitar's body bouncing upon each step.

I was the last man standing—or rather, the last slug sitting—in front of the TV. Aunt and Uncle had drifted off to bed an hour earlier, Uncle Art with a can of beer and Aunt Jo with a can of soda. Their room was, like Robbie's, upstairs...Robbie's on the east end of the short hallway, Aunt's and Uncle's on the opposite end. I was tired but resisted retiring. Robbie would, I feared, awaken as I entered and keep me awake as he noisily fell back to sleep: the vehement scratching of head and back, the coarse clearings of throat and nose, the pleas that I finish his remedial homework. Poor Robbie, the loud lummox, the bewildered self-abuser. He was one of those peculiar lost creatures for whom we feel sympathy only from a safe distance.

That evening, I began sleeping on the couch, an uncomfortable practice for me and an irritating practice for Aunt Jo. She didn't explicitly forbid me from sleeping there, but as I awoke on many mornings, she'd be twenty feet away in the kitchen, banging on pots and slamming the refrigerator door. I sloughed off her cues for a while then decamped, taking up residence in the basement. Creature comforts were few: a bed without a frame, cardboard dressers, a grotesquely ornate brass floor lamp. From a neighbor's garage sale, I purchased an old oak writing desk. The desk charmed me: deeply engraved into the writing surface was a heart. A crooked arrow cleaved the beating organ, and inside the heart was a scrawled declaration: "J.L loves M.E." I never learned the identity of J.L. nor M.E. But that declaration cheered me many a dank afternoon as I sat at that desk studying, writing, or, increasingly, strumming Kim's old black guitar to wordlessly hum the lyrics that orbited my brain.

And so life progressed, from a high school education instantly forgotten to a handful of college courses. Robbie took on a frayed string of low wage jobs: morning newspaper delivery, late night sub shop delivery, bicycle repair shop gopher.

To my surprise, Kim belatedly decided to take a few classes at Dad's university; she'd spent a year making excuses but apparently withered under Dad's insistence. Eventually, we developed a habit of meeting for dinner in the student union before our Monday night classes—Foundations of Civilization for me, Algebra I for her.

"You like school," she mildly accused. "I knew you would."

Later that semester, she abruptly asked if I'd write some song lyrics.

I wrapped the greasy burger wrapper into a ball and missed the wastebasket. "I can't write lyrics."

"Probably not, but that hasn't stopped you. I know you've written some." She explained that she'd written dozens of songs in the last few months but wanted to try something new: start with lyrics and build the melody and chords from the words. "You know, like get a feel from the words, from the mood, and take it from there." She looked slightly past me, gathering her thoughts. "You know, that's why I brought you that guitar."

"For what?"

"To get you in the songwriting mood."

Six: Snapshot

On a balmy May afternoon, I sat on the back stoop drinking a stale cola. Robbie approached and casually remarked—or rather, in his fashion, babbled and stammered: "Uh yeah, more beer'll be there because it's in a keg at her, at Kim's party."

"Her—"

"Freshman dropout party."

Could this be true? All through the year, Kim and I shared Monday night dinners before class, critiquing my growing batch of lyrics. She was in yet another band, and rehearsals had gone well all through the spring. But she'd said nothing about dropping out.

"How'd you hear about this?"

"The invitation."

"You opened my invitation?"

"Then I opened mine."

I abruptly stood and walked past Robbie into the house, being careful to carom my shoulder off his. Through the side screen door and into the kitchen he followed me, stepping so closely that the toe of his shoes twice brushed my heels. Suddenly seething, I whirled about and grabbed two fistfuls of his shirt.

"What?" he wheezed, averting his eyes from mine. "What?"

"What? What?" I mimicked, gripping his shirt tighter. He finally risked looking at me directly. Jesus Christ, I abhorred his thick wrinkled forehead, his fidgety rabbit nostrils.

"Stop it!"

"Let me tell you 'What? What?'" Pushing him against the wall, I did. Facts that once simmered now boiled: my absent carefree father, my boozing head-case mother, my indifferent sister. And now, the rounds of chores: domestic and academic, live-in help to the Aunt and live-in tutor to Cousin Imbecile. He covered his face like an inept boxer and, laughing, I released him.

The phone had apparently rung several times but I'd not heard it—anger had scalded my ears. The caller accepted the answering machine's invitation to leave a message at the tone.

"—so I don't know if you're coming. If you do, then—"

Kim.

"—bring the guitar. Maybe we'll get a chance to, you know, work on some music for your lyrics."

I picked up the phone: "So you really are dropping out?"

"You should drop out too."

Indeed: declaring herself sick of school, Kim was quitting. She'd just "bum around and loaf", she explained, get a part-time job and concentrate upon her music. Dad, she noted, wasn't pleased, but he reasoned that Kim would perhaps come to her senses after a year of minimum-wage lifestyle. "Barbara, that little priss, she's like, Oh it's okay, I took a year off school too and I'm just fine. She just wants me to move out of the house."

"Barbara's still there?"

"She's such a Stepford wife, such a fake. When Dad empties the spit out of his tuba valves, it's like, she gets this little zombie smile and you know she's going to stew about it for a week then just explode. Little bitch."

After Kim hung up, I rummaged through the refrigerator. Robbie had yet again consumed all but one of my private-stock colas. I pushed my hand past the plastic jug of dun-colored milk and captured the last bottle.

Robbie hurried by: "I wanted that last one," he complained as he departed through the side door.

"You got the first five," I barked back, but he was already in the detached garage. Now I nearly regretted roughing him up, but then again, I'd at least not actually hurt him. I heard him start Aunt Jo's car in his characteristic fashion: a grind of the starter, a pained roar of the engine as Robbie stomped the accelerator. A moment later, he backed recklessly out of the garage and, straying three feet onto the neighbor's weedy lawn, down the driveway. He drove with the dark urgency of someone with nowhere to go. He'd speed down the street, take a wide oafish right onto Morgan, then a last left onto highway 111 and keep traveling, traveling, past the final outposts of bland, over-night subdivisions. Eventually, he'd pull over to the shoulder of a gravel road, and maybe he'd turn up the radio and sip the beer he'd filched from the garage fridge. Or silence the radio and roll down the window to relish the late afternoon's breeze, fragrant with burning leaves.

And here the picture grows dim. Truth be told, I had no idea at all about Robbie's destination. Probably to the mall's arts supply store for more sketch paper and charcoal sticks. The details of his jaunt are mine, actually...the details of where I'd have driven if entrusted to Aunt Jo's car.

But I wasn't. Even if I'd been audacious enough to borrow a vehicle on the sly, I couldn't: Aunt Jo and Uncle Art had taken the latter's truck out for the afternoon...a matinee, apparently, followed by a post-movie dinner at Burger Mosh. Auntie and Uncle had, once again, failed to invite me...this, after Robbie had nasally refused their offer. It would've been pleasant to accept an invitation, and more pleasant to reject one.

At least now, with the house deserted, I could play Kim's guitar undisturbed, so I strode up the stairway and pushed open Robbie's bedroom door. Upon the floor: mismatching socks, a lone shoe, balled-up sheets of homework, a sketchpad. Upon the wall: his latest depictions of Amazonian wrestlers. But his *oeuvre* was expanding with new sketches of chipper gals on a bright beach. I enjoyed the retro details: the plaid one-piece swimsuits, the hale figures, the red and white drink cooler, and the volleyball net tall against the background of a cloudless summer sky. The sketches were more enjoyable than one might expect...Robbie's beach bunnies were clichés, of course, but clichés of a more pleasant pedigree, when sex symbols were not rendered grotesque by silicone or tattoos or bulimia.

I sat on the bed and, after flipping through a few more drawings, saw a bulging cardboard box in the corner. Inside were photos: amusingly, most of the photos depicted the television. Seems that Robbie spent hours before the TV taking photographs of his favorite programming: football games, chick volleyball...and videos of various lip-syncing female "singers", most of them plug ugly, with breasts and buttocks bulging from shorts and tops.

Beyond these TV highlights were family shots: mostly Uncle Art and Aunt Jo and even a few of the Edwards. And a recent shot of Kim: she sat upon a couch, empty cola bottle in hand. Beside her was the pant leg of somebody—Richard? Kim grinned self-consciously at Robbie, whom I imagined panting behind the viewfinder. I recalled Robbie's sweaty declaration about Kim's "boobies" and, sure enough, this photograph did indeed highlight Kim's aforementioned. A brief investigation unearthed more photos of Kim. Most damning was a photo showing Kim with her back turned to the camera. It was your ordinary flubbed snapshot, occurring when the subject turns away, camera-shy or distracted. The camera's crude flash illumed her white blouse, and plainly visible beneath the white fabric were black bra straps.

Even as I gathered the photos of Kim and shoved them into my back pocket, nausea radiated from my stomach to my torso to my limbs.

Seven: Dropout Party

We—meaning the Brocks, and Jeff the mercurial lodger—arrived for Kim's dropout party at 1:00 p.m. on a sunny Memorial Day. Several cars had already claimed their place in Dad's freshly tarred driveway, so we parked at the end of the bright suburban block.

"Nice house," Aunt Jo remarked as we approached the walkway to the front door.

"It's not bad," Uncle Don grunted. He glanced about him uneasily, as if planning an escape route.

"Yeah it's not bad," Robbie dutifully repeated.

Never having seen the house before, its sheer ambition took me aback: the gleaming picture windows sheltered by a grand awning, the three-car garage, the brass light fixtures, the broad bed of roses, tulips, moss and white stone that claimed a quarter of the yard.

These days, I'll confide to you, the house strikes me as not ambitious but neurotic...a grotesque monument to class anxieties, complete with absurdities such as an underground sprinkling system and—just to make sure that the equally insecure neighbors grind their teeth before bedtime—a grid of lights that "tastefully" illuminated the flower garden from sundown to sunup.

But yeah, at that moment, I was pretty impressed.

I'd been carefully carrying my boxed pizzas, so I'd fallen a few strides behind the Brocks. Aunt, Uncle, and Repulsive Robbie stood stiffly upon the big front stoop. Only the screen door separated the Brocks from the party inside, yet they hesitated.

I now stood with them to form a huddled mob. Suddenly both ashamed and angry, I hesitated too. But I feigned easy comfort and, pizza boxes stacked in the crook of one elbow, swung open the door and stepped inside. Music and chatter greeted us. We loitered in the foyer, a brightly lit riot of faux-tropical plants in hammered brass planters. Just ahead was the kitchen, where a giggling gaggle of Kim's peers stood drinking soda.

"Hey there's trouble!" Kim emerged from the crush and strode forward, arms stretched to greet the Brocks and myself.

"Your house is just, it's just so lovely," Aunt Jo sang in a nearly comic opera voice.

"Uncle Art, let's get you a beer," Kim suggested.

"Sounds like a plan." He accepted the beer that Kim, like a magician, produced from I didn't know where.

"Hey where's my beer Kim?" Robbie bawled nasally. His Adam's apple bobbed wildly as his question dissolved into giggles.

"Here's the pizzas." I nodded toward the stack of boxes in my arms.

Kim thanked me with a cry of "Yummy" and relieved me of the food. She turned about with military precision, calling over her shoulder to us to come in and make ourselves comfortable. I broke away from the Brocks and followed upon Kim's heels as she placed the boxes of large pizzas—seven in all—upon the oak table. *En masse*, her friends descended upon the food. They were armed with paper plates, plastic forks and knives, and a gleeful gluttony.

Ah what a pleasure it was, watching Kim's friends: *Female* friends, in denim jeans of black or blue, and in tee shirts of white or blouses of gossamer green or chaste pink. And though the episode was maddeningly brief, and I likely sentimentalize the details...it was an epiphany. Pagan hormones pulsed through my hands and loins and brain...the girls, you see, were momentarily free of excessive social graces—they were *hungry*, dammit!—and they were ablaze with Ancient Greek vitality, ripping through pizza and tossing back beer.

Beer!

Leaving the Brocks to fend for themselves, I filched an unclaimed import that had, apparently, been momentarily put aside by—by who? Hell, I didn't care. I pressed the flesh of my palm upon the bottle top and twisted. The beer was a bit warm, but still deeply satisfying to sip while evaluating the girls, who'd now pulled chairs in a crude circle about the kitchen table. One girl, blessed with an arresting contrast of round freckled face and long lanky frame, talked intently with my sister. Kim glanced about the room, her gaze ever so slightly dragging over me, then offered a quick smile. I exploited her familial gesture to bump my chair closer.

"Hey everyone, this is the man of the hour," Kim informed the bevy. "He's my brother Jeff, and he made the pizzas."

"I knew you were good for something," freckle face teased Kim. "You've got a brother who can cook."

The girls heaped praise upon my pizzas and, striking a modest pose, I raised the beer to acknowledge their congratulations even as I feared being tongue-tied.

Kim leaned toward me, half out of her chair. "Hey, Dad'll be pissed," she whispered, then paused to push the black bangs off her eyebrows.

"What?"

"He'll be pissed if he sees you drinking."

"That's such horseshit."

"I know it is but—" Abruptly, she sat up straight, nearly like a trained circus dog, as Dad entered the room. "Hey Dad, look who's here."

"Finally you made it here!" Dad noted with unnecessary volume. We extended his oar-sized hand, and we shook. Or rather, he shook and I hung on. "It's great to see you, really!"

My beer, a yeasty fizzing truth serum, loosened my tongue and stiffened my spine, but I resisted the impulse to inform him that, as an old-fashioned young person, I'd expected a formal invitation from my father a long time ago.

"Get this young man a beer," he jovially called to nobody in particular.

Kim feigned offense. "You don't think twice about letting him drink, but if I want a brew—"

The tall girl laughed heartily.

"I think he's had some already," Dad observed, eyes narrowing behind his reading glasses.

"I cannot tell a lie—because I've been caught."

Nodding humorlessly, Dad excused himself.

"Way to fool the Professor with charm," added the lanky girl.

"I'm sorry, but you're so beautiful that I forgot your name."

"Patty." She rolled her eyes good-naturedly, and her cheeks momentarily flushed, throwing her freckles into relief.

"Your brother's pretty funny," another girl called to Kim across the table. This particular specimen of the female species was—well, she was plain, though as my brain bobbed gently upon the foamy rising tide of beer, I supposed that she was not without her charms. She had breasts, for instance. Of that I was sure.

Another herd of guests arrived, and the kitchen grew crowded with errant elbows and feet. The gals and I abandoned the kitchen for the living room, which was rendered nearly narcotic by the congeries of throw pillows in every corner, heavily textured afghans draped across every chair, and the warm light of halogen floor lamps in each of four corners. From the stereo came an ardent melody...Rachmaninoff. Music and beer and the company of girls converged: a transcendent thirty seconds I've often tried to recreate, but with rueful results.

Adults clustered in flocks of five or six, chatting and drinking. University types, I knew: they shared with Dad that polished sheen of good manners. They nodded greetings and voiced congratulations to the dropout girl. Kim circumambulated the room, pausing to greet each guest.

I looked about for Patty. Ah yes, there she was upon a corner couch, the length of her legs pushing her knees out well beyond mine as I sat beside her. She and some other guests—male and female—had staked out a fogy-free zone.

"Oh it's you, brother of dropout girl. Back for more praise?"

"I wish it were idolatry."

The evening grew louder as the adults drifted out and Kim's friends remained. Dad'd been, fortunately, an MIA den mother and so I drank with easy-going verve—at least, verve for me: six beers in two hours. And that was plenty. I chatted freely with Patty, who periodically rose from the couch to gossip with girls or flirt with boys, but to my delight always returned.

Kim made her way toward us, blinking through the thickening cigarette smoke. A guy was following her...Richard Ray, spoiled Mama's boy and inferior musician.

"Richard, this is him. Jeff," Kim sputtered. She was drunk, introducing me to Richard even as she clumsily sat down.

"Kim, I'm up here." Richard tapped her shoulder.

Kim, precarious upon the cushion's edge, now slid downward upon her rump and sagged against my knee. "I dropped my cigarette," she wheezed, wiping absently at her mouth. "And I'll, I'll burn down the house."

I stood and bent forward at the waist, my range of vision advancing like a fly's from the back of Kim's crown to its top and, continuing forward, to her ruddy face—rendered upside down, of course, as I leaned over to mockingly study her.

She cackled at my face's descent from the smoky air. "Stupid fucker," she bawled happily, "get your knee out of my back." She gained her feet and careened across the room, bumping into several guests like a pinball, then disappeared into the kitchen.

Richard extended his hand. "Nice to see you again."

I nodded and assured him that I too was happy to see him, though I couldn't recall the occasion of our last meeting. I asked Richard what he was studying.

"Music. Right here at the university."

"You're a musician?"

He nodded.

"I thought you just played bass."

"Ouch!" Richard offered, playing along with me. Certainly, he'd endure my hassling, as he was almost certainly bedding my sister. He perhaps viewed me as a potential diplomat in his nascent courtship. "I might even have your dad next fall as a professor."

I leaned slightly starboard, trying to see beyond Richard's shoulder. "Speaking of whom!"

Dad weaved his way through the living room, which was awfully hot with guests and smoke. His brow was fixed in a way I'd rarely seen and his eyes were hard.

"Help me clean up a mess in the—" Several roaring laughs muffled the rest of Dad's sentence. He led me through the kitchen down a short set of stairs to the family room, which had been converted to his practice room: in one corner stood his tuba upon its bell, in another corner his euphonium, and a black digital piano, *sans* bench, obscured the view to a small TV. And upon a desk sat a computer that Dad used for recording music: from the back, like fleeing garden snakes, ran several tangled black cables. I wondered just how well his girlfriend Barbara liked this collocation. And speaking of Barbara: where was she?

I'd not seen her all evening. An odd anticipation—half-excitement, half-foreboding—distracted me from Dad's complaints. Gotta ask Kim, I reminded myself, about Barbara and where—

I collided with Dad like a tail-gaiting driver. I mumbled apologies but he hadn't even noticed. He'd stopped before gray concrete steps that led to the basement. Dad soughed, wearily ran a hand through disheveled hair, and descended. I followed a few steps behind.

Cacophonic voices greeted us. Kim, Patty, a few other girls, and some late-arriving guys had collected, like a weary rugby team, in a poorly formed huddle. And beyond the huddle's periphery extended a pair of legs in blue jeans and shoeless feet in dirty white tube socks.

Robbie.

The huddle dispersed as Dad approached, and I bemusedly noted that each of the guys just kept on moving past, hurrying up the steps and laughing about "the dumbass on the floor."

Robbie was indeed the dumbass on the floor, and despite that concrete floor's cool temperature, Robbie appeared in the grip of a radically elevated temperature, with luridly rosy cheeks and moist brown bangs. A string of yellowed saliva hung from his chin to his shirt collar.

"How can you land on own puke?!"

"Just shut up and help!" Kim yelled, standing to the side.

Just shut up and help, I sarcastically mouthed at her—I'd have bellowed my echo at her, but Dad's eyes counseled silence.

Dad donned a pair of yellow rubber gloves and worked his hands beneath Robbie's shoulder blades, while I bent over to grip Robbie's feet. Securing his grip, Dad called out one-two-three and we dragged Robbie six feet to the side. Robbie gurgled and belched.

"Get the bucket," Dad barked at me, not missing a beat.

I looked around the basement...a concrete structure with gray support beams and bare bulbs in the ceiling. I scrutinized the far wall, which was covered by makeshift wood shelving.

"The bucket!"

"Where is it?"

With a jerk of his head, he gestured toward that wood shelving, but Kim had already grabbed it, and she tossed it to me. But her aim was lousy and the bucket sailed three feet past me to strike Robbie.

Robbie clutched his head, mumbled that he hated graham crackers, and rolled onto his side.

Dad asked me to fill the bucket with water, and he studied cousin rumpot. "At least he's not bleeding," he sourly noted. I remained silent, standing beside the laundry tub as the bucket filled. Kim stood beside me, smelling of aqua vitae and odium. Her voice a half-whisper over the racket of water filling the bucket, she said she was sorry Dad had yelled at me, that it was all her fault.

Presently, I brought Dad the bucket, now foaming with hot water and laundry soap.

"Sorry I barked at you like that."

"It's okay."

Mop in hand, Dad attended to Robbie's slop. Kim and I stood and watched, saying nothing. Dad mopped for several minutes—longer than necessary—and I sensed that he prolonged the dismal chore so he could enjoy the company of son and daughter.

Kim perhaps had the same thoughts...she opened her mouth as if to talk. But she lost her nerve and contrived to cough.

"Too many cigarettes?" Dad joked.

She nodded.

"Here, have another."

Robbie grunted and sat up. He looked at Dad, then me, then Kim. "Oh hi Kim," he managed, then he lay back down, flattened hands between his ruddy cheeks and the gray floor.

Dad looked about the basement as if to find a chore other than dragging Robbie upstairs. "Well...I guess that does it, except for—" He rolled his eyes.

Dad and I grabbed one arm each and hoisted Robbie to his feet. Dizzy, Robbie asked when the party would really get rolling.

"When you leave."

Kim shushed me to silence and, a few feet behind, trailed us up the steps. Finally, twelve laborious and painstaking steps later, we arrived at the top, ragged passenger in tow. I looked about the practice room and knew that Dad wouldn't let Robbie within ten feet of his instruments.

"Where should we drop him?"

He nodded toward a corner, which was occupied by a fake fern.

Kim passed us and quickly moved the fern away, then tossed a few throw pillows into the corner. "Prop him up a little," she instructed as we freed ourselves from his suddenly flailing arms. "He won't choke if he pukes."

"Uncle Art and Aunt Jo will be so proud of their Robbie," I laughed, catching my breath.

"They left an hour ago," Kim remarked.

"And left this drunken oaf to throw up all over the house."

"It's okay," Dad mumbled. He was suddenly exhausted, face drawn with fatigue lines and swill sag. "Let's not, uh, worry about it, you know, at..."

"At this moment," Kim interjected.

Dad looked up as if to locate Kim's voice...she had hurried up toward the kitchen. "Yeah. At this moment."

Eight: "She'll stab her own windpipe."

I woke around eleven. Sitting up on the couch in Dad's practice room, I saw an unopened beer bottle on the coffee table. A twist, a few swallows...my hangover, which had a physical heft and clamminess, was washed away like so much half-dried mud upon a car fender. Then I saw a pack of cigarettes standing at attention, like a dutiful platoon to be sacrificed in my dry reeking mouth.

The house half-slumbered in the lonely pang that follows festive evenings. A few footsteps overhead, coming from—where? I had no idea, as I'd not been upstairs.

On the other side of the room, woeful Robbie groaned. I left Robbie to his struggles to make my way up to the kitchen, pausing only to drop my cigarette in a paper cup. The ciggie hissed and died, and I stepped lightly past the kitchen table and into the living room.

Kim was straightening up. Moving briskly about the room, she flipped beer and soda cans into one of four plastic garbage cans she'd placed in each corner.

"I'll help," I volunteered.

She paused to strike the pose of a basketball pro standing at the free throw line and, slightly springing upward, she tossed a beer bottle toward one of the cans. The bottle tumbled end-over-end and crashed into its resting place.

I looked about for more bottles. "So what's the deal with Barbara?"

"Seems that dear Barbara has moved on to bigger and better things."

"Such as?"

"Tenure track at some phony girls' college on the east coast. She'll teach them how to hold their French horns in such a lady-like fashion."

I tossed bottles into a garbage can.

"She wasn't around much anyway." Kim stepped toward me, eyebrows arched and voice low: "It hadn't been good between them for a while, and she never could stand me. Whew, the fights they had."

"What about?"

"Everything, just like with Mom and Dad." She paused. "Maybe Mom wasn't always the bitch we thought she was."

"Sure she was."

She strode past to retrieve several bottles marooned behind a chair...remarkable, I thought, how chipper she was after a night of boozing. Her hair, briskly combed, hung straight from the bifurcating part atop her head. She was changing, I realized...taller, thinner, but still tomboyish. Still sister Kim, but now slightly a stranger after my years of exile.

"Hey Kim I gotta, um, where's the daft tune?" called Robbie from just around the corner.

"There's a bathroom downstairs, just off Dad's practice room." Then Kim asked, "Why're you such a prick to him, anyway?"

"Because I live with him."

Pointlessly, she stared out the picture window. The sun had burned off the morning's loitering fog, and the green lawn glistened beneath the gentle artificial mist of the underground watering system. Three grade school boys, perched upon over-sized bicycles, pedaled furiously. Moments later, a grade school girl gave chase upon foot.

Kim leaned forward to catch final glimpse of the little girl on the street, then turned toward me with a darkened face. "If Mom were here, our little jam band would be complete." She sat at one end of the couch and I at the other. "But she's so nuts." In a bruised voice, she shared the grimy details: after a month of outpatient therapy, Mom's condition declined and she was hospitalized at Three Oaks, a private hospital that catered to prestige afflictions such as bulimia and leisure class kleptomania. But Mom's insurance fund—never stable—collapsed when Mom lost her then-current job as a plumbing contractor's office manager.

Mom was obliged to decamp back at home, where she undertook the thrift approach to therapy: drugs prescribed with rash enthusiasm by a certain Dr. Megarivicz, a doctor-in-a-box whose office shared a strip mall with a Chinese food buffet, a Dollar Deal discount, a medical supplies outlet, and a Hillbilly Bob's auto parts.

"That guy, he's not even a cow doctor," Kim asserted hotly. "He just flipped through his pharmaceutical brochures and thought, yeah hell, let's try that out."

Isolated and broke, nearing psychic enfeeblement, Mom submitted to the good doctor's spontaneous recipes. Kim hazarded a guess at one of the drugs: "Zolar or something like that," by which she meant Zoloft. Mom's broad-minded doctor also let her create cocktails featuring Zoloft and Risperdal, popular examples of that class of drugs known by the elegant jargon Selective Serotonin Re-uptake Inhibitors. But the inhibitors were not selective enough—or perhaps too selective. These mood-enhancers did indeed enhance her moods, though in the wrong direction: she grew nearly comatose with depression.

"I saw her once when she was, like really fucked up on that Zolar. She just sat in her old crummy housecoat and stared at the TV like a zombie. Her lips were all cracked and she lived on discount cigarettes and aerosol cheese from a can."

Mom's fortunes modestly spiked when, upon the recommendation of another of the cow doctor's patients, she asked for different medication. Her wish was granted, as the doctor handed her a fistful of a drug that "sounds like somebody's name. Like Travis," as Kim explained. I guess Kim's signified was Trazodone, a drug that, I've come to learn, eases both depression and agitation. And that certainly summed up Mom: depression and agitation.

Kim's narrative reached its climax with Mom's having moved into an apartment. "The house was just really getting her down, being empty and all. She sold it, you know."

I didn't.

"Part of the divorce settlement." She brushed lint from her pant leg. "So anyway...last time I saw her, I asked why she tried to kill me. She said I was being just melodramatic. I was pissed."

"Just what she wanted," I coolly observed. "You get mad at her, then she's got another martyr's tale about kids who never visit."

"Then she said, you know, don't sweat it, she gave up on me a long time ago. I'm just a whore, I'm just a sow. And so she feels nothing for me and if she ever does, she'll stab her own wind-pipe."

With colas and the occasional cigarette, we idled away the afternoon by listening to some CD's Kim had copied from Richard's cyclopean collection. At her mention of Richard's name, I smirked.

"What?"

I assured her that she knew. Precisely what she had to know was that Richard the roué harbored ever-deeper urges for my sister...he'd rarely let Kim escape his vigilance last night and now I recalled how at one point, I'd tapped Richard's chest with my finger and told him I knew exactly what he had in mind. He played dumb, of course, something he's born to do.

"Hey that's a good guitar, isn't it?" Kim blurted. She leaned forward, her frame suddenly coiled with energy, her right ear squinting toward the speaker. "Oh yeah, do you hear that?" she rhapsodized. "It's an A seventh that kind of, it floats above the D's and G's. Simple really. Just lay down the D and G and track over with the A."

"Huh."

She illustrated her tiny tutorial by mimicking a fleet fingered run of single notes in A seventh. "Lately, I've been playing some metal solos. You know, really balls-out and squealing."

I raised a disapproving eyebrow.

"Yeah I know it's a cliché," she laughed. "But I really like, you know, pastiche and stuff. Shit I could just drop that hammer down right onto a song...It'd be easy," she insisted, more to herself than to me: "Just use shareware imitation Pro Tools and do it right on Dad's computer."

From behind me, a voice—atremble with clot—demanded to be heard: "My friend Brad's got all of Pro Tools up on his own server. Takes a long time to download though," he cautioned.

"He's got Pro Tools on a server?"

"Yeah. And he's my friend."

Kim smiled. "What, giving that expensive software away, is he an anarchist or something?"

I asked if Robbie's friend might simply loan Kim the CD's containing the software.

Robbie's moist adenoids gathered strength so that their owner might continue. "I mean, yeah sure, he'd give me a copy."

"My computer, it's trashed," Kim mused. "But we can put it on Dad's. And we'll have time to do it, since you'll be staying here for a while."

"Huh?" I blurted.

"Yeah, you and Robbie are staying here for the weekend. But the first rule is that I get the shower first before the hot water is used up." She stood and whirled about upon one foot, leaving me with Robbie.

The silence, brutishly amplified in my hot ears, compelled me to speak: "Yeah, it'll be cool, Robbie."

"Hey thanks man!" he spurted, voice hard with anxiety.

Nine: Sundays

Reader, you've certainly observed that my family—both immediate and extended—had a child problem. The adults looked upon children as occasionally charming but typically tedious. As many children can be. Certainly, exceptions exist: Kim, with her rare talent, could never be a bore. But the less talented of we humans are, I now understand, often very boring, especially for those adults who themselves have no talent as parents.

Like burdens, we were passed around, the pattern beginning with Robbie and continuing with me. I do know that both Mom and Aunt Jo harbored some artistic ambitions: my mother's singing and Aunt Jo's photography. I will concede here on the record that Mama Righteous could indeed sing...very well in fact. I've got an MP3 of her singing the noir-ish standard "Haunted Heart," and her vocal is conventional yet impressive: plenty of range, very respectable technique, a sense for the lyrics. *There*. I said it. She could sing.

As for Aunt Jo's alleged artistry...Not once have I seen her photography. I've merely heard, mostly from Aunt Jo herself, how "compelling" her work is. Our Robbie's interest in photography, I assume, came from Aunt Jo's rousing self-praise.

According to my theory, the parents loudly or quietly resented us kids and the tedium we imposed upon still-young lives. Over the years, these frustrations simmered and occasionally boiled over, leaving messes to be mopped up. And so when Mom's marbles tumbled from her brain, never to be accounted for, I was off to Robbie's with the shabby understanding that their favor would, at some point, be returned.

That's my cobbled-together explanation, at any rate. Kim's assessment was more direct: "They're just puny little failures."

Robbie's quasi-squatter status can be traced back to the weekend of Kim's party. The matter was never discussed, really...it simply happened that Robbie stayed over the course of that first weekend. It further happened that a brawny pathogen assaulted both Aunt Jo and Uncle. Bed rest, fluids, pills, elixirs, vaporizers and vodka were the order of the week. With a determined two-fisted tug, Aunt and Uncle stretched that one week into two, then three.

At that point, Robbie went home...I recall that Dad had to drive him, as Aunt and Uncle were still too ill to drive. Dad returned, remarking that Art and Jo looked fine to him, but then again, he held degrees in musical performance, not medicine. Robbie's absence cheered me enormously. Yet after a week, I actually missed the twerp, if only because his ineptitude in all matters so amused me. But it was something a bit more...his absence gave me sufficient perspective to realize that I admired something about him: his devotion to drawing. Not the drawings themselves—one can ponder female wrestlers only so long—but his real commitment to a craft.

As it happens, Art and Jo's health was far more fragile than assumed, and after a dramatic setback (migraines, cramps) Aunt and Uncle told Dad that they needed a rest and retreated to the cool mountains of North Carolina. I recall with documentary clarity that particular phone call: Dad was in the midst of oiling his tuba's valves. Upon learning of the relatives' need for convalescence, Dad spilled the valve oil all over his right pant leg. Then, jaw set, he nodded hotly into the phone as Aunt Jo—her authoritative voice rendered mannish by cigarettes—jabbed at Dad's ear. Dad said little but the occasional "Of course" and "I understand" and "We're still a family after all."

He set the phone down with remarkable restraint, though I noted tics marching across his face.

"What?

"They're going to North Carolina for the next three weeks, and would it be too much of a bother if—"

"—if we drove a stake through Robbie's forehead?"

"If Robbie just, uh, stayed put for a while. Because, as you know..." With deliberation, Dad placed his forefinger upon his chin and looked toward the ceiling to gather profound thoughts: a theatrical simulacrum of Aunt Jo. "...as you know, a divorce doesn't mean we're still not family."

"Sure it does."

Two hours later, Robbie stood upon our porch gripping a bulging suitcase. The suitcase's weight compelled him to tip, Pisa-fashion, to the left. I held open the door and even managed a greeting nod. "Yeah great to see you too bro!" he exclaimed. He took a lurching step and dragged the suitcase behind him as if it were an anchor.

"What's in that?"

"Weights. I work out all the time now."

"Since when?"

He took three more labored steps and released the suitcase. "I started this morning. Gotta get in shape this summer."

Kim called hello from the kitchen.

"Hey yourself cuz!" Robbie honked back. Forgetting about his suitcase, he hurried into the kitchen, jabbering to Kim about his workout regime.

In short order, Robbie re-established his presence with an irritating offhandedness, like a princeling restored to his Lilliputian throne. Nonetheless, in my more meditative moments I suffered pangs of empathy: I too knew the discomfort of being passed off like an unwanted heirloom. As I'd done at his parents, he initially slept on a couch but eventually moved into the basement, building a security fence of blue plastic milk crates around his bed. He sketched, he watched TV, he ate my favorite cereal, and he used too much milk. And otherwise, he followed Kim around the house, asking her if she wanted to watch a movie on cable. No, she never wanted to. Robbie abandoned that gambit and began asking Kim to play guitar. Kim enjoyed an audience, and she usually accepted his hoarse requests.

A pattern emerged: Sundays became music performance days, in which Kim first and Dad second practiced their respective instruments. Kim's latest second-hand guitar was a Gretsch electric hollow-body with a burnished maroon finish. Slouched upon on a stool, she cradled the instrument and played so quickly and precisely that her fingers seemingly multiplied, like a centipede's legs, to approach one hundred. Early May's unusually torrid temperature compelled us to turn on the central air, and we had to augment its overmatched efforts with an electric fan that rotated upon a narrow plastic neck. Kim's hair—she'd taken to combing it straight back and securing it with a red ribbon—inevitably loosened and fell. When the fan's air reached Kim, her hair streamed behind her for a few moments then fluttered downward.

Kim's musicianship had approached the virtuosic. As you'd guess, Richard always found himself in the neighborhood on Sundays. One Sunday he arrived with a Fender bass in hand— literally in hand, as it had no case—and he accompanied her: their first attempts focused upon three-chord rock and pop tunes...typically, whatever ditties cluttered rock radio at the moment. Kim soon tired of these, and she moved restlessly to hyperkinetic rockabilly riffing, salted with long trebly surf lines and peppered with punk chords. Richard could do little but cloddishly follow, his squint jumping from Kim's left hand upon her guitar neck to the sheet music upon his metal music stand.

The musical duo piqued Dad's interest, and he took to listening—though he exercised due discretion by sitting upon the short stairway that led from the kitchen to the practice room. Perched out of eyeshot but not earshot, he sipped a flavorless light beer and only after Kim's badgering did he offer a critique. "Kim, you muffed the segue to the new key, that's got three flats not two! But your tone is, it's really good. It's *professional*."

"What about Richard?" Kim asked after basking in Dad's praise.

"Not bad."

"C'mon, give it to me straight," Richard stoically insisted.

"Not bad...the notes could be a little, uh, a little rounder. You know?"

And after digesting Dad's critique, they'd resume playing for another half-hour, at which point Dad, excited by the musical interaction, declared that he too must play. After a quick run through B flat, he performed several songs. Robbie lost interest and couldn't sit for even a polite three minutes, but Richard listened with admirable attention—so long as Kim stayed to listen.

Ten: Missing the Gig

By the middle of June, Kim and Richard, along with a gaggle of tone-deaf beer spillers and hoarse bong suckers, were rehearsing in Richard's basement. In fact, "basement" captures none of the over-wrought consumerist Hell to be found there: the basement was fully "finished," as they say. As I recall from my meager number of visits, the walls were painted in a warm near-salmon. The half-dozen chairs and accompanying tables made the creatures comfortable. Additionally, Richard had cobbled together a very serviceable recording studio based upon two over-priced Macs and music recording/mixing software. Kim and gang rehearsed in one cleared-out corner, using an amplified computer-generated drummer in place of a real drummer. A few kids who claimed to drum loitered and cadged beers from the basement 'fridge.

Kim was for obvious reasons voted the vocalist: everyone knew of her earlier prodigal years. Her vocal chops were really extraordinary; properly motivated, she nailed near flute-like heights and moody baritone lows. At some point, I realized that she'd modeled her vocalizing upon Dad's euphonium playing. This process likely went back to earlier years, when she'd lay upon a Dalmatian-patterned beanbag chair and, one leg lazily crossed over another, hum along as Dad practiced.

Kim's band, as yet unnamed, landed its first gig at the end of June. Kim was, not surprisingly, astute in choosing a venue: Dad's employer, the local university. "Those kids are so bored during summer session," Kim explained, "they'll show up for anything. Plus there's no drinking so they won't heckle us much and we can play some of our own songs too." With an actual gig facing them, the group recruited a summer university kid—a percussion major, thankfully—who listened to the group's songs a few times, enjoyed them, and arrived an hour before show time.

Such a haphazard approach to percussion didn't bode well for a debut. At any rate, I couldn't attend (exculpatory details forthcoming) and therefore heard only Kim's morning-after reportage. She was quiet at breakfast, offering cursory remarks, so Dad abruptly stopped pressing for specifics. After a half-minute's silence, however, Kim pushed away her empty cereal bowl and pronounced the gig a "near-success."

"How's that?" I asked.

"The place was half deserted. But..." She stirred her coffee with her finger, a slow smile lifting the left corner of her mouth, then the right corner.

"But what?"

"We played pretty good, and well—I played fucking great!"

"Easy with language," Dad dutifully requested.

"Sorry 'bout that but I did. I wowed them, especially on our own songs." She narrated the entire performance, the details of which I now boil to their crystal essence: alternating between currently popular radio fare and original songs, Kim nailed everything on guitar and vocals. "And I mean fucking *everything*."

"Language, please."

"And did I tell you? Some balding little guy—he teaches voice?—was there because he knew I was, you know, Professor Dave's daughter."

"Doug Johnson?" Dad suggested. "Master of basso profundo."

"I don't remember his name, but yeah, he said I should really major in voice."

"That's worth thinking about," Dad agreed with due delicacy, perhaps hoping that Kim would again take classes.

"Anyway, we're playing there again at the end of the week, and yes Dad—you can come this time." With that cheery invitation, she finished her coffee.

"Thank you," I said, suddenly prickly.

"Don't start with that shit."

"—because I *did* invite you but you had to work," Kim tartly reminded me, her diction surrounding "you had to work" with sarcastic quotation marks. She did her best to glare at me, but her impending gig was already crowding out all other concerns. "Anyway. You have a standing invitation to my gigs," she announced, palms turned up and out, like a welcoming host's.

"Now they're *your* gigs," I deadpanned.

"I mean our gigs," she belatedly laughed.

In fact, I had every intention of attending the gig. Simple curiosity compelled me somewhat, but more fundamental was Patty, the tall girl with whom I'd ineptly flirted at Kim's birthday party...she was going. I'd seen her only once since that evening: she stopped by in the middle of the week to visit Kim, but Kim was rehearsing.

"Tell her that, you know, sorry I missed her but I'll see her at the big show on Friday night."

"I'll see her there too."

"Family support," she remarked. "It's nice that you all get along."

"Except when we don't."

Exploiting her half-head height advantage, she winked downward at me. "Well then, see you later maybe. So 'bye!" And she was gone, leaving behind a bang from the screen door and the scent of a smoldering menthol cigarette.

And now to the exculpatory details to which I earlier alluded, the cause of my having missed Kim's inaugural gig: I'd gotten a summer job at Franco's pizzeria. See, all the music in the house that summer—Kim, Dad, Richard, even Robbie, the rudimentary plucker of orphaned bass guitar—all the noise excited me and I grew hungry for my own axe. True, this desire was absurd, as are many deeply-felt desires. I had the old black one from Kim, but that guitar was begrimed by Robbie's filmy palms—and his grotesquely pale fingers that never seemed quite clean. If I just had my own guitar, a virgin axe unsullied by Kim's expert fingers and/or Robbie's smelly paws...well, it would be solely and exclusively *mine*, and therefore properly broken in to the demands of my own peculiar musicality.

And to that fanciful piffle I add this prosaic fact: one day I just got pissed about something. Maybe mollycoddled Richard stole my last bag of B-B-Q chips. At any rate, I gave the black guitar a hearty heave-ho right through the basement doorway. The guitar tumbled with thrilling violence down the gray cement steps and stopped with equally thrilling violence against a basement support beam. Improbably, the instrument remained whole—structurally if not musically—and suffered a lacerated back and a busted tuning peg. The neck must've suffered a bend, though, as the guitar never stayed in tune for more than ten minutes, but Robbie never noticed.

Pizza and me...we've enjoyed a rich history. I applied for the job at Franco's on the slightest of whims, having spent an afternoon growing atwitter in the chain bookstore/café, hunched at a little round table with big cups of black coffee and big stacks of girlie mags. No, nothing so vulgar as *Peeled* or *S-L-*-T*. Instead, I relished the glossies that featured dillies garbed in threadbare clingy tees or buttock-climbing shorts. Flesh that retains a measure of mystery is the most rousing. The bookstore was the major tenant in a new strip mall, several of which now lined the asphalt tributaries that flowed from town outward into flat barren county land. Three doors down from the bookstore was Franco's Pizzeria, garishly cheerful with red booths and white tabletops. *Help Wanted, Experienced* announced the semi-grammatical notice, taped to the front window.

Partially obscured by a half-wall over which the cook placed completed orders, a stocky guy in his mid 40's whistled while he chopped green onions. I leaned against the counter, silently counting the seating arrangement: ten tables and twelve booths.

"Yeah can I help you?" the fellow called from the kitchen.

"The help wanted sign," I replied, gesturing with my thumb toward the window. "Still looking?"

"Just a minute, okay?"

Presently, the fellow ambled upon aching feet to the front counter. "Yeah, I'm still looking. I'm Franco, by the way."

"Jeff."

"Got kitchen experience?"

"With pizza sauce or dish soap?"

"Depends."

"Both," I lied. His big brown eyes widened and before he could ask for details, I briskly listed three of the finer dining establishments in my previous—and fictional—hometown suburb: "Well, in Rochester I worked at Anthony's, started with dishes and pretty quickly did set up for the evening. And Michael's, dishes again and then helping in the kitchen, mostly set up."

"Ever cook?"

"Breakfast."

"I see. Well in here, I need a set up guy. I need him yester-day."

"Right." I helped myself to a menu, one of a dozen stacked upon the counter. "Hey, manicotti. Is it good?"

"It's excellent," he assured me. Several faint trails of flour crisscrossed upon the gray tee-shirt. "But in here it's mostly pizza and antipasto. Sometimes baked shells."

I snapped shut the menu. "Can I look around the kitchen?"

Franco hired me that afternoon and I started the next night: the evening of Kim's first performance. Like her inaugural, mine went surprisingly well. Despite the small dining area, the kitchen was sufficiently spacious. I arrived at 1:00—three hours before opening—and under Franco's light-hearted directives, went about my business, preparing the pizza dough, sauces, and slicing up the toppings. Franco was easy to work with, possessed of that sociable enthusiasm inherited from his Greek mother and Italian father. I even joked that his sauce recipe was a little light on both the basil and oregano.

"Jesus, I know that," he conceded from the back of kitchen, where he rifled through the freezer. "But these customers!"

"You mean idiots?"

"If you say so—hey Julia, you're here on time!" he noted with mock pique.

A mid 20-ish woman in a wrinkled aquamarine waitress uni-form happily told Franco to perform fornication upon himself, and Franco laughed with sufficient gusto that, in the act of slamming the freezer door, he pinched his little finger.

Julia appeared in the kitchen, remarking to Franco that he was inbred. I nodded and smiled and she nodded back...the overhead fluorescent lights, slightly abuzz, revealed her to be certainly beyond the milestone of her third decade. Her angular figure, seen from a distance, had deceived me: a wasp-waist, alti-tudinous arse, bony shoulders.

"Julie, this is my new set up guy, Jeffery."

"And this—" I nodded toward Franco, who gingerly clasped his wounded little finger against his apron. "—this is my new boss." I extended a hand, which she accepted with a firm shake and a firmer nod.

The phone rang.

"Here we go," Julia said, glancing at her watch. "Can't even wait until we open."

Franco, studying his swelling little finger, showed no interest in the phone.

"I'll get it," I announced.

"No you won't," Julia corrected. "We open at four, and it's not four yet—it's 3:50."

"That's right," Franco agreed. "In two hours, we'll be too swamped to breathe. At least, I hope so."

And so we were: that night, Franco's served up forty-five pizzas, twenty-eight antipastos, and four dozen dine-in dinners. Franco seemed to tire rather easily and by the roaring dinner hour of six, he'd torn through two boxes of tissue to sop perspiration from his broad swarthy forehead. But he never complained: actually, he was happiest during the peak of the evening. With little time to talk or even joke, he kept the kitchen organized: his assistant Bill, a veteran cook, was equally implacable, though his expression was of strain, contrasted to Franco's expression of pleasure. When a customer sent back a pizza—it wasn't supposed to have sausage, or so the customer claimed—Bill remarked acidly that he just loved the food service industry.

"I do too," Franco grinned, grabbing for another dough ball. "I love it."

Eleven: What the Righteous Really Dread

Soon, musical Sundays were packed with guests who became regulars: Dad's latest mistress, an adjunct low brass teacher at the University, was one such addition. She'd ease her sleek designer rear onto the steps, beside Dad's, and listen to Kim and Richard with a passable imitation of interest. Quite sporting of Dana, actually, and a mark of her good-natured teacher's heart. When Dad played, however, the cheery mask toppled to reveal a face deformed by stark concentration. Then, after Dad's final note, she'd chatter hurriedly, praising Dad's intonation and fingering—and yes, the term "fingering" inevitably raised a smirking eyebrow from Kim, who despite her musical maturity retained a winsome streak of social immaturity.

In addition to Dana, revolving members of Kim's group attended, as did Patty. She'd grown more lanky and more stoned...her midriff was longer than her blouses, her head lolloped, her eyelids sagged.

One afternoon, after Dad had grandly resuscitated the decrepit chestnut *The Carnival of Venice*, Dana turned to me and said, "Your turn."

"—Mine?"

"Right."

I waved away her directive, but she insisted.

"C'mon, you've been practicing up in your room on that new guitar," Kim contrived to remind me before the assembled.

I stifled a sneer and shrugged. My new guitar was a source of strife between Dad and me, as I'd financed it with a high-interest credit card a week after hiring on at Franco's. Dad heatedly claimed I'd be paying on it forever, to which I heatedly answered that I'd be playing on it forever.

"Show us the fruits of that labor," Dad challenged.

Against my better judgment, I found myself seated uneasily upon the stool. My audience numbered seven: Dad and Dana,

Kim and Richard, pimpled Paul (Kim's latest drummer), Patty and Robbie. I fumbled with the guitar strap, my suddenly claw-like hands betraying my nervousness. Robbie clumsily stood and left. His departure didn't relieve me...no, it boosted the room's collective I.Q., so I was even more uncomfortable.

I eschewed even a piddling warm up, announcing that this tune was as yet untitled. I fumbled my way through the ditty, which I'd composed in my room over the last few days. I fancied it a fledgling show tune. It began with passable imitations of ar-peggios and then, pace brightening, it segued into a hummable melody of primary hues. The tune brought to mind a pleasant in-terlude in an early 1960's musical: the dappled park on a Sep-tember eve, a park bench for two, the young man declaring never-dying affection for his beloved, whose blonde bob contrasts with the scarlet-streaked sky behind her. Then, just to save the melody from sentimentality, at the bridge I tossed in a dark un-dertow of minor chords, a specter of love foundering upon the rocks in the future...then back to the theme and a cheerful dust-up of mirth as finale.

The final chord's ghost hung in the air for a moment, and against my own will I searched my audience's expressions. All smiles, I was instantly relieved to see, though I feigned only modest pleasure at their applause.

"Very nice," Dana announced.

"Yeah it was like, old fashioned," Patty said. "But in a good way."

I nodded thanks to my audience and noted Dad's thoughtful expression—eyes half-closed, hands hovering above his lap, as if searching out notes on a piano. He nodded toward me and that was, I knew, a concession that I'd played passably well.

"Hey that sounded like something the band could use," Kim belatedly mused. "So could we?"

"I haven't written it out." I gently placed the guitar upright in the corner. "But yeah, of course. When the song's a hit, I'll demand only my fair share."

Ever the budding professional, Kim left the house an hour later with her bandmates in reluctant tow. "That sax player is showing up tonight," I heard Kim explain above the screen door's squeak and bang. Her bandmates' reactions suggested that a sax player was news to them. As the gaggle wandered off, I relaxed in the kitchen, eating stale peanuts from a salt-dusted jar. Though I had the night off, I pondered driving out to Franco's. The employee discount struck me as a keen idea, and of course the food tasted better outside the kitchen's heat and hurry.

"She so bossy," observed a voice behind me.

I turned slowly upon my chair. Patty leaned against the stairway's black iron railing. "Don't you think she's bossy?" she prodded.

"Only when she thinks she's right. Or wrong."

"You're funny sometimes."

"Then you'll really laugh at this." I briskly brushed my palms together and, before my courage flagged, announced that I was taking her out to dinner.

"Really? I hadn't heard."

"In fact, we're going to get the best pizza in town."

"I thought the best pizza in town was right here in this kitchen."

"You're right about that but the kitchen is off tonight, so we'll have to settle for Franco's."

"'bout time you asked me out," she said, taking a step forward to grin downward at me.

Franco's was bustling. All the booths were claimed by the usual late Sunday afternoon assortment of exhausted parents with loud hungry kids. Fortunately, there were a few parents whose heavy demeanor promised bruising violence if the kids dared speak at all. Scattered about were a few lovebirds along with an oddball loner. The loner was by all appearances not, I noted, dispirited to eat alone. In fact, he seemed a wholly satisfied epicure as he savored slow bites of manicotti and even slower bites of the antipasto.

"Sit up front," called Julia from the register. She jabbed the air with her forefinger, indicating that my date and I take a booth with a still-littered tabletop.

Patty glanced at the table and sat gingerly at booth's edge, then pushed away with a long pinky finger a half-finished plate of spaghetti, the top of which was covered with a bloody membrane of sauce and melted scamorze.

"Sorry, we got swamped." Julie wiped at her forehead and flashed a phony smile at Patty.

"It's fine," I said. "In fact—" Still standing, I mouthed "Be right back" at Patty and hurried into the kitchen for a tub.

"Hey!" Franco called as I hurried back out.

I cleared the table with aplomb, lightly tossing the plates and glasses into the white tub and was back with a table-cleansing damp cloth.

"Now that's better, huh?" I grinned upon my return.

"You're so versatile," my date beamed.

She was lovely, really lovely, sitting upright in the booth. Her posture served, of course, to dramatize her height. As we made small-talk about Kim's band, I observed that her height was apportioned in marvelously balanced fashion. Her upper trunk was longish but not freakishly so, and likewise her legs, both lower and upper halves. And atop her slightly elongated neck, the height of which rendered her exotic, perched Patty's rounded face. Ah, but that face was changing too...its adolescent fullness yielded to a more mature length.

"Your cousin, he's sure got a crush on Kim," Patty observed.

"Yes...Cousin Robbie. He's really—" I paused as Julia arrived for our orders. I don't recall now what Patty ordered, though I do recall that she ate with wolfish intensity. As for myself, I ordered manicotti with pizza sauce, not meat sauce.

"You were saying?" Patty prodded, her long fingers wrapped comfortably about her water glass's perimeter.

"He's an amusement."

She giggled.

"And he's not that repulsive, so long as you don't have to talk to him or see him or think about him."

She shrugged in agreement and we exchanged our plans for the fall. Having both fumbled through several college courses with no distinction, we'd made semi-momentous decisions about our academic futures: she'd major in math, and I would major in...I had no idea. "Maybe I'll drop out like Kim."

"I thought you'd study music. Your family, they're all musical."

I demurred, admitting that I was the dilettante musician in my clan.

"But that tune you played was really good."

"You said it was old fashioned."

She laughed and quickly added that the tune had real style.

"—Really?"

"Yeah."

"So do you," I smiled, but my cheeky assertion was drowned by the heart-stopping crash of plates from the kitchen.

Julia appeared moments later with our food. "You picked a good night to have off," she huffed.

"Uh, ma'am? More cola for my date please?"

After dinner, we sat in the car—Patty's father's car, actually—and I waxed sentimental about everything that she and I missed by not knowing one another until now. She grew chattier as the summer's orange sky faded by gradual degree to violet-tinged blue, and she suggested we go for a spin. As she drove out of town, beyond the newest bromidic strip malls and gas stations, she asked me to open the glove box.

With a push of the button, the glove box door lowered itself upon tiny pneumatic arms, and a hooded light bulb revealed a comically long joint.

"What, are you lost?" I deadpanned. "Don't you keep a map in here?"

"If it's a map to a sweeter world."

"Ha! That map, a fight would break out to see who could burn it first." I pulled hard on the joint and nodded approvingly at the query of her raised eyebrows. The weed was wonderful, I said. And it really was, with aromatic hearty buds.

"So who'd burn the map?"

"The usual. Christians, Islamists...religious types generally and of course the jackass PC crowd."

Narrow eyes on the snaking road, she lovingly worked over the joint.

"Patty, what do the righteous really dread?"

"You?"

"A world with no sinners."

An oncoming car's headlights flashed across her face, which was dreamy with dope and—I hoped, oh how I hoped—a hankering for me.

She drove with expert aimlessness, taking lazy long turns into subdivisions, pointing out houses she liked, flowers she liked, and ambitions she'd discarded: she'd been an aspiring stage actress (rehearsing bored her), a botanist (memorizing bored her), and an elementary school teacher (children bored her). For the moment, she was a math major.

"Numbers excite you?"

"No, but I don't expect much from them. And it's the hopes that hurt us."

She sped up, taking another turn and driving a measure too fast for my taste: the maryjane had burrowed into my brain. Glancing at her legs in the car's dark interior, I imagined slipping those long jeans off her. My musings were scattered like startled doves as she turned yet again—this time rather violently—into a driveway, nearly colliding with a bicycle leaning against the tan garage door.

"Is this—"

"Yeah." She pushed open her door and, before scooting out, leaned over and kissed me lightly. "The world isn't sweet, but you are." She kissed me again, even lighter, little more than a polite peck.

She stood waiting for me on her front porch. She was so tall and so pale, an orchid at dusk. Once we were inside, she called out a hello to nobody in particular. Nobody answered, and she murmured that they, whomever they might be, must be in bed already. "They're such sticks-in-the-mud," she accused, glancing at her watch. "It's only ten."

"Seems later."

"It will be in a while."

I accepted a golden bottle of beer and raised it in salute.

"You're welcome," she half-whispered, delicately reaching into the open refrigerator. She lightly cursed as she breached the refrigerator's depths, banging bottles and butter tubs. Presently, she extracted a large green bottle. "Wine? I don't know what it is, but—"

"It's excellent."

She held the bottle at half an arm's length. "How can you tell?"

"Because good company makes for good wine."

She happily shrugged "Whatever" and, with that characteristic slight nod, she directed me back through the living room to a stairway. Gray carpeted steps reached downward to warm and fragrant: strawberry incense. I stumbled on the next-to-last step and lightly steadied myself with a hand upon her shoulder, which seemed nearly at eye-level.

"Hands to yourself, mister."

"Sorry, I—"

Then she laughed and disappeared around a corner. A fumbling filled the air: the striking of a kitchen match illumed Patty, who leaned over a table to light an oil lamp. The flame leaped to life, and she snuffed the match's flame with two rapid shakes, like a nurse shaking a thermometer.

"Better?" The wine bottle, dangling by her thigh, added yet more length to her reedy arm.

"I've got no complaints. At least none about you." From my shirt pocket—littered with three rumpled dollar bills and a paper clip—I rescued the remnants of the joint we'd started during our drive. I lighted it and passed it to her with chivalric courtesy. Languid, she sank onto a flower-patterned couch, joint charmingly crooked in her mouth. Her eyes reflected the joint's flaring orange tip, but her gaze remained upon me as I followed her onto the yielding cushions.

She scooted nearer to the couch's back and I eased my weight upon her. Lids fluttering to half-mast, her eyes rolled upward as if to surrender to me their so-called whites, which were actually of the very faintest blue. After a prolonged kiss, she squirmed to gain some space and pulled off her cotton tee.

Through means of tugging and stroking, she conveyed her desire that I stand over her. She took a teasingly slow pull upon another joint (where did she keep them, I wondered...under the cushions?) then closed her mouth upon me. Hunched slightly forward, she rocked back and forth, hands cupping her breasts upward as if to help them witness our act.

Twelve: Suburban Damaged

Patty's leisurely quaffing of my glands left me swooning and sore, as if Cupid had pierced me with his serrated arrow. We met at least twice a week. I'd stop by Patty's, or she'd pick me up after work, and we'd drive and smoke, chatting easily about the upcoming fall semester or about our parents. After a few joints, my vision and attention were peaceably trapped in a tunnel: I saw only Patty...her limbs, her hips, her spontaneous smile. And upon her lumpy bed we eagerly tumbled. At odd moments of intercourse she'd without warning bellow ungrammatical strings of sex confessions or, more alarmingly, accuse me of coupling with another girl. The first of these accusations stopped me in mid-stroke.

She blinked a few times, caught her breath, and demanded that I continue.

"What do you mean by someone else?"

She giggled and slapped my thigh. "Nothing. I just like it."

"What?"

"I just like the, you know, the accusation of it. The kick of it." And smiling, she repositioned me between her thighs.

Patty's parents remained a muted mystery. If they were at home when I visited Patty, her mother would warble a "Hello" from the kitchen, where she seemed to invariably stand before the kitchen window. In the living room, her father would look away from the TV to nod at me in greeting, though his hesitation indicated that he had little knowledge of even rudimentary social graces.

"They're damaged," Patty once noted.

"How's that?"

She'd been sitting before a mirror, wrapped in a damp beach towel and combing her hair. "Suburban damaged." Her pale bony shoulders were a tactile marvel, and I gently squeezed and re-leased them, watching my fingertips' impressions fade from white to pink.

"Explain, please."

"Keep massaging my shoulders, mister, and I will."

I obeyed and she explained. Patty's parents were indeed "suburban damaged": encrusted with that brittle anomie that af-flicts the upwardly mobile and those who long to be. Her Dad certainly worked hard—he was the senior writer at the suburban paper, which compelled him to labor before a word processor in the day and to attend school board meetings and zoning ordi-nance meetings at night. Mom stayed at home, yet was rarely home: she was instead at church, directing the charity bazaar or the upcoming holiday celebrations or, on occasion, slumped over a ledger double-checking the church's finances.

"When Dad's 401K tanked, it got pretty bad."

"Pretty bad" covered a multitude of pains: a third mortgage with all equity lost, then an auto accident that culminated in Dad losing three weeks of work and his insurance.

"The car was totaled."

Far behind in bills, Dad financed a used car at a high rate and, like an exhausted hiker in quicksand, sank and sank and sank. Now, with Patty's junior year at the university approach-ing, Dad's nerves were shredding, though he stoically refused to entertain thoughts of Patty postponing her education.

"But I think I'm going to quit anyway," Patty half-whispered. "It's not like I can't get a job for a while and, you know, pick it up later."

I nodded, unconvinced, and massaged her shoulders with new tenderness. "You're still going, right?"

"Going?"

"Back to school."

"Yeah I am...I was thinking that, you know, it's easy for you," she said without resentment, "with your Dad being a fac-ulty member."

She was entirely correct, in a sense: Dad's status as tenured faculty member allowed me to attend tuition-free.

"Must be nice," she said dreamily.

"It is..."

Her head swiveled and, studying me over her shoulder, she raised a querying eyebrow.

"It's nice that it's free, absolutely. I guess I should've taken better advantage of it."

"Your grades?"

"Yeah."

"Did I tell you? He's giving Robbie horn lessons."

With a hand, she suppressed a forced snicker.

"Robbie likes it 'cause somebody's giving him attention." I recalled seeing Robbie last week: a beginner's battered tuba in hand, sitting beside Professor Dave and nodding as he pretended to understand the difference between a half note and quarter note.

"You don't like him."

"Only when I'm around him."

"No, your Dad."

"I used to hate him."

"And now?"

"I just don't know him, which works out okay. He doesn't really like or dislike me, either. With him, I'm just...I'm a piece of furniture. Just there."

We sat silently for several minutes. Then Patty edged a half-foot back toward me, drew her legs up so as to place her feet upon the bed, and rested her face in folded arms. "You've been really nice to me," she said. I heard the smile in her voice—and I sensed a lengthy shadow that fell across that past tense *been*.

"May I continue to be nice to you?"

"I hope you always will."

She sat up, arching her back and stretching her arms skyward. "My goodness I'm worn out." After a second stretch—this one more atremble—she stacked one pillow atop another, gave them a playful punch, and lay across her bed. Her feet (one socked, one bare) were restless at the bed's edge. I rose quietly to leave but was detained by long strong fingers upon my forearm. I relaxed beside her. Slowly, tension tip-toed from her muscles and, in the dark room, she appeared slightly shrunken. I kissed her mouth, which was fragrant with marijuana and melancholy, and she smiled through the umbral passageways of fitful sleep.

Thirteen: A Vision

Summer's remaining days sprinted by, leaving me tired and unprepared for fall classes. Meanwhile, Kim's stern work ethic earned her several local gigs that paid little in cash but plenty in word-of-mouth. Across town, the Hotel Perimeter was hosting a backwater convention for so-called "New Media" executives and consultants, with panels on technology convergence and digital paradigms and the latest rounds of shock-and-awe layoffs. Hotel management let Kim and company provide musical entertainment for the conference's final evening in the hotel's Acropolis NiteSpot club. The semi-regular house band, a tasteful and tepid jazz trio, refused to play that evening because management hadn't paid for previous work. The trio had stomped off in noisy indignation, the pianist tossing several cigarette butts onto the strings of the Chickering grand.

I learned of the gig the night before the performance.

"Where you been lately?" Kim demanded as I eased my sore self onto the music room couch.

"Working, pretty much," I shrugged.

"And fornicating."

I nearly aimed the same charge at her, though remained silent as I had no proof that she and Richard were so involved.

Then she tossed me a cigarette and took the stool opposite me, her guitar leaning against her knee. "We got a great gig tomorrow night!"

I lighted the cigarette. "Cheers."

"Some enthusiasm."

I sat straight up. "Seriously. Tell me about it."

And she did: the conference of new media boosters, the angry jazz trio...the gig was an impressive leap forward. Kim ran through her tentative play list, laughing that she'd revise it three dozen times before tomorrow night. But at the moment she planned on a set more interesting and eccentric than that of the typical cloddish bar band's: a few "classic rock" dinosaurs ("just to kick their asses") and, more cheekily, several originals that I'd not heard.

"So what are your originals like?"

"A mix."

"Meaning?"

"Well we got that saxophone player now, Billy Barnes. He's a real monster. He plays guitar and keys too."

"So the songs are, they're...?"

She stopped me with a raised palm. "They *hint* at different eras. Ghosts of fifties rock and roll with the saxophone and snappy snare drum. And some 60's harmony—you know, a quick *sha la la la la* and then some crunchy rhythm guitar, plus 70's stuff." She caught her breath and immediately gagged upon the final tar-choked drag of her cigarette. "Even some loud whiny grunge for those effete little asexual Gen X wussies."

"All in one song?"

"Of course not, stupid! No, these tunes wear their influences very lightly, thank you very much." She leaned forward, drawing upon the air with her freshly lighted cigarette like a professor illustrating music theory upon the chalkboard. "See, the trick is to have really catchy tunes, really catchy sets of chords. Simple stuff that you can get your ears around right away."

"Even Richard?"

"So we've got the hooks, hooks that you can hum along with. No problem with *hooks*..." Her forehead wrinkled as she reflected: "I've been working on some of these songs off and on for six or seven years."

True enough...I recalled her laboring many times on a given tune for weeks and months: shaping and sharpening a melody, out with the minor A and in with the augmented E fifth. And when the tune was utterly finished, she'd play it for Dad, whose ear for melody was foolproof.

"And then we just toss some of the different era stylings in. Like, when Billy plays that sax. Whew!" She gleamed with admiration for the fellow's evident chops. "It's not silly assed mannered squawking or yuppie smooth jazz upchuck. It *burns*."

"Sounds pretty wild."

"I've got a CD right here. Oh crap, where did it go..." She frisked her jean jacket pocket. "Here." She tossed me the shiny disc. "It's got six of our tunes and the recording is pretty clear."

"Where you record this?"

"Duh! The university. Dad set it up and we got a clean sound in the second band room. You know that smaller one down from his office?"

"So how'd your vocals finally come out?"

"You mean: can everyone hear your lyrics?"

"That too. But Doug Johnson thinks you should study voice, and he's pretty stern." Indeed, he forbade his own daughter from singing within his earshot, claiming that her voice was not even mammalian but reptilian.

Kim shrugged, trying and failing to appear modest. Her jaw's cocky jut spoke volumes. She continued to profess, but I didn't so much listen to her as to study her: the conviction, the verve, the abrupt grins and gleeful pounding of fist upon knee as she stressed a point: "And Dad was right, absolutely. He ordered me to have the band record live in the studio to get that, you know, to get the ambience and that, all that fucking *bleed* you just don't get with computers and the, uh, that cut-n-paste. I mean, *Jesus*!" She playfully smacked her own forehead.

At that moment, I divined that Kim Edwards would sniff the edges of the big time, perhaps even frolic in the rarified air of authentic stardom. To what degree, of course, I couldn't say. But that she would be a force far beyond our town was, for me, beyond question.

Later that night, after Kim's chatter exhausted us, I lay in my bed with headphones on and listened to her recording. I'd feared a slop bucket of styles—styles that wouldn't do service to my lyrics.

After the first listen, I immediately relistened, pulse rising.

This music was *beauty*.

No, it wasn't "beautiful" in the decorative sense, with bloodless mannerisms or *faux* sophistication. This music was audacious and vital, a brainy blend of styles united by hooky melodies, just as Kim claimed. Kim's guitar was right up front: it careened with exciting unpredictability from surf to punk to rockabilly. And as for the sax...it really did burn, evoking both 50's rock and acid jazz. And *evoke* is the key word: these songs didn't cloddishly cut-and-paste the styles but only insinuated them.

But best of all was Kim's dark lustrous voice: effortlessly ascending, suddenly plummeting, then straightening out to ride on top of a catchy chorus. Remarkably, her aesthetics matched her pipes: she didn't oversing or succumb to self-parody, as so many powerhouse vocalists do. In fact, she sometimes held back and, at crucial times when the instruments laid out, her voice was a low mournful longing.

I called off work that next night, contriving a raw throat and dribbling nose. Franco was briefly peeved, but then thinking aloud, conceded that an infectious set-up man was of no help. He wished me a speedy recovery, reminding me that he needed me early in three days because of a catering gig. Duty avoided, I sat at the kitchen table eating cereal as Kim came skipping down the steps.

"I'm coming to the show tonight."

"Oh that's so cool, you can help us with the equipment."

"—Such as?"

"You know, equipment. The instruments and amps and PA and—"

"Cables and strings and all that crap, yeah I know."

"That's great. Robbie's going to help too, so that's cool."

I sighed.

She paused from the peeling of her orange. "Why not?"

"They'll think he's a grotesque balloon-twisting comedian who arrived late."

"You're awful."

"He's more awful."

"In fact," Kim said, voice sharpening, "he's been very helpful."

I returned to my cereal and, after a few noisy mouthfuls, said I regretted my sourness and that I would help her with anything she needed tonight.

As if still irritated, she stared at the leaking orange in her palm, then upon her sun-burned face bloomed a crooked grin. "You ignorant hayseed. The NiteSpot's got its own sound system, so we don't have to haul as much." She held me in the sights of an imaginary .45 and pulled the trigger. "We're going to knock 'em dead, I assure you. So, anyway…did you?"

I nodded.

"And?"

"It's good."

She blew away the smoke from her imaginary pistol's barrel.

"It's *very* good."

I accompanied Kim to the Hotel Perimeter at four, and we found the other band members, along with Robbie, lounging in the ersatz Continental lobby.

"Living like rock stars already," I remarked.

"Get used to it."

We walked east down the long hushed hallway, past a coffee shop and, a minute later, past a pool that was barely visible through the wall's steamed glass. Finally, we ambled past oak double doors and into the Acropolis NiteSpot.

"Not bad, eh?" Kim inquired over her shoulder.

I paused in the doorway, taking in the expanse.

The room was larger than I'd expected, seating a hundred or so. Just how many New Media hustlers would attend tonight, we didn't know. We wove past the smallish round tables and approached the far wall, where the band would perform. The scuffed bandstand was awkward, rather narrow with a makeshift nose attached to the front, presumably for a vocalist. Still, Kim was pleased. She plugged in Richard's bass, thumped it to her satisfaction, then moved on to her own guitar.

"All right," she good-naturedly called out to everyone. "Where's my guitar cable?"

"Crap, I swear I'd brought 'em all," Robbie proclaimed.

I busied myself with pointless contemplation of the grand piano, which had been wheeled to the back. I played a few chords while the others briefly complained about the missing cord. Then a cheer arose as Robbie returned from the parking lot, cord dragging behind him like a vestigial tail. Cable connected, Kim called the band to the bandstand as Billy Barnes, the triple threat sax/keys/guitar player, sat twenty feet back. His pony tail fell forward across his left shoulder and he tugged it while listening to the band play through the room's storied "line-array sound system," which turned out to be little speakers hanging from the ceiling. His conclusion: everyone was too loud. He ordered all amps be turned down. "Only *you* need to hear the amps," he mildly chastised the musicians. "The arrays will do the rest, so down, down, *down.*"

After ten more minutes of fussing, the sound improved markedly and Kim, impatient during Billy's directives, now sang for the first time. She didn't name the tune... an original, evidently. The beat was slightly staggered, like a stroll; the guitar chords were bright; Kim's vocal was loping and cheerful. Then I recognized the lyrics, which I'd penned months ago, and which Kim had edited, dropping a phrase here and adding one there:

> *Last Tuesday he didn't call.*
> *She stared at the phone all night.*
> *But why not another chance to lie to her?*
> *His wife's out and he'll get his story right.*
>
> *And then he'll be with her, with her, with her.*
> *He lies best when he lies with her, with her, with her.*

Billy nodded. Kim abruptly ceased singing and the others staggered to a graceless halt. Kim shepherded the herd to a table across the room to yet again review the set list and, presumably, to bask in Richard's empty assurances that she'd perform admirably. Billy's presence, however, pleased me: he was a grad music major in Dad's department and, like Kim, had grown up playing. His years of experience, I saw, calmed everyone.

Parking myself at an isolated table, I evaluated the room. It was your standard-issue hotel lounge, though it had graceful touches: thick white linen atop the tables, topped off by thin-necked table lamps. Upon the ceiling was a cheesy yet charming imitation fresco. Several ancient Greek temples sat atop an incongruously green and grassy hillside.

Robbie, the band's agog aide-de-camp, suddenly stood before me. He'd dressed for a night out, wearing a pressed white shirt and overpriced black jeans that bunched comically at his hips.

"Hey, check this out." From his back pocket he produced a chrome flask. "Brandy."

"May I?"

"Well it was for the band, and..."

"They can't drink before a show, Robbie."

"I mean for afterward maybe."

"For heaven's sake, just a quick pull."

He surrendered the flask. Robbie's sweaty palm print upon the chrome irked me, but I still drank heartily.

"It's all gone," Robbie huffed.

"Thanks again. I'll go get you more in a bit."

He nodded peevishly, certain that I was lying, and shook the empty flask a few times. Then he stomped off to join the others.

The brandy was better than I'd expected: not your lackluster swill that tastes more like perfume than liquor. No, this was a subtle inebriant, deftly liberating my brain's limbic system.

Lighting a cigarette—Mary my Virgin Savior, tobacco is a Beatitude!—I again contemplated the room's Greek motif. I imagined a Bacchanal binge: mushrooms and wine, pawing men and panting women, the pagan *joi de vivre.*

Robbie again distracted me, this time with his nasal snicker. I snuffed my cigarette and eavesdropped upon the band.

"...besides the acoustics in here are pretty good, so your vo-cals'll reach everyone pretty easily," Richard said. "Stick with 'Blush' for the opener."

"Just like last time," Billy soothed. "Start with the jangly guitar, just a *little* reverb, and then smash. Drop the hammer with your power chords."

The latest drummer, Larry, agreed. "'Blush', it's killer," he enthused. "My brother was, like, it truly *rawwkkkks.*"

"God, I just hope they listen," Kim squirmed. "We have to hook 'em early, just like our last gig."

"That's right Kim, just hook 'em," Robbie urged.

"Pay attention, bandmates," Kim theatrically instructed. "There he is, alone at the table. Our brooding lyricist."

"The creep," Robbie bellowed.

Larry laughed. "That's right! The creep!"

I sat straight up to better enjoy the abuse.

"No, no," Kim said, her hands silencing the group's guffaws. "My brat brother, he gave me the confidence to sing. Remember that?"

I did.

"Now shag your ass up and join your bandmates, you gloomy *artiste*." She stood and waved me over with comic exaggeration—and her hair, heretofore pinned up, tumbled to her shoulders. Joking about her need for a trim, she patiently re-pinned her locks: head tipped forward, fingers adroitly at work, a slight silver pendant swaying beneath her tee-shirt.

At that nanosecond, when the pendant swayed a second time, the vision struck me. A vision of—

"What, are you just gonna mope by yourself?" she jibed.

—of my sister beneath me: I looped her hair around my forefinger and her palms enfolded my face.

"C'mon, hop to it," Kim insisted.

Alarmed, I opened my eyes to find my eyes were already open...the others lounged about the table, smoking and sipping, contentedly killing time.

Kim remarked to the group that I was off to fetch a tall girl named Patty, or words to that effect. I could barely hear anything, really, and I shook my head like a stunned boxer. But the vision was bright, vivid, pulsing...I couldn't shake it off. As if from a documentary foretold tumbled scenes of heathen bliss: my sister's hands were upon my face, my hands were upon hers. Her hazel feline eyes narrowed and, in a hoarse whisper, she asked if Patty—

"Is Patty really your girlfriend?" Kim teased from the table. My imagined Kim, the Kim beneath me, repeated the question.

I feigned to glance at my watch, which in fact was missing from my wrist. "Off to fetch my girlfriend."

Fourteen: To My Soul

As I drove to fetch tall Patty, sweaty panic enveloped me and twice I pulled off to the road's shoulder to chase—but never quite catch—my breath.

Kim beneath me, her hands upon my face.

The celestial call reverberated in my ears, and my very fibers hummed and crackled. I vowed to somehow answer that call: Kim was the most natural of excitements, and everything else—everything—was suddenly petty and absurd.

Yet: how could I even *begin* to broach the subject? Would her jaw drop in glee or, far more likely, in stunned revulsion?

At that moment, a cat sprinted across the freshly-resurfaced road, which glistened oily black in the low-hanging sun. The sudden braking brought my car's front end to a squealing halt, but the car's chattering rear end swung around in a big arc and upended a garbage can. Metallic clanging filled the hot air, and after making sure nobody was near my car, I slowly approached the curb and parked.

A garrulous geezer approached: "I saw all of that and, well, you did pretty good in not hitting that cat."

"Thanks."

The geezer was, as they say, awfully spry. He leaned over and righted the can with a quick tug.

"I dented your can."

He waved away my apologies. "That's fine, that's fine. I've dented it too."

"I dented your can."

The fellow leaned forward, palms upon the car's roof. "You all right, my friend? Are you—"

"No." I knew that social custom required I do more that repeat the crudest declarations, but mad lust had short-circuited my senses. "No."

"You're not?"

"What?"

He clucked, adjusted his palms' position upon the car roof, and clucked again. "Should I call someone?"

My face was sweaty, my neck slippery, but an inner voice counseled me to feign normality: "No sir, I'm fine. Really. Sorry for any alarm." Still hunched in my seat, I looked up at the old guy—the sun was directly behind him, rendering him a feature-less silhouette. "I'm fine. Here, let me help you with, uh—" I gen-tly opened the door, and the geezer retreated three polite steps. "Let me see the can that I hit."

"Oh you can forget about that can!" he laughed. "*That's* what I was really shook about." Thumbs hooked through belt loops, he turned half-way from me and nodded toward a girl of three or four. Tiny in loosely fitting jeans and grass-stained white blouse, she stood partially hidden behind a corner shrub. "The kid was running after that cat, and I was yelling to stop—"

I sagged.

"—and thank God you stopped." He turned back to face me. "Wish more people drove more carefully, like you do. " Recrimi-nations gathered in his expression. "Like that kid down the street. *Terrible* driver. His mother too, they should take away her cell phone."

I noted his distended shirt pocket. "Can I bum a smoke?"

"Uh?" He glanced at my slightly trembling forefinger. For the moment, all thoughts of Kim were trampled by the thought of hitting that little girl.

"Oh sure," he grinned. He handed me a cigarette, which I ac-cepted with extravagant nodding thanks, then lit his own.

"It's scary, isn't it?"

"How's that?"

"The cat, the little girl—" What with the sun steadily fleeing westward, and the sky's orange canvas now vibrant with scarlet undertones, the amiable oldster sharing a smoke...Well, reader, you know the sensation? That humbling gratitude we feel when skirting disaster? When we're agreeably beholden to an ounce of good luck? Had that cat come along a moment later, or had that dumb kid run a degree faster—well, as we mumble at such mo-ments: who knows?

My senescent friend nodded, and behind the rising smoke of his cigarette, his eyes regarded me cheerfully. "Thanks for staying alert," he said. "Wouldn't look too good if Grandpa was snoozing when little Kimmy got hit."

"Her name's Kim?"

"Timothy," he corrected. "His name's Tim. Here." He handed me a second cigarette and as I smoked it, I glanced several times at the child, now plainly visible as a boy, not a girl. What I thought was a blouse was a loosely hanging shirt.

"Tim."

"Uh huh."

"Not Kim," I pointlessly clarified. He nodded with bemused courtesy, and upon consuming the entire cigarette, I giddily said, "Tim not Kim, Tim not Kim," as I walked to the car. The geezer followed me a step or two, the hesitation of his gait suggesting concern or alarm, but he stopped as I hastened my pace from stroll to sprint.

The door at Patty's—a door like her, tall and pale and nearly noble—swung open upon my second knock.

"C'mon in. I just need to grab some—wow, you look really fucked up, Jeff." She leaned forward, her eyes uncharacteristically hard. "What, did you indulge on the way over?"

I retreated a step from her near interrogation. "Nope."

"Nope?" she gently retorted, eyes still upon me.

"Not that I won't." But she was right: I had indulged not upon actual drugs but upon imagined debauchery. No doubt I looked madly besotted, and again, that tiny inner voice counseled caution: "Let's go, dearest. Kim and company need our immoral support. And let me state with really shameful honesty that you look lovely."

"One tries." Patty's demeanor returned to its defining slackness: she rounded her shoulders and even hunched a bit to minify her height.

"Others try. You simply *are*. "

She snickered and suggested that I had to be high: "You're talking awfully sweet."

"Well, I confess that I feel rather romantic at the moment." Ah yes, the social graces: I possessed them in rich abundance. I stepped forward and, my hand lightly upon her hip, waited for her head to droop slightly.

I kissed her.

Eyes half-closed, she leaned upon me. "You really do like me, don't you?"

"You should remove the question mark dangling at the end of that statement."

"All right...You really do like me. Don't you."

"Sure. Even if you *are* a Republican."

"What's that they say?" Her lazy lean grew urgent. "Politics make for strange bedfellows?"

"So does sex."

We were running rather late for Kim's gig. Our tardiness was caused, of course, by a prolonged caucus in the basement laundry room. Driving back to the hotel, Patty's long fingers entwined in mine...what did I ponder? Love. Even now, with hormones relieved, my love for Kim towered brightly above all else. And though still partially stunned, I'd recovered my senses enough to realize that I'd always loved her.

Always.

"Hey we're almost here," Patty remarked, nodding at a fast food emporium. "Two more blocks after Burger Heaven." She heartily squeezed my hand. "I've got an idea," she revealed as I turned into the hotel parking lot. "Let's rent a room here tonight."

"Really?" I trolled to the end of the lot and found a barely whole parking space; an SUV, its rear bumper blanketed with dozens of little American flag stickers, filled the adjacent spot and its bulk left mere inches for me.

"Don't you think?" She squeezed my hand again.

Now, I confess that her idea surprised me. It shouldn't have, of course: our romance had hit upon all the clichés: the initial date out, the pleasurably aimless driving about, the furtive intercourse spiced with alcohol and marijuana.

"Yes, I do think."

"Good, because I already got us a room." She regarded me with great care, as if fearing my response, but I smiled broadly and, to disguise my disquiet, kissed her. In fact, my imitation of lustful romance approached the virtuosic. And so, doubts dashed, Patty suggested we go inside.

Jukebox racket leaked past the entrance of the Acropolis NiteSpot. With picturesque Tall Patty in tow, I eased open the oaken doors and, once a few steps inside, surveyed the room. The crowd was respectable, not spectacular: several empty tables, mostly in the back, though the front and middle of the room were respectably occupied. The band huddled beside the bandstand: Kim, obscured by Richard and Billy, talked while the others nodded. Then, like the star quarterback leading her team to the scrimmage line, Kim clapped her hands and the members took their positions.

"Thanks for coming tonight. We're really pleased," Kim announced, voice nearly girlish.

Patty and I wound our way to the bar and loitered among several chattering customers. The customers lamented the false promise of broadband and complained that wireless's days as a cash cow were numbered.

Abruptly, the bandstand was aglow: three spotlights—two a mellow amber, the middle a chilled mint green—illumed the cramped stage and Kim strode forward, guitar slung across her hip. The adjacent chatter about Linux servers ceased as the conference attendees studied Kim. The men in the room—they outnumbered the women by four to one, I guessed—engaged in that most primitive of evaluations: they judged her eyes, her bust, her hips, her petite knees barely revealed by her black dress's hem.

"Wow she looks great," Patty remarked.

I nodded with admirable neutrality but silently picked a nit. "Great" was wholly inadequate for the lovely woman who, adorned grandly in a simple strapless black dress, commenced with the chords of "Blush."

"Actually, I lent her my dress." She chuckled. "I grew out of it in ninth grade."

"I suspected as much," I said. Actually, I'd suspected nothing, but then again, the formality of Kim's wardrobe didn't typically go beyond a cashmere sweater. "I'd rather see you out of it."

She waved away my compliment but couldn't hide her delight...at that moment, I was certain, she saw halos revolving over my head. Simultaneously, I felt the tips of horns pushing upward, poised to pierce my scalp. Kim in Patty's dress, Kim in no dress...a really wonderful notion that could ruin three lives.

After ordering a pitcher of beer, Patty and I found a table thirty feet from the bandstand. Upon the table was a jeweled CD case. Examining the case under the dim light, I noted the case's mid-1960's theme: pale pink background, with cheerful green and gold flowers in the foreground.

"So that's a, that's a CD of theirs?" Patty queried. I nodded and handed her the CD. At that moment, Kim began singing:

> *Grab me the cigarettes*
> *Turn off that stupid TV.*
> *C'mere, sit closer to me.*

Patty's squint moved from the CD to me. "Hey, that's your lyric."

"Some of it."

> *I've got something to drink*
> *You've got flowered paper cups*
> *We'll fill them to the brink.*
> *Drink up, drink up the blush.*

The ringing chords, suggestive of 1960's pop, grew darker, weightier. Billy's choppy keyboard chords followed Kim's vocal to the uncoiling chorus:

> *Sip and swallow—slowly, slowly*

A brief drum fill boasted the tempo and power chords filled the room. Switching to sax, Bobby followed the chords for a few measures and Kim's vocals soared above the muscular ruckus.

She had captured the room.

"They're named Mad," Patty remarked.

"—Mad?"

She shook her head, pointed at the CD. "Pad. That's their name?"

"Yeah I guess."

Beer foaming about the rim of her glass, Patty scooted her chair closer. "You write her lyrics so I thought maybe you, that you named the band too."

"Nope." I pushed the CD aside, amused by its retro design: an affectionate nod to pre-feminist femininity. "In fact..."

"What?"

"I don't get it. The name."

She studied me, beer poised at her mouth. "—It's a girl thing."

I shrugged, awaiting her explanation.

"You know. Pad. Feminine hygiene etcetera. Here, have another beer."

"How very *punk*," I laughed.

With an extravagant hoisting of the pitcher, she filled my glass. I smiled my thanks, and we listened to the band—Pad, that is—kick "Blush" into overdrive, upon which Kim's vocal danced:

> *You're a born again delight down here dear,*
> *Blushing and babbling, dumbstruck with awe*
> *Your girlfriend pales beside me:*
> *Can't even spell 'Epater le bourgeois'*

The band fell silent, and so the audience's attention was affixed to the final six syllables of Kim's lustrous tone. Like all fine show business moments, the syllables were long yet not long enough, and therefore created want.

Pride and lust urged me to stand with clamorous applause, but a few networking nerds/suburban sophisticates beat me to the gesture. Kim bowed to the clapping and then, with a sweep of her arm—a gesture stolen from generations of game show hostesses—she invited the audience to applaud for the entire band.

"Thank you thank you thank you," Kim beamed. "You're so nice that we'll play a second song." Left hand above her head, she snapped her fingers and the drums introduced the next tune: "Unsilent Partner."

The evening's joys escalated. The music itself moved me...I was consistently charmed by the songs' sly references to musical eras gone by. And Pad's musicianship that night was remarkable, showcasing the songs, not the band. As for the lyrics...false modesty just wouldn't ring true, so I'll admit that they bristled with swinging word play—even those Kim had chopped and diced.

But Kim as vocalist! A lyricist and loon could desire nothing more. Even Pad's critics, who sometimes sniffed (I turn now to my carefully preserved scrapbook) about the band's "self-conscious braininess," or its "impulse to show off," conceded Kim's vocal mastery. In fact, here's a quote from the obnoxiously hip—and in this case, entirely accurate—music rag, *SellOut*:

> Kim Bender has no serious vocal competition. Period. She's got virtuoso chops without the virtuoso's narcissism, with vocals that can evoke loneliness and lust at the same time. Her vocal chops even overshadow her jaw dropping guitar fusions of surf, punk, and rockabilly. Vocal comparisons are tough to come by, but (this is *weird*, we know) she reminds you of Patsy Cline in a completely different idiom. There's the power and swing, the warmth and humor that suggest a smart-ass winking of the eye as her alto rattles the rafters.

And Ms. Cline is long *dead*, the critic should've added for proper perspective.

"Here," Patty whispered. Into my palm she pressed a cigarette, the tip of which she'd earlier dipped in liquefied hashish. "It's waaayyy good."

I closed my eyes: Kim standing before me, the black dress tossed to the floor.

"Geez you look really fucked up," she giggled, a gaily admonishing finger in my face.

"Oh I am. To my soul."

Fifteen: Prelate, not Pervert

"What was the name of that one? It was really good," Patty enthused as the audience applauded. A guy behind me stood, a steadying hand upon my shoulder, and whistled his approval. So did the reveler's companion, a mannish woman whose hand briefly found clumsy support on my other shoulder. Both begged pardon simultaneously, and I half turned around to cheerfully shrug away their concern.

"More beer?"

"We've still got a half pitcher left, so of course."

As Pad hit its stride, the audience's enthusiasm grew. Word had filtered out to the lobby of worthwhile entertainment, and knots of vacationers, weary business people, and a few aimless townies took up several tables in the back. With the evening's concluding song—a subtly Latinized cover of "Speak Low," with Billy on keyboard and Larry eschewing snare and stick for cymbals and brushes—my would-be inamorata bid the audience good night and announced that, for the price of a single light beer, the band would happily autograph copies of their CD.

"Ha! That's clever," Patty said. "Look."

"Yeah, it's their CD."

"A CD with a single song, but you trade it in for another one with more songs. See?" From the CD case she peeled a sticker that made the generous offer. She cleared her throat and, like a cable network news babe, straightened her shoulders as she recited from an imaginary Teleprompter. "In entertainment news, the up and coming rock band Pad performed for an audience of thrilled geeks and clogged sinuses. Adding to the excitement: the performance served as a party to celebrate the release of—" She glanced at the CD, discerning in the dim light the tiny text. "—of the band's six-song debut, *Epater le bourgeois*. For the Entertainment Until Suicide Network, this is ball Patty."

"I liked that Freudian slip."

"Was it a slip?" She looked about the room, suggesting that we congratulate the band on our way out.

And so we did. Or tried. In fact, Kim was marooned at a table near the bandstand; several of the new media geeks had pulled up chairs to sweet-talk her. One balding fellow with a deeply cherished pony tail—it was held in place with an asinine ruby-studded band—had shouldered his way to a chair beside Kim. He yammered at her, rudely feigning "warmth" by touching her shoulder as he emphasized a point. As I approached the table, Tall Patty casting a shadow that bisected the fellow's frail back, he pulled out his wallet and redeemed his single-song CD for the six-song CD.

Kim accepted the putz's folded bills and passed them to Robbie, who flattened out the bills and placed them in a gray metal box. Then he passed back a copy of the CD to Kim. She was in her affably cocky mode, popping her gum and basking in the praise.

"Great show, really great show," the putz declared. He loitered, hoping to contrive another reason to touch Kim's shoulder.

"Great pony tail, really great pony tail," I announced with mock jocularity.

His back stiffened and he turned about to look up at me—and he blinked, taking note of Tall Patty who stood towering just behind me. One of his compatriots smirked at me, but a second companion smirked at Mr. Pony Tail's tepid machismo.

"Sorry, do I know you?" the putz tepidly challenged.

"You're sorry you don't know me?"

Kim raised an eyebrow.

I pulled a chair up to the fellow and extended my hand.

"He's my brother," Kim explained.

He accepted my hand, which he tried to squeeze manfully.

"And the lyricist," I added as his hand fell back upon his lap.

He offered feigned interest. "Well, the lyrics are, they're pretty clever."

"They sounded a little, like, foreign sometimes didn't they?" one of his companions complained. His complexion was doughy, with several blooming pimples, and he spoke with his hand partially obscuring his face. "What language were they in?"

"American."

"No really. It was—"

"French," Kim said.

"What did some of it, you know—what did it mean?" the pale fellow asked Kim.

She laughed. "Don't ask me, I don't speak it."

"Me neither," I added. "I only write it."

"You're a regular wise guy," Pony Tail complained. He regarded me for a lingering moment, eyes peevish and cowardly, then returned his attention to Kim. But Kim had lost interest, as she'd gotten his money. She now chatted happily with four or five others who'd stood with remarkably good manners in line for a full copy of *Epater le bourgeois.*

"—can't believe you remember that!" Kim cackled, suddenly upright on the edge of her seat.

"Yeah, that must've been at least three or four years ago," one of her fans remarked. "And Jason was in that band too, with, uh—" The fan, a chubby young woman with streaks of blue dye on black, snapped her fingers. "Jeez, who was that guy?"

"Tony?"

The woman nodded. "That's it. You guys were pretty good."

I felt a playful tug upon my belt loop and, a half-second later, Patty's narcotic whisper in my ear. "Jeffrey? *Suivre.*"

I waved goodbye to Kim, but she couldn't see past the latest ring of converts, all of whom brandished legal tender. I allowed myself to be directed gently, then vigorously. We took an elevator to the second floor and, immediately upon the hushed opening of the elevator doors, Patty coltishly bolted down the hallway to our room. My balance had deteriorated badly during our elevator ride and I had to walk slowly, with a supportive shoulder against the hallway walls. How could she even walk, I wondered, after all of the evening's refreshments?

She surprised me again when, upon stepping from our room back into the hallway, she threw at me her tomato red brassiere. It landed at my feet. I bent over to retrieve it but managed only to wrap one of its straps around the toe of my shoe.

"Someone call the manager!" Patty called through cupped hands.

I struggled with the strap.

"There's a pervert in the hallway!"

"The word is prelate, not pervert."

Patty must have towed me ashore, as I have no further
memory until three or four in the morning. Stretched warmly
upon me, she smelled of bath soap and bourbon. She told me to
listen to the music, but I could hear only the wheezing air conditioner. It filled the blackness with white noise and pushed cool
air upon our limbs.

"Hear it?"

I squinted my ears...surging strings and horn, rumbling percussion, a pianist leading the way...As if to aid my concentration, she firmly clasped my face. Rachmaninoff ascended, tinny
yet vital, from the transistor radio upon the bedside dresser.

With a quick push and roll, I was on top, and I reached
through the darkness to boost the radio's volume. An intruding
beam of light sliced through our imperfectly drawn drapes: headlights from a car just outside our window. The lights briefly illumed Patty's face, then darkness again reigned. Yet in those
three seconds of illumination, upon Patty's face sprouted thrilling features: black brows and narrowing eyes of incandescent
hazel.

I awoke the next morning to find Patty sitting upright,
sheets wrapped loosely around her torso. I bid her a good morning. Her smile was broad and naïve, as only first love's smile can
be.

"Let's never move out of this room." She reached stealthily
beneath my blanket.

"We can charge your Dad's credit card."

"That'll get us another day or two. Then what?"

"Use another of your Dad's credit cards."

"Let's find a place of our own." Her grip grew urgent.

I closed my eyes as she pulled faster. Laughing throatily, she
slacked off. Then faster again, faster and longer...and at the crucial moment Kim's face appeared as if on the widest of movie
screens.

"What do you say?"

Upon the screen, Kim eyes narrowed as I stroked her face.
Then the scene changed: as if watching from the ceiling, I saw
her hunched over someone...me...and she framed my face in her

hands and kissed me, her hair wet and freshly combed. She paused from her kissing to shrug off a white terry cloth robe. Now my sibling straddled me, her hands tensing upon my chest.

Abruptly, another viewpoint: Kim's face above me, lips pursed as she accepted all of me.

"What a mess you've made."

The movie screen went black.

I opened my eyes to see Patty wiping her hand with a thick wad of tissue paper. "That's the loudest yes I've ever heard."

Sixteen: The Routine

In the mornings, I would lay studying the cracks in the chipped ceiling...the crack's center was inches from the inoperable ceiling fan. From that center, the cracks radiated in all directions, their pattern growing more capricious as they reached the corners. I'd promised myself to paint over those cracks as soon as I fixed the ceiling fan—but until I met the latter promise, I saw little point in keeping the former. The mysteries of wiring often occupied me until nine-thirty, and I struggled to get comfortable on the lumpy pair of mattresses that lay frameless upon the wooden floor. Failing to find comfort, I'd flip open my lyric notebook and light up the appropriate inspiration: a joint for a first draft, a menthol cigarette for revision.

Patty was always gone by eight-thirty for her job at a property management office. Her employer oversaw a string of apartment complexes on the edge of the county. The state and federal governments subsidized the complexes, guided by the principle that even the poor merited new housing, especially if the poor were females with three children fathered by any given three of a larger indeterminate number of feckless beaus. I once joked to Patty that we ourselves reside there: the apartments, I guessed, would grow shabby in a few years, and so we should enjoy government largesse while we could. She rolled her eyes, remarking that my distaste for do-gooders would make me allergic to a place with a "mission and a vision", as the brochure piously proclaimed.

She added that the county Mounties were frequent visitors, especially at the end of the month when the young mothers' welfare checks arrived. The checks were a siren song to the otherwise indifferent fathers. The checks funded some noteworthy block parties. One such party began in a single apartment, but the hostess's *corps d'elite* expertly fanned the party's flames, and the shindig spread to several apartments and into the court yard.

"The cops showed up," Patty narrated, "just as some moron tried to roll a keg across the lawn into the street."

"Was it empty?"

"No, a car was coming and—"

"I mean the keg."

"Stupid...I don't know. So a car was coming and ran over the keg."

"And a cheer went up."

"Then boos. The cops found a couple bags of grass along with some coke. Enough grams to make it interesting."

"Restrict drugs to smart people...that's the solution."

"Anyway, a couple tenants got kicked out, but there's a line waiting to get in."

"Let's cut to the head of that line."

"You'd be bored. Stupid people lose their charm pretty quickly."

Not that Patty really needed to dissuade me. For the moment, I was content here in our peeling doll house, a rental eight miles outside the town limits on highway 22. Our be-it-ever-so humble was built in 1940 and had over the decades been host to generations of young couples. It had also, presumably, been host to generations of the chronically unemployed and unemployable, as its condition was disheveled: the converted coal furnace, afflicted by black lung disease, coughed up soot, and the chronically wet plumbing seemed smuggled from the former Soviet Union.

But the price was right and grew even more right when the owner, after enduring a vacancy of three months, agreed to snip another forty dollars from his original quote.

Upon rising, I crudely straightened the sheets and blankets. Then it was off to my classes at Professor Dave's campus. I was taking three this fall, though Dad had insisted that I take more. "After all," he pointed out, "it doesn't cost you any more, so why not just pile on the classes? You should probably take five."

"I'd rather take just two."

"Two?"

"Yeah. It's not like I have to hurry before I run out of money."

Dad's voice lightened, a sign that he had again drawn that velvet curtain between himself and me. "Well whatever suits you, I suppose. You know best."

My classes were your standard university fare. As in my previous courses, I found abundant stupidity in heightened form, and only rarely did I confront intelligence or talent. At times, the intellectual climate was barely post-vertebrate. My classes were: creative writing, history of the Enlightenment, and Sociology II, the last of which assumed a dreary "multicultural" position. Reader, as you can see, there was little to occupy anyone of my immoderate intelligence and even more immoderate philosophy. So I had my fun where I could find it, usually by mocking the politically correct or feigning slack-jawed amazement at a prof's inane analysis.

Now, to continue this executive summary of my routine...after classes I returned home, where Patty was sometimes in the kitchen, struggling to control the water's boil as she prepared spaghetti or eggs. I'd join her and sometimes take over the second half of meal preparation. On other occasions, Patty would have a greasy sack of fast food waiting for us. We'd sit at the unsteady table in our cramped kitchen, trading stories of our day, though quite regularly our late afternoons were darkened by the news that Patty's mother or father had called her, demanding that she return home.

"They'll give up on the idea eventually," she'd say, her tone betraying her uncertainty. "They just don't get it." She'd wait upon my supportive nod or quip and be satisfied. Poor Patty: her home life depressed her; her parents' plans for her depressed her; in fact, nearly everything depressed her. She was suburban damaged too, especially by the most sacred suburban commandment: *Thou Shalt Live to Impress Strangers.* But after a tentative week or so of cohabitation, in which she seemed stunned that she'd displeased her parents, she nearly relaxed.

I placed no demands upon her—none. And that gratified her—initially. Over time she recognized that, to use an appalling term, "relationships" are in fact built upon demands. And after our modest meal? Ah, to our bedroom, where we stretched out on the mattresses to watch TV. We'd view the news or an absurd talk show while savoring our chronically meager marijuana cache. On other days, we had barely time for a nod as I was off to Franco's, where I'd been promoted to pizza maker, freeing Franco to concentrate upon his more elaborate dinners, such as manicotti with wine sauce. Or, if not at Franco's, I made a mock effort to do my "homework", and I turned that into a game: I'd read a few pages, reward myself with a tipple of drugstore wine, then continue. Typically, the textbooks' inanity drove me to create a cognitive challenge: reading the books backward.

Patty, meanwhile, propped up several pillows and read a paperback, her feet hanging beyond the mattress' edge. If she found an interesting passage, she'd recite it. Now, her recital required that I feign polite interest, but I didn't share her taste: she favored melodramatic thrillers teeming with hard-bitten (though tender-hearted) police detectives and deranged (though genius) villains who committed strings of murders—"brutal" murders, actually. Sometimes, when her selected prose grew beyond my patience, I produced my smeared plastic bag and rolling papers. I'd take a quick puff and then let Patty consume the entire joint. Marijuana was her chocolate, though chocolate was her chocolate too: I quickly learned to bring home a bag of foil-wrapped chocolate kisses. She happily consumed both snacks and then, blissfully satisfied, she forgot to recite further.

In this fashion the months drifted, and in this fashion I grew restless.

I disguised my restlessness with an easy good cheer. Indeed, I found some grounds for my well-meaning deception: sexually, I could do whatever I wished with Patty, and I reminded myself that I was lucky to enjoy this comely girl with long limbs and guileless nature. Indeed, Patty would be a balm for most men, but no balm existed for my ailment.

Kim was ever on my thoughts. Indeed, she soon colonized my dreams. The dreams became dreadful enchantments, taking on a texture, scale and color that reduced waking hours to a pallid still life. In the most painful dreams, she tearfully avowed her love for me before I could do the same. With words trapped sideways or backward in my mouth, I'd watch in silent grief as she fled a featureless locale, shouldering her way through a milling throng that had gathered to curse me. I'd wake with my heart swollen to the choking point. If Patty stirred, I'd lie with a corpse's rigidity and wait for her breathing to regain its deep slow measure. Or, if I was too agitated to sleep, I'd position myself between Patty's always welcoming thighs. Presently, she'd clasp my shoulders and I would drain myself of all libido. Afterward, as I drifted off with her leg tossed lazily across my flank, a clammy certainty struck me: a certainty that Patty would deduce for whom I really ached.

Patty grew lonely for her family, her longing made stronger by her new habit of airbrushing her parents' faults and exaggerating their virtues. Adding to her dysphoria were impending Christmas Eve and Christmas Day...she'd invited her parents to visit, but they coolly begged off, claiming that they were obligated to visit a certain Aunt Betty.

"They *hate* Aunt Betty..." Her eyes dampened, as she'd never spent Christmas without her family.

"It won't be so bad. We'll have fun right here. In our own place."

She nodded, awaiting further declarations.

"And it'll take a while to open all the presents I got you."

"...Liar," she smiled.

"No, it will." In fact, I'd purchased a pile of gifts for her. I'm generous by nature, actually, and I wanted to distract Patty (and myself) from the holiday absence of both our families: Dad had picked up a holiday gig in New York—a gig he'd wanted for a couple years now—and Kim was charged with keeping an eye on the permanent guest, Robbie.

"What about a New Year's party then?" She immediately retracted the thought, noting that any of our likely guests would have previous engagements. "Besides, you'll have to work..."

"Then we'll make it a couple days later."

Losing enthusiasm, she studied the floor. "Then we'll have to get the furnace fixed..."

"So we'll get it fixed." The furnace had grown ever-more unruly as the temperatures dropped. It frequently pulled too much current and forced the circuit breakers to fulfill their purpose: break the circuits.

"I'll get money from my Mom," she suggested.

Money was a sore spot, as the previous month I'd loaned Kim two hundred dollars for a refurbished amp—as luck would of course have it—and she'd not yet paid me back.

"No, I'll get it from, uh, from Robbie."

"Robbie?"

"Yeah," I shrugged. "He's got lots of money. He's become quite the upstanding citizen under my Dad's tutelage. He's got a job and has learned to feed himself and everything."

She kept studying the floor, which meant that she didn't approve my idea, but she didn't voice a veto.

"So we'll have that party yet." I patted her shoulder.

"Maybe."

"It'll be the social event of the year. We'll disinvite all the best people."

Seventeen: "He follows you."

I hit the semester's home stretch hard, studying nearly each day and, on the odd occasion, continuing into the silent AM after work. My pride, I discreetly concede, was often at odds with itself. Pride compelled me to feign breezy indifference toward studying and grades. My classmates, however, *lived* to complain about academic pressure.

The complaints commenced when one or two scholars, bulging book bags strapped upon their backs, wandered into the student union. Presently, another one or two appeared. Eventually, the assemblage numbered a dozen or more. Seated around a big round wooden table, the aspiring savants catalogued the "eight hours last night" they'd studied, or the "twenty-one hours" over the weekend. I'd listen amiably, then observe that I'd not studied eight hours over the last two weeks.

"But your grades...!" the chorus would murmur.

"My grades suck."

Murmurs and restless glances ricocheted about the group, along with a stray grin or two. They enjoyed my irreverence, I think, nearly as much as I enjoyed mocking their studiousness. Eventually, however, I took to confounding their view of me and ended the semester strongly. In the semester's final weeks, I earned several "A"'s, a fact that I casually revealed as the others, in the grip of genuine or hysterical exhaustion, complained of overwork.

"Yeah but you've got, what? Only three classes?" Fred whined. Fred was terribly tedious: thin and sallow, with matted auburn hair. He was in my history course, and until now I'd managed to avoid him. "I've got five."

I was stung just a bit, I admit, by his tasteless observation, though I resisted pummeling him verbally. I merely noted that, in addition to my three classes, I also had a job and was a vital member of Pad, the up-and-coming rock band.

"What's that?"

"Pad. A band."

Most of the scholars were nonplussed, though two co-eds looked at me with new interest. "That band at the Acropolis?"

I nodded. "They're the house band for a while."

The co-eds, as it happened, had recently endured a double blind date at the Acropolis. They were taken there by their dates because one of the fellas had heard that the band was very hip. As it turned out, Pad rather confused the coxcombs but impressed the gals. One had even purchased the CD.

"I lent it to my roommate, and she lent it to the radio station and they're playing it quite a lot."

"The campus station?" Fred sniffed. "Who listens to that?"

"Until recently, nobody," I smiled. Then I turned to the gals: "Did they do the bait and switch routine? You know, have a one-song CD at the table that you turned in for the six song CD?"

"No," one answered. "They just sold them after the show."

"But hold it," the other assertively interrupted. "You wrote the songs?"

All attention narrowed upon me.

"The lyrics."

"Why're they all in French?" the assertive gal pressed.

"They're not. At least not when I wrote them."

"Seems like a lot was in French."

But her friend was enthusiastic. "That's so cool!" she declared. "And so's the band."

At that moment, buoyant upon the crest of celebrity, I nearly invited the entire group to my impending post New Year's Party. The words stood at eager attention upon my lips, waiting to be voiced: "You're all invited to my party, with musical entertainment provided by Pad." But I couldn't: Kim would balk at my last-minute plans, and the band was probably already booked, such was their growing local popularity...a popularity that genuinely surprised me. The desire to host a Pad party stayed with me the rest of the day: I imagined a heady bevy of beauties along with a few males...a 3:1 ratio seemed right...and all eyes were upon Kim, just as all ears were upon her resonant vocals. Meanwhile, I'd stand slyly in the corner to imbibe upon the soaring aesthetic bliss.

"Going to class now?" someone asked me.

"Sorry?" Ah, these visions: so often disrupted by rubes.

"Are you going to history class?" Fred repeated.

I sighed. "I suppose so..." I stood and nodded goodbye to the group.

About the history prof: He was Dr. Tracy Smith, who at the end of one session looked upon me with lively interest: "You're the Edwards boy!" he announced as I walked past his lectern.

I paused, turned and nodded. "Hello."

Dr. Smith struggled to clamp shut his bulging briefcase. "Sure, I remember you."

"From last week?"

"Huh?" Then he laughed, waving away my jest. "No, it's just that once in a while my wife and I would come to the campus music performances, back when your father was new on the faculty." The briefcase refused to cooperate and sprang open. Dr. Smith leaned over to retrieve the spilled papers and continued: "He was a really fine player. Still is, I'm sure."

I grabbed a sheet of paper that skipped airily across the floor.

"Why thank you." He accepted the sheet and tried again to close his brief case. With a percussive slam, he finally triumphed. "I like music myself a quite a bit."

Courtesy compelled me to accompany Dr. Smith as he ambled out of the classroom and down the hall to his office. "At any rate, it finally hit me that you must be his son. I remember you used to be in attendance with your sister and your mother."

I followed him in silence for a few moments. "Been to any performances lately?"

"Can't say that I have. My wife had a stroke several years ago."

"I'm very sorry."

"Why thank you. And so it's difficult for us to get out." We'd arrived at his office at the end of the hallway, and he paused before the door. "Do you play also?"

"My sister is the musical one."

He nodded, smiling moistly as he fumbled with his ring of keys. "I remember her too. My wife and I always remarked at how well behaved you two were during those performances. You couldn't have been more than, what?" He smiled at me as if I were a rarely-seen relative. "Nine or ten." He set down his brief-case and caught his breath. "Is your sister studying music here?"

"She was. Now she sings in a rock band."

His eyes and thoughts drifted for a few seconds. "I hope she's doing well."

"Yeah, she is actually. They've got a steady gig in town."

He smiled at me again, nodded, and opened his office door. Upon his desk were several crooked towers of books.

"I'll say hi to Kim for you."

"That's kind of you." He nodded again and gently shut the door.

Dr. Smith, I later learned, was almost entirely homebound. His wife had indeed suffered a stroke, and one far more devas-tating than his mild tone suggested. Bedridden, she required round-the-clock care. His quiet devotion to a loved one soothed me for a long time: in fact, nearly up to this very minute.

And about my creative writing class: it was one of the under-graduate's two most prized desiderata: the easy A...only the easy lay is more relished. I simply wrote and revised lyrics. Mr. James, the hack adjunct who taught the course, invariably scrawled upon my work: "This is good stuff keep it up revise more."

Sociology II finished my trivial trivium. It was my favorite class, actually, as it embodied that comic compound of academic mush and sanctimony that I so enjoy. In my midterm exam, for instance, I had enormous fun lampooning just about every tenet the course offered. I was careful, of course, to directly address the questions, yet my answers served the larger purpose of lay-ing a foundation for something more interesting than regurgitat-ing inane class notes. I recall laying my completed bluebook atop the others and, upon being asked by Dr. Charles how I'd done, I humbly shrugged and deferred that decision to her.

My jesting diatribe upset my Professor more than I'd hoped. She started out the next class session by "sharing" with the class some "interesting arguments" from the mid-term blue books.

"I won't reveal the names of the authors, of course," she as-sured us, "because the identities of the authors aren't relevant.

It's the arguments we should be interested in because they really lay bare some of our, uh, our culture's deepest myths."

My classmates shifted uneasily. With a placid smile, she recited a few lines from one of the exams, pausing to note its "cogent marshalling" of evidence to support the claim that post-colonialism has doubled back to its Eurocentric roots and finds expression in reality TV and expensive home workout gym equipment.

But her smile darkened as she opened a second bluebook and, as she recited, I recognized my work.

"Given the academic radical's asinine poses of working-class solidarity, one cannot be surprised to find an equally phony 'celebration' of a folk culture's 'local knowledge', such as the 'local knowledge' among many African cultures that the female's clitoris should be partially or wholly sliced off and the vagina sewn up. Such a practice becomes a surprising though paradoxical support for the radical feminist claim that sexual relations are always and forever about power. What could be a greater expression of power than sewing shut a vagina?"

I sensed the squinting of ears and glanced about. Some classmates stared at their desks, while a few grinned openly. Dr. Charles cleared her throat, and voice rising just shy of shrill, continued:

"One cannot imagine the wine-and-cheese leftist subjecting his own daughter to such a 'diverse cultural practice,' which betrays the ultimate condescension of the tenured Third World celebrant: the refusal to live by one's words. Indeed, the standard-issue academic critic can 'celebrate' such practices only from a safe distance, preferably at the yearly academic conference held at four-star hotels. Still, one must admire the sheer scale of their hypocrisy; they can simultaneously call for social justice and a second round of Vouvray."

Her face grew pink then red as she recited the final few sentences. By the time she pronounced "Vouvray"—or rather, mispronounced it—she was nearly shouting. A stifled giggle caused her to look up, her beady eyes reduced to a pair of savage black marbles behind her oversized spectacles.

She cleared her throat, put down my exam. "This exam is, uh..." She waited for another minor swell of giggles to die down.

"It's colorful and it's got a, a distinctive voice. It's also a textbook example of the *ad hominem* attack."

My eyes met hers.

"What grade did that one get?" came a call from the back.

Dr. Charles refused to engage my gaze any more and did her best to smile. "Did you write it?"

"No."

"Then it's not your business."

I got an A-minus on the exam, by the way. Dr. Charles detested what I wrote, but even a PC flunky such as her couldn't help but admire my diatribe. Admittedly, getting an A on written exams was simple. Dad had told me several times that most faculty, deeply dispirited by post-literate scrawlings, were viscerally relieved to read student work that boasted both the complex and compound sentence.

Still, Dr. Charles was occasionally a challenge. My midterm exam seemed to rouse her, and in the semester's final weeks she quite often proselytized directly from the lectern, using it as her bully pulpit to advance her "progressive" views. I suspect that she feared an open confrontation with me. She even took to bringing a bound copy of her doctoral thesis to class and read highlights to sycophants who loitered after class. Typically, these toadies hadn't bothered to turn in any homework, and they hoped—correctly, no doubt—that Dr. Charles would find it within her to award a "B" in return for shameless bootlicking.

On one occasion, she remarked to a worshipping herd of five or six that she had "problematized" the most bedrock assumptions in scientific discourse.

"...Wow," a classmate finally managed. He nodded slowly, as if nearly paralyzed by the labor of understanding our prof. "So that's why we, why we can't say stuff is really wrong."

"Wrong?"

"Yeah, like, how we just jump all over primitive stuff, and—"

"So-called Third World," she gently corrected.

"—so-called, yeah sure. How that stuff is really just adaptive," he worshipfully added. The other students nodded on cue.

"Certainly, we should at least be pretty careful about dismissing cultural practices as just, you know, as mere savagery."

"Yeah," the head toady nodded earnestly. He opened his notebook to record insights for further study.

"Especially in the sciences, where so much discourse is empowered by the appeal to scientific authority."

I'd paused a few feet from the lectern, upon which Dr. Charles leaned. Against her own will, she glanced at me in mid-sentence, and the sudden deepening of lines upon her forehead spoke of her wish that I leave. So I stayed, even sitting at a desk a few spaces back from the front row.

"Did you have a question?"

"Does aspirin work in the Third World?"

She blinked.

"What about antibiotics?"

"—Certainly."

"Antibiotics are context-free," I observed. "They work no matter the cultural context. Period."

"There must be context," Dr. Charles weakly countered, "because nothing comes out of acontextual, uh—"

"And to think," I continued, looking about at my classmates, "that dead white males conceived and perfected the double-blind study! What a blow against social justice."

She gathered her books, smiled curtly at the group, and departed. Her appearance was momentarily alarming: the lectern had hidden the enormity of her calves and ankles, and the contrast of her middling torso and meaty lower limbs was appalling.

The apple-polishers gathered their books and hurried out; a guy reminded a girl about the weekend keg spree at the Theta Chi house. One student, however, stayed behind.

"It's about time somebody shut that bitch up," he loudly enthused.

"Agreed."

He studied me, as if wondering how to continue our conversation. "Hey, you ever read the campus *Herald*?"

"Not really. Why?"

"Got a minute?"

"Got a smoke?" I'd been hungering for a menthol all day but had no money in my pocket—or anywhere else.

"No, but just come on with me. I'll get you a smoke."

I stood and extended my hand. "Jeff."

"I'm Tommy. Let's get you that smoke."

We walked across campus, chatting amiably about our classes and slacker study habits. Tommy was still excited by my ribbing of Dr. Charles. "Everybody hates that bitch."

"Yeah, maybe..." I shrugged.

"Well I do. You do, don't you?"

"Not really. She's entertainment, I guess."

"I hate her. I'm getting a D."

I nodded, glanced at the ground. After Tommy uttered a few more oaths and curses in honor of Dr. Charles, our conversation turned to music. He remarked that he'd seen a "weird band" at Rouch's, a bar across town that aggressively courted up-and-coming bands from Chicago and New York.

"Pad?" I suggested.

"Yeah, that's it. You know them."

"The singer is my sister."

He stopped short.

"Why?"

"She can really sing, I'll say that."

"You think they're weird, though."

"Not her," he hurriedly assured. "The music is...I mean, they can really play. Your sister? She's a monster on that guitar."

"But they're weird," I joked with mock offense.

"Maybe that's not the right word."

"Eccentric?"

He nodded. "But the bottom line is: they *raawwwk*. And..." He pointed at a drab, red brick building. "Here's where I'll get you a smoke." I followed him to the side of the building: Old Oak, which was a dormitory: a chick dormitory at that.

"What, are we going on a panty raid?"

"I wish. No, we're going downstairs."

Gray cement steps quickly brought us to the cramped editorial office of the *Herald*, the university's thrice-weekly newspaper. About a dozen students sat in haphazardly arranged cubicles, hacking away at their computer keyboards. Tommy invited me to have a seat. He returned presently with a cigarette, which he held with some awkwardness between his thumb and forefinger. I thanked him and, after patting down my jean pockets, found a book of matches that had drowned during last week's wash and rinse cycle.

"Whoa, there's no smoking in here," Tommy noted.

I sighed. "It's okay. My matches don't work anyway."

"No, wait, it's okay," assured a female voice. "Go ahead and smoke right there." A gal strode briskly forward, a ready hand-shake in her right palm and a smoke-eating gadget in her left. She placed the smoke-eater upon the table beside my chair, turned it on, and lighted my cigarette with a *faux* gold lighter. "Make yourself comfortable."

Which I did, or at least I tried. Tommy and the chick stood watching me, as if I were an exotic. So I just sat smoking happily, waiting for an introduction.

"Karen, this is Jeff."

Karen again forcefully shook my hand and assured me that I was just what she was looking for.

"You're looking for a smoker?"

She laughed too loudly, glancing with merriment at Tommy. Then she rolled an office chair from an empty cubicle and sat before me. "No, I'm looking for some new staff writers on the *Herald*, and it hasn't been easy. But then Tommy told me that you'd be really good at, uh, upgrading our writing staff."

"I didn't know you wrote for the paper," I remarked to Tommy.

"I cover the athletic teams. It's easy because they always lose."

"I'm really flattered that you'd think of me Tommy, and—"

"It was my idea to bring you over here," Karen corrected. She leaned forward. The faint remains of her morning's shower soap drifted past me. Without turning toward him, she sharply asked Tommy to get her a coffee.

"I'm flattered, but—" Jesus under glass, this girl was pushy.

"Ever read H. L. Mencken?"

"I've read his name."

"He was a journalist but more than that. He was a kind of, oh you know, a critic and really important intellectual through the 1920's and 1930's and so on. Anyway, the *Herald* is really pushing to revive the journalistic spirit with, you know, some really punchy writing that's not afraid to take on the status quo."

I nodded, wishing the back of my chair were not against the wall.

"Mencken made fun of the puritans of his time and from what I've heard about you, that's the, uh, you have the kind of spirit I'm looking for."

"I don't quite get this. Are you turning this—" I pointed past her shoulder to the modest expanse of the *Herald*'s office—"into a wax museum?"

"I don't follow."

"Me either. What I mean is: are you trying to find people to mimic famous journalists?"

"Their spirit, not their style. Like, I'm trying to find some-body who would do a bit of the Mike Royko approach too, you know, taking on city hall corruption from a real no bullshit, a real guy on the street angle. Here on campus, that would be tak-ing on the administration."

"And the Mencken mimic?"

"You wouldn't mimic. It's the spirit. He took on bigger issues like the world war and political parties. And the stupid compla-cent middle-class. The, uh, the booboise." She snickered. "And how religious fundamentalists were an awful drain on the coun-try's intellect."

"I didn't know Christers were running this college."

"No, but the PC types are and—"

"Ah ha." I sat up. "I follow you."

"Yeah?"

"He follows you," Tommy assured, returning with coffees. "Just this afternoon he took on Dr. Charles."

"God she's a joke," Karen agreed, turning to look at Tommy. "And to think she got the best teacher award last year."

"She sucks," Tommy summarized.

"I have a question," I announced.

Over-caffeinated Karen whirled about to face me. Her chair rolled slightly forward, and her knees came to rest against mine.

"What's the pay?"

"It won't be great," she apologized. "It's just student pay scale, you know." As she revealed this irksome detail, her eyes hardened upon me, as if to pin me in my chair. "But you'll have a fresh supply of cigarettes from me personally."

Eighteen: Then Came the Shriek

"So when did this guy die?"

"I'm wondering now if somebody murdered him."

Sitting upon opposite sides of a library table, Patty and I flipped through a few books and magazine articles to glean something about H. L. Mencken. The research was an excessively mixed bag: the consensus was that Mencken was a fearless though erratic critic of Christianity and the dimwittedness of ordinary Americans...

"That part I like," I said.

"Your new friends sure pegged you right in that regard."

...as well as an anti-Semite.

"The Jew-baiting though," I sighed. "That's weird. Hey, maybe your Dad knows something about Mencken."

"Why?"

"He's in the business."

Her smile was sour. "So, you want me to call him up and ask?"

"Not really."

"Then why did you—"

I raised my palms. "Sorry. No offense meant."

"For once."

"Jesus Christ," I whispered, leaning across the table to clasp her hands. "I said I'm sorry."

"Yeah well..." She looked away. "I can't tell anymore when you're serious."

"Look, if you're mad about something then just—"

She jerked her hands free of mine. "Quiet," she whispered, glancing about her.

"Okay, I'll be quiet," I offered through clenched teeth, "if you'd just tell me what you're pissed about."

"Nothing."

"Or let me put it this way: how have I failed?"

"Forget it already. I'm sorry. My fault."

I resisted the desire to say *Of course it's your fault* and shrugged, struggling not to sneer. We sat silently for several minutes, I flipping through the books and Patty pretending to read a fashion magazine. Finally, she attempted—rather feebly—to feign interest in my impending role of campus scourge. "So...what're their names again?"

"Who?"

"At the newspaper."

"Tommy and Karen."

She nodded mildly, returned her gaze to a scuffed encyclopedia of 20th century journalism. "Look at this. Here it says he tried to get Jews out of Europe."

"What, so he could kill them faster?"

"No, nothing like that." She read silently for several more minutes, still suffering from her sour mood: her face was a bit slack and her eyes lifeless. "He was no saint for sure but, ya know—" She closed the book. "He did write to several high and mighty types to demand that the U.S. give asylum to Jews."

"Better than most did."

"True."

I read a bit more. Patty grew restless, fidgeting in her chair like a child in a dentist's waiting room. "How much longer?" she finally asked, long hand covering another yawn. "Sorry. I'm just tired."

"Then let's go." I hurriedly stacked our books near the table's edge. I had promised Karen that I'd come up with story ideas over the holiday break and, with Patty's mood inexplicably poor, I'd looked forward to distracting myself with such some lazy solitary brainstorming. But I knew that despite her impatience with the library, she'd only bellyache further if I suggested she just sneak a nap in one of the stale study lounges on the upper floor. "C'mon. Let's go, Stretch," I whispered without malice.

We walked out into the night. A gust chilled Patty, and she grasped my hand. As we quickened our pace across campus to our car, the snow grew mischievous, altering its downward angle to harass our reddening faces. The sky was an endless awning of charcoal-streaked black that obscured all stars and, it seemed at that moment, all hope.

We drove in silence out of town, listening to the hum of tires upon asphalt. "Wish the heater worked better," I finally said to break the silence. She murmured and looked out the side window at the blurred queues of a fallow corn field. Finally, I pulled into our gravel driveway. Our house looked forlorn, shivering in darkness beneath a huge leafless oak tree.

"Do we have to have the party?" Patty stared at the house.

"Why?"

"Good." She patted my lap, opened the door, and hurried inside.

I watched from the car, my view obscured by the now rapidly falling snow. The flakes struck the windshield, slid downward, and disappeared. On the side of the house, the bedroom window glowed from the overhead light...Patty was, I knew, already getting into bed, where she'd shiver beneath piles of woolen blankets. On winter evenings, her pale limbs were simply too long: they took hours to warm up.

I recalled that Karen, the amusingly assertive newspaper editor, had given me a third cigarette. I retrieved it from my shirt pocket and, upon lighting it, got out of the car to lean wearily against the fender and watch the smoke disappear into the chilled black. Knowing I'd be unable to sleep for a while, I got back into the car and drove to a newly opened gas station. The station's garish lights cheered me a bit, and I made an effort to step lively inside.

Behind the counter stood a pimpled kid with the requisite nose and lip piercings. "Hey," he grunted in greeting.

"Pack of menthol."

"What brand?"

"Whatever's cheapest." I scrounged through my pockets in search of change, but I retrieved more lint than legal tender. The kid waited with admirable patience as I dumped the contents of both hands onto the counter and separated coin from refuse. My fingers, still chilled, were not quite up to the task, and I dropped some quarters to the floor. When an impatient couple, stinking micro-waved burritos in hand, stood behind me, I laughed and waved them through. And even after I'd gathered all my coins into a pile, I was thirty cents short and the pimpled kid bailed me out by crediting me with the balance.

"Thanks amigo," I nodded gratefully.

"That's cool."

"Is my credit good for a coffee too?"

"C'mon, man."

"That's a 'yes', isn't it?"

He tried to stare at me with disapproval, but when I pulled my empty pockets out of my pants and let them dangle inside out, like a silent movie actor, he laughed and nodded toward the coffee. I thanked him profusely and promised I would return the next day to settle my debt.

"That's cool."

The house was dark as I pulled into the driveway. Whorls of smoke streamed from the tilting brick chimney. Half-consumed coffee in hand and cigarettes in pocket, I quietly entered. For a moment I felt like a philandering husband sneaking home after a hotel lark with a minor.

Inside, the silence was unaccountably minatorial, and as I padded in fraying white socks upstairs to bed, the steps' creaking urged me to turn around and leave. I stealthily pushed upon the bedroom door. Ah, warmth: in a corner, the space-heater glowed red as it labored to push the temperature above sixty.

Patty sat fully clothed upon the bed's edge. For a moment, I thought she was simply brooding, and then I saw the phone in her hand.

"—feel differently about it now that, you know—" She clamped a hand over the receiver. "Don't spy on me!" she hissed. A fault line of peevishness marred her face and, in the dark stark room, she looked very much like the women she despised: the suburban-wrecked soccer moms, suffocating in ennui.

I mocked her with a quick pose of the busybody, palm to my ear and eyebrows raised.

She asked her fellow conversant to please wait for a minute. "C'mon, I'm talking here."

"Then please do continue," I invited. Ah, a potential melodrama, I realized: the young man returns to the sullen love nest and finds his mate talking furtively upon the phone. All that was missing was the hastily packed suitcase...

"What're you doing?" she demanded, now almost shouting.

"Nothing." I opened the closet door. No suitcase. Maybe it was under the bed?

"Stop it! Can't you see I'm on the—" She slammed the phone upon its cradle, and the sound of cracked plastic bounced off the ceiling. "What are you looking for?" she yelled, standing.

"A reason to leave the room." I faced towering Patty. In the dim light, her silhouette was imposing: I couldn't see her face's features yet felt her ire.

"Here's a reason to leave the room." She yanked a drawer from a dresser and tossed clothes onto the floor. Then she grabbed something, and that something struck my face. "You sick fuck!"

A white envelope fluttered to the ground. Through the envelope's opaque body I saw outlines of photographs: the photographs I'd rescued from Repulsive Robby.

She slapped me. "You've always had a thing for her!"

Another slap, though this one merely grazed my nose as I took a neat step back. At that moment, what with Patty in full blaze, I saw no reason to feign ignorance. "They're called photographs. Maybe you have some yourself. And if you do—" I warily regarded her flaring nostrils— "may I slap you?"

From her pocket she pulled the photo of Kim's back, the black straps prominent beneath the white blouse. "Just a little better angle," she raged, "and I could see her tits!"

"Do you want to?"

"You've got a thing for her. Look at this!" Red hand atremble, she held the picture inches from my face. "You cut it!"

"I what?"

"Cut it! You cut everyone out so it just shows, it's just her!"

The photo before me indeed had been cropped: only Kim's back remained in the photo. I'd taken scissors and reduced the photo's framing to the essential. And even as I stood looking, the memory of trimming it surfaced: I'd been stoned. Thoughts wandering inevitably toward my darling, I found myself looking through the photos and, desiring a more concentrated object of affection, I trimmed that photo and carried it around in my back pocket for several days.

"Even that night I met you at her party..." She shut her eyes to conjure the scene. "She was drunk and fell down and sat against your back. And you just—" Image conjured, she now righteously shook it away.

"Yeah, I pushed her away. Pretty erotic."

"I could see it."

"You're insane. Thoroughly."

The night of the dropout party, Kim had indeed, as dropouts do, gotten drunk and fallen against my knees as I sat beside Tall Patty. Yet at that point, I'd harbored not an inkling of desire for Kim.

"And I was stupid enough to—" She turned away from me, wiping at snot. "—Stupid enough to hope I was wrong. And for a while I was so happy 'cause it seemed like I was. I thought, Jesus Christ! Patty, you're just imagining things. He's pretty weird all around anyway. So he's a little attached to his sister, so what? It's 'cause his family is so completely fucked up, I mean even worse than mine."

"You're demented. And keep her out of your delusions."

"But a couple weeks ago, when you came home after you've had supper with her, it's like, like you wouldn't fucking *touch* me and you treat me like I'm an idiot."

A shiver slithered up my neck.

"And there's only contempt on your face if I *dare* try to speak to you, like you've been stuck with a consolation prize when you could be with your fucking musical genius sister!"

Another slap, this one meaty and loud. "Filth! You're both filth!"

I retreated down the stairs, taking three steps at a time, then ran to the car. Once inside, I tried vainly to light a cigarette: my hands shook and I yelled at them, drill sergeant style, to stay still. I managed only to snap the cigarette in two. Cursing again, I started the car with a violent twisting of the ignition key.

Then came the shriek: female, apocalyptic.

Patty ran barefoot from the porch toward the car. As she closed in, the car's headlights rendered her ghoulish, her pale face disfigured by tears and rage. I yelled at her to get out of the way and stomped the accelerator menacingly. The engine roared, but Patty stood boldly before my car. Her height added menace to her visage: she was a hysterical specter, snowflakes dotting her unruly hair.

She reared back like a baseball pitcher, her lengthy arm briefly disappearing behind her into darkness...then the arm whipped forward.

"Whadda you crazy?!" I bellowed.

A rock struck the windshield.

Another rock crashed against the windshield, and an erratic web of cracks instantly filled the glass.

I jammed the transmission into reverse and backed away even as Patty ran toward me, her feet a cadaverous white-blue as she took big awkward steps to avoid the driveway's stones. With ten yards between my car and Patty, I jammed the transmission into drive and almost stomped the accelerator: the spinning tires, I realized, might spray her with gravel, so I eased from the driveway onto the road. In my rearview mirror, I saw Patty, like a flustered high wire walker, come to an arm-waving stop at the road's edge.

Ahead of me stretched county road 20, its black surface glistening beneath melting snow. The road's yellow dividing line curved into the moonless horizon. Stunned by the sheer scale and velocity of this evening's calamity, I followed that line for hours. When the eastern horizon's dense blackness gave way to a dispirited gray, I pulled off the road and smoked the very last of a very poor batch of dope. The dope produced a sinister image: the future as a silent grinning thug, poised to step around a corner, baseball bat raised.

Nineteen: Quite Mad

Mornings had changed.

I awoke tired and listless to my marrow, even if I'd skipped work and hit the hay before 8:00 p.m. The mattress smelled of sour sheets and grievous betrayal. I'd scrubbed down the mattress with hot water and dish soap, but always that odor malingered. So on several evenings, I simply decamped upon a makeshift bed of clothes and blankets and—after one night of bong abuse—twigs and newspapers. On Fridays and Saturdays, I typically worked until well past midnight and was sufficiently exhausted to sleep on that accursed mattress, though not before spraying it down with disinfectant.

At these moments, I felt quite mad. But the smell was there, without question.

Patty left behind the avernal mattress and little else: the drab plastic dishes and water-stained drinking glasses were gone, as were the five pieces of weary furniture that she'd brought from her parents' home. The kitchen, too, now lacked its second hand Formica-topped table, which we'd purchased at a garage sale one lazy Sunday. The house's bareness amplified my every step and cough, my every thought and regret. When she mailed a letter to me, informing me of the date she and her family would arrive to claim the furniture—and a warning that I must not be present—I nearly stayed in the hopes of dissuading her. But I honored her demands and in fact was out of the house the entire day, not wanting to risk the humiliation of being seen by Patty or her family.

So now, alone, I'd rise just after day break or, if I got lucky, would scrape together a paltry joint and fall back asleep until ten or eleven. Mornings were awful: their dewy promise, normally bright with potential, merely reminded me of how hopeless my own yearnings were.

I passed the Christmas season utterly alone save for my hours at Franco's. At odd moments, as when sitting in the chill house (furnace unrepaired, funds failing), I wondered what the others were doing: Pad, certainly, was busy gigging, as I'd heard of two shows on the university radio. Pad's local success cheered me and, on one solitary Saturday, I heard "Unsilent Partner" twice on WXXR, the largest commercial rock station in the region. Feeling left out of the excitement, I called the station and requested that the song be played again. The DJ agreed, noting that the band was home-grown talent.

The guy's voice assumed its self-conscious on-air DJ jive: "— they've got *major market* in their future."

"Major market," I listlessly repeated.

I recalled writing that lyric. It was a Saturday, rather like this one, although my solitude then was a balm, not an abrasive, as I was still at Aunt Jo's and therefore often hiding in the basement.

She's at her best before ten.
Damp towels tossed to the floor
Ashtray tumbling, slam of the freezer door
The movie's starting, the popcorn's burnt again.

"What just happened? I don't get it."
I do my best to explain,
But she stops me to complain.
"Tell me again? I still don't get it."

Unsilent partner—
Talking over me.
Unsilent partner—

Kim took the chorus's five simple syllables and hung them upon one of her most endearing vocals, with the "un" starting low and, with that first step, her voice rose ever higher, lingering just behind the beat with each successive syllable, then soaring with "partnnneeerr..." Meanwhile, her guitar—a buoyant blend of surf and punk—careened alongside the chorus.

I'd lost track of time in my musings and was surprised to find the phone, now emitting a robotic cheerless flat tone, still in my hand. "Unsilent Partner" had ended, and a dork with adenoidal complaints promised another commercial free hour. I pulled the plug on the radio—the volume knob had long ago expired—and took another aimless drive until the dashboard's red needle tickled "E". I pulled into a gas station and scrounged for coin: It took all the change gathered from my denim jacket pockets and from beneath the car seat to produce six dollars and some cents: half went for a pack of menthol cigarettes and the other purchased gas. With little to interest me at home, I pulled the car to a corner of the station, adjacent to a brand-new dumpster, and smoked half the pack.

Once, when I had no grass to stave off my loneliness, I called home, wondering even as I dialed what I would do if Kim answered. But nobody answered and, upon hearing the answering machine's invitation to say hello, I hung up, both saddened and relieved to get no answer.

The forlorn house often compelled me to take long pointless drives, yet I didn't again risk calling home. The possibility that Patty had told Kim...that thought chilled me and several times woke me from haunted sleep. At times, when the anxiety escalated to bubbling dread, I unplugged the phone. Though I longed for conversation, I feared that I would place the receiver to my ear and be assaulted by Kim's curses.

Or by her icy demand that I eat poison.

But Kim never called, and I interpreted that fact as near-proof that Patty had told her about the snapshots. Of course, snapshots themselves are innocent, but in a specific context, they can point to guilt.

Indeed, my impulse to hide them stoked Patty's suspicions. And admittedly, I had no other snapshots of family members or anyone else, Patty included. And the other little things: my loaning money to Kim, my weekly campus dinners with her and, who knows? An indefinable melancholy on my face at the mention of her name? These commonplaces pointed to something peculiar, and once her suspicions were alighted, Patty stoked them with every detail she could find or invent.

Twenty: New Year's Day

Beginning around nine, the phone rang on the half-hour on New Year's Day. I searched within myself for reasons to answer and found none. At the rate I was smoking, I'd soon have to leave the house for a new pack and, if I was careful, I could kill off at least two hours. But the day offered no opportunity for worthwhile distraction: after purchasing my cigarettes at the gas station, I drove across town to the strip mall but, as I approached it, my spirits flagged. The stores were of course closed, and they looked abandoned, shuddering beneath a sudden dust-up of snow. I backfisted the steering wheel—I'd looked forward to steeping myself with some coffee in the bookstore's cramped "café" while flipping through magazines.

Realizing I could spare no more gas, I drove home and, with a cheery madcap call of "Happy New Year" to the house's drab front, marched forward ho. I even assumed a military cadence, arms and legs straight, chin up.

"Hut two three four..."

The marching orders invigorated me, so I marched around the front yard in straight lines and right angles of geometric perfection. After an impressive 360 degree spin upon one heel, I saluted myself and took a cigarette break. I smoked with polished discipline, standing at attention, facing the tepid eastern sky, cigarette straight and true in my mouth's corner. I calculated I'd be able to march enough to earn sufficient smoking breaks that required another trip out. After a final march, my tennis shoes leaving soldierly prints in the wet front yard, I declared victory and strode inside.

The phone rang as soon as I closed the door, as if the caller knew I'd entered the house. I looked over my shoulder through the rain-spattered front window, then scolded myself: I really *was* getting paranoid.

I grabbed the phone, calling "Happy New Year."

"Happy New Year yourself."

"—Kim?"

"What?" I heard someone laughing in the background.

"Sorry. To whom am I speaking if I might ask?"

"Your editor, Karen."

"Oh. Hello."

"Oh and hello yourself too, smartass. Listen. I've been calling you all morning. Are you hung over from some wild sex with groupies from your sister's rock band?"

"No, it's just me and my sister going at it today."

"Hey, that's cool, whatever. Listen, it's time to get to work on the paper. Are you ready to work?"

"Now?"

"Yeah now. What, do you have another orgy?"

Karen's bossy energy would, I knew, usually exhaust me. At this moment, though, it cheered me.

"Well what do you say?"

"At an orgy?"

"Ha. C'mon, some of the staff is here, so come on over. It'll be fun. We've even got some journalistic inspiration left over in bottles and if you're hung over, then just drink until you're not." Two people laughed in the background, and an image came to mind: a cramped college apartment, the air thick with cigarette smoke and good humor.

"What's your address?"

I easily found the apartment building and parked near the block's corner. Not wanting to be an unprepared guest, I brought with me a few quarts of discount beer and what remained of my marijuana stash. The stash was in miserable health: mostly stems and seeds and meager green leaves disintegrating in the baggy's dusty corners.

The apartment was your typical student housing fare, a brick building that, with dozens of identical structures, occupied several blocks near the university. I bounded up the walkway and rapped on the door. When no one answered, I banged harder. Silence. After one more bang, I shrugged and, turning slowly, wondered if Karen were a practical joker...certainly, one could easily imagine her loud enthusiasms turning pugnacious and even malevolent.

"Hey you dope we're over here."

I looked to the next apartment. Karen stood waving at me. I squelched a chuckle: she'd jam-packed her ripe figure into a cowgirl get-up—faded jeans and denim shirt—and her hair, streaked with various shades of blonde, was held in place with a cook's hairnet. A black vest hung across her torso, a dime store sheriff's badge glimmering in a fleeting break of direct sunlight.

"What, you can't follow directions?"

"I thought you said 204."

"I did. You're at 206. C'mon, you're just in time for breakfast."

I followed her inside and was greeted by the smell of bacon and eggs. In the living room, three people sat in a ragged circle upon the threadbare gray carpet; in the tiny kitchen, a few others stood chatting while waiting upon a wheezing drip coffee maker.

Karen clasped my elbow. "Everyone, this is my fantastic new columnist, Jeff Edwards."

A hoarse chorus of hellos.

One chubby fellow, his broad back barely contained in a black tee-shirt, craned about to look at me. "Karen's told us all about you."

She steered me toward a third-hand couch and gestured for me to sit. She sat immediately beside me and, after several impatient glances at her wristwatch, called the meeting to order: "C'mon shut up everyone and let's get to work."

Tommy was among those who came in from the kitchen. He waved at me with a free hand; his other hand held a nearly-drained beer bottle. He took a seat upon the couch's sagging arm and waited for Karen to organize a sheath of notes upon her lap.

"First of all, Happy New Year everyone," Karen began. "We've got a great semester lined up for the *Herald*." Felt-tip marker in hand, she called out names, matching monikers to faces: the chubby guy was Mike; adjacent to Mike was a painfully hung-over blonde, Cindy; across from Cindy was a perky co-ed, Roberta...she bubbled with fatuous enthusiasm at every idea floated that afternoon. Alan, tiny face obscured by a surfeit of dyed black hair and chrome face rings, raised his hand at the call of his name.

"A few people couldn't make it today," Karen observed with mock sympathy. "It was too far to drive, apparently."

Actually, I was marginally impressed that this gaggle of students had congregated in their editor's apartment: most students were still off campus with their families, enjoying or abhorring the holidays. As Karen continued, a mood of serious purpose settled upon the group and, pushing my bag of grass deeper into my jacket pocket, I concluded I'd made a gross miscalculation. Karen kept the meeting moving briskly. Her habit of finishing other people's sentences helped keep matters moving and, when chubby Mike's freshly-opened bottle of beer geysered upon the floor, Karen pointedly waited for him to stop laughing.

"Beer on my carpet I don't mind," she announced. "But can we stay focused? We have a lot to do." Then, frivolity crisply crushed, she continued. She spent several minutes interrogating her staff on story ideas, proposed solutions to production snafus, and ridiculed budget cuts demanded by campus bean counters.

She faced me, her knee abutted against my thigh. "And what are your plans?" She leaned forward, her thin booth-tanned face comically close to mine.

"Can I get fired before I'm hired?"

"You really haven't thought about—"

"Of course not."

The group chuckled. Karen held my gaze a second longer than necessary, then shrugged and capped her pen.

"But I have an idea now," I announced. And I did. "In the spirit of my putative model Mencken, I propose a series of investigative articles focusing upon prominent campus figures and—"

"Figures?" Karen interrupted.

"Like at the sorority house!" chubby Mike roared. To ensure we understood his tepid pun, he reached out to squeeze two imaginary breasts.

"Although 'investigative' isn't the correct term," I said, instantly correcting myself. "'Attitudinal' is better. Anyway. What this boils down to is puncturing all the *amour propre* creeps, from the politically to patriotically correct. You know, the self-righteous asses who aren't used to being ridiculed in print."

Karen's eyes narrowed upon me. "Who's your first subject?"

"My first victim will be Professor Charles."

The group loudly assented. The good Professor was, it seemed, the object of profound loathing.

"I think we've worked hard enough for New Year's Day," Tommy announced. He'd been silent through the meeting, discreetly leaning into a shadowed corner while sipping beer.

"But you haven't revealed *your* plans," Karen barked, though her body English suggested she wasn't actually angry: she finally got off the couch's edge and relaxed rather heavily against the couch's back—and half against me. "I love my new writer," she sighed with mock girly-girl silliness, then scooted a polite inch away.

"Well, the usual," Tommy said. "Our, you know, the university's really fine basketball team and—" He fell silent and waited for our gaze to turn upon him. "And there's this band I'd like to do a feature on. Pad."

At the mention of Pad, the meeting lost focus. Everyone in the room, it seemed, had heard "Unsilent Partner" on the radio over the last week, yet only Tommy knew that I was the cunning wordsmith behind the melody that produced such craving for second-helpings. And of that fact he now informed them.

"Cool!" several people declared for the next several minutes.

"It's not bad, is it?" I humbly smiled. My modesty rang so false. Jesus sweating in the mosh pit, I thought...the song was *happening*.

"How much have you earned on that song?" somebody called out.

I sipped upon the beer that someone had thrust into my hand. "I really have no idea...Probably nothing."

"Careful," Tommy joked. "The band always gets ripped off."

The group fell nearly silent and Tommy's expression was suddenly sheepish. "Hey, I'm just kidding."

"No, you're right," I agreed. "They usually do."

Eventually the discussion drifted to other topics, and I resisted the temptation to ease the discussion back to Pad. Or rather, back to me. I found myself implying that I'd provided "Unsilent Partner's" lyrics and basic chord structure. This revelation impressed the group even more...flitting about the perimeter of my brain was the nagging realization that lyrics don't impress nearly as much as music. Hung-over Carol surprised me by loudly and nearly correctly humming the song's chorus. She even nailed, with comic hand gestures, the alternating voices in that chorus.

"I could actually sing it," she said, greasy hank of hair falling across her pale forehead, "but those lyrics, I don't quite get them." Then, apparently startled by her own candor, she looked up at me bug-eyed and blurted, "No offense."

"None taken," I smiled. Fortunately, nobody requested elaboration about my creating the chord structure. Silently censuring myself, I said no more about my song-smithing talents. Even more fortunately, Karen asked somebody to look in the kitchen cabinet above the refrigerator.

"Mercy!" Mike yelped from the kitchen.

"No mercy!" Karen throatily laughed. Without looking up, she hoisted an arm behind her and, laughing again, she brought into view a bottle of Old Bushmill's whiskey.

"I've gotta drive," Carol groaned.

"You were drunk when you got here," Karen noted.

"Sorry. I just can't drink any more." Carol rose upon stalky legs and wished everyone a good day. Before Karen could cajole her, Carol was gone. Her hearty swing of the door pushed in a supply of cold fresh air.

Everyone else remained for a first shot—saying "no" to Karen was difficult, especially when she brandished whiskey—and the affair grew louder. I said little for a while...the depth of my own joy surprised me: the holiday season had been so gratingly lonesome, and now I was in a comfortable cramped apartment with fellow students who were...who were what? At least they weren't idiots. I enjoyed their enthusiasms and banter. Settling into the cushions, I smiled with my eyes closed, nodding in agreement when asked if I were all tuckered out or ready for another round. Time came unfastened and tumbled freely in several directions. Tensions melted, voices peaked and ebbed, the occasional hand playfully roughed up my hair or poured me another whiskey.

At some point, my nostrils twitched to the scent of marijuana and I stirred. The room was nearly dark and, as I righted myself, the voices heretofore hovering about my head fell silent.

"Finally waking up?" Merriment.

"Sorry?" As I found my bearings, I also found that my pant leg was damp. "Goddammit…"

"Oops. That's all my fault," Karen apologized, voice incongruously tiny. "I spilled a little bit of beer on you."

"That's okay."

"And we helped ourselves to your grass," someone added. I didn't recognize the voice.

"That's okay too."

"He's awfully agreeable," the new voice noted.

The shadows confused me…fleetingly, I recalled getting upon all fours as a kid and then studying the world upside down between my legs. That same sensation descended upon me now, and I asked if I might have a glass of water.

"No you cannot," Karen joked.

"Please?"

"Oh all right," said the stranger. "I'm Laura, by the way. The bitch's roommate." Laura hoisted herself from the floor and ambled past me. I heard the splash of water in the sink, the fumbling of a glass—then a crash and a curse.

"Dumb bitch," Karen called. "God you're stoned."

"Yeah I am."

Stoned yet resolute, Laura now stood over me with a plastic cup. Water slopped over the cup's rim and onto my already wet pant leg. The threat of a hangover—the existential dread, the headache sniffing about my temples—loomed darkly. I drank greedily then stood with some difficulty and went to the kitchen for a refill. I drank the second glass slowly, swishing the fluid about my mouth as if it were mouthwash: ah, mouthwash!

"Pardon me," I said, hurrying from the kitchen to the bathroom.

And there it was upon the toilet tank. Turning on the faucet for aural camouflage, I uncapped the sturdy plastic bottle and poured rather too much of the green solvent into my mouth. The splashing of water into lavatory failed to produce sufficient racket, so I turned on both spigots full-bore, then gargled half-bore.

Feeling nearly refreshed, I recapped the bottle and helped myself to stick deodorant: thoroughly girly-girl, of course, but the scent was perky, and at this moment I needed perky: Karen and Laura, my nose told me, were burning another joint.

And another.

The afternoon segued to evening. The three of us sat upon the floor, backs against the wall or against furniture. Laura, to my astonishment, produced a bulging bag of aromatic redbud: the resin-thick delight that produces erections in dedicated dopers (The phenomenon, lest you laugh, is real: I recall an article in *Archives of Psychoactive Research* that studies the phenomenon and suggests, with due caution, that marijuana's aphrodisiac qualities merit further study, especially in those cases where standard therapies such as Viagra are contraindicated for men over fifty).

My two friends were wonderful companions for dope smoking...all pleasure, no paranoia. We chatted about whatever subject staggered across our partially-functioning radar: classes, money and the lack thereof, politics, the arts. Twice or thrice, the subject of Pad arose, and I was forced to endure Laura's quizzings about the music business, of which I knew nothing.

"No offense but I hadn't really heard of them until, you know, just now." Sitting like a guru, she took a moment to straighten and stretch her legs, then re-scissored them. "But I'm really impressed. Somebody doing something artistic."

Karen murmured agreement, her eyes nearly invisible in the almost blackened room. Tiring of sitting against the wall, she lay on her back for a moment, then turned upon her stomach, chin resting on both hands. "Wouldn't you just love to strike it rich?" she asked me. "And then just...I don't know, just live and enjoy."

"I probably won't make a dime from this venture," I suggested, "but of course I'd love to strike it rich."

"Would you give some to charity?" Laura wondered.

"God no. I hate do-gooders and all the harm they do"

"You're kidding," Laura insisted.

"No, he's completely serious," Karen said, now again upon her back. She gazed at the ceiling. "He's evil."

"He's just stoned."

"I'm stoned, true." I re-torched a joint that had blacked out in the ashtray. "But no, I wouldn't give it to charity. Not much anyway. To a struggling museum, yes. I'd do that."

"I'd smoke the best dope," Laura dreamily whispered.

"You already do," I laughed. "This stuff is—" I sucked deeply; the embers glowed and popped. "It's bliss."

"I'm horny," Karen announced.

"That's impossible," Laura insisted. Facing me to accept the joint, she explained. "She paddles herself at least, what? Three or four times a day at least."

"Like you."

"True." Laura passed the joint to her roommate.

Karen sat up and finished off the joint in three greedy pulls. "Really, sometimes I'd chuck it all for just one big screw."

"What have you got to chuck?" Laura teased.

"About twenty bucks until the end of the month."

"And you, Jeffrey?" Laura asked, eyebrows mischievously cocked. "What do you have to chuck?"

"Just my morals."

Laura's and Karen's thoughts converged upon me. Oh it was wonderful, reader, to continue this repartee and see one woman glance at another as if to say, *Get lost! I thought of it first!* And the other would feign exquisite indifference even as she shot a warning at her rival.

As the playfulness rolled onward, the women alternately girlish and whorish, I stepped outside myself to watch them contend for me. Oh, I was funny! Stretched out upon the couch, whiskey and ice in hand, I watched the three of us laze upon the floor, passing around a joint or cigarette or drink, each gesture charged with a carnal communality. Naturally, the communality intensified, and the passing of cigarettes led inevitably to the passing of kisses.

"Pass it on."

We three grew entangled as the torsos rolled upon one another, our faces in her tee-shirt, her tee-shirt in my teeth. She over me over her.

"Pass it on."

And me sitting on the couch, watching, smoking, drinking. We sure were a happy-go-lucky trio, chattering between lurching gropes or feigned prudery. I moved from the couch and stood over us. We were a thicket of limbs and laughter. I lowered myself to hands and knees, my nose inches from ours, and—

"Pass it on."

—and the black hair fell away and Kim looked up at me.

"I said pass it on."

A poke in the ribs. I blinked and found myself, inexplicably, back on the couch, Laura beside me. She cursed under her breath, wiped ineptly at the ashes that had fallen upon her blouse.

The joint was, it transpired, a cigarette, and I held it at a distance, as if it were a conundrum.

"You're pretty shy for a freakin' mutation."

I stood up and, stumbling sideways the length of the couch, nearly tripped over Laura's sockless feet. She righted me with lingering paws. The room was entirely dark save for a low band of light beneath the closed bathroom door.

"She's passed out in there."

I knocked, then banged, upon the door but got no answer. Unable to wait any longer, I pushed open the door. Karen had indeed passed out—she slumped against the toilet, snoring. I eased her to the side and then stood over the toilet.

"Ewww you fucking perv!" Laura roared at me from the other side of the locked door. Then, behind me, Karen stirred and scrambled upon her hands and knees to escape. When I came out, hands still wet from a rapid rinsing, the living room was deserted. On either side of the stunted hallway, both bedroom doors were closed but the television was on: a televangelist thrust a Bible into the air and assured his congregation that Jesus, forever young, celebrated the New Year with them.

"—Hello?" I delicately called.

Nobody responded, so I gathered my coat and left. I walked crookedly, brain and limbs pummeled by drink and drug. I also took a wrong turn and walked several blocks before realizing that my car was in another neighborhood. Re-tracing my steps, I passed Karen's apartment and found my car at the end of the block. A trace of snow had fallen, and I wiped off my windshield with my arm.

"Finally up?" someone called from across the street. Karen.

I sheepishly nodded.

Karen assured me that I could've snoozed all morning; the couch was pretty comfortable, she noted. Then her gaze grew harder and, placing her steaming cup of coffee upon her car's hood, she crossed the street to study me. "You're not going to get all weird on me, are you? Because it's okay, Jeffrey. I understand, believe me. Most guys fuck first and ask questions later...you must really respect her."

"—Thanks." I couldn't grasp her meaning, and the sensation of having lost time rattled me. I glanced at my watch, which was of course absent.

"You're welcome," she chirped, nose wrinkling and hand upon my shoulder. Then she leaned forward to hug me and, nearly stupefied with confusion, I returned the gesture. But our hug was comradely, not erotic: just as quickly, the hug was over and she retreated.

Twenty-One: "Like you're dying and too fucking dumb to *stop* dying."

"**Y**ou're not going to get all weird on me, are you?"

Sitting in my rental, I laughed. What had I done? The list of potential deeds was considerable. Made chatty by booze or weed, had I dared confess my love for Kim? Or discussed my spooky knack for conjuring Kim in the midst of real or imagined coupling? Or even grown maudlin and pedestrian, tediously recounting my "unhappy childhood"? No, that was unlikely...too much like a daytime talk show confession, the earnest aesthetic of which repulses me.

Whatever the cause of Karen's solicitude, my ponderings could wait. I was pleasantly spent, as one feels after a session at the gym. I stretched upon the couch that Patty had inexplicably left behind and dragged a fraying quilt across my torso. I slept all day, stirring occasionally to enjoy a cigarette, look out the window at the blasted gray day, and then lie back down. The phone, I was vaguely aware, rang during the second round of my nap, but I ignored it. It was persistent, and I guessed Karen was calling to invite me over for another pow-wow with dope, drink, and chaste footsie. Finally, I just pulled the phone cord from the jack and slept for several more hours.

Violent sounds are peculiar, yes?

One feels them before one hears them. And so I leapt from the couch, heart stopped in mid-beat, as I felt then heard the terrific banging upon the front door. I flipped the porch light switch beside the door and peeked through the blinds...Jesus Christ, no light at all. The cheap bulbs always blew after a week. More banging. The sheer aggression of the banging gave me pause...this couldn't be Karen, certainly.

"Who is it?" I called through cupped hands.

A stifled whine of frustration...female. Patty?! I tried again
to see through the blinds, this time peering with genuine caution: I imagined Patty having grown even taller, standing seven
feet tall with bricks in each hand.

"Patty?"

"Patty?" an irritated voice mocked me.

I opened the door to the night. Cold air rushed past.

"Patty?" the voice mocked again.

"Sorry," I said, inviting my guest in with a chivalric sweep of
the arm.

"You're such an irresponsible ass," Kim snorted. "Don't you
answer the phone? *Ever?*" She walked past me, fast food sacks
swinging in each hand. "I've been calling you for days. Here."
She thrust a sack at me.

"Thanks." I shut the battered door. "I thought Lizzie Borden
was on the stoop."

"Got any lights in here?"

"Just a sec..." I hurried to the far corner and turned on an
unsteady floor lamp.

Kim surveyed the barren room. "What, you sleep on that?"
She pointed at the couch.

"It's for naps. Here. Please sit down." I removed the balled-up
quilt from the couch and, asking for just a moment, hurried into
the kitchen. I returned with metal TV trays and a roll of paper
towels for napkins.

"Why thank you." Kim sat grinning as I scooted one of the TV
trays before her. She placed her cheeseburgers on the tray, waiting for me to sit at the couch's opposite end with my own tray.
"Hope you like Burger Stud, I didn't have money for much else."

"That's more money than I have. And yes, I love Burger
Stud." Which was true, at least for this moment. The burgers'
fatty stink was wonderful. I ate enthusiastically, almost loudly,
and blitzed my two cheeseburgers before Kim had eaten half of
her first.

"Here, take my other one."

I smiled, shook my head.

She lobbed the burger onto the tray, and I thanked her.

She nodded, chewing lazily, studying me for several seconds.

"What?"

"She took most of the furniture, huh?" Kim rolled her eyes back and forth to indicate the length of the nearly empty living room.

"Yeah."

"I talked to Patty the other day."

"—And?" As in a suspense movie, ominous cellos sawed to and fro and a cold shadow crossed my soul.

"And she said—oh my God are you all right?"

I tried to answer, but a wad of burnt burger jammed in my craw.

Kim thrust her stein-sized soda cup at me. The liquid fizzed at the clot in my throat and, like liquid drain opener, bubbled backward up my throat and out my nose.

She upended the TV tray and ran into the kitchen. Seconds later, she was hunched over me, shoving a glass of water against my mouth and sharply slapping my back.

I got one swallow down, then another, but Kim's slapping grew heavier, and it felt as if she'd struck my back with the flat backside of a shovel—but the slappings freed the clotted burger, and I could again breathe.

"Okay okay!" I garbled, fending off her blows. "Truce."

Kim reluctantly sat down as I gasped and hacked.

"...You sound like this," Kim finally said.

"What?"

Big plastic cup in hand, she sucked noisily through her crimped straw. "Like you're dying and too fucking dumb to *stop* dying."

I reached for my hamburger.

"God I can't believe you're going to finish it."

"I'm hungry."

"Yeah, well—" She turned slightly away from me, nodding, as if to share a joke with herself.

"So what did she say?" I prodded.

"That you suck. And that—" Kim patted at her shirt pocket, then at the pockets on her discarded jean jacket. "Got any ciga-rettes?"

"Under the couch. What else?"

Smoke rolled from her nostrils and her eyes narrowed. "You just suck really really *bad*." Kim's laughter—so juvenile and joy-

ous, so pleased-to-tease—warmed the bare room. A moment
later, I too was laughing, and doing so for many reasons: clearly,
Patty hadn't told Kim of the snapshots. And clearly, Kim was
happy to see me. Buoyed, I laughed long and easy, happy to be
the victim of Kim's playground ribbing.

"I tried to stick up for you, but gave up. Pretty quickly."

"Thanks."

"Here, have a smoke with me, you disheveled loser." With a
show of great generosity, she handed me one of my own cigarettes. "Actually, she just said that you're a very bright young
man and all that patronizing shit, but that bottom line, you're
just another guy who's not ready to commit."

"Not to her," I quietly agreed, though only my voice was sub-
dued. My spirit was too big for my body, my relief was beyond
expression: and of course, I couldn't express it. But to just sit
here with her, laughing and joking and smoking...I could've
kissed her.

"You heard about Uncle Art and Aunt Jo?"

"They drowned Robbie?"

"They kinda left Robbie with Dad for a while. Permanently."
She smirked. "Anyway. I'm wondering how long Dad can put up
with it." She stood, ambled over the window to look out into the
blackness. "So what's life like out here in the boonies?"

"It's cheap, so I can almost afford it."

"How much?"

I told her.

She stood there, facing the window for a moment, then
turned to face me: "Need help with the rent?"

I shrugged. "Patty wasn't paying her half anyway, so"

"No, I mean: I need a place to live for a while."

"—I, I guess I can put up with you for a while."

Her gaze held mine for a long moment, as if testing me for
sarcasm. But no sarcasm darkened my voice or face. Then she
opened the front door and took a step outside. "I've got my stuff
with me. Guitars and clothes and laundry."

I replaced the failed porch bulb, and we unloaded her car. As
we walked back and forth, Kim dished: Dad had reunited with
Barbara, the French horn player. Barbara, it seemed, had finally

gotten serious about her playing, and therefore needed a more supportive environment than that secured by her "prissy finishing school" employer.

"Dad pretended that he wanted me to stay, but he was glad because his little lady was home." She dropped two guitar cases just inside the front door. "You should've seen the skank Dad was seeing before dear Barbara came back."

"Skank?"

"Skank. Some bar slut on the eight-year baccalaureate plan." She snickered. "Dumb as a box of rocks, and those whoppin' circus tits...Robbie, his jaw dragged between his feet whenever she was around."

"And what *about* Robbie?" I paused. "He's not gonna end up here too?!"

"Nope. He gets that monthly check. Uncle Art and Aunt Jo, they just wanted out from under it and Dad agreed to take the money. Turns out Robbie's the son of a junkie debutante with a rich Daddy. From New Orleans."

Seems that Jo and Art, nerves and bank account threadbare, had brazenly tracked down the debutante and the rich Daddy, now confined to a wheelchair with oxygen, agreed to extend the payments for ten more years. The debutante was newly engaged to a recently-widowed physician, and Daddy would spare no expense in marrying off his girl.

"Dad...he's pathetic," I smiled, adjusting the load in my arms: four ancient grocery sacks filled with make-up, pimple cream, deodorant, underwear, reams of folded sheet music and music magazines. The armload obscured my vision, and I nearly tripped over a practice amp that Kim had left in the middle of the room.

"But Dad, he's making it all up to me in a big way."

"How's that?"

"He's my manager."

"Watch your money."

"Oh and did I tell you? He won a commission to compose a piece for the Fort Wayne symphony"

Several times, Dad had competed for such commissions: local, national, private, public. He'd come close one year with a concerto that was, at least to my ears, very strong: he'd written it for trombone then belatedly realized it sounded better on the euphonium. After some re-working of the closing *presto*, he sent it to the judging commission and...earned second. Second merited a handsome certificate and no cash.

After finally emptying Kim's car, we sat upon the couch and smoked the rest of my cigarettes. Kim chattered breathlessly of Pad's unexpected success—"one catchy little song and it's like, damn! Rust Belt records in Chicago wants an album."

"I'm not surprised."

"Yeah, it was right after Chicago."

"Chicago?"

An errant ash tumbled from her rapidly bobbing cigarette, and she brushed it from her lap. "It was just before Christmas but I couldn't get a hold of you and we had to move *fast*."

Pad gained the fateful Chicago gig after an AR twerp with Rust Belt downloaded MP3's of "Unsilent Partner", "Blush", and "Looks Like a Tommy" from Pad's website, set up by Robbie's computer geek acquaintance. The AR twerp liked what he heard and e-mailed the band, asking Pad to travel to Chicago for a regional music conference.

"So we did it, just like that." Kim snapped her fingers. "We piled our equipment into our cars and drove non-stop and got there that morning. And didn't get paid a dime."

The regional music conference, Kim explained, was actually a corporate beauty pageant. For street-cred marketing reasons, it was presented as grass roots and anti-corporate.

"We were lucky," Kim reflected, "because we'd just played the last three nights and were punchy and loose. But we had every single note under our fingers."

"So you really signed?" I leaned forward.

Kim blinked at me, then glanced at the floor. "Dad wouldn't let us." She smiled ruefully, as if wishing Dad hadn't butted in. "He became our manager at that second, actually."

"He was right."

"Really?"

"'Unsilent Partner' is all over the radio. If that label wants you now, other labels'll want you."

Twenty-Two: Signed

During Kim's first month in my place, I saw her rarely, as Pad monopolized her time. Nervous excitement coursed through me. Sometimes it soared to the euphoric or staggered to the near-hysterical. Once, after Kim casually remarked that she'd hang herself before "letting myself get like Mom, so skanky and gross with black teeth," I laughed too loudly and, even as I tried to quiet myself, my merriment boiled over into cackling and coughing.

"So that would be funny?" Kim huffed. I had to assure her, tears of manic cheer welling, that I was laughing at her quip, not at the thought of her looking like Mom. Rigid upon the couch, she studied me an awkwardly long moment, seemingly ready to curse or spit.

"Seriously, I didn't mean anything by it."

"Fuck you."

"You first."

I cajoled and teased her in properly rough sibling fashion until she good-naturedly rolled her eyes.

"Well I've cut down on the cigarettes and haven't really put on any weight," she belatedly observed.

Ah, female vanity...it trumps all else. Crisis averted, I remarked that I was off to work, leaving Kim to experiment upon her acoustic guitar with open tunings. "I just love open E lately! All these unexpected little happy accident sounds."

Through an *ad hoc* crash course in self-control, I learned to monitor my emotional uprisings by retreating to the bathroom. At such moments, my joy transcended mere infinity, and as I sat upon the floor gathering myself, I felt like a lonely wayfarer who, against all odds, discovered his Elysium.

Kim, meanwhile, seemed on balance happy in her new home. She'd spend many mornings back at Dad's, mixing songs on the

computer or practicing guitar, and return by mid-afternoon, hair
stringy from running restless fingers through it. We'd talk and
then I'd be off to work at Franco's or she'd be on the phone with
Richard. Yes, measly Richard was still in the band and, I feared,
ever more in Kim's life. On several occasions, I'd return from
campus to find him and Kim sitting at the kitchen table, killing
off my freezer-burned burritos and discount colas. Then they'd be
gone, back to Richard's for basement rehearsals.

I attempted to camouflage my dislike of Richard and, for the
most part, succeeded. As winter fitfully faded, my radar remained on high alert for advancing storms. Wisely, I refrained
from asking about Richard, judging that she herself would at
some point reveal any budding romance.

Of course, I exploited my hours in the house alone to search
Kim's bedroom, up the steps adjacent to mine. Few details
emerged…I found no spermicide nor prescriptions for the pill; I
found no carelessly discarded condoms or tell-tale stains upon
sheets. I found only the odd guitar pick, empty facial scrub tube,
or chocolate candy bar wrapper. She kept a surprisingly clean
room, with CD's neatly stacked in a corner. Her modest wardrobe—jeans, mostly, with simple cotton blouses or tee shirts—
hung with military precision in the narrow closet. On the closet's
floor, sensible scuffed shoes: a few flats, although perched upon a
shoe box were newly purchased brown leather sandals, and I
imagined them upon her pale feet, her toes crowned with red
lacquered nails.

I performed these canvassings at least twice a week. Once,
while bent over a drawer of underwear, I foolishly allowed a
cigarette ash to fall onto the fabric. A flame sputtered to life despite my sloppily tossed cup of coffee. I had to yank the drawer
from the dresser, toss the contents onto the floor, and stomp out
the flames. Alarming images of my house—reduced to a sooty
smoking heap of bricks, wood and shards of glass—haunted me
for the rest of the day.

Meanwhile, my journalism lark secured welcome entertain-
ments. My editor Karen was whip-smart. Unlike most student
editors, she wasn't cowed by the colorless clerks called adminis-
trators who oversaw the university nor by the feckless sheep

called faculty who obediently brayed when so ordered by said colorless clerks. As with me, that academic blend of cowardice and self-righteousness amused her. Indeed, when I reported that Susan Charles refused my request for an interview, Karen merely smiled and directed me to make Charles's refusal the first line of my feature.

"What feature? She won't meet with me."

"So what? Improvise or just, hell, find someone. This campus has plenty of fodder. Here's some inspiration." She handed me a menthol cigarette, lighted it, and then, slapping my ass as a coach slaps his quarterback's, sent me laughing out the door.

The campus certainly did offer more fodder. Dr. David Butchart, newly arrived Dean of Academic Diversity, got my attention. My resulting piece about him, a clipped copy of which is now snuggly protected beneath clear plastic in my notebook, was a sensation. I started the interview in a low key fashion, asking the Dr. about his previous campus.

He professed pride in a job well done, as he'd "succeeded in establishing a diverse academic climate, one that respected difference and welcomed intellectual ferment. I chaired the English department for eight years. I also wrote this textbook." He leaned back in his black leather swivel chair and pulled his book from a shelf. "See?" He held it before me, wanting me to admire but not touch the text. So I jerked it from his pink hand and examined the drab green and gray dust jacket: *Diversity in Context: Three Progressive Arguments, 1946-2001.*

"How much does this cost?"

"Well, that one isn't for sale, but the campus bookstore can certainly get a copy. In fact," he continued, warming to the idea, "it would be an excellent supplement to the senior seminar for Literature of World Cultures." He made a mental note to himself. "Undergraduate education is my real passion."

"Can I just look at it?"

I flipped through it while the author struck a sagacious pose, hands clasped and chin lofty.

Dr. Butchart, I surmised, wasn't a mere academic mountebank; no, he saw himself as a radical storming the rampart of oppressive Western Civilization. And like all true believers, he lived to evangelize. So I played dumb.

"We've gotten a bad rap in the press, of course, but that's to be expected, given the interests of entrenched power structures. They tend to circle the wagons when under attack."

"They have wagons?"

"...Well, in a fashion. What I mean is, that power structures protect their own when they're criticized. When their interests are transgressed and exposed."

I glanced at my notebook and knotted my brows. "Sorry but can I borrow a pencil?" Borrowed pencil in hand, I asked, "How do you spell that?"

"—Transgressed?"

"No, 'borrowed'. I want the reader to know you let me borrow a pencil." I shrugged. "It's funny, but it doesn't sound like it should have only one R, does it?"

His face sagged, but he bravely pressed onward, explaining that power was embedded in discursive practices. "Given the fact that they're presented as neutral, as non-contestatory—"

"What are?"

"The discursive practices. Because they're assumed to be non-contestatory, the power relations are simply accepted. As givens, perhaps even as axioms. That's when they're most oppressive, of course."

"Could you give me an example?"

He grinned, daring to hope that perhaps I could at least transcribe his examples accurately. He referred to "barbarism" as an especially telling exemplar: "See, that word is employed in the attack upon cultural practices that the West sees as beyond the pale. Beneath any warrant. But there's a lot of ethnocentrism in that word, and—"

"What would be barbaric?"

"It's spelled like this: B-A-"

"No, I mean, what would it, uh, what would be something that we'd call barbaric?"

"Think of the Third World."

"Where is it?"

"Sectors of the Middle East and Africa. And parts of Asia."

"They're pretty far away," I nodded knowingly.

He cleared his throat and lightly brushed at his desktop with an open palm. "Anyway, there are in these places some traditions that might be called barbaric by the West, but we can't be to quick to exercise narrow judgment."

"What kind of barbaric stuff?"

He raised a silencing palm and continued. "You see, because our judgment imposes those supposedly neutral discursive practices upon local knowledge."

"Isn't that something?!" I looked up from my reporter's notebook, on which I'd been pretending to write notes. In fact, I'd been writing lyrics, but now paused as if to re-trace the steps in the Dean's argument. "I need an example. My journalism teacher said I'd fail this assignment if I didn't have examples."

"Yes, it's important to provide—"

"I can't fail this class again."

Over the next half hour, Dr. Butchart grew frayed by the dull dauber before him. Growing ever more frustrated by my failure to grasp his arguments, he offered a striking example of "so-called barbarity": the Muslim stoning as "adulteress" of the unfortunate woman who dared be raped.

"The practice of judging 'transparent' barbarisms implicates us in our own barbarism."

"—What for?"

The Dean enjoyed a patronizing guffaw. "What I mean is: as a first principle, we must respect local knowledge, and we must recognize that our own judgments carry with them potential violence."

With a hearty laugh, I discarded my yokel pose.

Dr. Butchart silently inquired, with squinting eyes, as to what so tickled me.

"Oh, it's verging upon gallows humor, I know, but—"

"Gallows?"

"Yes, gallows. But imagine this woman buried up to her neck and asking anyone for any kind of help, and—"

He wiped again at his desk, as if wishing to suddenly shoo me away.

"—and some crusading do-gooder from, I don't know, the ICRC tries to intervene but then the executioners open a book, and they quote from it."

His opened his mouth to speak but said nothing.

"They recite from *your* book."

"...Mine?"

I ran a forefinger down a page to find an appropriate quote. "'For even to imagine that we can judge the grossest examples of so-called barbarism,'", I recited, "'is to insert one's own assumptions into local knowledge.'"

"There's a context to this discussion, and—"

"'Indeed, the most prudent counsel would be, at this late date, to concede that the Western World, given its claims of Enlightenment values, is in no position to impose didacticism upon others. But we shall, alas.'" I slapped shut the book. "Nice use of *alas*."

"You're deliberately doing violence to my argument."

"Just imagine those rocks smashing your neck and shoulders and being pretty desperate, and then one of these pigs puts down his rocks to recite from your book. Pretty soon everyone's feeling a lot better. True, the raped woman's head is smashed in, but she dies for local knowledge. And that's what counts."

"You may leave now."

"But do I have to?"

"Please leave now, Mr. Edwards!"

I left him fuming, and once outside, laughed to imagine his expression when he realized I'd departed with his book.

When I arrived home, Kim was sitting in the middle of the living room floor, guitar across her lap and mirth across her mug. I nodded a greeting, stood to watch her practice for a sweet minute, then walked past her to the kitchen. Upon the kitchen table was a plate of sandwiches: thinly sliced turkey, cheese, and hot mustard upon fresh rye.

"Go ahead and eat those, I already ate," Kim called.

"All of these?"

"All? There's only two there."

"There's four."

She tittered. "I was so stoned." Then she galloped across the room to stand before me in our little kitchen. "Good news!" she announced, chin and eyebrows comically raised.

Sandwich in my eager hand, I nodded for her to continue.

"Actually, two good news...or newses? Well, the band is recording ten new songs in a Chicago studio—"

"Very cool."

"—and we have a record deal."

"Get out!"

"Yeah, with Rust Belt, but with better terms." Dear Kim was upon a chattering high, compelled to yap not so much from the marijuana that still tickled her frontal lobes as from the elation one feels upon waking to a cloudless blue horizon.

"So what are they? The terms?"

"Hold it, just a sec." She hurried into the living room and returned with several pages of perversely tiny print.

"So Dad read this?" I scanned the first page, then the second.

"And Terry Slagle."

Terry Slagle had represented Dad during his divorce negotiations. "So..." I flipped to the third page. "He knows music contracts?"

"Well enough. Between him and Dad, they got better terms."

"Which are?"

Her face reddened and she laughed. "Uh, I'm not really sure! We can go over it later. But the best part is—" She raised a hand for dramatic emphasis. "—that Martin Anderman is running Rust Belt!"

"Huh?"

"You're so knuckle-dragging stupid!" Kim cheerfully accused. "He's practically a legend, a real independent!" She explained that Martin Anderman was a former record executive who'd gone down with the corporate ship of his company when Internet file swapping erupted; alone, he'd argued against suing teens and argued for embracing technology, not fighting. "So they shitcanned him." At loose ends, Martin accepted an offer from another shitcanned executive and, after refinancing their homes, the duo formed Rust Belt Records. "He stopped by the studio for a bit but didn't hassle us at all. In fact," Kim grandly announced, "he said Pad could be the new Smashing Pumpkins."

"We don't live in Chicago."

She cockily crossed her arms. "Not yet. Martin, he's thinking long term."

Doubts marched across my brain. Still, I nodded with a masterful forgery of unguarded enthusiasm. What the hell. If this guy Martin believed in bands enough to sink himself into debt...and if Dad and Terry Slagle looked it over...I re-scanned the first page and found nothing but the formal declarations that lawyers use to inflate their billable hours.

"We can go over it later," she declared. "Spoilsport, don't you get it?"

"Yeah, I got it," I grinned. "You got signed."

She abruptly leaned forward and, as if I were a child, pinched my cheeks between thumb and forefinger. "No, *we* got signed. We're a band. You're in this too." Thumbs and forefingers relaxed then again squeezed with renewed traction. "Stupid! Ha!"

Vision obscured by my sister's hands before my face, I nodded and asked that she tell me again.

"Tell you what?"

"That we're a band."

Eyes ablaze—their hazel hue in contrast with her ruddy face—she joyfully repeated, in a sing-song voice, "We're a band, we're a band." Her blood rose, her body warmed, and I basked in her excitement even as I burned to press my face to hers, to stroke the declivities of her neck.

Then my face was free. "Oh yeah," I said as casually as I could, my voice nearly cracking. "How did you come up with the name?"

"Name?"

"Pad."

"Last minute joke, really. Billy's wife, she came up with that retro CD cover with the daisies. And I saw it and went, it's like a design for a box of pads. She was pissed but then I kinda liked the name. You know, it reminds you of some awful retro ha house slave with her middle finger in your face."

Then she was off to grab the ringing phone. Yes it was true, Kim assured the caller: they had signed a contract and—this was a new detail—recording began in a month.

Twenty-Three: Invitations

Good news marched arm in arm with more good news. Not only was Pad a signed band, but my profile of David Butchart was the best kind of campus hit: some politically correct hysterics stole the newspapers from several of the campus drop-spots. Nobody claimed responsibility but rumors pointed to the Student Progressive Caucus. As far as I could tell, the Caucus was a bleating herd that recited the pronouncements of sociology professor Paul Martino. On a hunch, I made a Friday afternoon appointment with Dr. Martino.

I arrived ten minutes early. His office was at the end of a dank hallway that, at this hour, was deserted. His office door was layered with photos, clipped newspaper articles of conservative wrongs, and rote celebrations of "cultural diversity"—your tedious Establishment Left clichés. Indeed, his office door was a brash exercise in self-adulation. For instance: an aged photocopy of Martino marching in an anti-war parade. Flanked by comrades on either side, he bellowed at a stone-faced cop, who was cut in half by the photo's border. In another photograph, Martino stood at a podium in an auditorium; the photo offered no clues as to the occasion, though that hardly mattered: the real subject was Martino's own exaltation. The third photo was different: at a school playground, he sat awkwardly in the sling of a swing set, a young child laughing upon the Professor's khaki-covered legs.

Restless, I stepped outside to smoke. Nobody appeared for another twenty minutes, and I enjoyed another cigarette, this time not bothering to step outside. At 3:45, I scribbled a note:

> *Thank you for agreeing to meet me today. I'm very sorry that you were unable to keep the appointment. Could you offer a reschedule?*

I pealed an ancient Kerry-Edwards sticker from his door and, using it as tape, stuck my note directly over a glamour shot of Che.

If not for Pad's unexpected success, Dr. Martino's evasion would've nettled me. But I was merely entertained by the good Professor and his apprentice PC clerics. My article about Dr. Butchart—"Celebrate This!"—had struck some tender nerves and, unable to practice prior restraint, the clerics practiced late night thievery. Karen wrote a righteous editorial for Friday's edition, though I never bothered to read it, as I was—and remain—allergic to breast beating.

A few campus acquaintances joked with me about the theft. Somebody clipped the article and pinned it inside a glass display case in the student union. Protected by lock and key, the article attracted a few readers over the next several days, and my scholastic roundtable friends congratulated me on upsetting the herd. On this particular afternoon, I dawdled before the display case to bask in my jaunty philippic, a brief portion of which I offer you (Yes, I have the article in my scrapbook!):

> Like most priests of PC, Dr. Butchart is devoted not to literature but to the pulpit. Indeed, so devoted is the Dean to his calling—defending diversity against Western culture—that he refuses to condemn such practices as *suttee* (wife-burning) or the Muslim gang stoning of an "adulteress": a woman raped by a wealthy and influential neighbor. Now, perhaps you and I, unsophisticated rubes that we are, might think, "C'mon! It's just not right to bash a rape victim with rocks until she dies." But as Dr. Butchart clarifies, "The practice of judging 'transparent' barbarisms implicates us in our own barbarism."
>
> In other words: celebrate diversity!
>
> And grab a rock! *No, not that one! The bigger one!*
>
> Dr. Butchart's argument is wonderful news to thugs 'round the world, who can quote from the Dean's politically correct orotundity, *Diversity in Context: Three Progressive Arguments, 1946-2001.* "Western culture's efforts to label various culture practices

as barbaric or primitive should give us special pause,
as few cultures are so hostile to The Other as ours."
    In other words: *Rape first, murder second!*

I bought a coffee and joined the regulars at our roundtable. I
was amused to see Tommy, one of my fellow newspaper scribes,
sitting with them.

The group entertained him: the griping about all the hours
studied, the demands of keeping a high GPA...he chuckled discretely as Fred, seemingly none the better rested after the holiday break, agonized over his numerous graduate school offers.

"Look at these," Fred complained, spreading upon our table
several glossy brochures.

"Bad break," Tommy deadpanned.

"It's not that bad," Fred conceded, "but how can you really
tell, you know, which one is best? They all say they're the best."
With an elderly sigh, Fred nodded his departure to the group.
"Big test next week...long weekend."

The group grunted and mumbled. After Fred had disappeared through the rain-dappled side door, the group laughed
and jeered. "What a dork," Carl Haugen smirked. "I mean, I'm a
dork, I know that. Okay? But he's hopeless."

"Hey it's the rock star," somebody behind me said. Ah, here
they were...the two girls who, last semester, had seen Pad at the
Acropolis NiteSpot.

They sat down, loudly dropping their books upon the table.

"You know my name," I smiled, "but I don't know yours."

"Brenda," said the chipper gal.

"Linda," said the assertive gal. "But we forget your name."

"Rock star," I answered, trying—and failing—to keep a
straight face.

The group jeered a bit, and soon they fell into the habit of
complaining earnestly about their work load. I listened politely,
sipping my coffee, and stole wry glances at Tommy, who several
times smirked.

"I don't know why you people study so hard anyway," Tommy
finally broke in. "You're not going to get any jobs anyway. The
economy sucks."

The group fell silent.

"Let's make a bet," Linda grinned. "Who can land a manage-ment gig at Burger Stud first?"

"You won't be qualified. What are you studying, anyway? Philosophy or something like that? Something just totally use-less?" He nodded at her stockpile of books.

"Botany."

"Now *that's* practical."

Linda leaned forward, her torso's considerable girth briefly tottering the table. "Your insult failed. And what about you? You're a, what?"

"Journalist."

"Like Jeffrey?" queried Brenda.

The group laughed and the nascent hostility spent itself. Presently, I quieted the group with a sharp slap upon the table. Brenda started and squawked "Gawd!" at me, and I mimed a "sorry" even as I slapped the table again.

"Everyone at this table is invited to a party," I announced. "Tomorrow night at 7:00."

"That's cool," several of the group responded simultaneously.

"My address is 217 West 250 South."

The group was nonplussed, as it was composed entirely of out-of-towners.

"It's about ten minutes from here, straight north, then just turn down 250 South and drive for about a mile. It's an old beat up place with no neighbors."

"Should I bring my notebook?" Tommy asked.

"Why?"

"I mean, I could interview your sister and, you know, get col-lege credit by drinking!"

"I'd rather get drunk by drinking. But sure. Bring it."

Twenty-Four: "Look."

"Oh great, a bunch of college punks."

"Yeah, like me." I sat on the couch as Kim pushed the asthmatic electric sweeper into a hallway closet. "So there's no need to make the wrong impression."

The closet door squeakily swung open and Kim shouldered it back shut. "Have you looked over that contract we signed?"

I hadn't.

"I guess it's okay but, like, Dad kept whittling down the band advances, said they're a trap."

"So how much is the advance?"

"It's got to cover everything, Jeffrey, everything. Like the recording and the producer and the promotion and touring and fucking toilet paper and food and—"

'How much?"

"Not much. About thirty."

"—Thousand?"

She nodded, her face alive with both pride and anxiety. "It's not major league, you know. It's not half a million. *That's* major league."

With impressive speed, my sister's band was already thirty thousand in hock.

"What? It's too much? Or—"

"It's fine, *really*. You guys can play—well, except for Richard. So the recording costs might come in under that figure." Unlike typical rock "singers", who required aural goosing with harmonizers, compressors, and software edits, Kim would slam-dunk every vocal.

"You really think so?"

I winked. "Congratulations."

Kim's anxieties would, I knew, shadow her until she sipped a relaxing beer or two. Fortunately, I'd already stocked for the party: beer, several bottles of yuppie California wine, and—for a special toast—a single bottle of Old Bushmill's whiskey. My bruised credit cards nearly fainted under this latest assault, but I didn't care. Besides, I'd squeezed in some extra hours at Franco's, even taking the rein when Franco attended a cousin's confirmation. Which reminded me: "Franco says he wishes he could be here and he says congratulations."

"Tell him thank you. And I'm sorry to fret, and I know I'm bitching, but look at that contract, would you?" She rolled her eyes and, for a chilly ghosted moment, my mother's posture of pique—jaw set, arms criss-crossed upon the chest—possessed Kim. I ambled to the kitchen, poured a dark beer in a freshly washed mug, and offered it to Kim.

With an easy swig, she exorcized that hint of Mama Righteous. "Mmm," Kim nodded. "That's good. Don't let me drink too much though." She grabbed the phone to invite a batch of her own friends.

Tommy arrived unfashionably early: 6:30. He ameliorated the *faux pass* with his open-faced cheer and his cocaine, wrapped in a mint gum's inner foil.

"This is a drug free party," I half-whispered, Kim just beyond earshot in the kitchen.

Doubt wrinkled Tommy's forehead.

I nodded that he should take a few steps backward, farther from the kitchen. "I'm serious. Kim'll just throw you out if—" My grin betrayed me, and Tommy slouched in relief.

"I thought you were serious, man." As if anticipating the evening's first powder dram, he brushed a forefinger beneath his nose. "It's really good," he declared, earnest as only a narcotics snob can be. "Just one toot and you're, well, you're just—" He snapped his fingers.

"Is someone here?" Kim called.

I presented Tommy to Kim.

"Tommy Webster." He extended a hand.

"Kim Edwards."

"Oh, so you two are related?" Tommy's feeble jest obliged Kim to laugh.

"We used to be siblings," I said.

"How's that?"

"We were separated for a few years, during what used to be called the formative years."

"Yeah, teenage wasteland years," Kim added.

"So when does the rest of the band arrive?"

"Dunno. Billy probably can't make it, you know. Cynthia."

"Who?"

"The wife." Kim voiced *wife* like *knife*. "But Larry's making it for sure. Free beer." She surveyed the room. "Why're we standing? Let's sit down." At that moment came several raps upon the door.

"I'll get it. You two sit down." I pulled open the door.

"Congratulations rock star!" came the chorus of Brenda and Linda. Loud and large in designer denim overalls, Brenda stomped right past me, with laughing Linda a few dainty steps behind.

"Beer and booze in the kitchen," Kim instructed from the couch.

Another knock upon the door, and I yelled that the guests should just come on in. And they did, stumbling into one another to form a slipshod conga line: Karen the editor, then her roommate Laura, then a guy whose hand was entangled in Laura's, then—Robbie?

"Hey, it's my *bro!*" Robbie threw his arms around me. "Long time no see, bro!"

"Really?"

Another clutch, awkwardly prolonged. "And thanks for inviting me!"

While enduring his embrace, I saw Kim on the couch, suppressing a smile. I grinned back with some hostility, but when Kim extended a middle finger toward me, I took the hint and roused myself to be hospitable. "Good to see ya, bro."

Another bang upon the door, and I waved in Larry the drummer, his date, and then, incredibly, dreary Fred. "Hey Larry, hey Larry's date, hey Fred!" The contrast of Larry and Fred compelled me to laugh: the former bristling with rock attitude in his black tee shirt and black pants, the latter bristling with anxiety in an incongruous Eisenhower jacket.

"Jeff, he looks stoned already," Larry joked to his date.

She smiled placidly. "So do you."

"Long time, no see and all that," Larry beamed, slapping me on the back. "Diane, meet Jeff. And visa versa. Jeff is like, uh, the heart of the band."

"Nah. I'm just the spleen."

"Yeah c'mon in the door's open!" Larry bellowed through cupped hands, and more guests streamed in. I excused myself and sought out my sister in the growing throng. Ah, there she was, holding court in the kitchen with several guests who'd I'd not seen arrive. A percussive burst of laughter filled the kitchen and, as I shouldered my way forward, Kim introduced me.

The crowd, happily co-ed, slapped me upon the back. Someone handed me a shot glass slopping over with amber fire and, before tossing it back, I thanked everyone for their good wishes.

The group cheered as I sank the Old Bushmill's with effortless brio.

"Remember how green and puking you got last time you drank that stuff?" Kim grinned.

"Of course not. I'm an optimist." Downward flowed the second shot, leaving a scorched-earth trail in my throat.

The kitchen grew hot and muggy, and with each rising degree my mood followed. Ah, another drink and somebody was bellowing into my ear about tapping the keg. A stranger's arm— no, wait, it was Robbie's—hooked around my inner elbow and we weaved past the revelers to a squat aluminum keg, which stood unsteadily upon a blue plastic milk crate. Excitement rose as I screwed the tap into the keg...some joker or two had apparently shaken the keg into a yeasty lather and white foam ejaculated across the room.

"Guess who?" queried a hot boozy whisper, and I struggled to turn half way around.

"Into the mosh pit!" Karen grinned, pushing me toward a gathering mob.

The whiskey had degraded my ability to ambulate. Indeed, I felt as if I'd stepped off a sadistic amusement park ride. I squeezed my skull between two sweaty palms and managed, with my upraised elbow, to clip a guest across the forehead. She and another fellow cursed me and I paused to apologize, or rather, I tried to pause: my palsied legs stumbled forward as—

"Turn it up!"

—shimmering chords and Kim's rousing vocal rose above the racket, and the revelers roared approval: "Blush" drove the crowd into arm-thrusting, head-jerking dance. From my left, a thin pale arm snaked across my shoulders and hung loosely upon the back of my neck; an unidentified female, blessedly jiggly in a damp red tee, banged her hip against mine. And on my right, a sweaty masculine arm—Robbie!—rested upon my neck. And here we all went...a drunken can-can!

"Turn it up!" Robbie bellowed, deafening me.

We kicked higher and higher, trying and failing to keep time with "Blush"'s stop-start bridge. I kicked too highly, my foot striking a reveler's rump. He twisted around and, seeing me, laughed and cursed me, then laughed again. Like a child held aloft by two adults, he hoisted his feet from the floor and ran in place, a drunken hamster scurrying inside his exercise wheel.

And upon the song's heady final note, cheers all 'round.

Needing a respite from the heat and elbows and roars, I escaped through the back door to the porch. Thin black clouds shrouded the chalky moon. Several other guests mingled in the dark soothing back yard.

"Got a light?"

I turned to face Kim, who leaned against the porch's primitive wooden railing.

She lighted her cigarette, which flickered and popped. Then, after a hungry pull, she handed it to me. The tobacco burned slowly, gloppy with liquid hash, and my lobes hummed and sparked.

Unsteady, she leaned further against the railing and into the shadows. "Thanks for a great party." Though I couldn't quite see her, I sensed her smile.

We finished the smoke. Rather than depart, she simply stood looking at me, a glint upon her eyes.

"I—" *I love you*: the words pounded upon my skull's interior, demanding release.

"...What?"

The words clawed forward to hang half-way out my mouth. Kim emerged from the dark to stand beneath the small kitchen window; through the window's blinds, light fell across her shoulders and arms.

Just how long we stood, I can't say. Probably no more than ten seconds, though in those seconds my hopes soared and the sapphire sky shimmered. And stars spun like silver pinwheels.

"Look."

She gazed heavenward.

The house was still packed, but the cast had changed a bit... I recognized several kids from the university. I ambled about the living room, dazzling the guests with my wit and verve as Kim, radiant, accepted endless handshakes and hugs. Several times, the crowd urged Kim to sit upon the couch's back and sing with an acoustic guitar, but she begged off, claiming to be too drunk. Meanwhile, I consumed another shot and feasted upon a badly rolled joint.

"Hey gimme that!" Seemingly from the ceiling, Kim swooped down upon me and stole a hit upon the joint. Then she scampered off to dance with a half dozen guests.

"She's gonna hit the big time," murmured Tommy.

At some point, the lights went out and jazz replaced rock. Indeed, the time was right for some jazz trio stuff, and this was good: "Autumn Leaves", covered by the Bill Evans trio. As those chords danced atop the bass, my senses pierced another realm. As if through a kaleidoscope, I watched the now gently dancing guests splinter and fragment into ever-smaller pieces that recombined into novel shapes and pulsing colors. The effect charmed me enormously...I held the kaleidoscope in my hands, turning it slowly to again fragment and recombine the guests. Then my own person strayed simultaneously in several directions to observe the scene: couples holding hands in corners, other guests chattering and gesturing and spilling beer and cigarette ashes upon one another...Ah lovely Kim, what a sport! She now danced with Fred, who kept wiping back his damp hair. It had grown long, I noticed, nearly touching his shoulders.

Suddenly, the room was bright. Tommy had foolishly turned the lights back on.

"Christ, turn that off!" someone demanded, and both music and light were turned off. Several guests took that as their cue to depart and Kim gamely reminded everyone to drive carefully, even as she sipped upon a long neck.

The TV was on. An aged minister, glasses glaring beneath poorly arranged studio lights, talked to us of Jesus. I rose from the corner, where Karen and someone who arrived late were half-dozing, backs against the wall.

"Why is that thing on?" Tommy complained about the TV .

I turned down the sound and kneeled beside the screen.

A few people rose upon failing sea legs and I bid them a good evening. But rather than leave, they simply moved closer.

"Religion is the world's oldest profession," I announced, now standing. "But in being high-jacked by the timid bureaucrats of the cloth, it's lost what made it vital: *beauty*. It's beauty that makes our lives worthwhile, it's beauty that's been high jacked by the clerics of the cloth and the politically correct."

"Christians and Muslims, and of course the politically correct...They've made a vice of virtue."

Kim cleared her throat. "Try not to offend our guests..." She glanced behind her at a restless quartet.

"Yeah," someone complained from the back of the smoky room. "What you're saying is pretty, uh...I mean, it's fuckin' offensive." A fellow stepped forward and, despite his companions' embarrassment, announced that he was committed to social justice. "Yeah go ahead and joke. The atmosphere grew awkward. "You're just avoiding the truth of what I'm saying."

"And the truth of what you're saying is—?" I prodded.

He impatiently gestured at his companions to shut up. "You can't just laugh at people's religions and at their, at their politics. I mean, you just insulted two great religions."

"Now you're flattering me."

"Fuck off." The complainant raised both middle fingers at me and, as his three companions unsteadily rose, stomped through the kitchen and out the back door.

I gestured solemnly toward our departed guests. "Hell hath no fury like a do-gooder scorned."

"That guy was a Muslim," Fred worriedly whispered.

A muttering rose from one corner and several others shuffled out the back door. I waited until their departure and, upon hearing the slammed door from the kitchen, smiled broadly. "Now we're among friends. And now, if my flock will simply wait upon me for a moment or two...Oh, here." I turned up the sound. The minister directed us to the Gospel of Paul. "Now flock, line up before me."

An amused complaint or two rose from the remaining dozen or so guests.

"Get your lazy asses up," Kim insisted. "It's party and you'll drink if I want you to."

A guest approached.

"Are you born again, my friend?" I uncorked the fizzing five dollar champagne.

He looked behind him, where his date stood laughing, then faced me again and helplessly shrugged. "I just like alcohol."

"Say five Our Fathers and three Hail Marys. And recite the Berkeley University affirmation to never harbor lust for pinup girls or non fair trade coffee."

"Can't I just have a little—"

His girlfriend guffawed and, grabbing him by the collar, roughly maneuvered him out of the way.

"Are you born again, my child?"

"Yeah but I'm drunk."

"Good! Then it doesn't count." I placed the bottle in her diminutive hands and she greedily chugged.

The line grew as merriment drew the scattered guests into the living room. We quickly drained the champagne bottles, but the guests graciously supplied more sacraments: a half-bottle of cheap domestic red, an unopened quart of imported beer. Karen, impressed by my absurdist instincts, pressed a twenty dollar bill into my palm, whispering that the party must have been costly.

Even dazed Robbie, shirt soaked by sweat and beverage, stepped forward upon confused feet. "Thanks man for inviting me!" he bleated. "Great party, man. Best party ever." He nodded with a drunk's earnestness and, without taking a single swallow, crashed to the floor.

Linda and Karen dragged him to the couch and took their proximity to me to thank me for a fine evening. In fact, evening was fleeing: a hint of gray was visible through the open window that faced east.

"I'm too drunk to drive," Karen cackled. She tried three times to open the door and Linda pushed her aside. Laughing, then nearly heaving, they stumbled through the open doorway and, repulsed by the fresh air, turned right back around. Linda disappeared into the kitchen and Karen decamped upon the couch, her hair unkempt and, like a mushroom cloud, defying gravity. "I'm taking *your* bed tonight, Mencken man!" she bellowed.

Kim shouted across the room through cupped hands: "You sure know how to work a crowd!"

Indeed. The revelers had dispersed to far dark corners to pass out or make out or both or neither. Others lumbered or tripped out either door to reclaim the lost art of drunk driving. Now, standing with Kim in the dark room, I cleared my throat and asked her to repeat as instructed.

And she did:

"Pray for me brother, for I have not sinned."

I handed her the bottle of Old Bushmill's. She raised it to her lips but, at the crucial moment, she refused to drink.

"You first," she insisted. "...Hey, slow down. Leave some for me."

Twenty-Five: "...no God after all."

Unable to recall walking or even staggering up the stairs, I found myself upon my bed. A pair of hands pressed my own hands down.

"Don't be fresh," ordered the hoarse whisper.

"—Karen?"

"Stupid." A giggle.

Alarmingly, the room was suddenly bright and I croaked a request that the curtains be drawn. Behind a tee-shirt, breasts pressed against my face, silencing me from further complaint. The tee's fabric was soft, worn thin by many washes, and the fragrant flesh beneath was hot upon my face. The room grew even brighter. I shut my eyes and reached upward to the legs that unsteadily straddled me...Music gorged the room—Rachmaninoff!—and my id was at fast boil.

Her hair pitched across my head. I held a lengthy lock in my right hand, twisting it between forefinger and thumb. "...It's you," I managed.

But the hair slipped away, then the torso was gone. I sat up, absurdly yanking the sheets to my waist for modesty. The bed quaked, as if possessed by an apprentice poltergeist, and I willed myself to step from it and seek refuge upon the hard floor.

"Are you sick?"

I took several deep breaths and, eyes straining, discerned the figure standing at my side. I held up a hand. Fingers intertwined with mine.

She moved lightly onto the bed and, her hand still gripping mine, she urged me to stand.

"You're a freak of nature," she condemned or commended.

I reached forward through the dark. Ah, the tee-shirt was gone! She eased back upon the bed and I lowered myself between her parting knees. With each long stroke, sister's eyes grew more

urgent, fixed upon my face, yet simultaneously taking in all the
morning's bliss: limbs, skin, laughter. I roared full-throated
emancipation of what was trapped within me since that evening
when—

"My sweet boy," she keened. "...Sweet."

—when, at the Acropolis NiteSpot, she'd stood to comb her
hair, and I could thereafter dream of little but Kim beneath me.
As she was now.

I woke and felt...ah, you'll laugh! But I felt born again: once
a libertarian, now a libertine.

Kim was on her side, face obscured against her tightly folded
arm. Her eyes opened. Hazel. Empyreal.

We watched one another for several minutes, blinking and
grinning, measuring the weight of our act.

I finally spoke. Propped upon one elbow, I revealed that she'd
enslaved my thoughts ever since that night at the Acropolis, and
that I'd lived despairing the thought I'd never have her—or
might live despairing the thought I *did* have her. "I mean, even
when you were right here—I didn't trust it. I thought maybe I'd
just lost my mind."

"...This is so weird," she whispered.

"So...when did you know?"

"...Years now."

"Years?"

"It's why I stayed away because, you know, it was so sick and
wrong. Or it was *supposed* to be. But everything else was so shal-
low. So awful." The words scurried from her, as if finally freed
from a jail cell. "Like with Richard—"

"Ugh."

"—with Richard, I'd wish by some magic it was you. We'd sit
around and play guitar or whatever and it was so *empty* and I
just effing *knew* it would be so much better with you..." She
rested a hand upon my hip. "And once that thought took hold, it
was like a root. It just went deeper and stronger."

Years!

"I pretended it was a phase. That it'd pass." She abruptly sat
up, letting the sheet fall away. "I even saw a shrink."

"And the shrink said...?"

"He said it was some fucked up desire for Dad's approval, which I knew was just the most idiotic Freudian voodoo horseshit, so I stopped going, but Dad made me go back and—"

"*Dad knows?*"

"No, stupid! Only the shrink knows." She grinned at my alarm. "This is more common than you'd think, as it turns out. So anyway. Dad just thought I was depressed for, you know, for like really regular boring bourgeois reasons. Like the divorce, his slut girlfriends, all that trivia I couldn't care less about."

"...Yeah."

"Remember that night? When Mom beat me up?"

"And you broke my nose?" I laughed.

"It was like, right at the moment I hit you, I was thinking this was it, this would really *end* it because if I can bust your face then I can't want you. So I hit you *extra* hard." Snickering, she recreated the arc of *ad hoc* weapon to my nose. "And even when you blacked out for a second I was looking at you and thinking Jesus Christ I *love* him, why did I do that? This sucks through a straw!"

Sis sat cross legged, pale and vibrant. I savored her belly's concavity, her breasts' slight slag, the chipped red polish upon her toe nails...and her voice's rich timbre, a voice that rendered each phrase musical. "After you moved in with Aunt Jo, I just thought more and more about you, about how you always stuck up for me. And sometimes you'd get really pissed, like, wondering why Dad didn't want you around. See, I pretended I didn't want you to move in. I was afraid he'd put two and two together and, you know, figure out what was wrong with me."

I nodded.

She studied me, and I blushed beneath her urgent gaze. "After Patty moved out—and wait a minute! What did you *see* in that skinny frump? I mean, she was okay in high school but what a fuckin' weirdo *frump* she's turned into."

Ah, so endearing that Kim could be jealous! She continued to berate Patty, hands animated and tone fervent. Then she enjoyed a belly laugh at her own expense. I found myself laughing as well, and our merriment grew manic before subsiding.

"So anyway, I was like, well let's just find out. I'm going to move in. It was *ridiculous* but I had to just, you know, to really face this down. It seemed okay at first because I couldn't see any trace that you felt, you know, like me and it seemed like, shit, it's excessively and totally weird but living here is, it's going okay. It might even get normal which meant *I* might even get normal, but then—" Her cackle was alarmed and joyous. "Last night."

"You got me drunk. And exploited me."

"And I thought, okay, this is *it*. It's like waiting in line for the longest, scariest roller coaster ride and there's no backing out 'cause you're on the ride and it's dropping you straight to Hell."

"Yeah."

She lit a smoke and abruptly queried: "Why'd she move out?"

So moved was I by our heart-to-heart that I nearly blurted out the truth: that Patty had found snapshots of Kim and had, as they say, put together two and two. But the fact that Patty had deduced my feelings from simple snapshots....it would shock and appall Kim.

I shrugged vaguely, my mind's gears grinding.

"What, you had a fight?"

"Several. Mostly about money. Sound familiar?" Of course it did: we'd heard dear father and mother argue about money—and everything else.

Goosebumps rose upon her arms, and she pressed her face against my collarbone. "...People, they'll find out."

"No they won't," I assured, stroking her hair. Lust soon announced its presence, and I turned her onto her back. My fever ran from red to blue to red again, boiling and cooling and boiling.

We stayed in my bed the entire weekend, rising only to visit the bathroom or the kitchen or to order out for a large pizza with everything from Giovanni's, Franco's fiercest competitor. Oh, the taboos we violated! Kim on occasion anxiously asked, in various ways, if it was really okay: "it" being, of course—

"It doesn't seem like, uh..." She raised a hand, requesting patience as she swallowed. "Mmm. That's good. Anyway, it doesn't seem like it."

"Incest?"

She winced.

I slipped another slice of pizza upon her sagging paper plate and laughed.

"What?"

"Oh, nothing really. I was just remembering what you said about standing in line for the ride that drops you straight into Hell."

"...And?"

"Don't worry about that. I've done a lot of research, and it turns out there's no God after all."

Twenty-Six: Bliss cubed

Kim and I eventually rose from our battered bed of bliss. Without actually discussing the matter, we assumed with exquisite artistry the roles of amiably feuding and occasionally embittered siblings. Each morning, we went about our business. She was, of course, busy with Pad—the contract, freshly signed, occupied her and several times she had me read it, perhaps hoping that if I read the contract enough, the terms would magically improve.

"But the contract's not that bad," I said one Friday morning. "There'll be money later. Your band is really good."

She beamed. Oh, when she beamed at me! Open-faced and open-hearted, guileless and garrulous. She chattered breezily, her guarded optimism finally unguarded. And the more relaxed she became, the harder she worked on her musicianship: indeed, Kim's guitar chops were now genuinely monstrous.

And I actually *was* satisfied with the contract. Some rudimentary research revealed that, above all, recording companies were happiest when a band was in hock. Why? Because the band must then submit to the company's heavy boot. The odds of commercial success, I knew, were forbidding, but those odds were goosed a bit by Pad's relative freedom from such debt. I made that point whenever Kim got nervous, assuring her that a low debt band was a freer band.

"That's why they want you to take advances. They're hard to earn back: bad for you, good for them."

Fortune followed fortune:

Every evening, I bedded my beloved. I adored each detail: the faint blonde hair upon forearms; the slight rivels that lined her forehead as she welcomed me; the restless left foot that hooked around my straining right calf; the belly upon which I caught my breath. No matter how many times I had her, I was merely slaked, never quenched. Afterward, as she chattered freely, I drifted between waking and sleeping, drugged by her voice, its chortling ultrasonics and giggling infrasonics.

I was up first in the mornings, blitzing through my tepid shower and scrape-filled shave so as to quickly surrender the bathroom to Kim. She relished long hot baths...by 7:00 a.m. she was in the tub, by 7:30 she had drained the cooling water and replaced it with scalding. By 8:00, she emerged in a robe, skin ruddy and radiant.

"Off to school already?" she'd joke as, hunched over the kitchen counter, I rather oafishly shoveled in the bran flakes and burnt bagel. "No time for a cigarette?"

I'd make time of course...we sat upon the crumbling front cement stoop and consumed two, three or four cigarettes a piece, our discussion drifting inevitably toward Pad: the band's blossoming musicianship and rising spirits. The group rehearsed every other evening from 7:00 to around 10:00. Wisely, they preserved their energy and therefore preserved their good will toward one another.

"The band's really coming together," Kim beamed one morning. "Nobody's pissy anymore 'cause we don't get freaked out by a bad rehearsal."

"And Richard's learned that C isn't F," I deadpanned.

"You're so fucking jealous of him."

"I used to be."

With a flick of her forefinger, her spent cigarette arced through the damp morning air. "I like you being a little jealous."

Life on campus, never serious, was now even more frivolous. I'd become a minor campus *cause célèbre:* semi-notorious campus gadfly and song-writing partner of the locally hip band. The theft of student papers inspired me to write a follow-up piece:

> *As anyone with an IQ above 70 can see, today's Or-*
> *thodox Left mirrors the 1950's Orthodox Right. Both*
> *see the world in the same way: a shabby summer stock*
> *of the mind, populated not by characters but carica-*
> *tures, their cheap stage garb topped off by horns or*

halos. This worldview is very convenient: no thought is required, or even encouraged.

My pal Tommy found the piece inspirational, using a discussion of its lofty sentiments to invite a fetching co-ed to his apartment for a political science study group.

"Jeff, I lied just a *little*," he guffawed. "But right away I pointed out that study groups can have just two people. And I scored."

And so the semester tumbled blissfully onward. My classes were a lark—I recall nothing about them but one, the History of Science, taught by a barely literate part-time Sociologist and full-time Marxist. He possessed no shoulders and nasally insisted that Newton's *Principia* sanctioned rape. I made him the subject of a piece, trying but failing to maintain a straight face for more than five minutes of an interview. I asked him if rapists actually read *Principia*, or if they got by with the Cliff's Notes summary.

"Gang rape, it isn't funny," he squeaked.

"That's a deep point."

The resulting article again produced a tempest in a PC teapot, and a few readers demanded that I resign my position. But a few others—the campus Republicans, to my amusement—rallied behind me. Karen, guided by her unimpeachable sense of campus politics, saw bigger things ahead. "Keep this up," she exulted, "and you might get picked up on campus wire services."

Paul Martino, who headed the Student Progressive Caucus, remained in my editorial sites. I'd spent all of February and March courteously brushing aside his evasions, though I stepped up the pressure when I became the subject of gratifyingly nasty discussions on the campus listserve. I was never mentioned by name. However, several students and Dr. Martino had detected a "rising tide of campus conservatism."

Indeed, the discussion proceeded at a lively pace through March and April, growing more urgent as my attempts to interview Martino grew more urgent. Karen subscribed to the listserve, egging on some of the more squishy participants with hectoring, right-wing calls for freedom of speech, freedom from the thought police, and—a clever gambit—the right for university graduate students to organize a labor union.

"You gotta check out the student union movement!" Karen blurted as I ambled into the newspaper's basement offices. "Look at this!"

Toward me she thrust a sheath of papers.

"I printed some stuff off the university listserve discussions and—" With a violent red pen, she circled a two-paragraph listserve message from our friend Dr. Martino:

> The next stage is indeed unionization of the truly dispossessed. We needn't be doctrinaire like Lenin about this, but even capitalist ideology admits to stages of historical developments toward more wide-ranging democratization of the workplace, from third world sweatshops to America's temp. worker offices.
>
> The question is one of tactics: where do we start? Because tactics matter. They can't be brushed off. If we wish to change the world, we must live in the world.

I shrugged. "So...what's the point here?"

"Oh c'mon!" She grinned at my supreme display of ignorance, which was supreme because it was genuine. "You don't get it? Jesus, how could you have *missed* it?"

How? Because I was still narcotized, having spent the early morning several inches deep in my sister's genitalia.

"If you could stop being the rock star for just a moment." She snorted and lighted a cigarette. I brightened, gesturing that I too wanted a smoke. We sensed the disapproving glares from the messy half dozen cubicles and stepped outside.

"You changed brands."

"They're cheaper."

"Jesus Christ," I huffed. "Give me just a *little* respect."

"—What?"

"Do you know how humiliating it is, bumming these cheap cigarettes?"

In no mood for jest, she pointed again at the two circled paragraphs. "Martino wrote this. This guy is just what you said he was," she vehemently nodded. "A complete phony. His bullshit about tactics, he's just weaseling out of it. The entire administration hates this student unionizing stuff, and Martino and the rest will just keep weaseling."

"Uh huh."

"And remember when you said that the liberal hypocrites would back off at the first sign that their hot air escaped the classroom?"

"Remind me."

She spewed a raspberry of equal parts affection and irritation. "Stupid. You know, at my little newspaper staff party after New Year."

I pulled hard upon the miserable cigarette, hungry for even the hint of real tobacco. "I remember drinking a lot."

"You were drunk, all right." Her voice softened: "Remember how you climbed all over me?"

Befuddlement. I recalled that evening as one of enormous drinking and enormous longing for my beloved. And yes, there did break out a gentle game of flag-football fondling: light contact, no hard tackles. I recalled the giggles and titters, the joints in mouth, passing them forward, lip to lip...

"Laura thought we scared you away." A hand briefly upon my shoulder. "You were such a dear. There aren't many true blue romantics like you, are there?"

"Not like me."

In mock pique, she lowered her eyebrows and glowered. "Just don't do that too much, mister, or you'll get a bad reputation as a tease."

"I've got a bad reputation already." With enormous strain, as if facing a scattered jigsaw puzzle, I managed to piece together and recall a moment deformed by crooked lust in which I...

"So you'll nail down Mr. Progressive, right? Tell him that you wanna discuss the SAEU. He's on the record as supporting it."

...in which I pleaded some discretion, explaining that I was in love with a girl, and therefore out of respect for her..."Most guys wouldn't think twice, but you really respect her," Karen had said: seriously or mockingly, I was uncertain.

"So hang him out to dry, Mencken man!" she cheerfully erupted, largish fist punching my shoulder. From her back pocket she pulled a sheet of paper. "This lovely document is a, a—Oh Christ. See for yourself."

With a thespian's clearing of the throat, recited the text at the top: "We, the undersigned, do hereby act upon the recognition that all labor is possessed of intrinsic dignity, intrinsic worth, and intrinsic value. Given this fact, we urge the administration of our university to act in good faith through dialogue, through mutual understanding, through a perspicuous view of the spirit of labor law, to recognize the legal right of the Student Academic Employee Union to collectively bargain on behalf of members of the SAEU."

"What do you think? About getting Martino to sign it?"

Glancing down the page, I saw that no signatories supported the ponderous prose.

"And he won't. And then you can have fun shedding light on his progressive values."

I smiled.

"I knew you'd like this."

"Oh I do. In fact..." I flattened the sheet against the building's pebbly wall. "Got a pen?" She did, and I took the pleasure of being the first to sign the petition. "How can he refuse me now? I've shown my commitment to the cause."

My life was bliss cubed: carnal, social, aesthetic. All my appetites were met and life bloomed into an ever-widening, lush garden path of delectations. Granted, on odd occasions my high spirits spooked me; at those moments, I feared infection by a germ of Puritanism. *How can you live like this?* a voice would rudely hector. So the voice and I debated, accused, and struggled, but I always triumphed, obliterating the nag through an insuperable mix of will and bonhomie.

Of course, never did I reveal the slightest telltale doubts in Kim's presence. I did once uneasily dream, during a late March rainstorm, that Kim had fled our home, suddenly repulsed and shamed by our violation of all known mores. The dream ended with an amplified slam of the front door, echoing the conclusion of *A Doll House*, as Nora slams the door upon her clueless husband. I woke from that dream with a start and, shaking the fright from my brain and heart, was doubly alarmed to hear the slamming of a door—a real door, an undreamed door. I was instantly out of the bed and halfway down the stairs when I heard the splashing of water: Kim was in the bathroom, and she slammed it merely because it initially refused to close securely.

When my darling padded back into our bedroom, I had recovered my senses. Indeed, I feigned sleep as she lay back down and, just as she turned upon her side, her breech-like pajama bottoms slid halfway down her pale backside. Oh, how I surprised her: in seconds atop her and within her.

Twenty-Seven:
"The *sine qua non* of my day-to-day *dada*."

The day I was scheduled to meet Professor Martino, Kim arose early and was at the kitchen table as I came down the steps. I wondered why she was up so early—rehearsal had lasted until nearly midnight—but before I could ask she announced that Pad would begin recording that very evening.

I sat down across from her and nodded gratefully as she slid toward me a chipped mug of hot coffee.

"Finally in the studio!" she beamed. "I'm so nervous but the more I think about it, I really think we can pull it off. I mean we've been rehearsing like crazy and have everything down so that we can just go in there and, *Bang!,* we can nail the songs without a lot of, you know, overdubs and studio gunk and not just suck the life out of the songs with take after take. In fact, Dad was saying..." She caught the cloud that darkened my face. "What? Dad's been really helpful with a lot."

"That's true. I know."

"He's really looked out for the band. It's not like, he's, like he's screwed me—"

"I hope not. That would be wrong."

Face suddenly crimson, she looked as it she'd swallowed a red pepper.

I waved nonchalantly. "I know what you mean."

Like seasoned diplomats, we made jocular small talk as the tension diffused. I remarked that today I'd be laying a trap for Dr. Martino, and if the interview went well, I'd be able to miss my afternoon class in good conscience.

"What class is that?"

I squinted my brain to recall. "It's a business law class."

"Thinking of Pad's future, huh? You can work out all hassles in future contracts." And she reached for my right hand, which was wrapped around the coffee mug. I accepted her grasp and reveled in Kim's quick sharp squeeze. Then her hand was gone. Even when we were alone, daylight demonstrations beyond the most conservative sibling affection unnerved her. I'd learned, therefore, not to let a hand or gaze linger over her for more than nano-seconds.

And it struck me: she looked different in daylight. The same woman, of course, yet somehow unaccountably unfamiliar, and I risked a loitering gaze. Ah, so lovely, her black hair swept straight back, her pony hanging like a rope halfway down her back...my psyche's matchless micrometer couldn't measure the change, but merely sense it: perhaps her slowly-growing confidence in all things musical and—who knows?—confidence in matters beyond the musical.

Our chitchat ambled onward. With endearing enthusiasm, she explained that the recording studio was in Chicago's Near North neighborhood. "Vic Valmot's recording us. He just produced a solo record for that crazy bitch who sang in The Margins."

"That woman who named herself Hank?"

"Very good, Mr. Showbiz."

"I read that a couple of those songs are going to be in a movie sound track."

"Yeah, the soundtrack for *Fleeced*. Anyway, after Vic gets his points, there really is no money left in the contract, but—" She shrugged. "That's the way it is, and I guess Dad knows what he's talking about." Indeed, Professor Dave—belatedly a father figure to Kim—had asserted strict managerial control over Pad. Nothing aroused his parental instincts like money.

"We're booking six long weekends—like, Friday night through Sunday night—for the recording." That Spartan schedule was at Dad's insistence as well. "Vic wanted two months straight, and Dad, he just laughed out loud. Said that's for amateurs who can't sight read or tune their instruments. He's like, if we can't get them done in time, then we're slobs. Actually, the last sessions are vocal retakes, if we need 'em, plus maybe a little extra tracking with guitar or, you know, with whatever."

"Well on that point I agree. You want to sound like a band, with performance quirks. Like Richard's flubbed bass lines."

"Oh and Robbie's coming along too."

"Every time?"

"If he wants."

The thought of our befogged cousin running riot through a recording studio…I smiled. "You are remarkable. Putting up with Robbie blowing his nose or traipsing around in one of his jester's outfits, with the shirt inside out."

"Dr. Martino?"

"Mr. Edwards?"

I stepped into the good professor's office. Upon the desk was a shambling pile of books that obscured Dr. Martino, but he made no effort to stand or even sit up straight. I stood inside his doorway, glancing about for a place to sit. Two plastic chairs before his desk were pressed into service as bookshelves.

He pretended to be distracted by a student essay and slowly pushed it aside. Then, rubbing his eyes and offering a tardy smile, he urged me to "just push those books off the chair and get comfortable."

I began removing the books one by one from a chair, but he urged me to "shove them to the floor," which I did with a sweep of the hand.

"Coffee?" he asked, turning about in his ancient swivel chair only to see that his coffee pot was empty.

"Yes, thank you."

"Well then—" He scratched his head then stood up, leaving a tuft of graying hair standing upright, like weeds missed by a mower. "How about we get some coffee at the student union?"

Dr. Martino was affable during our jaunty walk across campus. He affected an air of modesty, even claiming at one point that he was "pretty much a novice" in his particular academic discipline.

"Which is?"

He paused briefly in mid-gate to hitch up his baggy gray pants. "Well, officially I'm a sociologist but my real interest is, you know, it's cross-disciplinary."

I waited for further details and, getting none, remarked that I'd somehow avoided taking his sociology lectures.

He nodded amiably, suggesting that music must take up all my time.

"Not really."

"But you're Dave Edward's son, right?"

"Yeah, but my sister got all of the talent in the family."

"Oh, I can't believe that."

"You will in about an hour."

When we arrived, Friday afternoon saw the student union nearly deserted, though the solemn bookworm Fred sat by himself at our scholastic roundtable.

"Do you mind if we have company?" I asked as Fred approached.

"Not at all."

I introduced my two companions and, after we all took turns praising our coffee's freshness, I noted the campus rumor that Dr. Martino's group, the Progressive Caucus, had stolen the student paper some months back.

"Oh, these things do happen on occasion, that's true," the professor mused in a manner both lofty and casual. "You know, emotions run high and people feel, uh, the need to do something. I know that some people—maybe even you, Mr. Edwards— thought my group did it, but I really doubt it was an organized effort on their part."

"Why?"

He shrugged. "Because the students in the group talk to me quite a bit, sometimes pretty candidly. None of them said anything about it."

"I'm just wondering," I smiled, "if you brought it up to them."

"No."

Impishness tip-toed up my spine as, without warning, I switched topics. "You're a pretty vocal supporter of the SAEV, right?"

He missed only the slenderest of beats as he enjoyed a prolonged sip of coffee. "I'm committed to the dignity of labor. That's part of what I was talking about before." With his thumb, he gestured behind him, as if to retrieve a snatch of lost dialogue. "You know, about cross-disciplinary study? That's a big part of it."

"Of what?"

"The various levels that labor gets exploited at. It's at all levels." Warming to the discussion, he scooted closer to the table. "Not just in the Third World, but in the First World of course and especially in the hidden economies, where inequities drive excess labor."

"And what about here on campus?'"

"Oh, here too," he nodded emphatically.

"But faculty aren't paid that bad," Fred interjected. "I mean, I don't know what they're paid but it's gotta be not bad."

"Faculty pay is far behind administrative pay," Dr. Martino asserted. "I've done some, done some pretty decent work on that." Sitting ever straighter, he awaited the wide-eyed attention of his two student companions. "Some of my graduate students have done ground-breaking research into the growth of administrative pay relative to faculty pay relative to student tuition dollars and state support."

"But your pay's gotta be pretty decent," Fred persisted.

"Two of my very own graduate students just presented papers this month on this topic. At the ASLSC." He paused to explain what these letters signified...suffice to say that the ASLSC is merely another academic conference at a four-star hotel in New York City or Chicago or Los Angeles.

"The students are yours?"

"Nancy Cooke and Dave McAllister. You know them?"

"No, I'm afraid I don't." I let my confession of slight ignorance hang in the air before continuing. "I guess maybe I made some faulty conclusions about you, Dr. Martino."

"Oh it wouldn't be the first time people have done that!" His agreeable laugh became a merry roar, and his face reddened as he slapped the table top. "Being misunderstood, it's common enough in my field. Hell, maybe I misunderstood you, Mr. Edwards."

"I hope so."

He laughed again and asked if we all wanted a second coffee. I indicated that I would but, before Martino rose to fetch the refills, I placed on the table a sheet of paper: the petition for SAEV. Martino seemed not to notice the sheet and cheerfully disappeared around the corner.

"He's a pretty nice guy," Fred offered.

"So far."

A question mark darkened Fred's face.

"Here we are," Martino announced. "Three more coffees."

Martino sipped cautiously at the scalding drink as I looked over the SAEU petition.

"Ever see one of these?" I placed the petition before him.

"No, not lately." He glanced over the rim of his white Styrofoam cup. "Well, I think I saw a rough draft of something the SAEU was working on, but—Whew! That coffee's pretty hot."

"I've taken the liberty of signing it."

Martino belatedly picked up the petition and, after glancing at it, glanced at me.

"What about you?"

"It's an important issue."

"That's great. The SAEU needs some credibility with the administration." Ah, how I savored this moment: Martino restless in his suddenly uncomfortable chair. I faced Fred. "What about you?"

"What?"

"The petition." I snatched it from Martino's loose fingers and placed it atop Fred's pile of books.

"Oh." Fred, ever cautious, actually read the petition's preamble from beginning to end. As he read, Martino must've noted his own unbecoming squirming and, in reaction, became stock still as he stared out the rarely-washed windows. Outside the union, students streamed by in groups of three and four, with the occasional couple holding hands and chattering.

Finally, Fred was finished. "I don't think so," he said, voice tinged with regret. "I'm not really much of a joiner."

"What?"

"I'm just not much of a joiner." Turtle-like, he gathered his arms close to his body into an invisible shell.

"Fred, you're not joining the SAEU when you sign this. In fact, you can't. You're not a graduate student."

"Not yet."

"So you're going to be?"

"Yeah, next year." The turtle's limbs re-appeared. "I got accepted back in, well it must've been last December."

"Then sign it for your own good." I offered him my pen.

"You're a born union organizer, Mr. Edwards." Martino offered a queasy smile.

Under my stern gaze, Fred agreed to sign as long as doing so didn't commit him to joining. "I couldn't afford the dues, probably."

"Don't worry, Fred." I rolled my eyes at him, briefly but harshly. "You can always disavow your own signature next year." I turned toward Martino. "And your signature will make three."

"That's a good start, but—"

I slid the paper across the table with my little finger.

"—but I shouldn't. Not yet."

Notebook in hand, I nodded for him to continue.

"Oh you're doing a *story* on this," Fred interjected. "Do you have to include my name?"

"Only if you don't want me to."

"That's cool. I really don't want it to—What'd you say?"

"Professor Martino, you were saying about your refusal to sign the SAEU petition?"

"I haven't refused."

"So you're signing it?" I looked up from my notebook and, as I smiled, I saw it: the hate. The hate began with his suddenly peevish little eyes and radiated to create a nasty little aura. "That's *commitment*."

"You know, as a journalist, you shouldn't be advocating a position one way or another."

"Then neither should you, Dr. Martino," I said quietly. I placed the notebook in my lap. "If all you're going to do is talk, then you shouldn't advocate a position, either."

He opened his mouth to speak but remained silent.

"Look, do you support the teaching assistants or not?"

"Nobody on this campus is more committed to labor rights in the context of social justice."

"You don't have the courage of your clichés."

"My colleagues were right about you, Mr. Edwards."

"And my colleagues were right about you."

"They said you were, oh..." He began counting on the fingers of his right hand. "Deliberately difficult and combative. Awfully arrogant. Self-aggrandizing. Narcissistic."

"I love being talked about."

"You really *are* narcissistic. Does that bother you?"

"No. Narcissism bothers me only in other people."

"Hey look," Fred abruptly announced. "People are out there."

I glanced out the window to the courtyard. Students walked past, as they had all afternoon, but nothing was out of the ordinary. Then I realized that the escalating hostilities bothered Fred, and he wished merely to redirect our attention, if only for a moment.

"Your friend is right, Mr. Edwards. This conversation is pointless, so we should end it."

"As I said: my colleagues were right about you."

He snorted.

"You're a fraud...an upwardly mobile Marxist who just can't live without cheap student labor."

"Oh, and your heart bleeds for our grad students, right?" he tepidly challenged.

"No. I'd work a bait shop before I worked for fakes like you." Before I realized it, I'd slammed the table with my fist.

Martino regarded me with new wariness. "No need to get hostile, Mr. Edwards."

"Who's hostile? I didn't hit you."

"You're a very angry young man."

Fred tapped my shoulder. Several students loitered nearby, eager to overhear the disputation. Seizing the moment, I didn't disappoint. Indeed, I invited the students to gather 'round. Most stayed in the background, but a co-ed trio—two guys and a gal—accepted my offer.

Martino, coward that he is, hoped for safety in numbers; he even waved good-naturedly at the students, asking if they'd not been enrolled in his Sociology 211 last year.

"I don't remember," one of the guys said.

"That's what all his students say," I offered.

The trio laughed and awaited further entertainment.

I turned to the trio. "I was just saying to Professor Martino that he should sign the petition to let grad students organize."

"What are they?" the gal asked.

"Petitions or grad students?"

"I'm not sure."

"Yeah I think he should sign it," one of her companions said. "I mean, half my classes are taught by grad students."

"And they suck," the gal said.

"Maybe if they were paid a tad more," I suggested, "they wouldn't suck."

"They'd still suck," the trio asserted in unison.

The good professor had retreated and was halfway across the room, rapidly approaching the exit. I apologized for my sudden departure, but assured the group I'd be right back. "Beer's on me!" I told Fred.

The trio and the half-dozen other students in the background murmured and smiled at my mention of beer. I broke into a relaxed trot...Martino's florid rear, seemingly trailing its owner by a yard, banged against the rapidly closing door of the union exit. I caught up with him in a few strides. He glared at me and, as if facing a strong wind, lowered his head and drove his hands deep into his jean pockets.

"You know, if you'd just acted with a little tact, and not just fucking attacked me, I would've signed that petition," Martino harrumphed.

A bright wave of euphoria roared in my skull.

"Jesus, you're a real creep, kid."

I grinned.

"Irresponsible asshole."

"Last week, I bought beer for minors at the 7 Eleven."

"I don't doubt it."

"Then I bought dope from the minors."

"It didn't help."

"And then I went home and I, uh, I proposed to my sister."

He waved me away.

I clasped his arm. "I'd make an honest woman of her, but she'll only live with me in sin."

Ah, the annoyance that spread across Martino's face: the humiliation of having his "liberal" nostrums so rudely exposed before several undergraduates, and now his having to endure a daft discussion of sibling matrimony.

"Get away from me or I'll call the police."

I hurried to gain a few yards on him, then spun about. He kept stomping forward and I skipped backward at Martino's pace. "Don't leave yet. People like you, you're the *sine qua non* of my day-to-day *dada*."

Martino abruptly halted. He studied me with rising contempt, and I could see the rusty gears turning beneath his balding pate: How has this punk, he wondered, so thoroughly bamboozled me? Eventually, he gathered himself and wished me a good day. With complete sincerity, I replied that his wish had been granted.

When I returned to the student union, Fred and the stragglers were waiting. "What about that free beer?" one of the students asked.

I glanced at Fred, who sat smiling with books atop his lap. "Yeah, I'm pretty thirsty, and besides...you always inspire me to stop studying."

"Careful, or your grades will be like mine."

"Impossible."

"Okay, the beer is free. But first I need to get it." The students muttered a bit, but I assured them my offer was good. Of course, I added, a few dollars for gas money would be much appreciated. A few laughed and pressed folded singles into my palm. "Great. You guys know where the newspaper office is?"

One guy, attired in sloppy gray sweats, said he did. "Dude, I'll lead the way."

"Give me twenty minutes."

Twenty-Eight: Where the Intellectuals Gather

I arrived with three six-packs of bottled beer, two discount bottles of wine, and a few packs of cigarettes. The gaggle waited by the office's drab steel door and even called out a little cheer when they saw me, half-obscured by the paper sacks cradled in my arms. My key stuck in the lock a bit, and I had to wriggle it to the point of breaking, but finally the lock yielded and we tromped into the deserted newspaper offices.

I set the sacks on Karen's desk. "Make yourselves at home," I called over my shoulder while discretely rifling through Karen's desk. Ah, there they were: matches.

"So this is where the intellectuals gather," Fred remarked in mock awe. Uncharacteristically loose-limbed, Fred sauntered to a desk across the room and, with an incongruous whoop, sat down in a squeaking office chair and scooted back toward the rest of us. The others took his cue, and the guy in gray sweats—Bob—dragged an abandoned classroom desk to the middle of the room. It served as the refreshment stand, and we organized our chairs in a ragged circle around it.

I contentedly sipped and smoked. The group talked of summer plans: the boring jobs, the more boring parents and hometown friends, and the impending post-graduation life that made one tingle with hope and trepidation. I remarked that I'd decided against graduating at all; I was enjoying my dissolute life very much at the moment. My declaration compelled the group to drink more earnestly, and as the smoke and suds rose, conversation drifted toward the faculty who were loved or loathed. Presently, one of the students who'd been quiet mentioned a certain Professor Edwards. I squinted my ears.

"Edwards is okay, pretty much," he grinned. "One cool thing, he took today off because of some musical stuff or something he had to do."

"So you play?" I queried.

"Tuba mostly, but I'm trying out the trombone, though not very well."

A female beside him smiled. "I heard you in studio last week and—"

"What?"

She shrugged, sipping on her beer. "Oh, nothing."

"Man, you were in there!" He looked away, chagrin darkening his face.

"Yeah. But you weren't that bad. No, really you weren't." Apologetic, she patted his shoulder. "Listen, I'm no critic. All I've ever played is tuba, so don't take any stock in my opinion. I leave that to Professor Edwards."

Fred leaned forward in his chair. "Watch what you say. There's a spy in our midst."

"What's that?" the girl asked.

"A spy." Fred nodded toward me.

The door's scraping distracted us. "Jesus, is there an orgy in here?" someone called.

"Not again!" a second voice added.

I sighed. "We're all busted."

Tommy and Karen approached. Tommy was enthused to find the group. "Where's my beer, bro?" he cheerfully demanded of me. I pointed at the desk inside our circle.

"Finally that dumb desk is put to good use," Karen remarked. "It's been in here for years and I don't know how it even got in here." She too smiled at the group, though cautiously. She was, I saw, uneasy with the crowd of strangers. Nonetheless, she took a chair and, as she sat down, I offered her a cigarette.

"Are they spies too?" someone asked.

"Spies for the administration," Karen joked. "We're doing an expose on binge drinking, and I'm here to live the story."

"You've been living it all week," Tommy added.

"No, they're not the spies," Fred announced. "It's this guy, our host. His dad just happens to be Professor Edwards."

The female tubist studied me. "Nice to meet you. My name's Kristen." She extended a hand. "Your dad's really a strong player."

"So do you play too?" Bob asked.

"No, I'm the non-musician. There's Dad and there's my sister, Kim."

"His sister is a rock star," Tommy announced.

Remarkably, all but one person in our drinking quorum had heard of Pad. Even more remarkably, half my companions didn't know that Kim was a faculty brat—her fame reached beyond the narrowly local.

"Our host is the band's lyricist," Karen added. "So he's a celebrity—a minor one, that is, along with his rock star sister."

"That's so cool," Bob offered, and the group agreed.

"Hey, does she have any groupies yet?" Karen continued, voice rising. "You know, sex on demand?"

Tommy offered to join the groupie fan club.

"Or are you keeping her on the straight and narrow?"

"I think her work habits keep her on the straight and narrow." The group was plainly curious about Kim, so I offered a speedy thumbnail sketch: music lessons from grade school onward; singing nearly as long; serious guitar player since 7th grade.

"Yeah man," Tommy enthused. "That guitar, it's like, nu-metal with rockabilly or something."

The male tubist snapped his fingers. "Is that her that's been on the radio a lot? That tune with, yeah, that kind of punkabilly in the break?"

"Probably 'Blush'," I suggested.

"That's it," he nodded. "Blush." He squinted at me. "You wrote the lyrics?"

"Uh huh."

"That's cool," he allowed. "But some of them, I don't get them."

"You're supposed to admire them, not understand them," Karen remarked.

I glanced at my editor, wondering why her mood was sour. "That's true. But sadly, dear editor—" I swiveled to face her— "it's the inverse for you: we understand you but don't admire you."

She modulated her tone and added, belatedly, that "Blush" was indeed a very fine tune. "And with that..." She looked toward her desk. "More beer anyone?" She rose and gathered several beers in her arms, then walked about our circle giving each guest a fresh bottle.

"Oops," she said as she came to me. "We're all out."

"Yeah, whatever Karen, if you want us to—"

"Just kidding!" she said too merrily. She produced a bottle from behind her back. "Just don't drink too much. You owe me copy this weekend."

Indeed. My hatchet job on Martino was due Sunday evening.

"So how did it go, anyway?" she asked, hovering over me.

"Ask Fred."

Fred's consumption of beer had reddened his face, and his big white teeth against suddenly ruddy complexion rendered him grotesque. "Oh yeah," he half-whispered, wiggly. "Martino, he's a working class hero and you should've seen him when Jeff asked him to, uh...oh crap." Beer spilled then foamed upon his lap.

Karen rolled her eyes. "So did he?"

I held the petition aloft. "Whose names do you see there?"

She squinted. "Mmm...Conspicuous in its absence."

Fred removed his socks to soak up the beer from his slacks. "You should sign it, uh—What's your name?"

"Karen."

"You should sign it."

She ignored him. "I really do need that copy by Sunday, Mr. Mencken."

I saluted crisply.

Karen clasped her hands like a retiring hostess. "Nice to meet all of you, and just make sure you—I mean, you, Tommy and Jeffrey—clean up after the party."

"Yes mother," Tommy snapped.

And she was gone.

"Bitch," Tommy snorted after the door shut behind Karen.

The group shrugged, suggesting Karen seemed okay to them.

"She was a little hostile," I agreed. "What, is she maxed out on her credit cards again?"

"I don't know," Tommy said, "but she was ragging on the way over here."

"And why were you guys coming over here, anyway?"

"To work on the paper," he sighed. "It's Friday night."

"Who works on Friday night?" I laughed.

The beer was gone, and a few of my new friends graciously went out to buy more. They returned with several quart bottles, the contents of which they poured into plastic cups. The gathering reached its peak around ten, with loud squawking and spontaneous dancing around an even more spontaneous fire that Fred started by impishly lighting a grocery sack. I barely managed to dive across the room to pull the battery from the smoke alarm, and Tommy snuffed the flame with a metal wastebasket.

"That's all I need, man," he complained as he lifted the wastebasket. Smoke briefly obscured his face. "Jesus, if Karen saw this."

"Fuck Karen," Fred laughed.

""If she saw this, we'd be busted and kicked out of school."

Tommy's palpable alarm was a wet blanket upon celebratory spirits. The three or four females, with charming solicitude, instantly went about cleaning up our refuse: the discarded bottles, the errant cigarette butts, Fred's socks, the plastic cups reborn as ashtrays. The men half-heartedly offered assistance, but the women waved us off.

And just like that, the party ended. Tommy and Bob wished everyone a happy summer, and Fred followed them out. He in turn was followed by a co-ed who'd not spoken two words. She'd sat pensively with us, smiling on cue but seemingly ill at ease. Yet now, as she stood, I marveled at the sumptuosity that was her body and the élan that was her freely swinging hair.

"Hey Fred, wait up," she called.

Fred turned with drunken grace upon one heel. "Finally you talk to me after all semester!"

She caught up and the two were briefly log-jammed in the poorly-lighted doorway. Fred took a half-step back, bowed like a gentleman, and she exited first, chattering over her shoulder that she'd wanted a joint all night.

"Night Fred," I called, rather wan at his departing silhouette.

"And to you." He waved with the finality of one who didn't plan on seeing me for a long time.

I turned around and nearly collided with the two remaining guests: Kristen and the male tubist.

"Whoa! Sorry 'bout that," I apologized. "I thought everyone had cleared out."

"Sorry. Didn't mean to stay too long," Kristen said—even as she sat down, both palms discretely smoothing her skirt.

"I'm sorry, but I didn't catch your name," I said to the fellow. "My name's Jeff Edwards, and well, I guess you know my dad."

"Mike Watson." He glanced to his side and, upon sitting down, inched his chair closer to Kristen's. "Nice to meet you."

"I'm sure my dad has mentioned me," I said with a straight face.

Mike offered a meager nod, then apologized for the fact that my dad had in fact not.

I laughed. "I'm just kidding. He never mentions me." I turned to Kristen. "Does he?"

A half-second's hesitation. "In fact, he mentioned you yesterday during the grad student seminar."

"Get out."

"Yeah. He's said that, well, he's mentioned it a couple times." She glanced at her feet. "I mean, in the context of styles, of learning and musicianship and of practicing. Like, he was talking about how his teacher was an ace sight reader, while he himself could get away with things because he has perfect pitch."

"I *hate* people with perfect pitch," Mike sighed. Then he hoisted his bottle in a toast to all people who, like himself, were stuck with relative pitch.

"And he happened to mention his son. Who would be you," she pointlessly clarified. "People with big ears who really can soak up music without—"

"Without trying, yes," I finished for her. Then I assumed a pose close to my father's: legs crossed, one elbow resting upon a knee. "But that's not *enough*. One must practice, practice, practice. People who hum have big ears. People who play, they *practice*."

"But how many people write lyrics for a hip rock band?"

The beer having loosened social niceties, one noted that Mike was keenly interested in Kristen; she, as it happened, was courteous but uninterested, though she did accept his suggestion that they "get together before finals and maybe practice. I'm working on this piece, it's a trombone concerto."

She smiled in recognition. "Working on *adagio* or *presto*?"

"*Presto*."

"Yeah, it's a nice piece." She chuckled. "The good professor Edwards likes that piece a lot."

"Yup," Mike nodded. "Doesn't he, Jeff?"

"I suppose."

And then Kristen rose, thanked me for a great evening. She even joked that she'd inform my father of my laudable work ethic. "In the office past midnight!" And Mike, as aroused drunks do, tried not to appear in a rush as he rushed to follow Kristen out. "Bye, see ya Jeff!" he called, then the two were gone.

Curious, I rose and peered out the basement's narrow windows, which were at eye level. Ah, there they were, ambling down the gently serpentine cement walk. They paused beneath a vapor light. And though I couldn't hear a word, I enjoyed Mike's labored wooing: his overwrought gestures, his anxious affability, his abrupt silence as he hung upon Kristen's every word. Presently, three other students approached. Mike's spirits visibly flagged as the students stood yammering. After several minutes—during which Mike gamely persevered, wanting to be courteous yet wanting to drag away Kristen—the trio departed. Kristen waved as she hurried away, apparently assuring Mike that they would indeed get together and practice before the semester ended. Mike stood alone beneath the vapor light for a few minutes, looking about, his hands restless in his pockets.

I loitered about the *Herald's* office. Commandeering Tommy's desk, I read some news of the day on the Internet and kept telling myself that I really should get to work. The now-empty office saddened me, and an aching swelled my heart.

Eventually, I fired up the word processor on Tommy's machine and began:

> On his crowded campus web page, Dr. Paul Martino is unabashed. He is a self-proclaimed champion of social justice. Indeed, his resume bristles with commitment. For instance, his longstanding activism against Third World sweatshops has energized students nationwide.

And what about academic sweat shops? In other words: what about graduate students who teach two to three undergraduate courses for a paltry stipend and waiver of tuition (but not books)? In that context too, Dr. Martino is a leading dissident voice, having contributed what he calls 'groundbreaking' research into the matter.

And yet: he refuses to support student unionization right here on our very campus. In fact, he refuses to sign even a modest petition that merely asks that the administration examine, in good faith, the issue of student unionization. When I discussed this matter with Dr. Martino just this past Friday, he—

The piece took longer than I'd expected: I spent ninety minutes gathering data from various activist websites about Martino's "leading role" in dissidence, and contrasted this research with his refusal to sign the petition. I even found an old photo of Martino, portly body bulging in a sweaty tee-shirt, linked arm-in-arm with local government officials in South Africa. "On to the next battle!" trumpeted the caption. "Leading American academic assists grass-roots leadership."

Finally, around three a.m., I completed the piece. I uploaded the piece to Karen's e-mail and left a hard copy on her desk. After a last quick look about the room for errant beer bottles and cigarette butts, I left. The morning air was cool and enlivening. I passed the library's large flower bed, and the flowers' fragrance sharpened my senses. I reached down and plucked several tulips for Kim. At home, I couldn't sleep; I burned with her imminence: her face beneath mine, her beautiful hands upon my back and neck, her black hair scented with Pantene and menthol cigarettes.

Twenty-Nine: In Sixty Seconds

"I'm so tired," Kim announced as she stepped clumsily, battered guitar case in hand, through the door Monday morning.

I'd been dozing upon the couch, the radio turned to the university's morning music program: Glenn Gould's eccentric and wonderful interpretations of Beethoven had soaked my psyche.

"That Beethoven crap again."

"Crap?"

"And here, have one." She abruptly shoved my legs from the couch and sat down, then gave me a Styrofoam cup of coffee. "Careful, I got pop on it. And mustard."

"Thank you. And welcome home."

"I'm so tired," she repeated, but she didn't seem tired. Indeed, she was frisky. "The session went great! Or at least, a lot better than I'd hoped! Vic is cool. Very cool."

"I'm all ears."

And indeed, chatty Kim would've rendered me all ears, regardless. Wired on caffeine, nicotine, and elation, she detailed Pad's inaugural Chicago recording session. The band had wisely taken a day off from rehearsal, so they hit the studio rested. Vic Valmont, fresh from an industry buzz-setting recording setting with Day Glo, wanted Pad to be the right cross of his one-two punch.

"First thing he did, you know what? He got us all together in the studio and he pulls out a copy of our CD and we listen to 'Unsilent Partner.' Said it was some of the best vocals he'd heard. Then we listened all the way through the CD, and he pointed out stuff that was good and bad, and Dad—"

"Got pissed."

"No, he pretty much agreed." Vic, it turned out, was first chair trombone in high school, and when he learned that profes-

sor Edwards was a pro, Vic and he established a respectful rap-
port. "And then we got set up and we played a couple tunes from
the CD and tried to follow his suggestions about improving them,
like the high hats in "Aim for the Ditch" and the bass in—"

"Everything?"

"Oh shut up. The bass in, uh, in a couple tunes and he even
had me slow down on some guitar parts. He'd say, 'The notes
have to *sing*.'"

"Sounds like a brass teacher."

Onward she chattered and smoked until near lunchtime, her
narrative ranging from the number of songs recorded—"Only
one, but it's good"—to the spaciousness of the converted Halsted
street loft in which they recorded. "He lives in the loft too, isn't
that cool?"

I nodded.

She rolled her cigarette back and forth between thumb and
forefinger. "You missed me," she observed, eyebrow raised in satisfaction.

I snatched the cigarette, finished it with one long pull and
eased her out upon the length of the couch. Then I reached to the
tiny table beside the couch.

"Tulips?" She gathered them in both hands and held them to
her face.

Work that evening was demanding, but I enjoyed it. I appreciated Franco's geniality, his enthusiasm for the mundane task
of boiling spaghetti or, with three expert strokes of the big
wooden spoon, stuffing cannelloni shells with cheese. The evening grew hectic when three extended families came in, along
with the typical medley of penny-pinching elderly and declassed
beer burpers. Around nine, I took a break and made an Italian
sub upon a freshly-baked loaf...ah, the meats! Fragrant salami
and proscuttio!

Examining my creation, Franco threatened to add it to the
menu.

"You wish," I joked, enormous paddle of meat and bread in
my mouth. "I'll never give up the recipe."

We closed shop at one. Energy still high, I rolled out dough
for pizza.

Franco was incredulous. "You're still hungry?"

"My sister asked for a pizza." I shrugged and, after wiping a knife off with my spattered apron, sliced some pepperoni. After slipping the finished pizza from the paddle onto the stone, I threw together an antipasto: aralli, grissini, sopressata, yet more pepperoni, dry sausage, baby genoa salami, bruschetta.

"Nice salad," Franco smiled.

"Nice salad," Kim whistled as I placed my creation on the kitchen table. "Jesus, have some! I can't eat all this." I noted I'd eaten plenty already and insisted that she was welcome to it all. She attacked the pizza and antipasto with zest. Made merry by the food and the solicitous love it embodied, she allowed me to crouch trollishly behind her, hands cupped upon her breasts.

"Geez, don't hurry me," she laughed, pushing away the empty plate. "Here, have a cigarette with me."

Still crouched behind her, I did.

And so the next several weeks' pattern was established: a silent house on long aching weekends as I waited for Kim. As I expected, the recording sessions suffered several unhappy episodes, and Vic Valmont grew increasingly impatient with Richard's maladroit bass-plucking. Once, after beer had rendered her unusually frank, she admitted that Richard was just not up to speed. Still, she felt loyalty toward him, as he'd help find Larry and, admittedly, he assisted in extra-musical ways by keeping the band's equipment organized, tuned, and the sheet music and CD-R's well-organized.

"He'll get the tunes down." Kim's eyes narrowed. "Vic, he's not a cut-and-paster. He really wants a real performance from start to finish."

Satisfied, I said nothing.

"Oh, but there's some good news. Dad's got some tour dates."

I blinked with surprise.

"Vic, he's pretty happy with the recording and the band and so, yeah, he gave Dad some phone numbers to call. Clubs and a few booking agents and all, all that stuff."

"One step closer to world domination," I smiled.

Victory was gained on campus, too. My hatchet job on Professor Martino elicited outraged howls from his yippy lapdogs, but it elicited loud enthusiasm from much of the student body. During finals week, a few strangers offered handshakes and backslaps. Karen, too, was pleased and assured me that she wasn't angry at me for having a beer fest in the *Herald*'s offices.

"If that's what it takes to get copy like that, then have a kegger next time," she enthused. "Everybody's either pissed at the paper or in love with the paper. I got word we're up for the Midwest Regional award for most improved publication. And that's good on a resume, I can tell you. Especially my resume."

Karen sang only my praises for the semester's remaining days. She allowed me to write a restaurant review of Franco's that started out straight, but halfway moved from reality to surreality with a portrayal of the chief cook—Jeffrey Edwards—donning a chiffon dress and singing weepy arias to startled customers.

And then one balmy afternoon, Karen pounced upon me outside the *Herald*'s office.

"Congratulations!" she chirped. "You've made me a success!"

"Details?"

"I got an internship in New York City this summer! And your pieces, they helped a lot." She paused, gathered herself, then spoke in careful, measured tones: "Because, as I told them, I encourage risk-taking but demand accountability." She laughed. "They loved that line!"

She abruptly grabbed me in a manful hug and planted a long kiss on my cheek. Then leaning back to survey her buss's effect, she laughed and planted a second. "Such a cold fish," she teased, reluctantly releasing me. "And who'd think that beneath that air of blasé detachment beats the heart of a romantic...Yes, a romantic who still carries a torch for the one who got away."

I shrugged.

"So what's her name? Patty, wasn't it?"

"No."

Karen's high cheekbones rose even higher in merriment. "Well whatever. That's what someone said at your party." She let her remark flutter in the air as she turned away. "But you're *still* coming to my end of the semester bash, aren't you?"

"Still? I didn't know anything about—"

"Oh shut up!" she happily jeered. "I decided on it just today. Hey, you'll be the special guest."

"When is it?"

"Gee, Jeff. That was so enthusiastic."

"No, really. I'll invite Martino. I'll bury the hatchet—right in his skull."

"The party will be…"

I don't recall what she said, as I had no intention of attending. Karen's innocuous flirtations alarmed me, and I suddenly abhorred being the object of her—or anyone else's—drunken speculations. I waved goodbye and turned in the opposite direction, not knowing to where I was walking. To the front of my lobes clawed sordid scenarios: Tall Patty, for example, arrives at Karen's party, stoned. Suddenly she shrieks: "He's fucking his sister. And in my dress. *Constantly*."

The ambiguity of the imagined accusation—just who wore the dress?—left me even more uneasy. Clammy dread seized me and I couldn't find my feet. Or the rest of me.

"Hey Jeff," a passerby waved.

I nodded, feebly lifted a greeting hand…waited for spine and legs to regain their wits. What a comical sight I must've been, motionless save for the fretful licking of tongue upon my lip, as others passed by nodding, smiling, scowling, or ignoring. My senses briefly freed themselves from their stock-still shell and floated a good ten feet overhead. Even as I saw myself standing oh-so-stupidly in the middle of a campus walkway—the air fragrant with May's bloom—I couldn't will myself to walk. I just stood there for ten minutes. Or so it seemed. Retrospectively, I've reduced the incident to a mere minute.

But the event's brevity didn't matter. In sixty seconds, fear can highjack joy.

Thirty: A Call

Karen's party was apparently memorable. Tommy left a message on my answering machine. He noted that my absence was peevishly remarked upon by some revelers until 3:00 a.m., when the police arrived to forcibly turn down the stereo.

"Dude, call me!" Tommy urged. "The police unplugged the stereo because Karen got rowdy and pulled off the volume knob. Hey I'm working here through the summer, can't stand the thought of going back home. Call me."

Meanwhile, Pad pressed onward with Vic Valmont. However, Kim grew more agitated, and a creeping pessimism clouded her assessment of the sessions. On a muggy night—the ceiling fans roaring like propeller blades, the air conditioner sounding its death rattle—she returned from a session exhausted. The session had stretched into six days; Richard had claimed or feigned illness and left the remaining members to soldier on without him—not difficult, I would've guessed, but his absence produced social if not musical tensions and Pad finished only two songs. Now, two songs in six days is very good by contemporary rock band standards, but of course many bands are nearly illiterate, musically speaking.

The bands with serious label money spend months and many tens or hundreds of thousands of dollars in tony recording studios with the latest in mixing boards, digital sound enhancements, vocal tuning software, instrument tuners, video games, imported water, vocal coaches, caterers-on-call and shrinks-on-call. The producers and engineers flog, scrub, goose, and anesthetize the meager songs.

Every emotion faked, every peak a shabby heap of histrionics, and all traces of an actual band—the swing, the roar, the ambience—are irradiated.

And the bands *without* serious label money?'

They have to bang out a recording in two weeks…and usually sound like shit.

"The songs, they're not gussied up, just cleaned up." Kim tossed me a CD-R. "Pretty much a live sound. But I don't want to hear it now."

"Oh c'mon." CD-R in hand, I hunched before the stereo, fiddling with the equalizer. A crackling drum roll leapt from the speakers.

"No really," Kim protested. "Now now. Not with you."

"Not with me?" I silenced the music.

"You won't like it."

"For Christ's sake, Kim, can we just listen to this?"

"Yeah, go ahead." She shrugged apologetically and turned to go upstairs. "You listen if you want, I'm gonna take a bath."

I restarted the recording. At the moment the drum roll filled the room, the phone rang. Ignoring the call, I listened with squinted ears to the first cut. I'd not heard the melody before, and it took me a few verses to recognize the lyric…yeah, it was "Nap After Breakfast."

> Beer on bran flakes for me,
> English tea and Irish coffee for you.
> I'll clip coupons
> Then hit the mall for a spending spree.
> And for you? A nap after breakfast…

I'd lazily anticipated the melody would be colored blue by some minor chords, though not—Heaven would forbid, if it could!—any lard-assed 12 bar blues clichés. Kim forbade any such exhausted ideas: no overt blues riffs, no moronic boogie, no bellowing hard rock choruses. But the lyrics, which I'd conceived as minor-key melancholy, were paradoxically transformed by the tune's big bright melody and nimble, stop-and-start verse. Then the chorus, pared to a superbly catchy hook:

> Nap after breakfast
> Yeah…eahhhhhhhh
> Snores until noon
> Yeah…eahhhhhhhh

Halfway through the chorus, the instruments laid out: first the bass (always wise), then Billy's for-texture-only piano chords, then Kim's windmill strumming. "*Yeah...eahhhhhhhh...*" The lone vocal peaked with a ragged roar, accompanied only by Larry's walloping drums. Upon the vocal line's final syllable, the drums discretely morphed to Western swing for three bars, then faded.

I rewound the tape, listened again, then again...the tune produced a hot whimsy. I wasn't even annoyed that Kim had cut half my words from the chorus, and the drums' tempo change concluded the tune on an intriguingly ambiguous emotion.

"Please pick up the phone!" Kim shouted from the top of the steps.

"Machine'll get it."

"Please?"

"For Christ's sake...!" I lowered the volume and, having sat before the stereo like a swami, my aching legs nearly failed me.

"Hello?"

"Good evening."

"Professor Edwards?!"

Dad cleared his throat. "Listen, can we talk?"

"Sure. Uh, let me get a cigarette." I clamped a hand over the receiver and looked around for a pack. Nothing. "Okay, I'm back."

"No, what I meant was, can we talk in person? Now?"

I heard Kim padding about upstairs, and I knew she'd soon don her white terry cloth bathrobe. My *élan vital* stirred for her, all the more because she'd been gone longer than usual.

"How about tomorrow?"

Muttering. "Tomorrow's an early day, gotta be at my office by nine-thirty and I've got a meeting at ten with the graduate committee."

"Then how's eight-thirty? I'll even bring coffee."

Eight-thirty, he grudgingly conceded, was acceptable.

Upstairs, Kim sat on the edge of her bed. "Was that Dad?"

Ah, what a poor dissembler: eyes upon me with a guilty imitation of innocence.

"How'd you know?"

"Don't snap at me. I didn't know he'd call tonight." She made a considerable show of not facing me.

"What? Why're you pissed at me?"

"I'm not pissed. I'm just really really tired and I don't feel like you climbing all over me."

I gestured for a cigarette. She listlessly tossed me the pack.

We smoked silently. We'd not before negotiated a rough patch in our peculiar romance. Such negotiations are difficult enough, but when brother and sister play house, such negotiations are especially difficult. One doesn't know how to even *begin* to begin.

"Well since you're not talking..." She glanced toward me but not at me and, with a shrug, pulled back the sheets to lie down.

"I'm talking no less than you."

Now in repose, she pulled the sheet up to her neck. "You're always right."

"And it's my only fault."

"What are you, anyway?"

"Sorry?"

"Fuck, look at us. What we're doing, it's off limits."

"But what if *nothing* were off limits? We'd be so bored."

She yanked indignantly upon the sheet. "I'm serious." Beneath the sheet, she crossed her arms across her chest. She looked wrapped as snugly as a mummy.

"Jesus, we lived apart and barely saw each other for, what? For years."

"So suddenly we're not, uh, not that." She could not bring herself to say "sibling" or "brother" or "sister" —nor could I.

"All that time apart from you, it changed almost everything."

"Almost."

"I don't think there are words for what we are. "

"Look in some psychiatric manuals. You'll find lots of words."

I couldn't stifle a snort. Kim, so brilliant in all things musical, could be so dense in other matters. The love we had—its scale and convivencia—made this moronic planet habitable. And there she lay, so snippy and stupid, so ordinary.

"Why the awful moralism?"

She glanced at me, then toward the drapes rustling in the evening's breeze. Beneath the sheets, her posture softened. She didn't resist when I stretched out beside her. Still, gallant beau that I was, I didn't press myself upon her. The breeze had picked up and, in the dark room, the drapes now fluttered like a playful ghost.

Thirty-One: "Because you hate her."

My early arrival would surprise Dad. He'd wanted eight-thirty and instead would get—I glanced at my watch—seven fifteen, with fresh brewed coffee to boot. Dad's suburban neighborhood was awash in dappled sunlight and glistening dew. Now that school was out, the streets were rather quiet: a husband or wife off to work, a lawn chemist spraying a yard, a young mother strolling her infant in a white-wheeled carriage.

Not having been to Dad's home in a long time, I drove right past it into an unfamiliar block of even larger, even more anxious-to-impress homes. At a cul de sac, I swung around and drove back more slowly, studying each house. Ah, there was Dad's bright home, the shrubs square and motionless, the flowerbed crowded with colors: red and white roses, white azaleas, neon lycorises. The driveway was freshly resurfaced, shiny black. Incongruous in the driveway was a drab cream compact, rust fizzing around the wheel wells. I parked behind it, noting the university parking sticker. Huh. Dad must've economized on his car, given the evident price of maintaining his absurd suburban castle. I grabbed my cardboard drink holder (stein-sized coffee cups ensconced within) and stepped lightly up the walkway to the front door.

The door was slightly ajar, so I stepped inside and announced my presence.

"Jeff?" Dad called from upstairs. "Is that you?"

"Dad? Is that you?"

"Make some coffee for us?"

"I brought some." I removed my shoes and, as Dad suggested, made myself at home in the kitchen. Doing so required that I inspect the *faux* chrome refrigerator. Not bad. Its gleaming interior held a variety of food and refreshment: breads, bagels, meats, apples, cheeses on top trays, and imported beers and "fresh squeezed" orange juice on the bottom. And further back, inside a grease-stained tan box, a pizza from...what the hell. From a competitor? Yeah, from Pizza Butt. Offended but hungry, I pulled a slice from the box.

"Hey," Dad called again from upstairs. "Can you, uh, can you get something in the basement for me?"

"What?"

"I said, Can you get something from—"

"No, I mean, what do you want from the basement?"

"Bath towels. I thought I had some up here, but..." His voice trailed into silence.

I was halfway down the stairs when, overhead, I heard the gallop of feet upon the steps. Figuring he'd found the towels already, I turned right back around and headed up the steps. Rounding the corner from the top step to the kitchen, I turned to see the front door violently slam shut.

Dad's heavier tromp came next, and he pushed the door fully shut. "Hi Jeff," he managed.

I stepped past Dad and, smiling, pulled upon the door's big brass doorknob. "And hi to you," I said to the young woman who stood tensely upon the stoop.

"Hi."

"It's Kristen, isn't it?"

Kristen stared at her feet, so I turned to Dad: "Kristen's here."

"You're early," he noted.

"I blocked your car," I said to Kristen as I opened the screen door. "C'mon back in. I brought us coffee." Tentative, she stepped inside. "As for you, Dad...you'll have to make your own."

"No, I won't be taking any," Kristen half-whispered. Upon retrieving her purse from the top of the fridge, she hurried out the door. Her dripping hair—ah, the call for the towels!—left a wake of droplets upon the polished wood floor. Without waiting for me to back out my car, she simply pulled as far forward as she could and, after a torturous series of cramped advances and retreats, gained sufficient space to drive out—right across Dad's lawn.

"She's pretty high spirited." She'd left a tire track halfway across the lawn.

"How do *you* know her?"

"I got drunk with her a while back."

Dad blinked.

"Did you get drunk with her too?"

"When did—"

"I mean, is this a casual fling born of faculty-student beer parties, or is it—"

"Maybe we should just talk about what I called for."

"Should I call her 'sister' or 'mother'?"

Dad shouldered past me, yanked a chair away from the kitchen table, and gestured for me to sit down. Ignoring him, I grabbed the chair opposite his and, coffee cup in hand, took my seat. He fidgeted for several seconds: long enough for me to note that dear ol' Dad, heretofore forever young (or at least forever adolescent), was beginning to look if not act his age...the thinner higher hairline, the slight sag about the eyes and chin, the nascent paunch beneath the wrinkled cotton shirt.

"I take it you didn't call me to talk about Kristen."

Dad heavily sat. "True enough. And I'm not—I mean, we're not—going to talk about her. Period."

I shrugged in breezy agreement.

"I called to talk about Kim. And you."

Reader, at that moment did adrenaline course through my limbs? Yes. But I maintained an affable insouciance, certain that Dad couldn't possibly know.

"She needs your help with, with something."

"She doesn't act like it."

Dad paused in his clumsy prying of the plastic lid from coffee cup, then shrugged. "She was going to, but I agreed to talk to you about it. Not that I want to."

At that moment, cousin Robbie tromped down the steps. "Hey is that you? I thought I heard you down here! Bro!" Resplendent in red plaid pajama pants and a sleeveless tee, he approached quickly, hand extended.

"Yeah. How are you, Robbie?" I stood and accepted Robbie's handshake. He shook with absurd good cheer, a left-leaning grin cleaving his big face.

"Bro! Not bad! I'm working at the newspaper, you know at the warehouse? Assistant manager now."

I smiled.

"I hate the hours but I've got a good delivery crew right now."
He joined us at the table for about fifteen minutes, regaling me
with stories from his job at the newspaper warehouse. "Aw, the
excuses some of the carriers come up with! I mean, who could believe them?" Indeed, the excuses were pilfered from inept fifth
graders: broken-down cars, lost maps, roadside collisions with
deer, lightning on clear mornings, etc., etc. "Hey you know? Once
I had to cover a route and drove right by your house! Should've
throwed you a paper!"

"Catch me next time?"

"Oh I will for sure. Hey did my buddies stop by yet?"

"...I'm not sure." Oh. He was now talking to professor Edwards.

"Not yet Robbie, but you know, they're probably running a
little late."

"Yeah. Craig said after work he was hitting the club and..."
Robbie's words grew indistinct as he departed.

Dad briefly rolled his eyes. "He's a good kid. But I sure wish
Art and Jo would reconcile."

"So what if they don't? He can live with one of them."

"I know, but—" He cleared his throat. "He wants to stay here
and I can't turn him away."

"What's he worth? Three hundred a month? Not bad!"

"Can we return to the thing that I called you to discuss?"

"Go."

"I'm going to ask you to talk to, to your mother."

"I hate her."

"I know."

"Then why me?"

"Because you hate her."

"Duh!?"

"Because Kim's afraid to, and your mother'll just throw me
out immediately, she'll never listen."

"Talk to her about what?"

"Money. For the band." He sipped the coffee, studied me over
the cup's rim. "See, that contract didn't have much money in it."

"Details, please."

"Your mother's brother—you know, Uncle Lou?—died and
left her quite a bit of money. Remember him?"

"No, I mean details about the contract. The recording costs."
Dark thoughts and violent impulses ricocheted about the interior
of my skull, and fleetingly I imagined smashing Dad's face
against the edge of the kitchen table.

He left the kitchen momentarily, returned with reading
glasses halfway down his nose and a thick tube of papers in his
hand. "Ever read this? The contract?"

"Not really."

He harrumphed with sour triumph. "Should've. It's your
band too."

My fingers drummed the tabletop.

He pushed his reading glasses upward and, with a clearing of
the throat, recited some figures. I will now offer you, reader, the
pertinent facts while excising the tedious and immaterial accusations that occasionally broke out between father and son:

In regard to recording cost essentials, Pad's contract called
for:

> $24,000 for studio fees
> $11,000 for equipment rental
> $19,000 for the producer's advance

Dad boasted about cutting back by persuading the producer
to let Pad sleep in his studio loft. Only Dad took a hotel room—
"A pretty drab place on Halsted," he sniffed—in which the band
showered and escaped for mid-afternoon breaks. Now, as a
minimum wage lackey, I found all dollar signs both impressive
and alarming. But the figures really were minor-league.

"How much more money does she need?"

I braced myself for an appalling figure: another $15,000?
$20,000?

"Ten thousand."

"Is that all?" I shrugged. "C'mon, why don't you put in some
money?" I opened my hands upward to take in the rather posh
house in which we sat. "You're hardly broke. Cough up some
Robbie money."

"I'm *completely* broke. And I couldn't teach this summer because of Kim's band stuff, and I've got my own recording to finish
off, so I've got no time for gigs."

We sparred for another half hour or so. I was aghast at the thought of seeing my mother: the scaly hag, the sniffling drunk, Mama Righteous who nagged and drained all around her. Finally, only for Kim, I agreed. Dad thanked me fulsomely, adding that Kim and company really were recording well, but a few flies in the ointment had marred matters: Richard's bass playing and Kim's periodic outbreaks of studio nerves.

"When she's just playing, everything rolls. Aside from Richard, especially in the beginning, the kids really know their songs. And they can *play*. But the producer has his own ideas sometimes. And her vocals, they're taking longer than they should."

"What's the producer say?"

"He says, 'Let's try that one more time' a lot."

"No, I mean, what does he think when the vocals are finally done?"

For the first time in our conversation, Dad smiled: "Whadaya think? That she's one of the best singers around. Period. That he's taking every little precaution to make sure the record captures her voice." Dad added a tantalizing detail: the regional tour dates he was arranging might be bigger than anticipated. "Almost every date was as a support act, but with 'Blush' getting a lot of college airplay and with Vic's name to drop, well, now the dates are getting reshuffled to featured act."

"Seriously?"

"These dates aren't Carnegie Hall. They're clubs. But yes, they're flipping over into headliner status and they all have actual sound systems with actual techs to run them."

I grinned.

"Which is why," he continued, voice growing grave, "this money issue is on the crucial side."

"...Okay."

"Hey that's great! And no kidding, ten thousand really should do it. I didn't want to go to the record company for more. I really wanted to bring this thing at budget, even under budget, and I think we're only a few weeks from being completely done."

I pushed myself away from the kitchen table, taking my now-cold coffee with me. Dad escorted me to the door, patting my broad shoulders the entire time. "And take it easy. Just think of it as business. A simple meeting."

What a jackass he was. The "simple meeting" would be a collision. "I'll see her next week."

"Tomorrow would be better. The sooner it's over, the sooner Kim will relax and the sooner—"

I raised a silencing hand, nearly covering Dad's face. "All right all right all right. Jesus *Christ*."

Dad's raucous laugh filled the foyer. "You're a great brother."

"Give my best to Kristen," I managed, shouldering open the screen door and hurrying away.

"You're a sport, you know that?" he called after me.

I waved away his good cheer and didn't notice the trio of denim-clad ragamuffins loitering on the porch. None looked to be over 16 or 17; they shifted about with exquisite boredom, cigarette smoke wafting gently overhead. One asked me if Robbie was ready.

"For what?"

They glanced at one another, then the ringleader—the clichéd thorns of tattoos on both arms—spoke up. "Ready to party, you know? *Party*."

"'till he pukes. Hey...front me a cigarette?"

"I've only got one left," the ringleader said.

"That's all I need."

He considered refusing but, sensing my mood, he surrendered the last smoke.

Kim sat on the living room couch. She'd just jabbed out a cigarette in the heaping ashtray, but as I sat beside her—my face distorted, I suppose, by the inchoate emotions with which I wrestled—she instantly lighted another.

"You never let on what you people cooked up for me."

Kim rubbed at her face. "I haven't seen her in so long and the more time that's passed, the more I figured I'd never see her again. And to see her now...I'm afraid what she'd say to me, what she'd yell at me about."

I snorted. "Like she knows!"

"But that's just the thing. If I never have to see her again, she never *will* know. It's like she just—" Kim slowly extended her arms, as if pushing away an enormous boulder. "—Like she's just gone. So she *can't* know." Then Kim abruptly faced me, scrutinizing me so closely that I was nearly embarrassed. "Thank you. So much."

"It's okay."

"No it's not. It's awful. But thank you thank you thank you." With each thanks, she squeezed my hand. "Oh, and did I tell you? Thank you."

I laughed.

"So when are you going to see her?"

I slowly freed my hand from hers. "Right now."

Thirty-Two: A Visit

Most aptly, brooding clouds gathered in the summer sky, and by the time I traveled the 55.7 miles to her apartment, rain spotted my windshield. Her apartment building was what's charitably called a "non-descript affair" and accurately called a dump: four units, two at the ground level and two above, with scrawny shrubs framing the scuffed entrance door.

Scrawled upon a strip of masking tape was *Mrs. Edwards, Unit #4.* I took the steps two at a time, refusing to let my own loathing impede my plan to quickly begin and end this matter.

The door—incongruously decorated with several adhesive plastic daisies—opened upon my second round of knocks.

"My word." She wore a wide brimmed hat, and her hard eyes darted beneath the brim's shadow. "My son."

I extended my hand, and her grip was limp and cool.

"Please. Come in." She retreated two steps and gestured me inside. "Can I get you a drink?"

"No thanks." I shoved a pile of unread newspapers from a chair and sat down. "Mind if I smoke?"

"No. But I don't have an ashtray—" Hand fluttering about her mouth, she stood in the middle of the room, scouting for something to serve as an ashtray. "Right there." She pointed at me.

"What?"

"Right next to you. That little paper box."

Inside the little paper box was a dry lump of shrimp fried rice. I lit up and settled, as best I could, into the chair as she pulled a folding chair halfway across the room to set before me.

"So...how are you?" Her hat remained upon her head, though she did tip it back to reveal her face.

She looked...well, she looked crazy: the failed dental hygiene, the nicotine-stained face and hands. Most notable, though, were those eyes: still hard, still bright, still eager to hate.

"I'm fine, thank you."

"That's nice. I'm doing better lately and—"

"I came here for money."

"—so it probably doesn't hurt to have this, this little drink." She glanced at the drink, then back at me.

"Money for Kim."

"Why?"

"Because you've got money."

"Is she in some kind of trouble?" She stiffened in her chair, the Mama Righteous pose taking form: chin jutting, nostrils flaring. "Is she pregnant?" Her voice rose in excitement. "Because if she is, then I'm sorry, that's just life. That's how your father and I started out, and that's just—What's so funny?"

"I'm pretty sure she's not pregnant?"

"Are you lying?"

"No. At least, I sure hope not."

"You're being evasive."

"No, I'm being direct. She is not pregnant, she is not in any trouble, but she needs money. Ten thousand dollars."

"Why didn't she come herself?"

"You scare her."

"That's so like Kim. So melodramatic."

"Not really. You tried to kill her."

"Now *you're* being melodramatic."

"I know the court didn't think you tried to kill her." I leaned forward, squarely facing Mama Miscreation. "But I saw it."

"And you tried to kill me."

"No, I just tried to cripple you."

"Oh, but you did. If Kim hadn't stopped you..." She grew small in her chair, like a slug curling in upon itself. She'd aged far beyond her physical years, certainly, though had lost none of her haughty petulance. "If she hadn't stopped you, I'd be dead."

"Then write a check for ten thousand dollars."

"Jo is handling the money, not me. She figured that I wasn't, you know, maybe I wasn't up to handling it all."

"How selfless of her."

"Did you hear, she's divorced?" A lilt brightened Mom's voice. "Must run in the family. We're all so inept in human relations."

I nodded.

"So she's not pregnant or not in credit card trouble or, or whatever. Why the money?"

"Her music career."

She sat motionless for a minute, silent, eyes losing their focus upon me as her thoughts turned elsewhere, someplace far beyond this dank room and shabby reunion. "Career," she murmured to someone not present.

I lighted another cigarette and waited. I'd decided that, if need be, I would simply ransack this four-room dungeon until I discovered her checkbook. Presently, Mom rose to mix herself another drink: upon the dingy kitchen counter sat a white jug of orange juice and about a dozen little bottles, apparently stolen from an airline. She emptied three of the bottles into her red plastic glass, then added orange juice, which was of a suspect greenish tint.

"Are you on medication?" I asked as she rejoined me. "I mean, other than booze?"

She shook her head. "No. I've given up on the drugs...the anti-depressants, the anti-psychotics. They worked in the beginning, but after a while..."

"After the third or fourth cocktail?"

She studied me, eyes enlivened by self-satisfied offense. "Such a smart ass for someone who wants money. But yes, that's right, the pills don't work so well. Besides, I like to drink." She prattled on a bit longer, then surprised me by announcing that she was taking the "talking cure."

"Psychotherapy?"

"That's correct. We talk. My group and the shrink, and sometimes just the shrink and me." Her voice descended a few levels and—my hair stands upon my neck even now—she sounded rather like Kim. "It helps to talk about it. You know. Just talk."

I nodded.

"The empathy of another person who's willing to listen, it's really something. Makes you feel almost good sometimes."

And within her flat statement inhered a request, one that I could barely abide. Yet for Kim's sake, I did so: I listened. She talked with typical self-exaltation for a while, yet as she saw that I wasn't interested in debating but merely listening (or so I pretended), her demeanor softened and she grew, in the next hour, nearly bearable. Against my own will, I found myself chuckling at her recounting of psychotic episodes. With you, reader, I share the best: given the state of permanent anxiety under which our nation now lives, Mom one night turned on the TV to find that the government had raised the national threat level. Tense, she drove to the store for a twelve-pack and over-heard the pimply teen behind the counter chatting on the phone.

"The kid was talking about some planes that, I don't know, that the government had been suspicious about. I didn't think much about it at that moment."

But the notion of a suspicious plane tunneled into her frayed psyche, and by the time Mom got home, she was trembling.

"I climbed out the window and sat on the roof, drinking and watching for hijacked jets."

By sunrise, beer and fatigue drove Mom back inside, but a pattern was established: each night, around ten, Mom's diffuse worries about jets grew into hard certainty, and she spent several evenings hunched upon the roof. If rain fell, she wore a rain-coat.

"Some neighbors saw me one night out there, and then the next night. They got scared I guess. A policeman showed up and I thought—" Her laugh was rueful. "—I thought he was a terror-ist and when I crawled back inside through the window, there was another cop in there. They weren't very friendly."

Mom was persuaded to undergo yet another round of medical treatment, but as she had little money, little treatment was available.

"I was just so tired. But then I remembered how a depressed little guy—a queer priest or something—how he got help. He wrote suicide notes. So I did the same and right away, *bang!* I got treatment. That's what I did when I got bored, in fact. I wrote a bunch of them."

"Have you picked out your casket?"

"If you swallow a few pills or run a knife across yourself, the notes are like first-class tickets. Zoom! Right to the front of the line." She faced the sliding glass door that opened onto a tiny deck. "It's starting to rain."

Not knowing what else to do, I too studied the tepid rain and ashen sky. Presently, Mom cleared her throat and without warning came down to the sharpest of brass tacks: "I won't give you the money."

Coolly, I concentrated upon my cigarette. "It's not for me," I finally observed. "It's for Kim."

"She's got her father."

"He's broke."

"All that money on that silly house and his silly rich girl-friends. Your father, he has no interest in life *at all* but music and women half his age."

"That's why he's broke."

"Kim can get a job."

I clasped my hands most humbly, hoping to strike the right pose of both patience and altruism. "None of this money is for me. It's for Kim. Not Dad. Kim. She's making a record, it's pretty much done, but the money's running low."

She leaned forward, her posture suggesting a witch hunched over a bubbling black cauldron. "Your father's the manager? Kim's a fool to trust him with any money."

"How'd you know he's the manager?"

"Robbie told me."

"Robbie?"

Her crouch deepened. "Yes. He visits me once in a while. He comes over with Jo and he's told me all about it. Already."

"Robbie's a moron."

"Yes, and he's happy to chatter about all kinds of things. He said that your father—"

"What? That he's ripping off his own daughter's band?"

"No. But I know your father. He's a very *cheap* man, with money or time or attention. Unless you're an illiterate co-ed."

"Then I'll handle the ten grand. What, you think I'll cheat Kim out of the money?"

Her eyes were simultaneously cold and hot. "Someone told me some very terrible things about you."

"How wonderful for you."

"A girl named Patty."

Nausea and bile crested in my stomach.

"Things just too sick. Not that I believe them. At first I did, but after a while we just had to choose not to believe them. What else could we do?"

"*We?*"

"Jo and I."

"And what awful things did Patty reveal about me?"

"You know."

"No I don't. I mean, there're so many. That I'm an embittered son? Or a failed musician or campus smart aleck?"

"Don't flatter yourself."

"Or that I'm crazy. Maybe a bit like you? Have you ever floated out of your body and seen yourself at a party or, I don't know, standing on a sidewalk unable to move but floating above yourself?"

"What?"

"It's happening right now."

And it was: perhaps I willed it, and therefore perhaps the experience was more one of wishful thinking than fact, but I now stood by that sliding glass door, glancing over my shoulder at the rain. The rain now fell violently, eddies and tiny rivers forming all about the parking lot below. Meanwhile, fourteen feet across the room, I sat on the edge of one chair while my mother curled wretchedly upon another.

And what was I saying to her? I can't claim accurate reportage, as my brain seethed and my hands demanded revenge upon the hag's throat. But the general drift of my demands was clear: write the check for ten thousand dollars.

"What you and Kim are doing," she accused. "It's a scandal."

"The check."

"I won't. I could write two checks for that amount. But I won't."

"Write one."

"Patty, she seems like such a nice girl too."

I watched myself leap, infuriated, from the chair. I followed myself from the chair into Mom's bedroom. I was yelling for the purse, and she was a half-step behind me, refusing to give me even a dime. I was filth, she accused. Kim was filth.

"And you're a lunatic. Listening to a jilted pothead girlfriend."

"How I ever survived among you people, all you slimy chunks of filth. I think of you or Kim or your father and I—" She shuddered. "I can't feel clean, even after five showers."

"The checkbook!"

She refused to cooperate, but her eyes betrayed her: she glanced toward a dresser at one end of the bedroom. With three steps I was across that tiny room. Atop the dresser were inside-out tube socks, wrinkled blouses, unopened stacks of mail, candy bar wrappers, empty cracker boxes, a yellow legal pad.

"Where is it?"

Again she refused, and when she lay a hand upon my shoulder, I stepped back. Then, with a wide sweep of the arm, I cut a swath through the debris atop her dresser. When Mom stumbled toward a pile of movie gossip magazines, I followed her—and, standing in a corner, I watched us: Mom grabbed the checkbook from beneath the magazines.

I twisted the checkbook from her hand.

"Stop this," she whined. "This is so silly. I mean, I know what it's like to have ambitions, to want to sing."

"Write a check for ten thousand. For cash."

"I wanted to sing. Nobody gave me any money."

"*Now.*"

"I'll tell your father what you're doing to Kim!"

"And while you're at it, tell him that you sit on the roof waiting for Islamists to carpet bomb your apartment with a thousand Korans."

"I'll call him right now."

On an impulse, I grabbed the yellow legal pad that had tumbled to the floor. I watched myself flip roughly through the pages as Mom muttered and wiped at her flush face. I began to read:

> *Everyone is so full of shit, I was the ONLY ONE who knew, the only one who took action! NOBODY listed—*

"It's 'listened', not 'listed.'"

"I should've choked that little bitch harder."

"Write the check or I'll choke *you* harder."

> *Nobody in our family HISTORY has my talent, nobody and I will never forgive you for not supporting it. For not standing up! For ME! You*

won't even do it when I'm died! I only wish I could
I could I could see your stupid face when you see
I'm dead but even God who can do miracles will
deny me that one gift.

Mom sat heavily upon the bed. I continued to read.

Jo   you   just   don't   care   and   you   don't
UNDERSTAND what MY pain is and how could
you even laugh at me, why is breast augmentation
stupid if you're pushing fifty???

"Stop it!" Mom pleaded, suddenly wonderfully pathetic and, I
sensed, wonderfully malleable. I ripped a check from the checkbook and made it out for ten grand in cash, then bellowed at her
to sign it front and back.

"I won't."

"You will."

She bawled, snot dripping to her lap. Finally, she rose from
the bed, flattened the check upon the dresser and signed front
and back. I immediately grabbed the check and announced we
were going to the bank.

"It's closed," she sniffled.

Hand upon her shoulder, I lightly pushed her out the bedroom to the front door. My observant self—amused, jaunty—
joined me as I walked Mother out.

"I lost my keys."

"I'm driving."

"I can't remember where my bank is."

I looked at the check: the Fourth 1st bank, which had
branches on nearly every street corner in the Midwest. After
shouldering Mom toward my car and into the passenger seat, I
drove around town for exactly eight minutes and spotted a
branch office. The bank cashed the check without a fuss—the
teller even greeting Mom in a familiar voice—and then we were
back at Mom's apartment.

"I should've choked both of you. No, all three of you."

I reached past her waist and pushed open the car door. Defi-
ant, she gripped the steering wheel, as if to barricade herself in-

side my car. I peeled her fingers from the wheel and, laughing, stiff-armed her out of the seat. She quite visibly bounced upon the parking lot's asphalt. Through the open car door, I waved goodbye at her with her yellow legal pad. She made one feeble lunge for the pad and I sped away.

Upon being shown the money—ten thousand dollars in immaculately stacked hundreds—Kim whooped and cheered. She thanked me, praised me, blessed me, and undressed me. The chilly shadow that sometimes haunted our private life was cast out, as if by a joyful exorcist.

Thirty-Three: Only Four Weeks

The ten thousand dollars were not merely an aphrodisiac for Kim; they were a musical catalyst. Freed of money worries, Pad's recording progress leapt forward and, in an outburst of high artistic spirits, Kim established a new regime of song-writing. She even began penning lyrics: in notebooks, on the back of sheet music, on grocery sacks and once—when no other material could be found—upon Mother Dear's yellow legal pad.

"Oh my God!" Kim gasped, mouth to hand, as she flipped through the pad. "Suicide notes!"

"No, suicide threats. Let's hope she writes one good enough to use." I took one and, upon clearing my throat, read several lines. It took me a moment to capture the shrew's intonation: throaty from too many cigarettes and feigned profundity. But after a few false starts I had Kim in mirthful tears.

"You're so awful!"

"She's more awful, and so is her syntax...I'll help her write the perfect note. Then she can kill herself with proper grammar."

"God, what a crazy fucking self-righteous *bitch*." Kim snapped shut the notepad. "But you know, that gave me an idea...just scream her suicide notes over some dark chords. Speaking of which..." She sat up straight on the couch, plugged in her guitar, and peeled off a slithering chain of diminished chords.

"Very ominous."

"All these new chords and melodies are tumbling out. I could add another five tunes to the record right now."

I swelled with a peculiar heart-felt blend of brotherly and loverly pride. "You're already thinking of the next record."

"Gotta finish this one first," she sighed.

The sessions indeed wrapped up quickly, just as Dad predicted and, with its recording in the can, Pad queued up with countless other bands, itching to defy the sobering odds against financial success. The band would labor mightily, the members promised one another: they would tour from mid summer to early autumn. He sweet-talked a retired colleague into renting out his RV. The colleague never quite grasped the nature of the RV's usage; Dad let the fellow befoggedly believe that Kim was part of a touring low brass group, entertaining seniors in Branson, Missouri and similarly sedate towns.

Dad seethed with such schemes. His concern for Kim's career was rather out of character but certainly admirable. I guessed that his larger motive, though, was to diminish Mom's contribution. Though he'd insisted that I secure that ten grand, he never again conceded its importance: once the money was in hand, he dismissed it.

"Kim, your career is barely fetal," Dad sagely noted one morning. He, Kim, and I were driving to Chicago to hear Vic Valmont's final mix of Pad's full length debut, tentatively entitled *Femme en Blanc*. "Foundation is everything. Pinch the pennies now and the dollars will follow. Maybe."

And look at that: he was smoking, a sure sign that he was in a holiday mood. "The money left over can be used for a bit more promotion. Some air time on college radio before your shows, for instance, and a few extra CD's for the show. Oh, we get the CD's at a discount."

I sat up so as to be heard over the air-conditioning's whistle. "So the band'll do everything?" I was skeptical. True, many rock bands daydream about luxurious tour buses, three-man crews, and even extra cash for guitar amp rigs and a celebratory party before the tour's first gig...but Dad's cost-cutting might be counterproductive. "Look, the tour's four weeks. They'll get tired. Plus, Billy's wife is going."

In the rear view mirror, Dad smugly smiled. "As you said: it's four weeks. Not four years."

I glanced at Kim, but her expression betrayed only ambivalence.

"Debt, it just *kills* bands. If you get out there and you kids keep your acts together and play at your best, you'll sell some records."

"God I hope so," Kim muttered.

"Each record you manage to sell or get downloaded, it's one step closer to paying back that goddamned advance."

"Get Billy's wife to be your crew," I suggested. "She's big enough."

"Yeah maybe she can drive too."

"No, she will not be driving," Dad instructed. "You will." He gazed upon me from the rear view mirror.

"—Me?"

Kim whirled about to face me, mouth half-open. "You will—?" Then, fearing she exhibited a peculiar enthusiasm for traveling with her brother, she turned back and reminded Dad that the tour lasted into September. "He'd miss his classes."

"Can you take the semester off?" His question was a demand.

I was caught flat-footed. Naturally, I savored the idea of traveling with Kim on tour, of hearing her perform, of witnessing her rising star. Still, after completing eighteen credits this past year, I looked forward to one day actually earning a degree.

"What's the big deal?" Dad huffed. "Richard's going to do it." He faced Kim. "Right?"

She nodded, stared out her passenger window.

"He's worked it out with his instructors, and—"

"He'll be a grad student," I noted, "and music major to boot. In *your* department. So he gets some slack."

"You get slack too. You're a faculty brat."

Dad fell silent and Kim, I realized too late, was angry at both Dad and me: angry at Dad for wanting me to drop out of school, and angry at me for not wanting to drop out. Fine, I thought. Let them fume. I resumed my semi-supine posture, smoking and hoping that, upon my return from the road, Franco would hire me back.

"Here's our exit," Dad announced a few hours later. We'd been crawling through I-94's very slow traffic from Chicago's south side to Adams. Muscle-bound 16 wheelers, prissy SUV's, sedans, pickups, even the occasional motorcyclist...we all lurched and stopped, burped and groaned as progress was often choked off to the tiniest drip. Finally, after nobody acknowledged Dad's left-blinker, he did as everyone else did: simply rudely cut in front of the first nervous female driver he saw.

The studio was, as Kim had told me, in a Halsted warehouse, five minutes north of Greektown. Dad double-parked in front of a drab brick building with atrocious painted-over green windows.

Vic Valmont greeted us at the top of the steps. He had an easy familiarity with Dad and Kim and—to my amusement— with me.

"So you're the man behind the lyrics!" Vic shook my hand with practiced warmth, then held open the scuffed wooden door. Inside was the studio, peaceful beneath the natural light of sky-lights. The live room was expansive, with a drum kit and digital piano waiting for some company. The hardwood floor clicked pleasingly as one walked.

"Hey that's a new one," Kim remarked, pausing by the piano. "Billy would've liked it."

"Nah," Vic laughed. "He's purist. He likes the wood a lot better."

"Wood," Kim noted, "is Billy's lingo for an acoustic piano."

"C'mon in here," Vic motioned to us. "You guys just missed Martin Anderman."

"Martin!?" Kim sang with regret. "We're *always* just missing him."

"But he's happy with the record. Really happy." Chivalric, he held open the door to the control room. Plainly at ease, Kim dropped into one of several comfy chairs while Dad took another. "Hey, you like all this stuff?" Vic asked me.

"Sure," I nodded, scanning the mixing boards and stacked decks of equipment.

"It's some good stuff," Vic suggested, fatherly pride warming his otherwise nasal voice. Like a tour guide, he placed a light hand upon my shoulder and discussed some of the equipment. "We can do a lot here. We can record and import and export all the major formats. Your WAV, your AIFF and so on."

"Very impressive."

"But we didn't choke on digits. There are zero after-effects on this record," Vic declared with charming solemnity.

"They record like a jazz band," Dad proudly noted. "Live, pretty much. No handholding or remedial cut-and-paste."

Vic gestured me toward a chair and, once I was seated, he began the playback. He winced at a very slight hiss, assuring us that it would be soon gone. Five seconds later, Kim's guitar leapt from the overhead speakers. The guitar established the giddy punk rhythm of "Aim for the Ditch." In a few bars, the riffs grew trebly and corkscrewed: Kim's antic surf riffing, now joined by Larry's beefy beats. Then Kim's vocal, rage tempered with amusement, filled the room.

> *You'll miss me*
> *And turn around and hurry back*
> *Afraid you're locked out.*
>
> *You'll fly past the first exit*
> *Won't bother with the second.*
>
> *Keep your foot on the gas*
> *And aim for the ditch.*

Kim, Vic, and Dad listened with eyes half-shut, torsos slightly swaying to the music's romp and roar. When Kim's barbed guitar wrapped itself around Billy's chiming piano chords, Vic leapt from the chair, sending it spinning backward against the deck.

Dad started and Kim laughed.

"*That's* how guitar is meant to be played!" Vic testified.

I looked upon Vic with new respect, even gratitude. He was beyond dispute devoted to this music, and the devotion was infectious: I too felt rising exaltation as the playback continued. At one point, as Kim's vocal sailed atop the chorus of "Blush", I covered my suddenly hot face...the grain and hue and muscle of Kim's voice was, miraculously, fully present on this recording.

Vic nodded violently. "*That's* what we wanted," he nearly shouted at me. "That resonance in her voice, that ring." He cheerfully complained about the maddening variety of microphones he'd gone through, laboring to capture Kim's voice. Forty minutes later, the playback concluded, Kim smiled at Dad and Vic—and glanced at me, her eyes chilled.

At that moment I sensed that posterity would judge some of these tunes to be classics. Most compelling were the contrasts:

casually perfect vocals atop spare, even desolate instrumentation. Or: full-bodied but melancholy vocals atop spitfire, hair-
raising riffs and big bright major chords. And Vic had whipped
the songs into a unified whole: overt references to numerous musical eras were largely absent, replaced by the occasional mid
60's pop radio touch—charming girl group harmonies or a shade
of Burt Bacharach-ish piano. Even Kim's guitar was on a short
leash: she managed to sneak in her Look-Ma-No-Hands show off
solos in only three or four tunes.

I faced Vic. "Good work...you delivered the goods."

"I'm honestly excited," Vic said, "to think of you taking these
songs on the road."

"Finally you're telling me the songs are good," Kim teased.

"So I get a little tense sometimes. But it pays off, and it'll pay
off on the road." He turned to me. "Don't you think?"

I did indeed think. "I'm very much looking forward to it."

There, my eyes told Kim. *I'm going.*

On the drive back home, Kim briefly probed my resolve and,
seeing I was serious, she wryly smiled. Striking her expert pose
of affable sibling irritation, she warned me against setting a beer
bottle on the band's battle-scarred equipment. As for Dad, well,
he was pleased because he'd enjoyed another strategic victory in
his battle to keep his prodigy daughter free from corporate debt.
If that meant among other things having the son miss a semester of classes, so be it.

Two weeks later, the record company sent Kim two copies of
the CD. The record release party? That was conspicuous by its
absence; Martin Anderman, label CEO, apologized for the lack of
a party in a handwritten note: We're pinching pennies, he scribbled, and saving each dime for you. Just as well, I reasoned...having to sit in the same room with Kim and Richard
would've deeply irritated me, though I fleetingly mused that Kim
would've enjoyed my rising irritation and embers of jealousy.

Lazing upon the bed, Kim and I had our own record release
party: cigarettes at the ready, we listened to the entire recording
with squinting ears and soaring spirits. Vic had done a wonderful job: the grit and grain of Kim's vocals were indeed faithfully
captured; the recording was clean and fresh, spontaneity enlivening each rich melody, with space between each instrument.

Kim occasionally narrated a vignette about the recording: a flubbed vocal on one tune, a quick rewrite of another, but she largely remained silent. We listened three times in a row, and as we finally drifted off—her head growing heavy upon my neck, her leg draped across my waist—the melodies burrowed into my brain, where they played and replayed through my sleep.

Thirty-Four: Showtime

"Eyes on the road, hands on the wheel," Dad reminded as I took control of the RV that crisp Sunday morning. "Trouble? Call me on the cell phone. No trouble? Call me on the cell phone."

"We'll call," Kim assured.

In the back, Richard busied himself like a rodent, pushing suitcases and guitar cases this way and that to make room. Larry, drum kit secured in the little trailer hitched to the RV, counseled patience to Richard. "Dude. Just like...*ooze* out in all directions."

"Huh?"

"Oooze. You'll find your own space here."

Dad, growing smaller as I pulled away, offered a final wave.

Kim whirled about in her passenger seat and demanded that Larry pass his joint forward.

"How'd you know?"

"Oooozzzzeeee," Kim cheerfully mocked.

Behind us, staying a prudent fifty feet behind on the highway, were Billy and his wife. Everyone understood that Billy's wife was coming along to keep her a peevish eye on her husband. Curiously, I'd met her only once and never got to know her, as she never rode in the RV and typically insisted that Billy get to sleep immediately after the shows. Kim whispered that Mrs. Billy was unhappy about the tour, brief as it was.

"She thinks," Kim explained in a low whisper, "that he wants to get into my pants."

Pad's first gig was in Hamtramck, an archetypal working class town near Detroit. The hosting venue: Small's, allegedly an authentically hip place that drew both local and regional music fans. The record company had congratulated Dad the Manager on landing the gig, though as a veteran of hustling more highbrow stuff, he knew how to work the phones: persist.

After parking the RV a block away and ambling inside, I was slightly disappointed. Decent room on the stage, but the place was smaller than I'd allowed my self to imagine; too much of the expanse was, I noted, hogged by three pool tables. Still, the manager was warm, immediately welcoming Kim and the rest of us. His face was lined with night-shift fatigue though his voice was crisp and resonant. He invited us to check out the sound system, which Billy deemed as surprisingly good.

"Have a warm up," the manager invited. "The sound tech's ready to go."

Indeed: a balding fellow, big belly peaking beyond the edge of his black tee-shirt, motioned the band that he was ready. The group glanced at once another, shrugged, and returned in fifteen minutes.

I eased onto a barstool. Immediately behind me, the bartender purposefully cleaned his bartop with oil soap while, ten feet from my stool, another employee scrubbed at a stubborn spot upon the wood floor. Ammonia soon wafted toward me, setting my nostrils aflutter.

After a brief showdown with an uncooperative amp, Pad coasted at an amiable pace through "Blush" and "Unsilent Partner," Kim's bobbing head riding atop Larry's drumming. Billy blew several bars with his sax, then, as the band continued, he departed the stage to consult with the sound tech. Thirty seconds later, Kim's guitar was brighter and sharper and—thankfully—Richard's bass was ratcheted down. After a cheery "Bathrobe Yoga", Kim was feeling her oats. She shooed the others to sit down and called for the tech to kill the amplification.

Grinning as all eyes converged upon her, Kim shook the mothballs off "I Fall to Pieces." As she hit the chorus, her voice was clear and mournful, like a late night October wind.

The manager, sipping iced tea, did a double-take. As Kim brought the tune home to a ringing conclusion, the manager joined Larry and me. "She can really sing," he half-whispered.

After the sound check, Kim went for a solitary half-hour walk, establishing a pattern that lasted throughout our tour. When she returned, face freshened and nerves becalmed, she merely nodded at us that it was time to go. We found our hotel, a dreary yellow and white discount affair one minute off I-94. Expertly feigning sibling irritation, Kim and I checked into our room; Kim warned me against kidnapping the TV remote even as Richard—eyes sad like a loathsome puppy's—wistfully studied Kim. Richard and Larry would bunk together, and Billy and Mrs. Billy of course took their own room. Establishing another tour-long ritual, Billy knocked upon my door around five, inviting me to accompany him to Small's, where he would set up.

I agreed, though wondered why Larry didn't accompany us: his drums, after all, were by far the most unpleasant task.

"He's getting stoned with Richard," Billy shrugged. "Besides, it's easy. We'll set them up in ten minutes."

Back at the hotel by seven, I flipped pointlessly through the cable TV channels until eight as Kim soaked in the steaming bathroom. Then with the mock air of a high school chaperone, I knocked upon each of the band members' hotel doors, announcing that show time was nigh. They responded as I hoped, nervous energy and nervous smiles. We arrived at Small's at 8:30. Huddled in the parking lot beside the RV, we passed around a communal menthol cigarette, and even Mrs. Billy—usually marked by cool reserve—cracked a few jokes.

We entered through the back door, nodding at the manager and bartender, who were sneaking a smoke. "Good crowd out there," somebody called through cupped hands. "But the first band sucked." To my relief, the turnout was fine: the bar was crowded, and most of the tables were claimed. The first band's equipment was gone and Pad plugged in quickly. I took an abandoned chair at the back and studied the darkened stage...there was Larry, announcing the impending performance with a drum roll. About half the crowd kept chatting; the other half turned their eyes to the bandstand.

Larry clacked out one-two-three and Kim, emerging from the shadows beside Larry, cut a figure both dashing and shambling: baggy black work slacks fit for a mechanic, and a retro bowling shirt. Larry really put the boot into the drums, laying out the beat for "Share My Vice". Richard joined, bass in tune, the snappy ascending four-figure riff keeping respectable pace.

And Kim, her shirt's flames comically garish in the lights, sang atop the bass-and-drums rumble:

> *Share my bed?*
> *Share my vice!*
> *Watch me first,*
> *Watch my blood boil bright red...*

With that, Kim grabbed both guitar and audience by the throat with that dive-bomber guitar line, plummeting as if to smash against the ground, then pulling upward ...Ah yes, an attention-getter to be sure.

My emotions soared at the tune's half-way mark: the observers would, I could see, soon be revelers. Kim sensed it too: she smiled broadly, with not a hint of smugness...just an honest joy to play for people who listen.

> *...boils bright red,*
> *...boils*
> *...bright*
> *...boils bright red*

She pushed those last three syllables—a hooky Cm-Fm-D—nearly through the roof, and the indifferent frat boys beside me squinted their ears. Even the billiard hustlers paused, cue sticks at ease, to peer from the back of the room. And then my beloved peeled off a solo, a thirty-second salvo of high spirits and bracing ideas. Its sheer authority flummoxed the jabbering frat boys.

"That chick sings and plays?" one Theta Chi marveled, beer foam upon his chin. "Plays and sings *like that?*"

"Like that," I spontaneously laughed.

"Fuck yeah," another grinned at me. He raised his beer, which was, I deduced, the ultimate salute.

The time was ripe, I guessed, to hustle the pile of CD's I'd brought in. Three quarters of the way through the show, Pad sashayed into "Blush." About a dozen folks cheered at the chiming chords: as we'd hoped, the local college station had played "Blush" several times through the week, and the tune's hooks had sunk in deeply. The band was impressively relaxed, confident in the hundreds of rehearsal hours and, more importantly, confident in their leader's voice and chops. Kim's face was flush and her shirt soaked—the stage was much hotter, I belatedly realized, than one would've guessed. Larry's hair was a mop of wet curlicues but he smiled nonstop, his big shiny forearms making mincemeat of his drum kit. As always, Billy was self-effacing: almost motionless on the stage and half-obscured behind Kim, he never overplayed, never wore out his welcome on solos...indeed, as with Kim's playing, his sheer melodicism left one wanting more.

Richard? I don't recall much, save his occasional wide-eyed glances at his left hand, as if alarmed that he had just muffed a note.

I sold about thirty CD's and forty Pad tees (bright purple script with bright green and blue daisies) that night. A very successful night, or so I figured. I had little against which to gauge it. The crowd—or at least most of it—paid strong attention, and "Blush" got several folks dancing up front, where a small knot of fans soon swelled into a larger knot. The crowd stood mere feet from Kim and their eyes roved freely over her. I too burned to join the milling oglers...ah, to join the hormonally-buzzing group and know that I, only I, would be with her that night.

But I remained a good soldier attached to my detail: the little table in the back with Pad merchandise. A few times, one of the bouncers approached my little table and nodded a greeting. By appearances, he was AWOL from the WWF: a preposterously mighty fellow, at least six feet and a half, with a back as broad as Ohio.

As Pad ripped through its final song, a souped-up surf-metal instrumental called "Menthol", the bouncer grew alert: a scrum of fans, heads bobbing and fists thrusting, pressed against the stage. He leaned closer to me to be heard over the racket and whoops. "It's cool. Friendly vibe tonight." I nodded in agreement, noting the meaty scar above his left eyebrow.

We all stayed around for a round of drinks. A handful of fans, mostly males but a scattering of gals too, stopped by congratulate the band.

"Yeah that song, it's been all over the radio," one girl en-thused. She was very drunk yet seemed no older than 16, with pimple cream smeared atop her make-up.

"I hope it stays there," Kim smiled through her cigarette smoke. She looked spent, and occasionally reached around to tug at the back of her damp shirt, which still clung to her back.

A hulking guy, perhaps a future Detroit Lion, nearly up-ended the table when he merely brushed against it. "Really good band," he said with near combativeness. His companions, as di-minutive as he was large, agreed. "Really good band," they duti-fully repeated.

Richard, the poor unknowing fool, had incorrectly hoped that out here on the road, his romance with Kim might be re-vived...as Kim sat sipping her beer and nodding thanks to the well-wishers, he took a chair beside her and affected an air of romantic familiarity. She pretended not to notice his intent, even smiling with—dare I say it?—a sister's asexual good cheer when he patted her on the back for a job well done. When he did it again, she oh-so-subtly shifted away from him.

Mrs. Billy frowned as a fresh gaggle of gals loitered at the next table. "Well..." she announced, rising from her chair. "Ann Arbor tomorrow, right?"

"Pretty good, huh?" she whispered happily.

"Very." I began to tell her how lovely she looked in that bar tonight, how I was thrilled by the many pairs of eyes that roved over this young woman who, out of nowhere, sang and played like nobody else. She turned off the table lamp between the two beds and pulled back the sheets for us. "You were saying?" Then, grinning at her own vanity and my impatience, she shimmied out of her two-dollar bikini briefs.

And so the tour's essential contours emerged: hours on the Midwest's flat littered freeways, soporific stops for increasingly distasteful fast food (I lost ten pounds on the tour, as I found road food inedible near the end), and afternoon visits with the venue in question. Several times, as Kim napped, I sought out a storefront laundry (motel laundromats, bleak and damp, depress me). As Kim's and my clothing soaked, spun, and dried, I'd lean lazily against the storefront and smoke. Midwest August was now boiling, and the sidewalks were aflame with the afternoon sun's reds and golds.

In the early evenings came the set-up, performed always and only by Billy and me. Richard, pained by Kim's rejection, was haughtily anti-social, amusing himself with expensive cell phone calls to friends back home and an unaccountable absorption in *Rolling Stone*'s inane fashion spreads and boilerplate features about illiterate rappers and "politically-engaged" rockers. After set-up, more time-killing...I got in a good amount of reading at bookstores, stoking myself upon coffee and news magazines. I also clipped any of the irregular and frustratingly brief notices about the "upcoming band, Pad" appearing at that evening's club. Then, of course, I merchandised through the show, cash rolled into my wallet, and a half hour or more of sitting around to visit with whoever wished to say hello. Typically, the evening featured a local opening act: usually, some anonymous heavy rock outfit, though one pleasant night I enjoyed a gifted folksy group, led by (how wonderful!) a brother and sister. Their jaunty strumming and picking were a refreshing change from the oafish opening acts.

The shows sagged at mid-tour. In East Lansing, allergies dampened Kim's voice, and she took to whiskey and cough syrup. The booze and pharmacy speed worked at odds with one another, though by the end of the show she gained her bearings and daz-zled the crowd with a spontaneous cover of Hank Williams's "Lovesick Blues". As the tune's chords jangled and rolled, she kept time with a slap upon the guitar's body and a thumb-plucked bass line. Her voice finally broke free and she nailed both the tune's soaring yodels and plummeting baritone growls. The crowd cheered lustily, and somebody bought beers for us.

A red-faced celebrant trotted to my table, on which sat the stack of CD's. He grabbed one and tried to read the song list in the dim light.

"Does this have that tune she just did? That lovesick thing?"

"No. But it has twelve other songs just as good."

"I doubt it." He tossed the CD back upon my table.

The string of erratic performances raised our hackles a bit, but in the end we were sustained by Larry's joviality and Billy's calmness. It was Richard, predictably, who provided the tour's only soap opera outtake. Indeed, I now witnessed just how narrow his relationship with Kim—with the entire band, really—had grown: he was little more than an employee, nodding curtly at my greetings as well as at Kim's directives. One night, inspired by gin and a fan's stinking joint, he threatened to jump ship in Fort Wayne. When Kim merely raised her eyebrows at him, he maintained his melodramatic posture, chin outthrust.

Then he abruptly muttered "Yeah whatever" and retreated to his room.

The final gig was in Chicago's yuppie-infested Wicker Park. Dad phoned in the day before, exclaiming that Pad's buzz was now a roar, and the gig was at Donel's, an allegedly upscale establishment.

"Finally, we've arrived," Billy beamed.

Mrs. Billy tried and failed to smile.

And more good news: the day before the gig, a freelancer writing for the Chicago *Tribune* reached Kim for an interview via cell phone. Feet upon the dashboard, Kim answered several softball questions about influences, ambitions for the band, and so forth. Did she have, the writer wondered, advice for aspiring guitarists? Yes she did: "Do *not* improvise on scales. Improvise on melody." Then, getting whimsical, she asked the writer to hold on and tossed the cell phone over her shoulder to Larry, who chatted amiably about the weather, his favorite colas, and his interest in computers—in short, everything but music. "I just always wanted to do that," he later laughed. "Be a pain in the ass rock star."

Around six that evening, Pad ran through some tunes as the sound technician, skinny and earnest, kibitzed with Billy about the latter's ordeals on the road: broken equipment, missing equipment, just plain dumb equipment.

Donel's was indeed a step up: bright oak wood floor, tables and chairs in good repair, and even a kitchen that offered a self-consciously "working class" menu with enormous burgers and, for the chronic dieter, twelve dollar salads topped with a few shrimp. Still, I was pleased. The place was well maintained and orderly. The assistant manager, a fetching Swede with the ghost of an accent, had warmly greeted us as soon as we poked in our heads and called hello.

"Do you speak Gaelic?" I asked her as the band tuned up.

"Should I?" she smiled.

"Sure. I mean, the name of your establishment and all."

She happily shrugged and revealed that she spoke three languages but not Irish.

From the bandstand, Kim declared her satisfaction: "We've got every note under our fingers, *completely* under our fingers," she harrumphed. And she was right. Even Richard pegged every note and key change. I hailed the band to a back table and ordered a pitcher, then invited the comely Swede and somber sound tech to join us.

"Guess what I heard on XRT today?" the tech quizzed.

"The President's been arrested?" Larry hoped.

"I heard 'Blush'. And it sounded *good*."

"Actual commercial radio, goddamn!" Kim enthused. She downed her beer in three gulps and waved at me to refill her glass. "First Jesus died for my brother's sins, and now we're on commercial radio. Will miracles never cease?"

"Ask that after we get a royalty check." I stood and pulled my jeans pockets inside out; pennies and lint fell to the floor.

"No more beer?" Billy mock whined.

I smiled and pulled a ten from my shirt pocket, and more beer was on the way. Just as I refilled everyone's glass, Kim's eyes widened as someone approached the table. The fellow nodded and, after a moment's hesitation, sat down.

"Told you I'd make it," he said, a shade sheepish.

"Everybody," Kim announced, "meet Martin Anderman, CEO of Rust Belt records."

Martin dressed like a grease monkey or assembly line zombie: drab blue work pants and sagging tee-shirt. He nodded courteously at everyone and, as Kim introduced me, Martin extended his hand. "So you're the second half of rock's finest songwriting team."

"I'm the *first* half."

"—Sorry?"

"Just kidding," I laughed, accepting his handshake. "By the time Kim's done chopping up my lyrics, I'm just glad to be here."

"And we're glad you're here, Martin," Kim sang. "I was hoping you could make it."

Martin slouched heavily in his creaking chair and, beer in hand, said he wouldn't miss the gig for the world. He craned his head about slowly, remarking that he hadn't been in Donel's since spring. He bummed a cigarette from me and, as if the nicotine defogged his brain, his eyes widened. "Great news, friends. 'Blush' is getting airplay on KCRW and KROQ."

"That wouldn't be *world famous* KROQ?" Larry loudly asked.

"With broadcasts live from Hollywood." His news electrified Kim and Larry, who engaged in a round robin of high-fives and cheerfully raised middle fingers. He smiled at their antics as the sound tech earnestly informed me that KROQ was the foremost taste-making station in Southern California.

"I just love giving good news," Martin sighed, his longish legs reaching halfway beneath the round table. "I mean, KROQ is corporate, but good corporate."

"The *best* corporate!" Kim insisted.

Martin faced me. "Can I bum another smoke?"

He bummed smokes and visited for another forty-five minutes, enjoying the giddy chatter of Larry and Kim. He mostly listened, adding on occasion that he'd heard a given gig had gone just as well as Larry and Kim reported. Finally, with palpable regret, he rose from the table—pausing to drain the last hint of moisture from his glass—and noted he was late for a business meeting.

"So how *is* business?" Kim queried.

"Always a struggle." Then, with another glance at his watch, he sat back down. "*Always.* More stations are manned by robots, and I mean literal robots. Not just 'radio personalities' with lobotomies and idiot PD's. And most music is manufactured for fourteen year old boys. Just like movies. Same demographic: dumb and dumber. Et cetera et cetera et cetera" He shrugged, smiled. "That's my view, anyway. But we're hanging tough and might get some investor money next year..." He pronounced "investor money" with a blend of hope and skepticism. "What do you guys think about maybe, in a year or so, of having your gigs recorded and available ten minutes later for downloading to your MP3 player?"

"You *fucker!*" Kim beamed.

"I'm not saying it'll happen for sure, but if we get some out-side money..." Martin smiled amiably at Kim, his eyes dragging ever so slightly away from her to glance at me. "Money is good, but investors...they have their own demands. Mostly stupid de-mands."

Kim, impatient with Martin's somber musings, clucked and shook her finger. "Really, Martin. Rev up the I-Pod right now. We're going to play one for the ages tonight."

He winked at Kim. "I know you will."

I discretely refilled Martin's beer glass and noted that, musi-cally speaking, Kim's only fault was that she was never wrong.

"So I've learned." Martin drained his suds and said he really did have to get moving. "But see ya tonight."

Martin never did make it back.

As we were setting up, a phone call from his wife informed us that Martin's back—injured during a motorcycle accident two years ago—had failed him as he reached to the floor for his shoes. He was abjectly apologetic, it seemed, and sent an out-sized bouquet of fresh cut flowers over to Kim. She shrugged with only a shade of disappointment and placed the flowers atop her amp.

That night, the band peaked. Everyone, even moping Rich-ard, was inspired by Martin's talk of KROQ and KCRW and I-Pods. And sweet icing upon that evening's cake was the crowd: dense and muggy with taste-makers and wanna-be taste-makers. I guestimated the crowd at about three-hundred. Tell-ingly, the musical grapevine, a tangle both sweet and sour, had lured several hotshot Chicago musicians to the gig.

Kim and I stood offstage behind a tattered black velvet stage curtain. "Hey look, that's Julian Bender," she enthused.

"Lucky him." Mr. Bender's band, a roots-rock revival outfit, had just signed with Utmost and was feted in the local music press. "Since he's here, show him how to play and sing."

And she did.

A mere minute into "Bathroom Yoga", the band jelled: Larry's drums crisp, Billy's keys bright, and Kim's guitar muscu-lar. Richard, astutely, simply kept his bass lines round and otherwise stayed out of the way. And the band was upon a cleaver's edge of fatigue and excitement, and therefore both loose and attentive. Kim's vocal, with its ebullience and grain, brought an outburst of applause and whoops. She grinned and chatted with the crowd, which shouted back like a tent revival congregation.

"You're so talkative already," she laughed. "Must be all that beer." And with a quick tug upon her bowling shirt's collar, she cued Larry, who clacked out *one-two-three* with his drum sticks and leapt into "Aim for the Ditch." Inspired, Billy spontaneously added squawking, nearly free-jazz saxophone at the bridge.

Taking up Billy's friendly challenge to show off, Kim stretched out her guitar break on "Unsilent Partner". Her galloping notes became a wash of shimmering minor chords—-then silence. The audience whooped, demanding more, and she obliged with Middle Eastern chord voicings out of which snaked lines writhed and spat.

To use the vernacular: the crowd went fucking nuts.

"*Now* can we have beer money?" she laughed. Change and wadded dollar bills briefly showered the bandstand.

Over the last four weeks, Pad had developed its show-biz shtick. After a two minute smoke, during which Billy offered an amusing Liberace imitation, Kim grabbed her battered acoustic and sprinted through Beethoven's *Allegretto* from Sonata 17, tossing in a couple parodic heavy metal chords. The crowd, wet with beer and sweat, demanded a reprise of that little miracle.

"That's too easy," Kim winked. "Just gimme a second..."

The crowd shushed itself as she tuned down the bottom E to D. Then, showing off some ace contrapuntal picking, she limned a sliver of Bach's *English Suite.*

Julian Bender ran both hands through his expensively tousled hair. "She's a *monster*," he declared to three hangers-on.

On that wonderful evening, the crowd called back Pad back thrice and the final tune was "Looks Like a Tommy". Red-faced Larry huffed and Richard laid out at as Kim and Billy improvised a coda of Godzilla power chords. I imagined Japanese cars and busses crushed beneath monstrous reptilian feet...I dove into the fray. The crowd surged forward and back, forward and back. The music's roar became a perfect wave, and we were all engulfed: selfless, weightless, agog.

We loitered beyond closing time that evening, the manager toasting us several times too frequently. Fans clustered about to anoint Pad's performance the best of the summer, and I sold forty or so CD's. Kim dutifully autographed many of them and, her mood drunkenly expansive, she demanded that even Richard immortalize the CD's with his signature. Six or seven fans queried me about the inspiration for my lyrics.

"Stupid people, yuppies, suburbia, Marxist professors and—"

A celebratory roar rose over my answer: yet another pitcher of beer, its foamy head the very icon of revelry, was placed upon our table. Mrs. Billy, uncharacteristically free-spirited, refilled our glasses then planted a big sisterly kiss upon Kim's forehead. Soon we were far too drunk to even consider driving, a fact that even Larry conceded, so the manager called in two cabs for us.

Kim slept past noon. My skull was brittle, and I slowly extracted my torso from Kim's right arm and leg, both of which were draped across me. After a triage trio of cigarettes, I made coffee in our room's asthmatic mini-brewer. Kim drank two cups, her eyelids swollen with fatigue and booze, then peaceably fell back asleep. I moved slowly from the bed to the hotel lobby, my usually hardy spirits slapped down by my hangover. For a few minutes, I even flirted with existential despair, my stomach raw and my brain boiled. I plucked the morning paper from a blue metal vender. And here it was, a review of last night's show.

The critic, who'd earlier interviewed Kim via phone, praised her even as he waxed merely tepid about the band as a whole:

> *Pad arrived with some hype as the latest band produced by Vic Valmont, a key force behind the revived indie scene. The band's new CD, "Femme en Blanc", boasts a very live sound and plenty of melodic firepower. The evening's performance demonstrated that Pad's hype is only partially misleading. The power and nuance of Kim Edwards's vocals are beyond dispute, and her voice was a three-dimensional physical presence on "Blush" and "Lies With Him." Fortunately, unlike*

many vocal powerhouses, she has the good sense to not oversing. Additionally, she is a legitimate guitar prodigy, albeit an eccentric one who blends surf and rockabilly with hypertensive punk chords.

However, she constantly overpowers her band. The other band members, though competent, could sometimes do little but struggle to keep up. In the end, they didn't try, as Ms. Edwards offered for no discernable reason two imposing renditions of Beethoven snippets. Later, she left her band in her wake with a speed metal "Looks Like a Tommy", which she concluded in a brief raging shriek that made amplification redundant. More than one listener wondered aloud how many lungs the rather diminutive Ms. Edwards really has. Ms. Edwards' promise is indisputable; but her efforts to develop this promise in the company of her current bandmates is problematic.

So much for rock "journalism": the writer—a mid-thirtyish fellow whom I'd spied nursing a light beer and heavy acne—muffed the band's song titles and confused Beethoven for Bach. Worse, he dismissed Billy's talents. Indeed, Billy was a font of musical acumen throughout the tour, his sax, keys, and guitar adding bright emphasis and heavy punch, always when needed and never when not. Without Billy, Pad would've been immediately lost. A few days later, after I shared the clipping with her, Kim teased that I was most angry about a glaring omission: my lyrics. I conceded the point only generally, noting that my lyrics were rarely mentioned anyway.

"But when they are mentioned, well, the mention is pretty good. Witty and cruel." Her smile was oblique. "And that's *you*."

I stretched out along the double beds we'd pushed together, and rested my face upon her warm belly. "You should write your own lyrics anyway. I mean, you're chopping mine up quite a bit."

"Chopping?" she challenged, belly tensing.

"Okay. Revising."

Eyes half-closed, she traced a curlicue line along my fore-head. "For being so smart, you're such a dense dumbass...I mean, you're my *muse*."

Thirty-Five: Were There a God

I dropped Larry off at his apartment and, ignoring my own fatigue, suggested we unload his drum kit immediately. He sighed, tired but willing, and we sloppily unloaded his kit without inflicting serious damage, even as the night sky clouded to form a dour canopy. Then I dropped off Richard at his father's home. He'd been nearly silent the last three or four days, though as she stepped off the RV runner board onto his father's driveway, he did rally a bit.

"Good times," he managed. "Let's do it again soon."

"We will," I lied.

He waved as I pulled away and Kim sighed with both relief and melancholy. "His staying in the band is...it's probably not a good idea."

The RV hummed along the road to Dad's place, and the familiar roads, surprisingly, lifted my spirits.

"Hey look." Kim pointed at the front picture window as I eased the RV into the driveway. "He's waiting up."

There he was, Mr. Manager, parting the curtains to wave at us. Then he was out the front door to greet us.

"I was getting kind of worried," he said, bear-hugging Kim and, at the same time, slapping me upon the back. "C'mon in. I've got some pizza and some beer." He released Kim and winked at me. "You're road-tested now. You can probably drink more than me."

"A beer sounds good," I agreed, fibbing that I'd had less than sixteen ounces of alcohol during the tour.

Kim concurred, noting that I was a model designated driver.

"But now I'm the designated drinker."

Though all three of us were tired, we yakked vigorously at the kitchen table. Kim grew animated, her narrative already downplaying the frequent tedium of travel. "I want to do it again already!"

Mr. Manager grinned, soaking in all the details. "You've got three gigs in a couple weeks at the NiteSpot. You guys made the local paper a while back. On the 'fridge? The clippings are up there. Oh and there's some interest in Boston and Toronto."

I rose to read the clipping and retrieve another beer. "The clipping's not here."

"Must've meant to put it there..." Dad said, a gaping yawn distorting his face. "So anyway. No trouble getting paid?"

"No, surprisingly enough. Well, the guy in Indy pretended to be confused about the money, but he eventually came through." Draining the beer, I shrugged and—recalling Billy's travel advice to Richard—*oozed* back into my chair. "All the checks and money, all the receipts, they're all in the RV." I added that I'd sold about maybe two-hundred CD's. "We pretty much broke even. Maybe even made a little. I don't know yet."

Dad waved away my concern. "You're all back in one piece, that's what counts. And you're a real band." He rubbed almost violently at his eyes. "Forgive me. I've been up since six this morning."

Kim cleared her throat. "Probably time for us to shove off too." I recognized the subtle unease in her voice, a symptom of her almost constant anxiety of being outed from our maximally private closet.

"Stay here tonight," Dad insisted. "We can all have breakfast tomorrow." His inflection of "all" caught me ear. "Barbara's getting back into town tomorrow," he quickly added.

"She's been gone?" Kim lightly asked.

"Since Thursday. Brass clinic in Kalamazoo. Hey, she wanted to catch you guys, but the schedules didn't match." He rose, told us again how happy he was that we were back safe, and shuffled to bed.

Kim and I waited until Dad was safely upstairs, his bedroom door closed. Then she tossed me a cigarette and I got us two more beers. Kim mildly protested, claiming that she was too tired to drink, but I laughed at her protestations, claiming that I was too tired to smoke but wouldn't dare think of letting her smoke alone.

She leaned forward to accept my light. "How very gallant. And you wouldn't dare let me sleep alone either, would you?"

I pursed my lips in mock offense. "Under your father's roof?"

"Mmm hmm." She drained her beer in four long swigs.

"You're lookin' at me funny." My heart's sleepy pulse was instantly roused.

Already she was out of her chair and leaning over me, her mouth upon my neck and her hands squeezing my shoulders. Flipping off the lights, we scurried silently downstairs and felt our way in the darkness to the music room and then down the steps to the basement. Our recklessness emboldened Kim. She removed the cushions from an orphaned couch and, with a mad titter, lobbed them to me.

We awoke at the first hint of dawn, Kim's right leg across my stomach, her face against my chest. I prodded her awake with great difficulty but, when finally awake, she surprised me by grinning and kissing me with her hands upon my crotch. Now, this was all wonderful—my beloved so *bold!*—but circumstances demanded discretion. She reluctantly acceded and went upstairs to her old bedroom for a few more hours of sleep. I replaced the cushions and found comfort in a recliner chair in the music room.

Morning stretched lazily into early afternoon. Kim had been up for some time...she sat at the kitchen table, smoking and drinking coffee.

"Where's Dad?"

"He's been up for a while, very busy. Take a look outside."

I opened the front door: Dad had disgorged the RV. Upon the porch sat our suitcases, along with Kim's guitar cases.

"I guess," Kim said, "that Dad wanted that RV back right away." She added that Barbara had indeed arrived that morning: her car was parked on the curb.

I nodded, stepped outside to search through our belongings. Specifically, I flipped open the briefcase by which I'd scrupulously organized our tour's paperwork: the itinerary; the necessary phone calls; the ledgers; the checkbooks; the gig money and petty cash. All but the petty cash remained, and it was truly petty: sixty-one dollars in threadbare fives and singles.

Kim now stood behind me, stretching lazily in the sun.

"Ready to go?"

"Don't want to wait for—"

"No."

She regarded me for a few seconds then lazily stretched again. "Whatever."

We slept for the best part of three days, rising only to slap together peanut butter sandwiches, to shower, and of course to enjoy our privacy. I marveled at Kim's blooming insouciance. Before the tour, she'd maintained the habits of one who fears surveillance: killing the lights, drawing the shades and the curtains, donning pajamas or tee-shirts that reached her knees. But now, post-tour, she became a cheeky libertine. On our first morning back home, she lay starkly nude upon our bed, her pale belly and limbs in sharp contrast to the rich blue quilt beneath her. Her fears no longer darkened our pillow talk; she talked of the future not with trepidation but with buoyancy.

And to my amazement, Kim grew interested in Beethoven, Liszt, even Wagner. We spent all of Sunday afternoon downstairs, inspired by these colossi—and by a pint of sipping whiskey.

"So *very* good," she whispered as the 5th movement of "Pastorale" inflamed her.

Were there a God to thank I would pray:

> *Heavenly Father who*
> *gives all life,*
> *thank you for*
> *This life:*
> *Rest and drink and*
> *Bed with sister.*
> *My kingdom has come*
> *My will has been done and*
> *I bless You.*

Thirty-Six: "So just drop out."

After three days in Erotopia, I understood the lotus eaters, who peaceably lazed away all their lives. Kim my lotus...smelling of shampoo and cigarettes, her ready laugh still hoarse from the tour.

Still, ordinary life waited impatiently outside. The fall semester was two weeks old, and I groaned to ponder the maddening red tape that lay before me.

"So just drop out," Kim joked. "Like me. Forever."

"I'll drop out as soon as I graduate," I said, battling a recalcitrant shoe lace. "The journalism lark I did last semester—"

"You like it?"

"Yeah, at least as I practiced it. You know, for my own amusement."

"Bah humbug. I guess that means I have to get an actual job until, you know, until stardom and big bucks arrive at the door."

"Sooner than you think," I hoped.

The drive to campus was a pleasure: The sky was flawless September blue, clear and undistorted by humidity. I wondered if the newspaper gang had all returned. My own summer, busy with All Matters Kim, had no room for my campus acquaintances. I parked in the faculty lot, knowing that I would merely throw away any campus ticket, and made my way to the Registrar's office.

The Registrar's office—stale, with a small waiting area beyond which were messy desks and mirthless clerks—was empty. Still, I had to lean heavily against the ancient counter and clear my throat several times before anyone even looked up.

One matronly soul, her fat ankles bulging atop her gray flats, lumbered toward me. Her laborious steps fatigued me. My yawn irritated her, as she made a point of walking even more slowly.

Finally, with visible distaste, she asked if she could help me.

"Yes, I'm needing to register for the fall session."

A single eyebrow raised upon her fleshy face.

"I know it's late, but—" I grinned, leaning forward. "My father, Dr. Edwards? He's made arrangements with, you know, whoever it is that he made arrangements with."

"It's too late to register."

"On paper it is, I know. But Dr. Edwards has—"

She turned away and disappeared around a dreary gray corner. About fifteen minutes later, she returned.

"I've double-checked on this matter," she said, "and I'm sorry, but you cannot register."

"But I—"

"The final day was last Friday, and that was for exceptional cases only." She paused to awkwardly scratch at her back. "See?" She handed me a pamphlet. "Page two defines what we mean by exceptional cases."

"Dr. Edwards, of the music department? He's set something up for me."

"No, I'm afraid he hasn't. If you want to talk to Dr. Rowlands, you may. He's the Registrar."

Patience now dented, I nonetheless smiled agreeably. "Yes, I'd appreciate that."

"He's out of town until Thursday. I mean Friday."

"And that would put me even further back."

"That's correct."

"I don't see how that will help me."

"I don't either."

"Thank you," I managed, turning upon a squeaking heel. What the hell...Dad the Manager had certainly mismanaged this one. I hurried across campus to the performing arts center, which housed his office. He was out, and I left a handwritten note taped to his door. I walked aimlessly through hallways for several minutes, listening to the squawking of horns and stumbling of pianos in the practice rooms. Restless, I left the building and had a few cigarettes in the deserted courtyard, which featured a kitschy bust of Bach.

On a whim, I stopped by the newspaper office to inquire about Karen and Tommy. The office was quiet; a single student sat in the semi-dark, the ghostly glare of a computer screen upon his face.

"Is Karen around?"

Eyes lingering upon the screen, he asked, "Which Karen?"

"Karen the editor."

"I'm the editor. Jason Weinstock."

"Really?"

"But I know who you mean. She's not here anymore."

"No kidding. What about Tommy? The sportswriter?"

Jason's fingers tapped absently at his keyboard. "I think he flunked out."

I smiled.

"But Karen, she did way better than flunk out. She moved up. Yeah, that summer internship in New York? It went great and she made some contacts and she's working with some indie papers and in graduate school too."

I nodded somewhat wanly.

"Can't blame her for getting out of nowhere, can you?" he smiled, fingers still poised upon the computer keys.

"No."

"Listen, sometimes she e-mails some people here. Give me your name."

I did.

He took new interest in me, spinning about in his chair to face me. "Jeff Edwards? No kidding. It's funny, I worked here all last year but never ran into you." He rose and firmly shook my hand. "Yeah, you were one of her better writers."

"Thanks."

Jason leaned heavily into his chair and pulled one crossed leg atop another, like a Yoga student. "Wanna write for us again? I could really use you."

I explained to him my bureaucratic difficulties.

"Man, that's too bad," he sympathized. "You really helped her out with that Martino hatchet job."

I nodded, not quite sure of Jason's meaning. "How did I help her?"

"I guess Karen's advisor—I mean, her new advisor at her new school, you know? —He loved the entire concept, her setting you up as whoever she did."

"Mencken."

"Yeah that guy. But you know," Jason lowered his voice, "Mencken had a problem with Jews. Do you?"

"None today."

"Ha, you *are* funny. No, yeah, Karen's advisor loved the concept and she's doing the same thing in New York. Karen, I mean."

"Which is?"

"Scouting *talent*, man. That's what moves you up in the business. Scouting and nurturing the talent, you know, building a stable. I mean, that's her thing. She wants to edit one of the prestige news magazines, and that's what it takes."

"I suppose so."

Jason lightly tapped a palm with a fist. "Too bad you can't enroll. I could really use you. That piece about Martino!" He cackled, then grew instantly serious. "But a lot of people hated you for that piece too."

"Cool. I like living up to my readers' hatreds."

When I got home, Kim was snoozing on the couch. I made a sandwich—noting our paucity of groceries—then called Dad to alert him to my enrollment difficulties. He of course wasn't home or perhaps merely pretended not to be home, so I left a message. Irritation rising, I emphasized that whatever paltry money Pad had earned on the tour was owed to the band members.

Kim stirred upon the couch. "Hiya. What's up?"

"Just calling the manager."

She nodded, yawned.

"I'm going to the grocery store."

"Mmm. I'm hungry. Pick up some steaks. And more of that sippin' whiskey." She slyly smiled. "I'll have the charcoal ready when you get back."

Though I had only $30.00 in my wallet, I waved goodbye in fine spirits: I would charge the groceries to the business credit card. And what fun! I filled my crookedly-rolling grocery cart with meats, cheeses, cereals, breads, cooking oil, sodas, frozen snacks, coffee, birth control and rock magazines. This booty would last at least two weeks. I swiped the card through the electronic slot and, for a restive ten seconds, feared the charge would be rejected. But my fears were baseless: the card graciously accepted the $300.00-plus sum.

Adding pleasure to profit, the card also accepted the cost of filling up my car with gasoline. What joy, to charge so freely! I treated myself to three cartons of real menthol cigarettes, not those tepid off-brand "cigarettes" with 10 percent actual tobacco.

Back home, Kim indeed had the grill aflame in the leaf-carpeted back yard. I showed off my culinary skills by grilling two T-bones to just the slightest hint of pink. We ate hungrily, pleased to be free from the tour's nasty fast-food diet. Later, as dusk fell and our back porch light was obscured by the tumult of excitable moths, we smoked, sipped, and plotted Pad's next move. Kim hoped for an East Coast tour in the spring.

"Did our manager ever call back?"

"Nope."

Thirty-Seven: Pay for my Hell

September became October. I never did enroll.

Speaking in the drab voice of the bureaucrats he claimed to despise, Dad stated that the administration had recently re-evaluated its policy regarding free tuition for faculty spouses and offspring. "It's probably temporary," he soothed. "The state legislature wants to grandstand about costs, and it found the universities."

"It found *me*."

"Take a semester off."

"I've got no choice."

So I worked more hours at Franco's. Franco, bless him, welcomed me back warmly. I badly needed the work, as Kim had virtually no money yet coming in. The band had indeed made sub-minimum wage on the tour, and Kim feared that the gang would now lose interest. I reminded her that nobody held any illusions: the odds of money this early were extremely remote.

"But it's cool, isn't it, about the soundtrack addition?"

"Yes. It can't hurt."

Or so I thought at the time.

Vic Valmont had called Dad with exciting news: a movie producer wanted a Pad tune on the soundtrack of said producer's horror picture, *Speak for the Devil*. The picture's puny premise was that Satan, hopes flagging after several centuries, redoubles his efforts to recruit evangelists. To his delight and relief, Satan finds that the most enthusiastic recruits are the most righteous. Global pandemonium erupts: Satan wins over Cardinals, Imams, Holy Recluses, Vegans, and Ivy League humanities professors. The quasi-feminist subtext—an obscure order of unaccountably attractive nuns saves humanity with an Internet exorcism—promised a few laughs as well, though the laughs were perhaps unintentional.

"Gore, gore and more gore," Kim summarized. "And then a really graphic sex scene with a priest and a soccer mom with implants."

"A hetero priest? *Perverse.*"

This particular evening's performance was at The NiteSpot, now Pad's home base, drawing respectable crowds and earning a bit of money. Fortunately, I managed to attend...I was usually at work, flour caking atop my sweat. The NiteSpot was filled. "Blush"'s legs were gratifyingly long, and the band was amazed to learn from a local fan that "Blush" was rising on college radio.

"That's good, right?!" Larry asked as he fiddled with a pair of snapped drum sticks.

"It'd be cooler if college radio meant money."

"It could jump over to commercial radio. There's your money."

"But did I mention the sound track addition?"

"Nope."

"Yeah. Vic Valmont's got some rough tapes of a song you guys did with him, but it didn't end up on—"

"That instrumental?"

"Yeah. Vic said that a movie producer wants it for a horror picture."

"I love horror movies," Larry grinned. "But I'd love money even more."

"You know *that* story."

He did: Pad would get a minimal fee—perhaps $500.00—for the song. "Low budget flick, right?"

"A no budget flick."

Larry patted my shoulder. "Then the song-writing duo might make, what? Maybe another couple hundred bucks?"

"Not me. They're not my lyrics."

The set went well. Kim even remarked the next morning that she was singing better than ever. "Which is good. I'm doing vocals for the soundtrack next week. A rush job. Two days, tops."

"You can do it in one day." I brushed the hair off her forehead, and she scolded me for exposing a pimple. I replaced the hair. "So, let me hear the lyrics."

She shook her head emphatically. "No way."

"Oh c'mon."

Kim slid atop me, hands framing my face.

"Hey, can you work this Sunday?" Franco called to me as I came in at 5:00. "Can you do set up on Sunday too?" he added before hearing my answer.

"Yeah, sure."

"At the new store?"

Ah, the new store: Franco's goal for the last six months. He'd scouted several locations about a mile just outside of town. The area was the site of a prolonged residential building boom, with awkwardly outsized homes upon tiny lots. The class-anxious neurotics were stampeding in from all directions, with their budget-busting leased cars crowded in the driveways and tree-less cul-de-sacs. And upon the heels of the over-night neighbor-hood development were the overnight strip- and mini-malls. Franco had settled upon a prime corner lot, which shared an ex-pansive parking lot with the Super Sized Wally World. "All that traffic," Franco enthused. "It can't miss."

"I haven't even been over there."

He handed me a glass of cola, easy on the ice, just as I liked it. "And now's your chance, Jeffrey." He anticipated my half-hearted complaint, conceding that the new site was an extra twenty minute drive for me. "I'll give you a dollar for every extra minute. Twenty bucks."

Chronically short of cash, I agreed. "Who else is opening?"

"Julia. She's the new manager out there. Except on her nights off, then it's you. That's another extra twenty bucks a night." His eyes glinted at my smile: "See? Don't I treat my em-ployees well?"

Franco's new location became, in fact, my regular workplace. And the new store was actually a pleasure. The kitchen was no larger, but it was more comfortable, thanks to the big exhaust fans. The dining area was twice the size of Franco's original, and it certainly did pull in the business. Typically, we were busy by five o'clock with families, casual daters, beer buddies and shop-ping gals. Julie remained true to her waitress roots by refusing to stand aloof from the labor: she bussed and cleaned tables, she helped with drinks, she even fixed the electric can opener, which I'd broken with my first attempt to open a can of tomatoes. The kitchen crew was green but we got on amiably. The waitresses seemed reasonably content, as the pick-up area was spacious and, on occasion, the evening crowd left decent tips. Meanwhile, the contiguous stores quickly opened: bookstores, shoe stores, an "Irish Pub", a movie rental emporium, a computers & electronics store...the leviathan Wally World was the crown jewel.

On Sunday nights, Kim took to coming in for pizza with some old friends from high school and the university, though on some nights she came in solo. Sundays, she explained, were sad nights to be alone, and she enjoyed watching me hustling and sweating in the kitchen, spinning out pizzas, manicottis, and strombolis.

As this semi-regular habit matured into ritual, she brought with her sheet music, on which she'd scribble and revise as she had a salad and half-order of baked spaghetti. One evening, a couple of kitchen kids—eager to demonstrate their musical bona fides—claimed that they were the first to be hip to Pad.

"That song? 'Blush'? I got it when it first came out," George boasted to me. George was a high-school senior for two years running, as he spent nearly every waking hour with his stereo and his drop-out girlfriend. "Good raw production values." He hastily added that the new record was good too: "Her fuckin' guitar playing? She should be in *Guitar Player* every other month." Still, George had reservations: "I hope they don't get too commercial next time out. The industry, you know," he explained earnestly, "it sucks a band dry." George then proceeded to interrogate me: What was the value of my publishing deal? What was the producer's cut? Was the record moving from college to commercial radio?

His buddy Alan broke in, mimicking George's nasal valley boy dialect: "And can I date your sister?"

"Shut up," George demanded.

"And if he can't," Alan continued in his own voice, "can I?"

They tittered like grade school girls and I allowed myself an easy smile. At that moment Julia appeared, face flush, and warned us of an approaching party of eight. We groaned in unison and braced ourselves for the order. She faced the dining area, carefully recounting. "No...make that seven."

"Do I hear six?" Alan pleaded.

"Patty came in here," Kim told me as we closed up one evening. She pushed aside her empty salad plate, tossed her wadded napkin on the table. "Came in with a bunch of people but she saw me and then left by herself."

"Good."

"Mmm hmm." Kim gathered her sheet music and, as we walked out the rear entrance to our respective cars, she studied me with a coolness that I realized I must answer.

"Give me a cigarette?" I asked just as she opened her car door.

She nodded, barely visible beneath the dank November night, and produced a cigarette.

"Thank you. Now: give me your full attention?"

She nodded, eyes not quite upon me.

"I'm not happy—not at all—that Patty came in tonight. But I'm very happy she *left*. That she left the pizzeria and that she left me."

"Hey, what do I care?" she feebly joked. "I'm just your sister."

And against my will, it came out: "She knows."

"What?"

"Knows."

"What the fuck—!" She glanced left and right, then lowered her voice.

"Brace yourself." And before poor Kim could do as instructed, I said it. "When I went to get that ten grand? Mom told me."

"Oh my God," she could only whisper. "Oh my God."

I risked placing a hand on her shoulder, which she hurriedly shrugged off. "How in gay Christ's name could they *both know*?"

I could only dumbly and dishonestly shake my head as I watched stunned Kim stare her shoes.

"What are we going to do?" she finally managed.

"Laugh at the squares."

"Goddamit Jeffrey, for once would you please..." She smacked her forehead.

"Listen to me: Nothing's happened. So a jealous ex girlfriend and a certified lunatic have their suspicions. So what? Nothing's happened."

Kim studied me, eyes hard with fright and anger.

"*Nothing's happened.* Patty probably came in tonight by mistake anyway. She walked out and left with her friends, right?"

"So life just goes on," she half-whispered to nobody, rolling the words around in her mouth and brain. "It just goes on." She hurried to her car.

Kim was off to Vic Valmont's that next weekend to record the soundtrack vocal. She'd been sullen for several days, burning to blame me for chatty Patty's revelations to Mama Righteous. I kept calm and merely shrugged, suggesting that even the crazy and the envious stumble by mistake upon the truth once in a while.

"That's just great. When we get fucking *outed*, make sure you have more of your stupid little quips." With that, she rolled her eyes and stomped off.

The day before she left, however, the clouds dispersed and, lazing in bed, she even lit a cigarette for me, which was her overture for a chat. We talked easily enough of this and that, tactfully avoiding mention of Patty or Mama Righteous. I concluded that the impending recording session—and the fact that the sky had indeed not crashed—lifted her spirits.

And to my surprise, she called me Saturday afternoon to say the vocal track was finished.

"You're not serious."

"No, I am. And, it was—Goddamit, I just knocked over the ashtray."

I heard raucous laughter, tinny through the phone. "Where are you?"

"In the hotel bar. I tried calling you with my cell phone but the battery's dead and I was too lazy to go to my room. Hey, Vic's here and he says hello."

"And I say hello back. Can you hang on for a sec?"

She could. I grabbed my own cell phone and, offering a mock prayer to the absent deity, called Chicago information for the phone number of the Double Tree near Water Tower place. Yes, a room was available for tonight.

And yes, I had a credit card: Dad's business credit card, which he grudgingly kept open in the event of band expenses such as strings and drumsticks. In three minutes, the transaction was completed and, spirits air-borne, I returned to Kim.

"Okay, I'm back."

"I was about to hang up."

"So, you're staying at that dump off Halsted in Greek town?"

"Why?"

I glanced at my watch. "Because you're moving to nicer digs. The Double Tree, right by Water Tower Place."

"—What?"

"Just be there at the lobby in three hours. We'll have dinner and celebrate the impending release of your latest star vehicle." A long pause upon the phone, and a nagging unease. "Hello?"

"—Yeah I'm here. I had to go to the bathroom to, you know."

"Let me guess. Get away from Vic Valmont."

Her laughter echoed off the walls, which I imagined to be of salmon porcelain tile. "Vic's okay, really. He's just a little horny from the beer and—"

"And from your pipes."

"Naturally. It's what my pipes do to the unfairer sex."

My mood, an amalgam of high spirits and carnal anxiety, compelled me to drive a steady 80 miles an hour until I reached the outskirts of Chicago's far southern suburbs. Inevitably, the traffic clotted around 95th, but I was determined to be on time: suddenly, so much seemed at stake. I'd never treated her to an actual date, and I was gratified by her excitement when she grasped my plans. Emboldened, I drove happily upon the expressway's shoulder and exited at Lake Shore Drive. Hurrying northward, I nonetheless managed to enjoy Lake Michigan: the November temperature was nearly balmy, and the night's humidity cast the moon in a soft-edged glow.

My watch informed me I was due in ten minutes, and it took me the full ten minutes to navigate further north, then a few short blocks west. I pulled upon the curb and stepped out.

"Good evening. Welcome to Double Tree." A fellow with an overcoat and Nigerian accent smiled as I handed him my keys.

I hurried inside to the hushed lobby. The check-in desk was manned by an employee who looked faintly absurd in a maroon jacket.

"Edwards," I blurted.

He smiled with practiced courtesy. "Room 735."

"Know what?"

"—What?"

"Tonight, I'm staying with a rock star."

"That's very good, sir."

I turned happily upon my heel and—

"Whoa!"

—and lightly collided with said rock star.

Cigarette dangling with cocky *esprit*, my rock star took a half-step back. "You're late," she teased. "But I've got a table for us."

I followed her through the lobby to the entrance of the hotel's restaurant. Ah...this was pleasant: a small table, immaculate with linen and silver, right next to the floor-to-ceiling windows.

I pulled back the chair for my grinning date then sat opposite her. "Would madam like a drink before dinner?"

She glanced about her, noting the suits and pricey dresses upon the business folks and conventioneers. "This is kinda expensive, isn't it?"

"I hope so." I turned about in my chair, waved over a waiter. "Do you have champagne?"

"We do."

"Is it from France?"

The waiter, an amiable fellow with a wrinkled face and sagging stomach, nodded with new understanding.

And so began our meal: a bottle of champagne that Kim and I quaffed with refined gusto. Next came an appetizer, quite good really: an enormous potato topped with cheese that was, to my surprise, actually fresh. Then came the dinner: a yuppie designer pizza, light on taste and heavy on pretension. The pizza was anti-climactic but I didn't complain, as Kim's mood was exquisite: relaxed, yet nearly atremble with excitement about the future: "That track came out really good."

"Does it have a name, this track?"

"'Pay for my Hell.'" She snickered. "Vic, just before I left to come over here, he introduced me to the producer of the movie. She's from Chicago."

"She?"

"Yeah, it's a she. And she listened to the track right then and there at the hotel bar on her I-Pod. Says it should be the first song on the soundtrack."

I refilled Kim's glass—we'd switched from champagne to an after-dinner sherry—and we clicked glasses. "Cheers to you."

She accepted my toast and, with elaborate manners, claimed the bottle and refilled my glass: "And you."

I paused, placed the glass upon the table. For one of the few times in my life, I was at a loss for words. Because she'd said it. "I do," she whispered, leaning upon the table with both elbows. "I love you."

That weekend, we lolled upon the absurdly uncomfortable mattress; we window shopped on absurdly expensive north Michigan Avenue; we clowned like country bumpkins on the escalators of a Borders bookstore. And we rejoiced to find that Borders had two copies of Pad's CD, one of which I purchased. We lounged in the café, drinking overpriced coffee that smelled like plumbs and tasted like hot soda. Three stories below was Michigan Avenue's consumerist bustle. Within this expensive zip code, nearly everyone had the purposeful stride of the monied and those who wished to be. Kim sank into an overstuffed chair and nodded peacefully as I told her I was off to the basement to browse through the history books. Ninety minutes breezed by and I happily charged several hard covers to the business card.

Later, we enjoyed an early dinner at Italian Village, the corner booth intimate and the appetizers appetizing: aromatic with flavors both rich and subtle. I ordered manicotti and with the first few bites, noted its sauce didn't meet my standards.

"You're *so* full of shit," Kim happily accused, her fork quickly claiming a piece of manicotti from my plate. I returned the favor, claiming a slice of lemony white fish.

After dinner, we ambled slowly north, savoring the lake air's marvelous temperance. Too soon we were near the hotel. Wanting to prolong the evening, Kim nodded toward the Fourth Presbyterian church.

"It's *way* cool," she attested.

And it was: three Gothic Revival structures, with a spire straining heavenward a hundred or so feet above Michigan Avenue. We stepped into the deserted courtyard and sat upon a bench. The setting—Indiana limestone buildings, dark green lawn—was romantic and grave. We were silent for some time and, I confess, I felt a comic twinge of sacrilege while smoking in this stately campus of Our Lord. Kim suffered no such compunction and happily smoked several cigarettes, though she did scrupulously place the spent butts in her jacket pocket.

"Couldn't we just live here?" Leaning against my shoulder, she was cloaked by the courtyard's shadows. "It's so perfect." Her hair was the deepest black and, as she brushed away an errant bang, her hand was a ghostly gray. She sighed, leaned more heavily into me. "I miss it already."

So did I.

And I continued to miss it through November and December. Indeed, a few days before Christmas, I planned a return trip, but Kim caught a cold that, tenacious and humorless, refused to depart until well after New Year. She did little but sleep through the holidays, though she of course refused to cancel her NiteSpot gig and, in a three-day stint that nearly led to pneumonia, she landed holiday gigs across the state line. I attended the last gig, perhaps the sloppiest of Pad's career. She flubbed the lyrics to several tunes and even missed a solo.

"Fuck this is awful," she mouthed toward me, where I lounged twenty feet to the side of the cramped riser. She had a point: not only was the band suffering, but the crowd was sparse and indifferent. I shrugged, ordered another beer, and shouted at the band to soldier onward.

Fortunately, sloppiness was joined by merriment as the bar slowly filled. Kim, yet another cigarette ground out beneath her tennis shoes, lurched without warning into "Pay for my Hell". The band didn't fully know the tune and Larry gamely pounded out 4-4's while chronically confused Richard laid out.

The crowd responded lustily. Amused, Kim hoarsely declared, "The band that plays best plays least." Then she played it again:

I'll smash down your door
Kick you into the basement

To hear my last words.
What's a family for?

To Pay for my Hell!

The surprising diatonic melody rose to life. Billy caught the wave on rhythm guitar.

First your blood, then mine
Alive just long enough, long enough to see
First your blood, then mine.

The slicing notes were an uncanny embodiment of the lyric's ravings. As Larry and Billy stepped on the gas, the tune lunged violently and Kim went to work on the tune's five-note hook, bending and twisting it until it burst.

Abruptly, the guitar fell silent and, after a deep breath, Kim roared "Pay for my Hell!" The patrons started and blinked, as if Kim were berating them.

"Jesus Christ!" Billy declared, putting a congratulatory arm around Kim's shoulders. "*That's* how you play rock and roll!"

Then came cheers as Kim curtsied, her fingers daintily clasping the hem of an imaginary skirt. She requested beer money for the band. "They're so thirsty, and all I've got is pocket change."

Thirty-Eight: Goodbye, Ivory Towers

Her voice was shredded through the New Year, and she accepted my counsel to lay the band off for a month. We lounged, read, daydreamed. To maintain "appearances," Kim stayed at Dad's a couple days over the holidays while I stayed home, piling on the hours at Franco's II. Upon her return, Kim reported that Robbie—or perhaps Robbie's Internet-savvy acquaintance—had updated the heretofore languishing Pad web site. Robbie'd spent the day after Christmas taking digital photos of Kim, along with absurd poses of her with a guitar: the pensive folk singer, the distracted savant, the rocker with 'tude.

"I kind of begged off at first, but you now how persistent and whiny he is," Kim noted.

Indeed I did.

"Dad butted in with a couple halogen lamps and an umbrella. The pics are up on the website. God, I fucking hate seeing pictures of myself."

"How does the manager feel about that new guitar you want?"

"It was Christmas and I didn't want a fight."

"I do."

She raised an eyebrow. "How unusual."

Already, the phone was in my hand. Dad feigned pleasure to hear from me, claiming that he was at this very moment mapping out a tentative regional tour for the spring.

"Then she'll need better equipment."

I could sense Dad's sneer, though he mouthed partial agreement. I pressed him on the matter, noting that Kim had her eyes on a new Gibson SG Junior, to which she wanted to wed a Butlerized amp. "And a delay. Nothing fancy, just enough to split a couple amps by 20 or 30 mills."

"That'll take a more money than's coming in right now, so—"

"I'm not asking that lunatic for another dime."

"That's not what I meant." He cleared his throat, a sign that he was gathering his thoughts. "She called here a couple times over Christmas."

"What did she have to say?"

"Nothing really. Well, just to complain about never seeing anybody over the holidays."

"She hates holidays."

"Yeah."

"So...what else? Did she hector you for that ten grand?"

"Didn't mention it. Just called to, I don't know, just to bitch."

Even as I tamped down fears that Mama Righteous had claimed incestuous relations between her dear children, I sensed my opening: "If you'll forgive the lack of a segue, I tried to enroll for spring classes today."

"And?"

At that moment, I nearly slammed the handset against the phone but Kim was trying to nap on the couch—even as she kept one ear squinted toward my conversation.

"They wouldn't let me."

"I'll try to—"

"Stick it."

"—Excuse me?"

"I know what happened." And I did: I was *scholar non grata.* Just as I claimed, I'd tried to enroll, even arriving at the registrar's office fifteen minutes before opening. Walking in with a crisp stride and friendly smile, I announced my name and my intentions to enroll: "Thank goodness for that faculty brat tuition waiver," I added with self-deprecation. "I can barely afford the books."

The same drab matron stepped up to the counter to help me but, as she recognized me, her face thickened and fell. She asked that I wait for a moment. After a moment and fifteen minutes, the registrar herself appeared. A woman of unusual height and severity, she spoke to me with a barely controlled fury, as if just having yelled at someone.

"Hello, I'm Jeff Edwards and I..." I explained my wishes.

Dr. Rowland, fiddling with her clumsily large broach, nodded impatiently, merely waiting for me to finish so she could announce: "Your tuition waiver has been withdrawn."

"How might I—"

"Withdrawn permanently." She glanced behind her, where the silhouette of a familiar figure lurked behind the frosted glass of her office: the pot belly, the smallish sloping shoulders: Dr. Martino, upwardly mobile Marxist.

Upon hearing my reportage, brave father hemmed and hawed, refusing to concede what I'd learned from Jason Weinstock, the current campus paper editor: last year's muckraking had ruffled too many haughty academic feathers: "Yeah, I overheard it at a Christmas party," Jason had explained, fingers restive upon his computer's keyboard. "You pissed off Martino big time, and he's got clout here, right? He got on Dean Butchart's ass about this and—well, the Dean just flat out hates you anyway. Butchart played hard ball with your Daddy: shut up the kid or take a hit on the budget."

Upon hearing my narration, Dad ineptly defended himself. "I—I'd wanted to talk to you about that for some time, but—"

"Stick it."

"—but the Dean was going to slash my budget by thirty percent, so—"

"Did you stick it yet?"

"—so I'd have to lay off a couple part-timers. Jesus, even the grad assistants would lose their tuition wavers and stipends. What, you suddenly don't give a damn about grad students? All your harassment of Martino was a lark?"

"You *haven't* stuck it."

"So you don't care if the grad students get laid off," he accused, trying and failing to change the subject. "Or about their exploitation."

"Let's toss those three things in the air and see how they land. Oh look! 'Laid off' got clipped back to 'Laid.' And then there's 'exploitation.' Put 'laid' and 'exploitation' together, and—"

"Stop it."

"—and then there's 'grad student.' Doesn't that remind you of a certain someone named Kristen?"

"Don't threaten me."

"What'll you do? Keep me out of school?" I sensed Kim standing behind me.

"My personal life is none of your concern."

"There must be a really fundamental conflict of professional interests here, don't you think? I mean, she's not only your lay, she's your subordinate. And that's frowned upon these days."

"Watch what you're saying."

"Tell me if anything I say is untrue: lose your budget, lose your grad assistant lay, lose—oh, how to phrase it?—lose control of a potentially dicey situation? The Dean's very progressive and all that, but he's probably a Puritan in other matters."

"Shut up."

I slammed down the phone.

Kim kneeled beside me. "Wow. Kind of an exciting call."

"Don't think that I'm not proud of your music or don't want to be involved or—"

She placed a cool hand upon my shoulder. "I know."

After several smokes, I'd collected myself enough to note with some detached amusement that my undergraduate days, never glorious, were already over. Kim winced at the melancholy beneath my none-too-convincing blasé observation. "I know you liked school last time," she murmured. "You were really happy then, writing and all that."

"Hassling the professionally offended..." I mused. "I'm already nostalgic." But no such hassling lay before me. Instead, the horizon offered—at least for the present—more hours at Franco's II.

"You could always join the band."

My face was a question mark.

"I fired Richard yesterday." She studied me as I took in the news. "Actually, he quit. He knew I couldn't put up with his flubbing notes anymore."

"Or put up with his trying to get into your pants again?"

"Uh..." She chewed upon her lower lip. "You could cool down a little, don't you think?"

"What's he doing to do? Take up the mouth harp?"

Her smile was ironic. "Study music composition with a certain Professor Edwards." She studied me for a long second. "Richard can be the son Dad never had."

Thirty-Nine: Hello, Hollywood

Kim's squeal startled me: "The ad, it's got the band's name!" She flattened the morning paper upon the crumb-flecked kitchen table.

The paper's Weekender section featured an ad for *Speak for the Devil*. "Opening in One Week!" the ad shrieked. "From the New Master of Horror comes a New Vision of Hell!" Dominating the ad was a drawing—a very good one, I was surprised to see—of a bearded, aged priest. Behind him, a half moon glowed against a foreboding evening sky. The priest squarely faced the viewer. He gripped a bible in his left hand and a freshly severed human head in his right. The bible, not the head, dripped blood that fell into a widening pool before the priest's bare feet. The priest's glassy eyes betrayed religious ecstasy, perhaps because in the background, barely visible in the upper left corner, dangled several bare calves and shoeless feet. The limbs belonged, it seemed, to parishioners hanging from a tree, the branch of which extended across the top of the drawing.

"That's so cool!" Kim enthused.

The drawing was striking, in a style that I'd never anticipated: black and white, with long graceful lines and minute details: the priest's beatific smile, his left nostril's flare, the moon-dappled cover of his bible, and—a detail slow to dawn upon me—sinners who crawled in a serpentine queue behind the priest.

"And look at that!" Kim recited copy from the bottom of the ad: "Featuring the single 'Pay for my Hell' by Pad."

At that moment the phone rang: Billy's wife, who was unguardedly excited. "Look in the paper, Jeffrey, look in today's—"

"Yeah, we're looking at it right now, and—"

The calls came in all morning: from Dad, who half-way through his greeting was interrupted by Robbie on another line: "Hey bro isn't that great! That ad is, it's great! Put Kimmie on the line." Charmed against my will by Robbie's enthusiasm, I handed the phone to Kim, who simultaneously grinned and winced as Robbie spewed congratulations. Robbie grew so loud that I could hear each spittle-thickened phrase.

Kim chattered all morning with well-wishers. People to whom Kim hadn't talked in years kept calling, including an old high school chum who claimed offense that he'd not been told that the movie was coming out.

"I didn't know myself!" Kim cackled. "I thought it would be out in the summer but, ka bang, there it is. I'm not complaining...! Yeah, Hollywood beckons." She slapped a palm on her outwardly thrust hip. "And I've got one week to get my *fabulous* new wardrobe. And of course the studio will pay for it."

Movies, I saw, possessed far greater glamour than music, and I fleetingly allowed myself to imagine that Kim and I would launch upon a prosperous career as soundtrack composers. Granted, "Pay for my Hell" was a Pad oddity: music *and* lyrics by Kim Edwards...with amusing lyrical inspiration by Mama Righteous and her yellow legal pad.

That week was chaotic and joyous. Kim's cheer brightened all rooms and all conversations. Indeed, she was girlish and, at times, simply a girl: yapping on the phone with her newly discovered old friends and freshly made new friends. Then Dad called, briskly announcing that the first sales and royalty statement for *Femme en Blanc* had arrived.

"The figures are actually quite good. Twelve thousand copies at eleven dollars each—you'll recall, Jeffrey, that eleven dollars represents the discounted figure. All the retailers demand a discount, you know. But the downloaded versions, they're less."

"Yeah."

"—So at any rate, after all the number crunching, our sales produce $16,000, give or take a buck." He paused, and I heard the tranquil filling of a coffee cup. "And remember: I kept the advance low, so that's a big down payment on paying all that off."

"Fourteen thousand copies," I flatly noted. "What a scorcher."

"Yeah but—" The sound of pages being flipped. "Sales actually are up the last two months, on a, uh, on an upward spike."

"Yeah."

"Listen, if I'd agreed to more of an advance you'd be in the hole further."

I nearly asked about songwriting royalties, but instantly sensed that the figures would further aggravate me. I merely handed the phone to Kim.

Our life that week was a double shot of *joi de vivre*. Kim was the subject of two local newspaper features: one in the university's *Herald*, and one in the local suburban paper: Yes, the paper that by unpleasant happenstance employed tall Patty's father. Kim noted that each writer asked nearly identical questions, and she feared the stories would therefore be tediously similar.

Naturally, I've clipped the stories. They're of mere sentimental value, as each piece is marred by the blandness and bare control of grammaticality one expects from most papers. "Faculty Brat is a Star!" inanely announced The *Herald*'s piece. My acquaintance Jason Weinstock wrote the piece, and the wit that I'd sensed in him was largely absent, though he did in passing mention that Kim Edward's brother Jeffrey was a "former *Herald* muckraker." The suburban paper's piece was, if anything, more mundane. It misidentified Professor Dave as a member of the Art faculty, thereby making nonsense of the article's hook that daughter was following in father's footsteps. Happily, the writer redeemed himself by adding a quickie review of *Epater Bourgeoisie,* correctly though clumsily praising "Kim Edwards's powerhouse vocal power" and her "unusual guitar instrumentation."

And as I'd come to expect, silence on the lyrics.

The piece concluded with a plug for "Speak for the Devil," noting that the movie opened next Friday nationwide, including our local Cineplex.

The paper ended with a tiny Q & A: "Will our local celebrity be making an appearance?" the writer wondered.

"If everyone brings me a beer, yeah," the local celebrity answered.

"Actually, I didn't say *that*," Kim noted that night in bed. "About the beer, I mean." She finished her second Miller and, sitting up in the dark, poured us each a shot of Old Bushmill's. "Cheers." We clicked and drained glasses, then finished off the meager remainder of a joint. The blue smoke drifted lazily ceilingward.

"So what did you say?"

Bottle in hand, she gestured toward my empty glass. I shook my head and she filled her own. "Mmm, I love that stuff. I wish I could drink it and play, but I can't."

"You can drink it and do other things well." I stroked her bare cool back.

She finished the drink and lay her head upon my stomach. "I'm stoned. Thoroughly."

"So if you didn't say *that*..." I prodded, lightly poking her ribs.

"That I was kind of nervous and would need a beer first."

Sister's thighs opened to brother's hips. Sister's feet hooked around brother's calves. As she caught and rode his rhythm, her hazel eyes—bright in the black room—narrowed upon me. From above I studied us...

Presently, I saw me slide off her. What a sated Sybarite I was, hair comically disheveled like a nuclear plume! Kim turned upon her side, sly with a surprise. She grasped my right hand. She was whispering, and from my lofty vantage point I couldn't hear her.

"What?"

She lightly slapped my chest.

I glanced up at the ceiling. I was gone.

"I said: 'Now I can make an honest woman of you.'" She reached behind her to turn on the wobbly table lamp.

Upon my right ring finger was a plastic ring taken from a box of Cracker Jack.

"Now it's off to Vegas for a theme wedding," she laughed. "Maybe the Trump Plaza?"

"Who's in the wedding party? Alexander the Great and Cleopatra?"

"I was thinking JFK and Lee Harvey Oswald."

Forty: *Speak for the Devil*

Premiere night arrived. The Edwards family managed to affix bright smiles to their faces. Dad and I agreed to put aside our ever-widening differences—more specifically, I agreed not to mention Kristen as long as he bought Kim a Gibson SG.

"I suppose you're going to the Friday night showing?"

"Yeah."

Brief brooding. "I've got a prior engagement." He was playing with a jazz ensemble at a top-tab wedding gig. "Maybe we can all see it Sunday?"

His announced absence cheered me. I'd never needed him and now resented his efforts to help Kim. "Oh and I'm joining the band," I jested to keep him off balance. "Good career move for a college dropout, right? Join a band that at the end of the day hasn't made minimum wage?"

He offered a clipped goodbye before I could ask if Kristen was a member of his ensemble. Probably not, I judged; Dad disliked sharing the stage with a subordinate, sexual or otherwise.

A thin moment later, Richard called.

"It's great," he said, manfully humbling himself. "Big time, you know?

"I know."

"Yeah, so is Kim there?"

She graciously accepted his congratulations and asked (with evident sincerity, to my irritation), if he would be at the movie Friday night. No, he wouldn't: he had a date, but he would of course see the movie soon.

The members of Pad planned on an early pizza at—drum roll!—Franco's II. I actually took the day off, though I did flaunt my unrivaled versatility as lyricist, driver, and chef: I shared with Kim tentative lyrics to a new song; I chauffeured everyone (including Billy's suddenly chatterbox wife) to the restaurant;

and I took Pad's dinner into my own hands: family-sized antipasto (scamorze *and* mozzarella, light on the shaved black ol-
ives), two large pizzas, and a pitcher of beer. Oh, what a big shot
I was, waving away with bravura the offers of George and Alan
to make the dinner.

Crowded into the corner booth, our table wobbling upon un-
even legs, we ate hungrily and laughed noisily. At first I found
myself obscuring my new ring with a napkin or by resting the
hand below the table. Yet nobody paid the slightest attention
and soon I was happily filling and refilling everyone's beer glass,
pitcher in hand and ring agleam.

"So Kim," Cynthia remarked. "You fired Richard?"

Caught with a mouth full of pizza, Kim merely nodded.

"Nah," Larry corrected. "He just quit. As he should have."

We nodded and groaned.

"Yeah that's right," Cynthia continued. "He just, what? Just
didn't practice enough."

Billy, voice modulated and posture relaxed, guessed otherwise. "I've heard him play pretty well, really. And it's not bad,
not bad at all, on the record."

Larry snickered. "That's because five or six tracks—"

Billy winced and closed one eye, as if expecting a blow.

"—feature guest bassists."

"How's that?" I'd not heard this detail.

"You didn't know? Kim and Billy, they covered bass on,
what?" He turned to Billy, who needlessly studied the pizza upon
his plate. Cynthia, I saw, studied not her husband's pizza but his
suddenly tight jaw.

"It wasn't really that many," Kim suggested, pizza belatedly
swallowed. "Three at the most."

"Which ones?" Cynthia asked, draining a half glass of beer.

Oh, I realized. A *scene.*

"Yeah, which ones?" I brightly asked.

Larry held up a beefy hand, fingers extended, and counted off
the songs. "Five by my count."

"Whatever," Billy said through nearly clenched teeth.

Cynthia's bottom-heavy face, never attractive, grew ogre-like:
eyes smaller and mouth snarling. "Don't you shush me," she
snapped to nobody in particular.

Richard glanced about the room. "I told you that Richard laid out on a couple tracks."

"You said one," Cynthia loudly corrected, violent nostrils twice the size that nature typically allows. "You asshole."

"Cool it!" Billy insisted, carotid pulsing. "This isn't the best time, really."

She blew a raspberry at him.

Kim leaned forward. "Cynthia, please. You want to try laying down a track or two with us, then fine. Can we at least talk about this later?"

Cynthia loudly sloshed and swished her beer as if it were mouthwash. Under Kim's pleading gaze, she nodded and swallowed. "You're still an asshole," she said to her husband, who wadded his napkin and tossed it atop his empty plate.

"Kim I'm really sorry about this," Billy managed.

"Nah, forget about it," Kim laughed uneasily.

"You want me to forget about it?" Cynthia challenged.

"Come to think of it," Larry gamely tried, "it was only three tracks."

Billy, who fortunately occupied the booth's edge, abruptly stood and asked that the others not think too badly of him. "But I think, really, it's best that we pass on the movie tonight."

Kim, Larry, and I instantly agreed.

With discrete force, Billy gripped Cynthia's upper arm.

"But I wanna see the movie!"

Billy brought his wife to her feet and escorted her out. She walked willingly enough, although her unzipped jacket, flapping as she took long fast steps, clipped an elderly man's ear. The elderly wife angrily stared at Cynthia, but she and Billy were gone in another six seconds.

Kim scratched at her forehead as if to unearth an apt summarizing comment. "Cindy's a bitch," she finally observed.

Larry leaned forward, eyes merry. "But she's hot, don't you think?"

Kim blinked. "Listen, don't ask me. But no, she's a dog."

"Just how long," I asked, "has she wanted to be in the band?"

"Forever," Kim sighed. "Which I didn't really figure out until just a couple days ago. When Richard quit. Then suddenly Billy's like, oh man, my wife wants to join the band and she can't play for shit but she thinks she can and—" She raised a hand and, forefinger to thumb, created a clucking hen. "Richard, he wanted to quit even before the tour but Billy asked him not to."

Larry laughed. "She doesn't give a shit about being in a band. She's just scared to death that hubby will have fun without her. Which is the only way he's gonna have it." He looked at Kim then me for agreement. We obligingly laughed. Satisfied, he finished his beer then refilled everyone's glasses. The beer rendered him philosophic, and he advised each of us against marriage. "Music and matrimony," he mused. "They just don't go together."

"So it seems," Kim lightly agreed. "Our Dad sure couldn't figure out the equation."

"'Cause he was too busy chasing coed skirt, that's what I heard."

Growing gossipy, Larry asked why neither Mom nor Dad Edwards would attend tonight's premiere. Kim snorted: "Because they're failures. Puny little failures."

With that matter dismissed, Kim faced me. "We need a bass player, and since you're..." Nearly imperceptibly, she raised an eyebrow: a cue that her words arose from a hidden context. "...since you're already part of the band and, really, are part of the process."

"You play bass, dude?"

"Not really."

"That's good enough," Larry judged. "Man I'm thirsty. Anyway, Richard didn't play it either, not really."

Kim's hidden context grew expansive: "It'd be good for everyone, really: I mean, you're not in school right at the moment and we could get the songs down more quickly."

Larry began to ask if Pad's crack songwriting team had more tunes in the pipeline, but he belched.

Kim's eyes, growing ever wider and greener, betrayed a great desire that I accept the idea. "Hock your guitar for a bass," she suggested. "And while, you're at it, strike the pose."

"Excuse me?"

"The bass player pose. You know." Kim sat straight and, right hand dangling by her hip, played air bass guitar, her face a study of detached cool as she plucked imaginary notes.

"Play the notes in 'Blush' and I'll tell you if they're right," Larry mock challenged me.

I smiled despite myself and, as Kim asked, assumed the pose. My hanging right fingers plucked and pulled on imaginary E and A strings then, for good measure, reached upward for a G.

"That's a tougher rehearsal than Richard ever had," Larry remarked. "You know, he never could figure out that one, uh, that change in 'Looks Like a Tommy', and—"

"Time out!" Kim grinned. "It's showtime!"

We arrived twenty minutes to seven, surprised to see that parking was at a premium. The parking lot was long neglected and marred by softball and football sized holes. Larry, gamboling on unsteady booze legs, nearly collided with a car as he rounded the corner to the ticket booth. He laughed at his own near-hit then turned around: "Hurry up, there's kind of a line."

Kim instead gripped my jacket and with a step back, tugged me toward her. "So will you do it? Join the band?"

"You're serious?"

"What, you're smoking a joint?" Larry called, just out of sight around that corner.

We trotted toward him and, peering beyond his shoulder, I saw that a line had indeed formed at the box office. As we walked closer, someone in the crowd pointed at us.

"Hey, that's her," another person called, and then two raised arms gestured toward us.

Kim squinted. "Who's that?"

Jason Weinstock and—ah, poignant memories!—whip-smart Karen stepped half-way out of the line. "My man Mencken!" she cheered. She wrapped me in a robust hug. "It's so cool to see you!" She released me and, hand thrust forward, sought out Kim's hand. "I'm Karen, your brother's former editor. I was at a party of yours last year. And my God, congratulations to you!"

Kim smiled and introduced Larry.

"I was at the party too!" Larry announced and, head thrown back and arms wide, invited Karen to hug him too. Karen, assertive as ever—though hollow about the eyes, as if New York City made its demands—pushed Larry aside and eased us into the line. "Jason, where's your photographer?"

Jason looked about. "Not here yet."

"Probably got the times wrong," Karen suggested, though the suggestion carried the weight of hard certitude. "You had the times mixed up earlier yourself."

As the line moved forward, Karen explained that the *Herald's* photographer would be taking a photo of Kim, faculty brat made good. Kim weakly protested, claiming she looked awful, but Karen insisted that Kim looked wonderful.

"You really do," Jason added. I turned to find him, head slightly cocked, studying Kim's petite rear. His eyes caught mine, but feigning sibling disinterest, I merely asked if he were writing a review.

"I already wrote it," he half-whispered. "Copped it off a few Internet sites."

"So long as the review is good."

"Oh it is," he earnestly assured. "I mean, it's a teen slasher movie so what can you say? But I said that 'Pay for my Hell' is really good. And it is. It's catching a buzz. It's streaming all over the Internet the last few days."

"Good bye royalties," I wistfully observed.

The turnout was, it seemed, quite good. Tonight's fans were in gleeful spirits, with outbursts of laughter as various young co-ed tribes congregated in the lobby by the video games and concession stand. Several people took note of Kim in the lobby, as people do when they've seen a celebrity's photograph then realize that the celebrity stands before them in the flesh. Armed with absurdly expensive popcorn and soda, we took our seats.

As for the picture...suffice to say that it will never be more than a curiosity in the history of horror films. The acting was abysmal, with few actors grasping even rudiments of modulation or understatement: nearly every character bellowed at full boil from beginning to end and therefore possessed no reservoir of emotion when a knife hacked at a sweaty veined neck or when a demonic pervert clawed for hale and hearty breasts. The nuns who saved the world were compelled by various plot contrivances to disrobe until their breasts strained against gray tee-shirts.

"Oh I get it," Kim whispered to Larry. "A wet tee shirt contest."

"My nipples are hard."

Tonight's crowd—mostly tweens, teens, and twenties, along with a scattering of arrested-development thirty-and-ups—enjoyed the show, growing silent when so directed: a menacing shadow, a dark swelling of synthesized strings. They shrieked when so directed too, as when the possessed priest beheads the brave but hapless high school wrestling coach. The coach's torso stumbled about for three seconds, then collapsed with limbs starfished upon the now-bloody alter.

The priest, I should add, was portrayed by the movie's single skilled actor. Indeed, his beheading of a nun behind the church is a minor miracle of nuance—or at least, as nuanced as one can be while holding a bloody, flesh-flecked axe. The beheading of Sister Lydia began with the rote tropes of such films: the priest's mad eyes, the daft unsuspecting victim, the axe's head hovering high, shining in a soundstage's blue moonlight.

The priest's initial axe stroke was smooth and purposeful, and in a quick close up, his eyes widened gleefully, as if the nun had met her maker.

But the priest missed, and the blade cleaved his shoe. Pandemonium erupts as the screaming nun flees and the screaming padre follows in an agonized hobble. Victim escapes in the shadows of the church's backyard cemetery and, in doing so, she collides with a tall headstone. Panting priest soon stands overhead, axe sloppily employed. The priest demolishes half the headstone in wild swings as the nun rolls and bobs on the grass.

The nun sees a chance as the priest, in agony and desperation, loses grip of the axe, and the weapon somersaults into the darkness.

"Get the bitch!" someone up front yelled.

The priest did so, tackling Sister Lydia and battering her with a spiky chunk of destroyed headstone. At this point, the audience was thoroughly engrossed, waiting for the sister's inevitable rescue. But the rescue never arrives, and the priest pounds the sister's face into bloody gruel. After catching his breath, the padre struggles to the church's front yard, where from the trees hang several parishioners, one of whom is still alive and whose clotted shrieks fill the theater.

"This is *sick*," Kim whispered in complaint.

"This is sick!" Larry enthused.

Glancing behind me, I saw several patrons cover their eyes while others leaned forward, eyes not covered but bulging. The theatre was, I marveled, absolutely silent.

"I'll betcha it comes right now," I whispered to Kim.

The angry, lunging chords of "Pay for my Hell".

Then Kim's voice:

> *Pay for my Hell...*

My skin was gooseflesh. The hair upon my neck? Did it stand? No, it saluted in awe! Kim's voice snapped violently from the theater speakers.

> *What's a family for?*

"Oh yeah!" Larry whooped. To the alarm of the patron before him, he pounded out the beat on the back of the patron's seat. "Man that's me!" Larry explained. "That's me!"

> *Alive just long enough, long enough to see*
> *First your guts, then mine.*

The guitar ricocheted in several directions then settled down to repeat the chorus's hook. Kim, gathering her nerve beside me, even sang along for several seconds. Recognizing the voice in the movie as Kim's, several patrons turned fully around to study her.

On screen, the priest struggled to control another victim who, despite being hogtied, rolled about upon the grass with maddening elusiveness. And just as Kim's solo rose from its tightly coiled riffing, the priest's axe separated head from torso. From ten feet away, the head watched in disbelief as the body swung crookedly from the tree. A montage of shots and sounds: eerily, the priest's face changes from mania to beatitude; victims' legs swing ever more slowly until nearly still; the church's steeple writhes against a canopy of heat lightning; Kim's guitar's lines bite deeply as the priest kneels beneath the lynching tree to pray. Larry's drums break from straight four-four into a skull-crushing Bo Didley beat.

Alive just long enough, long enough...

The camera craned skyward: a ring of heads surrounded the priest, who was ecstatic in prayer. Meanwhile, in another church's basement, silicone-enhanced sisters of mercy prayed for the world's deliverance, which came in the form of a much younger priest made fearless by Psalms and steroids.

We sat as the credits rolled and—again!—came "Pay for my Hell", but this version was instrumental. Larry stood and slapped out the beat on the now-empty seat before him. Several patrons loitered about as the lights came up, talking among themselves and nodding toward Kim. A few even waved, and Kim jumped up and waved back at them, her grin so wide as to split her face into two radiant halves.

The pimple-faced employees, silly in their ill-fitting green vests, invaded with brooms and buckets.

"That *rocked!*" Larry exulted, thrusting his arms skyward like a victorious prizefighter.

In the lobby, a modest herd gathered to congratulate Kim. The paper coverage had gotten the word out about the faculty brat making good. A line of fans—perhaps fifteen or twenty—began at the neon blue refreshment stand and reached to the entrance. There in the dimly lit lobby, Kim accepted kudos and signed autographs. Larry joined her and signed his name too, explaining to bewildered fans that he was the drummer.

"You are not!" a skeptic challenged.

"Oh yes he is!" Karen assured. She waited with Jason at the refreshment stand, her oil-spotted bag refilled with popcorn.

The skeptic walked away. Taking no chances, Larry snatched away the newspaper article Kim had just signed and, clearing his throat, signed his name.

"And that guy," Karen continued, "he wrote the lyrics." A few patrons glanced about and followed Karen's pointing finger to me.

"Actually no, I didn't—"

"Yes he did!" Kim insisted, "And he's the bass player too!" Somebody shoved a child's pen at me—its barrel striped in red and white like a candy cane—so I happily signed my name to the clipped newspaper stories. A few fans, in the *de rigueur* black of exquisitely alienated youth, amazed me by presenting both *Femme en Blanc* and *Epater le Bourgeois* for Kim's signatures.

"We came here from Chicago," one of the sophisticates announced, her green hair taking on a neon cast beneath the lobby lights.

"—Chicago?"

Green Hair nodded and her companion, a young woman four feet high and three feet wide, grinned in confirmation. "The Wicker Park show? We bought our copies then. Oh and did you see the editorial reviews on Amazon dot com?"

Kim, smiling graciously, conceded that she had not.

"You should check it out. Anyway, we just love *Blanc*."

Blanc. The amusing reduction of the title from three words to one was a sign of Pad's ascending star: "*Blanc*" was a shiny bright signifier in the hipsters' *lingua franca*.

"Wicker Park, yeah, that was a good show," Kim enthused in feigned recollection.

Green Hair set her legs straight, rather like a military recruit, and announced: "You're the best singer I—"

"We," the companion corrected.

"—I've ever heard."

"My goodness," Kim beamed, "that's so kind for you to say."

A very tall young woman loomed from behind the duo. "Hi Kim."

"Patty. Hi."

Green Hair and friend moved on to the exit, having completed their musical pilgrimage, and Patty handed Kim a rolled up newspaper to sign.

"Good movie." Patty was stoned, eyes pink-rimmed and hugely dilated. She held the autograph six inches from her face and scrutinized it with great effort, as if she were looking for a hidden code—or as if she were illiterate. Larry gingerly plucked the paper to add his own signature, but Patty jerked it way, muttering, and took three steps to stand before me.

"*Filth*."

Larry looked up quizzically, wondering why this tall woman had deemed him "filth."

"I said 'filth.'"

"You lisped," I noted. "You're stoned."

"Sister fucker."

"You lisped again," I managed as Larry glanced at us. "Larry, she's a groupie or something. Remember her from Ann Arbor?"

He took a long second look and shook his head.

"Sister fucker!"

Kim briskly exited, a hand on Larry's forearm, and I followed them into the parking lot. I nearly shouted at Kim to stop running but, glancing behind me, saw Patty wobbling after us upon her stilts. Behind her hurried Karen and Jason, the latter's digital camera swinging from his neck.

Seeing her pursuers, Patty took a sudden turn—and stepped into a pothole.

"Jesus, who the hell are you?" Karen yelled, catching up to Patty.

"She's on PCP!" Jason blurted. "She's a crazy insect!"

Karen gripped Patty's arms, demanded that she calm down.

"What's she doing here?" Kim seethed.

"Having fun." I eased her behind a crookedly parked van. "Just stay put while—"

"Sibling sex, Pay for my Hell, sibling procreation," Patty babbled, trying and failing to step out of the pothole.

In a half-second Kim was past me and tearing at Patty.

Karen tried to stand between charging Kim and struggling Patty, but Kim shoved Patty aside. "Gimme ten seconds!" Kim demanded. She backfisted Patty's mouth.

By now, Larry had joined Karen and Jason in keeping Kim off Patty.

From behind a row of parked cars emerged a figure...headlights of departing cars illumed the appalling face and orifice-like mouth. "It's my humiliation, it's *my* hell!" she wailed. "You're all dirt!"

Kim paused in mid-attack to gape at dear mother.

"That little bitch stole my work and put it in that song and, and—" Mama Righteous waved a yellow legal pad in the air. "It was on paper just like this, like this! My life was on that, my fears and hopes and she, she just mocked it. Before the world!"

Spectators appeared, eager for a catfight.

"First my husband," mother testified, "then my daughter and my son." She called for Patty, who had finally freed her outsized foot from the pothole and cowered from Kim behind Larry and Karen.

"My fucking son."

I faced the harpy.

"You're filth, you're both filth."

I punched her.

She fell backward, striking a parked car with her jiggling derriere. Then she slid sideways along the car's fender and landed on the pavement face first, still gripping her yellow tube of paper.

"Goddammit cool it cool it be cool!" Larry demanded. He pawed at me in restraint but I mashed my palm against his face and stiff-armed him three feet backward. He tripped over a gaper and fell beside a mini-van—the owners of which watched the donnybrook behind locked doors.

"You fucker you hit your mother!?" Jason was in my face, his moist mouth working grotesquely at top speed. I took a half-step away, pushed him away in warning, but he followed me.

"Cool down man, cool down!"

My punch only glanced the top of his skull, but his brain switched from fight to flight. As he turned his back to me, I grabbed him by the collar and, in the process, entangled my hand in his camera's strap.

My hand was willful, more willful than the ragged chorus that surrounded me, screaming at me to stop. Far more willful than the hands pulling at me. A passing car's headlight illumed Jason's face: it turned from red to purple as the camera strap tightened further around his throat.

And now, levitating in the evening's cool twenty feet above, I witnessed it all: my trapping Jason upon the asphalt, my hands twisting the camera strap and Larry laboring to drag me off— and therefore dragging Jason with me too, for I refused let go.

"Jeffrey let go!" Kim pleaded.

I hunkered down like a face-hugging science fiction parasite, and his eyes rolled backward. Yet above, as I watched me choke Jason, I saw something else...aided by a stupid Samaritan, Mama Righteous stood upon trembling legs. Her filthy housecoat fluttered, and she shooed away the stranger's further assistance. Then she tore a single sheet from the legal pad and commenced:

All I did was that crummy little stuff like support you and gave you hope! But I was right always right you all are skanky money grubers, even Robbie knows that and he's technically a MORRON and IDIOT and that makes me a morron? No a sucker!! And to think that I gave you every idea you've had, both of you!

"She's got a gun!" somebody barked.

Ive had it and that means you've had it and theres no more band because theres no more brains, I am the brains and you stole ideas and ten thousand dollars and I cannot live anymore. the slime and stink of you two. Patty's right, you are filth you are filth.

I released Jason when the gun fired.

From my psychic perch, I saw the gun's flash and the crowd's collective flinch. I saw me scramble on all fours toward the hag, nobody stopping me, everyone in shock. I wanted to be first to see the dead hag's face, to see blood dribble from her blackened mouth, to see her brains scattered across the parking lot.

But she'd lost her nerve. She stood motionless, pistol at her side: "I'm not done reading!"

A second flash.

My God's eye view was abruptly gone, replaced by a vermin's eye view: before me were Mama Righteous's stubbled legs. With a sweep of my arm, I knocked her from her feet. She hit the asphalt hard, and I scrambled toward her then hopped on her chest.

Her eyes cart-wheeled, and I kept squeezing.

"She's dead!" someone screamed.

"Not quite!" I corrected.

Red foam rose upon her scab of a mouth. An errant page from her legal pad fluttered past.

The hands were upon me again: pulling, slapping, tearing. I feigned surrender and, for a fatal moment, the hands paused.

Then I snatched the candy cane ink pen from my pocket and drove its ballpoint into her face and neck and chest. Blood sprayed my arm and shirt.

"She's dead!"

Weirdly, the pavement felt spongy, like a trampoline. Even as I yelled for Kim, I fell into an awkward heap. Then all was dark and I felt the hands again upon me: a pair upon my back, a pair each upon each wrist.

Forty-One: Even as one Dies

"It's good to see you here every day. And it's good for her." Behind the front desk, the chubby nurse dispensed an unctuous smile. "Family members, sometimes they give up."

"Not me."

"That's good," she said, voice lilting and loathsome, like a Sunday school teacher's. "If you don't give up, then—" She capped her pen, put down her clipboard, and smiled. "Miracles *do* happen. The Lord works in mysterious ways."

"The Lord sucks." She looked away and lightly scratched at her cheek. A fleck of rouge fell to her clipboard. I hurried out, trying but failing to walk without a limp.

"She's been moved, Mr. Edwards. She's in room 211." But she wasn't, having been removed for still another round of testing. I hobbled back out.

The parking lot was lonely as a deserted playground, and in the corner waited my haggard car. The door swung open for me and I nearly turned around, determined to walk home. But my ankle now pained me greatly and I reluctantly returned.

"Here," she said, handing me a tightly rolled joint. "It'll make your ankle feel better."

"The last stuff you had, it wasn't very good."

Tall Patty watched me consume the entire joint. "Glad you don't like it much."

"I really don't. But how else can I stand your company?"

Huffy, she crossed her arms and stared out the passenger window. A gaggle of nurses stood chatting, their caps rendered autumnal beneath the parking lot lights. One of the nurses stepped away from the group as if to begin her shift, then she paused for more chatter. I recognized her as one of Kim's nurses.

"You just won't let me make amends, will you?" Patty groused, easing another joint from her purse. "I've been out here four nights in a row now and you won't give me the time of day. Jesus, how many times can a person say she's sorry?"

"Tell Kim you're sorry."

"I didn't tell your mother to bring a gun."

"You just told her that brother Jeffrey was fucking sister Kim, that he wanted to knock her up. Happy Mama Righteous, a grandmother at last. Did you two daydream about the baby shower?"

Emphatic, Patty slapped the dashboard. "Talk about humiliating, losing out to your boyfriend's *sister*."

She kept yammering as I finished the joint then took one of her cigarettes. I was thoroughly broke and savored Patty's contribution of sundries. Still, I held hope that some money from Pad would make its way to me: *Speak for the Devil* had enjoyed brisk box office, propelled by sensational Internet headlines such as, *Freak!! Rock Star Incest Murder and Suicide!*

That evening's horror was, it seemed, ironically sanitized by the context: a movie about Satan. This context produced a lively e-buzz, with exciting rumors of satanic sex and violence erupting nationwide. I persuaded Cousin Robbie to add to the buzz, drafting him to upload one of Jason's digital photographs to Pad's new website. (Predictably, the corporate Pad website was in the graveyard, but gratifyingly, fan sites sprouted daily). Jason gravely cooperated; he even surrendered to me the camera he'd used that night. "It's the least I can do," he conceded, near tears. "That night, I crossed that, you know, that journalist line from observer to participant."

The photo was of Mama Righteous, bloody face captured in the blunt flash of Jason's camera: her tiny eyes stupidly crossed, the pen barrel deep in her neck. I spent hours with photo-editing software to bring the pen's candy cane stripes into clear focus. I found myself hoping to release Pad outtakes with that very image burned onto the CD.

Meanwhile, that evening's disaster inspired antics nationwide, as at a San Diego high school dance. To suggest siblinghood, several couples arrived wearing sports jerseys with identical names on the back, and the mock sibling-couples commandeered the dance floor as the deejay cranked up "Pay for my Hell!" One of the young gals, judgment shattered by loud music and potent pot, planted a long kiss on her astonished brother. A saturnalia erupted right there on the gymnasium floor as couples morphed into triples and quadruples. The frantic principal fought his way to the center of the throng, screaming for a restoration of order. Apparently, the young scholars pretty much acceded, though the principal was later assaulted in the parking lot.

Patty interrupted my musings: "C'mon, Jeffrey. Let's drive to my house and hang out."

I considered her offer. Patty was a welcome distraction in my diminished state: hereafter, life offered merely the ordinary. I shrugged in blasé agreement.

She smiled.

She was such a stupid thing, believing that her simpleton's gesture—falling upon her back and opening her long legs to me—would balance the scales.

"Still not talking to your Dad?"

"He got all judgmental on me. I told him to shut up or I'd shit all over his flawless front yard. He's screwing the band out of royalty money for 'Pay for my Hell', I know it. *Billboard* says it's approaching sixty-thousand in sales, and even threw in a good review of *Epater*, too."

She murmured, nodded.

"But he says there's no money coming in yet. Scum."

She glanced at her purse, thinking.

"Anyway, I yelled at him to give me some Robbie money."

"Robbie money?"

"He gets money for taking in Robbie. Uncle Art and Aunt Jo, they paid him for a while and then when Dad got tired of it, they gave Dad Robbie's college fund on the condition that he'd keep Robbie permanently."

"...Oh my God."

"There was fifteen grand in there. Professor Dave, I'll bet he's spent it already on a new Besson euphonium."

"I feel sorry for Robbie, getting ripped off like that."

"I told Dave that I'd take Robbie *and* his money."

"You're really going to—?"

"No. I couldn't even if I wanted to. Robbie got busted for stealing cigarettes from the Wal-Mart."

"He's so stupid," she sadly noted.

"Three times now." It was true. Robbie had been twice detained for stealing smokes for his young friends, that trio of layabouts I'd met on Dad's front porch. "He's never had friends before. He just wanted to keep them."

Patty stared out the window, melancholy darkening her eyes.

"So, Robbie's doing six months, but Daddy'll be there for him when he gets out."

"Robbie gets jail and you get nothing," she said hotly. "You *fuck*."

"Did you mean 'fuck' as a noun or verb? Because if you—"

"You *love* telling your shrink that you, how you fucked your sister."

"I've never told anyone—including you, Miss Drama Queen— that I ever touched Kim."

"You *brag* about it. I just know it."

"Those discussions are off the record. And remember that rumors are just that: rumors. Started by a crazy dead hag and a six foot two inch pothead."

"You've got no morals."

"I've got no grass, either. Got any more at home?"

She snorted indignantly.

"C'mon, do you?"

Her eyes softened. "...Yeah. It's better stuff too."

"Before we go..." I pulled out a sheet of paper, crisply unfolded it. "Read this."

"Fuck off, loser. Look, all I did was cry on your mother's shoulder and, you know, say things I shouldn't have. But *this*—" She sneered at the paper. "—I mean, this is private shit. I can't read that bitch's suicide notes."

"How do you know? You haven't even tried."

"You're the sickest fuck. *Ever*." She shoved open the passenger door, which bounced upon its hinges and ricocheted back shut. Reopening the door, she marched off, indignation in every step, and I wished only that she'd left me a pack of cigarettes.

I was thoroughly broke, and with no money in sight from Professor Dave, I risked daydreaming about Karen's spontaneous business proposal: a few days back, Karen called from NYC to say hi. I was truly moved: few people talked to me anymore.

Even Larry, who I judged as breezily blasé, refused to return my calls, and Billy and Mrs. Billy let it be known that, if I appeared on their doorstep, they would shoot me.

"Mencken man, still offending Middle America," Karen cackled. I was silent, unsure of how to respond, and she chatted onward. "Hey, I found a review of your sister's CD in *Lower Fifth*."

"What's that?"

"A freebie NYC paper, you know, all ads and no sentences. But they did sneak this review in. Wanna hear?" Not waiting for an answer, she recited it. Used to bad news as I was, I clamped the phone stoically between chin and shoulder. But I was surprised:

Highlights are "Menthol" and "Aim For the Ditch", in which Kim Edwards and sidekicks play tug of war with bright melodies, pulling and yanking until the tunes fray and explode. "Pay for my Hell!" now included as a bonus track, is big and loud, a boulder rolling down a mountain, crushing everything in its path. As a whole, she continued, *the songs are a wild ride between the giddy, the satiric, and the barmy. Kim Edwards's lusty banshee on "Looks Like a Tommy" is aural Viagra.* Karen whooped. "Little sister's voice gave the guy a yard long hard-on. Which you'd understand." Concluding, she read, *The songs add up to an experience both bracing and vertiginous.*

"...Huh," I managed.

"Oh c'mon, it's a terrific review!"

"It won't help."

Even over the phone, I could hear the smirk. "...Okay, let's not talk about music. Let's talk about how tremendously fucked up you are!"

Surrendering to her relentless high spirits, I remarked that keeping a notebook was part of my therapy.

"That's so perfect!"

"What?"

"It could be a best seller!"

"You're nuts."

"Ha, that's funny. You calling me nuts. No, seriously, it could be very juicy, a rock and roll epic. And it's *gotta* have the sex in it," she demanded, suddenly the editor handing out an assignment. "The sex is a *must*." Indeed, Karen wasn't scandalized by the rumors, not even the true ones. "Maybe you really are both perverts. *Talented* perverts."

"You're like everybody else. Hungry to believe the worst."

"What's it like to get your sister off? Is it in the manuscript?"

"It's a diary, not a manuscript."

"So what? When you're out of therapy, just go through it and, you know, fix the spelling or put paragraphs in or whatever. And be sure to put me in it," she added, "but keep our little tryst to a discrete minimum."

"What tryst?"

"On second thought, just cut it out. I don't want the world or even your shrink to know I slept with a disreputable person."

"You didn't, so stop flattering yourself."

"This could lead to a television deal," she enthused. "I've gotten to know some TV people in New York. What about a cable movie that could, uh, what is it you love to do? Mock the righteous?"

"I hate TV."

"Do you hate money?"

I really have to, collect myself, but I've got nothing but headaches, headaches with claws, headaches with fish hooks. I thought writing it out, making sure it was true would help because it would help me make sense of the comedy and the wreckage.

But Dr. Rebecca, you're right. I should stay away from Kim's hospital room for a while because it, because of the floating. The ceiling traps me right over her and I can't look away, I just have to keep looking down at her and yelling for them to help her.

Her arms so skinny and dried out and covered with bruises from the IV's. And she's shriveled down to nothing under that stained hospital gown that I ordered them to change yesterday! When I can make it down to the floor, I bend over Kim and lift her eyelids. All the green is gone, her eyes are dead filmy yellow.

Kim's latest room was private and looked out to a rolling cornfield. Late afternoon's angular sunlight fell across that field, and haggard rows of stalks gazed dispiritedly at the gray western sky.

She was asleep. She was always asleep.

Such is the fate of the vegetative: to always sleep, even as one's heart beats and as one's hair grows. Even as one dies.

The portable radio upon the night stand was silent, so I turned up the volume and, clasping her hand, listened for an hour. Not once did she stir, and not once had she stirred since that night which had, until those awful three minutes, been among the most gratifying of her twenty-three years. I hoped that more than the most primitive impulses coursed through her damaged brain. I hoped that memories of her last conscious evening buoyed her: the soundtrack, her fans' adulation, the hometown autograph line. Now, four months later, she lay corpse-like upon the white hospital bed, wires and hoses and machines sprouting from her limbs and torso.

I sat gingerly upon the stiff-backed chair. Mama Righteous's bullet had left an unpleasant though hardly life-threatening wound. Upon seeing me charge her, she'd fired wildly. The bullet shattered my talus, a heretofore underappreciated bone that helps form the ankle joint. I recall no pain from that shot, though it pained me plentifully now.

As for Kim...she'd chased after me and grabbed wildly for the pistol. Mother shrieked and fired again. The bullet struck Kim's brain stem, and my beloved hurtled backward along the evolutionary path from animal to plant. You see, reader, the human brain stem oversees one's breathing, one's heartbeat, and one's ability to swallow—to name merely three vital functions. If she ever wakes, Kim will likely suffer severe deficits of intelligence, of movement, of sensation.

On that awful evening, even as my inamorata lay just three feet behind me, I didn't realize she'd been shot. I was hard at work with my pen, determined that matricide, not suicide, would be mother's *ne plus ultra*.

Kim's hair had grown back a good deal after the surgery and I'd managed to gather enough of it to create a pony tail. That gorgeous hair was now stippled with gray, and I vowed to her that I would dye her hair back to its lustrous black.

A nurse entered, duly took note of the patient's vitals. "So how're you doing?" she queried while updating Kim's chart. "Still getting those headaches?"

"Once in a while, yeah," I lied. I had a new headache every minute.

As she hurried out, a smile flickered across her otherwise dour face. "I'll bet you do."

As I always did, I updated Kim on my therapy sessions. I was the model patient, I jested, and enjoyed nothing more than en-tertaining the therapist. "She just loves the dissociation theory, can you believe it? But she's nice enough, and she means well."

Indeed, what a scamp I'd become with Dr. Rebecca! I let her believe she was leading me to a shocking insight: that the Ed-wards' incest was a response to a cruel family life in which love was routinely mocked by hateful parents. Incest, she'd announce, was the simultaneous act of rebellion and declaration of love for the one family member for whom I cared. Dr. Rebecca believed that, together, she and I would stalk my mind's dark corridor un-til we found a Key, an Answer. Her rationalist naiveté amused me...she couldn't grasp the simple fact that my love for Kim was beyond the understanding of anyone but Kim and me.

With stubborn good cheer, Dr. Rebecca clung to the Wester-marck theory. "He was an anthropologist," I explained to Kim. "Said that when people grow up together, their brains put each other into hands-off categories like 'brother' or 'sister' or 'sibling' or whatever."

I imagined how Kim would happily shrug then direct me to listen to her latest tune.

"And since we spent a lot of time apart growing up, Dr. Re-becca speculates that our brains didn't put each other in the hands-off category. I'm going along with her, more or less. I've got no choice." Rather than prosecute me for matricide and sun-dry lesser charges, the court ordered psychiatric therapy.

I can't stop the words. They just keep coming, the same words about what tomorrow has for me. And what it has for Kim.

"Look what I brought."

Kim couldn't be surprised. I'd brought them, my cache of photographs: the very photos that drove howling Patty to Mama Righteous. Sitting there, photos arranged like playing cards in my hands, I looked back and forth, from Kim to photo to Kim...from ephemeral past to pitiless present. "Maybe I should've told you the little story behind these pictures."

I imagined that Kim waved away my agitation.

"Maybe next time then. Anyway. This one's my favorite."

The snapshot captured her perfectly. She sat at Dad's kitchen table, guitar across her lap. The camera had distracted her: her left hand still held a chord upon the guitar's neck, and her right hand was raised to ward off further snapshots. The camera's flash bleached her palm white. She grinned broadly, *mon aimé*, her hazel eyes luminous with all the success that once lay before her.

My headache, previously licking at my skull's perimeter, sunk its fangs into my brain's pearly core.

"I guess you're probably pretty bored with these by now."

Another nurse came in, so I stepped outside for a cigarette. When I returned, I moved the chair next to her bed, and my knees touched Kim's thin mattress. Guilt and despair gathered in my brain...they pointed, taunted, bellowed. After all these hopeless months, after all these hopeless days and seconds, they'd cornered me. I had barely the strength to slouch. Fingers trembling, I lifted Kim's eyelids.

I studied her eyes a long time.

A long time.

I can't stop the words. The phone rings or I start my car— every sound says Nothing, Nothing. Or when I take a walk and my shoes scuff along the road, every sound says it, keeps saying it.

Nothing.
Nothing.
The Nothing.

www.ingramcontent.com/pod-product-compliance
Lightning Source LLC
Chambersburg PA
CBHW031111030726
47496CB00002BA/485